The Wizard's Son

A Novel by Kathryn L. Ramage

The Wapshott Press

The Wizard's Son

Published by
The Wapshott Press
PO Box 31513
Los Angeles, CA 90031

The Wapshott Press

www.WapshottPress.com

ISBN: 978-0-578-03293-1

06 05 04 034 3 2 1

Wapshott Press logo by Molly Kiely
The Northlands map design by Molly Kiely
Cover design by Michelle Mauk

For my father.

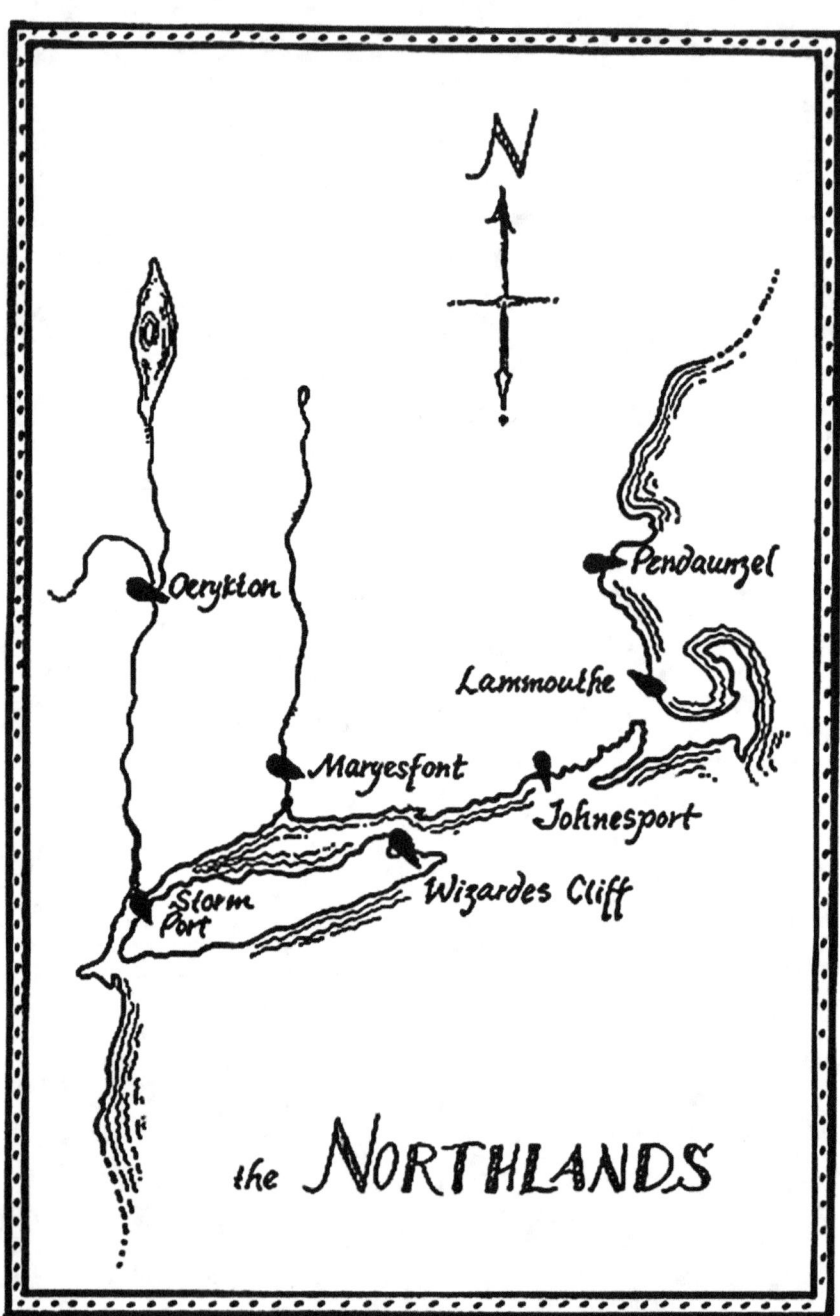

N

Oerykton

Pendaumzel

Lammouthe

Maryesfont

Johnesport

Storm Port

Wizardes Cliff

the NORTHLANDS

The Wizard's Son

Table of Contents

The Little One
1939

une

The little boy looked up in amazement as hooves clattered on the loose cobbles of the alley and a man in brilliant red rode into the yard. He had never seen such a colorful being before, wrapped from hood to polished heels in a crimson cloak and most wondrous scarlet mantle. A gold talisman glittered upon his brow in the early-morning sunlight. All about the little yard, common folk in home-dyed garb of brown and butternut were out to lift their storefronts and throw rubbish to the gutters, but the boy had forgotten them. He was transfixed by this stranger, who seemed larger to him than all of this small, dirty patch of Lammouthe.

Lammouthe was made up of narrow, tangled streets, mud-daubed buildings around little stone yards, a busy marketplace and a busier port. The boy had never been out of this maze, but at times he would venture to the docks to gape at the tall ships, the mariners who spoke in odd tongues, and the great, greenish-gray ocean, and wonder what was beyond: where did the ships and sea-folk sail to? He heard the names of faraway lands—Persia, Napoli, Arabia, Cathay—and he tried to imagine what they were like, but his imagination would not take him out of the only place he knew. He thought all the world must be like Lammouthe: an endless town by the endless sea.

But as he stared up at this stranger—so tall and handsome, radiant with light and strength—the boy began to believe that there might be other things than brown-garbed shopkeepers and the ever-present stink of fish, things more strange than foreign mariners, more beautiful than the ocean, more wonderful than the tallest ships. Surely this red-robed man must be from the most marvelous place in the world!

The splendid stranger turned to him. "Do you belong here, Child?" His voice was deep and gentle, but the boy inched timidly back into the shadows. "Do you know a woman named Nann Dafodylle? Is such your mother's name?"

"Mama is Nann Lyghtelotynge."

"And your name, Child?"

"Orlan," he whispered.

"Orlan." The stranger smiled. "I believe I am seeking your mother. Can you tell me which house she lives in?"

"Mama's ill," the boy answered. "Ellan says I mustn't `sturb her."

"I might be able to help, if you will tell me where she is."

Orlan pointed to the tavern. Ellan, the old woman who looked after him, was out at the yard well and she frowned suspiciously as the stranger approached. They spoke together and looked at him, and then they went in. Orlan had followed cautiously, a shy step at a time; now, unobserved, he slipped into the tavern after them, past the forehall where the great, empty ale barrels and casks were piled, and into the unlit stairwell at the back of the house. He heard voices, Ellan and the stranger, on the stairs above.

"`Twas her third, M'Lord, since the little lad. She was never one to be patient lying in for a child that had no father by name. She'd lost the other two right enough and she said she'd be safe for this, as it hadn't quickened, but she's been high in her fever since and no use to hoping she'd be well again. She said she'd call upon ye, though I never thought to see it true. Ye've never come to her before."

"I was not summoned," the man replied. "Nann has always held that power. I would have come if I'd thought she had need of me. I didn't know. What of the boy?"

"She was hoping ye'd take him as you ought. No mistake whose child *he* is."

"I will," he tried to answer, but Ellan interrupted angrily.

"None of that! Oh, I know how ye Lordlings do. Take yer sport of a pretty maid and if there's a child ye'll name it only as ye've no way to get `round refusing, then see it never troubles yer sight again. Take him? Ye never cared to know the little lad before. What do ye care for him now? I'll say right out t'ye, M'Lord, I won't have ye take him from his home and drop him in an abbey where he hasn't a friend."

Most of this was beyond Orlan's comprehension, but Ellan's last words froze him with horror. He knew that the Abbey was like a church, but much bigger, and children went to live there when no one wanted them. Mama had threatened to send him there before, sometimes when she was angry and sometimes when she was weepy and said she wasn't fit to have him. Was he so naughty? He always tried to be very, very good, and obey Ellan, and stay out of the way when Mama was sickly or sleeping or when she brought men upstairs from the tavern. He didn't mean to be troublesome. Would Mama truly send him away? Surely she wouldn't let this stranger take him?

Orlan wanted to run and hide, but his fascination with this wondrous, strange man and his desire to know what was happening overwhelmed his fear. Quietly, he crept to the foot of the stairs, and up to the two little rooms beneath the eaves where he and Mama and Ellan lived.

Above, Ellan and the stranger had ended their argument. A door shut. As Orlan reached the landing, he saw that Ellan had gone to her room. The other door, to Mama's room, was open. Orlan could see— the stranger knelt at her bedside with her silver amulet in his hands.

"Fare ye well, Dafodylle."

The boy was shocked. Mama had always worn the amulet on a faded black ribbon about her throat; Orlan knew the large silver disk, its engraved face worn almost indistinguishable by caressing fingers, so well as his mother's face, her voice, her scent. It was as much a part of her. But why was this man taking it? Why did Mama let him?

He stepped to the doorway; the floorboards creaked beneath his feet. As the stranger turned, the scarlet hood fell back and long, silvery white hair tumbled free. The eyes that shone into his were palest gray, like small pools of water, irises rimmed by bright blue. Orlan stopped at the sight, thrilling with sudden recognition and near understanding. No one except old, old folk had white hair, and no one, old or young, had such odd, colorless eyes. No one except this stranger, and himself.

The stranger held out his hand. "Orlan, come to me." Orlan obeyed. "Do you know who I am?"

"N-no."

"I am the Lord Wizard Redmantyl. That means that I am the most powerful of all living wizards. In my youth, I was called Lightmaster. I met your mother by that name." He took Orlan by the shoulders. "Orlan Lightesblood, I am your father."

Orlan knew that this was true; he could not doubt at those solemn, colorless eyes that looked so deeply into his. Mama had said many times that she had once loved a great wizard. People up and down the yard made jest of her braggings and called her Lyghtelotynge—*light-lover*—but Mama's story never changed. She told Orlan that he was of magical blood; he had the look of the wizard. His father had been so tall and strangely handsome, like no mortal man she'd ever seen, that she had loved him from the first moment she saw him. She had wanted a child like him, so silver-fair. One day, she promised, the wizard would return for them. Surely he meant to. Hadn't he given her this amulet to seal the bond between them? When he was done with his wonderful, magical adventures, she said, he would come back and marry her and name her son as his own. He would take them away from this miserable alehouse. Everything would be wonderful then.

"Mama said my father filled a room with fairylight–" Orlan found his mother beneath her pink-stained sheets. "Mama?" He would have run to her, but Lord Redmantyl caught his arms and held him.

"Your mother is ill," the wizard said. "She has asked that you come and live with me until she is well again. Would you like that, Little One?"

Orlan stared at the figure lying so still, face pale, yellow hair in limp curls. Beads of fever-sweat cooled on her lip. "She shan't call me back ever," he said slowly, trying to encompass an idea that tore at the foundations of his whole, small world. "Mama's dead?"

"Yes, Orlan, she is."

The boy was bewildered by all that was happening. Mama had wept and moaned all night and he could not sleep in his worry for her. She had never been so ill before. Then Ellan had come in to dress him and send him out to play. When he asked what was wrong, she only said that he must go and not be troublesome. Now, Mama was dead and this splendid red-robed wizard was his father. It was too much for his grief-stunned, eight-year-old mind to comprehend.

"Ye said ye could help her." His voice trembled hopefully.

"I cannot recall one who is past healing," Redmantyl answered.

"But if ye be most powerful–"

"Child, no wizard who has ever lived had power for that! Would I could bring her back, but it is impossible. She has gone."

Orlan burst into tears. In an instant, Lord Redmantyl swept him up. He was lost in the thick folds of his father's cloak, wrapped in darkness, pressed against a thunderous heartbeat. Sobs tore from him, wrenching his small body. The pain was unbearable. He struggled in the unyielding embrace. His fists thumped helplessly against the wall of the wizard's chest. He would have screamed, but then he felt the rough and unfamiliar sensation of a short-clipped beard brushing against his temple. Redmantyl whispered into his ear, words so soft and strange that Orlan could not make sense of them, yet he was comforted. He could not break free and his father's voice drew him in; he must surrender to this gentle magic.

He began to relax in the protective strength of the arms about him, and the sorrow which had cut him so unbearably was eased. He couldn't think of his mother lying so pale and still. He couldn't be afraid. Already, the sharp stabs of grief were blurring, soothed away by his father's touch. Each sob hurt less than the one before. At last, Orlan sniffled and stopped.

His father smiled tenderly and blotted the tears from his face. "Better now, Little One?"

The boy nodded. Ellan emerged from her room bearing a small, shapeless cloth bundle. "M'Lord?"

"In a moment, Goode Ellan." Redmantyl took the boy's shoulders again. "Orlan, your mother wished you to be raised as my son, as you properly should. You must come with me now." He tied the amulet about the child's neck.

Orlan fingered the smooth silver in confused wonder. "Mama's–"

"It was your mother's," Redmantyl agreed. "Now it is yours."

Ellan, on the landing, scowled. "I don't like it," she said.

"You can do nothing against it," the wizard replied. "He's coming with me whether you like it or no. Orlan, you must bid farewell to Goode Ellan."

Orlan lifted his head. He hadn't realized that he would be leaving her behind. "Ye'll not be going too, Ellan?"

"No, Child. I'll not be going."

"Why not?" He twisted to look up at his father. "Father, why not? I want Ellan to come. Please?"

Redmantyl glanced over the child's head. "I will need a nurse for the boy," he offered grudgingly. "You may see to his care yourself if you do not trust my intentions."

"If ye will, M'Lord," Ellan answered. "I might come along after I see to Nann's proper burying."

"Very well then!" Orlan paid little attention as Redmantyl searched his mantle's deep pockets, giving Ellan directions and money. "And I'll write out this message for you."

"I'm not one for such letterings," the nurse protested. "What's it about?"

"You must give this to the Lammouthe Justice. It states simply that I, Lord Redmantyl, have claimed the child Orlan. If any contest that, they will find me at Wizardes Cliff." The wizard pressed the spell on his signet ring against the folded strip to seal it. Ellan frowned at the smudged direction as she accepted the note, then tucked it into her apron.

"Now I'll be along before ye're missing me." She took Orlan's head between her hands and bestowed a last kiss. "God 'ild ye, and mind ye be yer best for M'Lord."

The little boy nodded.

The wizard took his hand. "Come along, Child." Orlan gripped his father's fingers and went with him down the stairs, out of the house, and out of Lammouthe.

It was July of 1939, a peaceful year for the Empire.

The Norman Empire was not so large as Spain or Russe but its people, for the most part, believed themselves more valiant, virtuous, and prosperous than any other. History declared it so. United by conquest and intermarriage in the nine hundred years since Guylliame, Duke of Normandy, had claimed the English throne and stormed the cliffs of Hastings in 1066, the seven kingdoms—Angeland, France, Gallys, Skotsland, Eireland, Burgundy, and the Northlands—stood proudly together above all lesser realms. Normandy was now a small and insignificant portion, recalled only when its overlords honored their legendary origins, for Normans relished the glories of battle. Bardly songs and thespian pageants celebrated the adventures of knights and shieldmaids, commemorated besieged cities and courtships and grand coronations. The modern world had not seen such spectacular times. For all their love of warfare, the Normans were a well-behaved people at peace; the first four decades of the twentieth century had seen the Empire with its borders secure, its taxes unimposing, and its citizenry left to conduct themselves according to their own responsibilities and sense of right. Guided by a millennium of laws, manners, and traditions, every subject, Lordling or cowherd, always knew the proper thing to do.

Orlan was vaguely aware of his homeland's exalted history. He had heard the old folk in the yard recall the grand days of the century past, before old Eduarde Redlyon had grown too weary to raise his sword for one more campaign against the Spanish, and he learned from gossip that the Redlyon's heir, Kharles IV, who had died that spring, had been better at bookkeeping than leading troops, and his younger son, Duke Dafythe of the Northlands, was as mildly mannered, but the boy-Emperor, also Kharles, promised to be a spit-fire hero in the old tradition. The child knew that he lived in the Duchy of the Northlands, and that the custom houses at Lammouthe were run in Duke Dafythe's name; the golden lions on blue shields over every door meant that they belonged to him. He had heard the name *Plantagenet*, but he thought it a grand, grown-up way of saying *royal*. To Orlan, Dukes and Emperors were as remote and fabulous as God: he sometimes felt their influence upon his life in inscrutable acts; there were things he must do and mustn't do, and if he asked why, he was hushed for his pertness and told to be good. Orlan had also heard impossible tales of powerful magicians and he imagined them—his father especially—to be as fabulous and unfathomable. Meeting Lord Redmantyl had not yet altered his opinion.

He hid in his father's cloak, frightened and miserable, as they rode along the Lammouthe Road. When at last he grew bold enough to look up, he found himself in an unfamiliar world. Beyond Lammouthe, the woods of the Northlands ran wild, broken here and there by little villages and open fields. Lush maple, oak, and birch trees blocked the sun and left dancing, dappled patches of light on the wide road. Deer scattered as they passed, and the noise of unseen birds and crickets rose riotous from the bushes. Orlan was so excited at the sight of a squirrel leaping in the branches overhead that he nearly slipped from his father's grasp, and he yelped in surprise and reached for a bright orange and black butterfly that fluttered past the horse's ears.

"Where are we going, Father?"

"To Wizardes Cliff, my home."

"You were there when Mama called `pon ye?"

"No, I was at Pendaunzel. My Lord Dafythe and I would settle a matter of inheritance that will be to my advantage if the young Emperor favors it."

Orlan gaped at this; Redmantyl might as well have said that he had flown to Heaven and spoken with St. Peter. "Where's `Danzel, Father?"

"In the north." The wizard waved a hand in that direction. "It's a very large, grand city. Someday, when you are older, I will take you there and present you to My Liege Lord Dafythe. He has his own son, like you."

"Has the Duke a boy too?"

"The Duke's son is a man full-grown," Redmantyl explained. "I meant that, like you, his mother and father were not married."

"Oh," the boy said. "It matters much?"

"For the Duke's son, it means that he cannot be Duke. When My Gracious Lord Dafythe dies, his daughter will be Duke of the Northlands. It will not be so important for you, Orlan. A wizard does not leave his title to his child."

Orlan squirmed to look up at him. "Father, are all wizards as ye?"

"What do you mean?"

"Are they all of white hair, as we are?"

"No, Child," Redmantyl answered. "Most wizards are as dark as other folk. Only our family is so fair."

7

"Are there many of us?"

"Not many. My father, my Aunt Loren, my cousin Tomasin, who is dead now, and her daughter Laurel, and my cousin Kaiese and her little girls."

"They all live with you?"

Redmantyl laughed. "No."

"Are they wizards, Father?"

"No. I am the only wizard of our blood. My aunt and cousin are magical, but they fear their powers and will not employ them. Laurel, I think, may be magical too."

"Shall I be a wizard one day, if I am yours?" Orlan asked.

"I cannot yet say, Little One. But magic is in our family and I would be proud to see you a wizard of power."

"I should like to be a wizard, Father, and wear red robes such as yers." He plucked at his father's sleeve.

"You may wear red, Child, but only if you are the best of all wizards when you are grown. This mantle is a sign of my place as most powerful. The lesser wizards wear black."

"What do these marks mean?" The wizard had embroidered strange devices upon his mantle with threads of black and white and gold. A small finger traced Greek letters, simple and complex geometric figures, runes, numbers, and other arcane and cabalistic symbols. "Are they words?"

"They are spells I have woven to protect myself," Redmantyl answered. "I have enemies among the lesser wizards, and Other, greater forces seek my destruction."

"But if ye're most powerful, Father, why do you need such spells? Are ye not strong enough without them?"

"Even the greatest power can be destroyed by deceit. I may be taken by trickery if I allowed myself to be weak and unguarded."

"E'en as ye sleep?"

"Even as I sleep. Then, I must draw a circle with spells beneath my bed and hang my mantle over me. I have such a spell, a pentacle, carved on my chamber floor at the castle."

"'Tisn't fun to be a wizard?"

"Not fun, perhaps, but most satisfying. If you have the talent you can be content with nothing except wizardry."

"Ye'll do something magical for me now?"

"If you wish." Redmantyl let the reins drop on the horse's neck and lifted his free hand. He turned his wrist slowly, and a sparkling orb of blue light appeared upon his fingertips. Orlan cooed, then laughed, but the horse shied and the wizard was forced to break the fragile spell.

He first saw the castle Wizardes Cliff the next day from the deck of the ship which brought them from Johnesport; his father lifted him up to the rail to see the tall towers, the sheltering battlements and the red-roofed halls atop the formidable cliffs. They were grown together, walls from rock, pale stone that shone white in the midday sun. It was a fairy kingdom in itself, high away from the long, green island and stretching up into the clear blue summer sky.

"`Tis–" Orlan struggled for a word, and failed. *Wondrous? Grand? Magical?* None of these could contain his awe. Even together, they could not describe. The castle surpassed every wonderful thing he had imagined.

Once their ship had docked at the foot of the castle cliffs, Redmantyl took him up the steep steps hewn into the face of the rock, up and up through the long, dim corridors of the castle, up stairway after stairway until Orlan believed they must be climbing so high as the clouds. They went swiftly; Orlan had only the briefest impression of rows of closed doors and astonished servants as his father carried him past.

At last, Redmantyl brought Orlan up to his own chambers and set him down on the enormous bed, which had moss-green curtains and posts like tree trunks carved with ivy, roses, and grinning satyrs. The wizard called out: "Simon!"

A young man in dusty-gray livery came in. "M'Lord? Ye be `ere?" He blinked at the little boy, but did not ask.

"An emergency called me from court," Redmantyl answered as he tossed his dusty riding cloak over the manservant's arm. "Simon, my son Orlan. We shall present him before the household, once he is made ready. As you see, he urgently needs a bath and some decent clothing. Do you think Kai's things will fit him?"

Soap and gauzy towels were brought in and the copper bathing-tub in Redmantyl's dressing room was filled to the rim. Orlan was first delighted; he had never seen such a bath before. But when he stretched one hand over the curled metal lip to touch the water, he withdrew quickly. "`Tis cold," he said. "I must wash in so cold?"

Redmantyl placed the palm of his left hand flat on the surface of the water. After a few silent minutes, he said, "Is it more to your liking now?"

Orlan touched the water again, then plunged his arm in to the elbow, reaching so near the bottom of the deep tub that he nearly fell in. The water was now warm. "Ye can do that?"

"Yes, I can do that. It is a simple trick."

"Simple," Simon muttered to himself. "Simple, `e says."

Then the wizard left Simon to assist the boy.

"Quick now, Pup, before the water cools," the servant urged. "I'll not be able to warm it so quickly as `Is Lordship does."  He knelt to help Orlan unlace his jerkin.  When the strings broke at his tugging, he threw them to the floor in disgust.  "`Ow'd a Lordship such as `Imself let `is own little one walk about in such rubbish.... Well, ye'll be washed more'n ye've likely been before, but we'll `ave ye proper clean."

Orlan had not known how dirty he was until Simon scrubbed his hair and scraped under his nails and threw his old clothes into the fire. Before his bath was finished, Redmantyl returned with garments borrowed from the Chatelaine's sons and a dark gray tunic belonging to the wizard's apprentice.

"It's too big for `im, M'Lord," said Simon once Orlan was dressed afresh. "That tunic nearly drags the floor."

"Godefroi's the only one of the house who wears the gray of a wizard's child," Redmantyl answered. "Can't you do something about it? We can't have the boy tripping over his hem at every step."

"I'll give a try." And the little boy stood perfectly still while Simon pinned and basted his too-large garments and combed out his damp and tangled curls. At last, the servant stood back and asked, "What do you think?" Orlan was relieved when Redmantyl pronounced him presentable.

They brought him down to the Great Hall and, there, the wizard made a formal speech of acknowledgement before the entire household: "I vow in the name of our most majestic Emperor and My Liege Lord Dafythe, Duke of the Northlands, in the name of the loyalty I bear to both and in the name of the honor bound into my place as premiere Lord Wizard. I own Orlan as a true child of my blood and I claim responsibility for him until he is of age. He will be one of my household hereafter. So swear I, Lord Redmantyl."

This was a ceremonial promise, as binding as a written contract. Afterwards, Redmantyl lifted the boy up onto his shoulder, said, "Well now, Orlan, shall I show you the castle?" and took him out to walk across the vast, sunlit plazas and along the battlements. The wizard pointed out every tower and hall and gave all their names. Orlan knew he would never remember them all. Surely he must be lost in this enormous castle if his father did not lead him by the hand!

That night, Orlan was put to bed in a small chamber near his father's apartment. He woke later in strange darkness. Nothing was as it ought to be. The bed was too large and when he reached out he found nothing but cold sheets around him. He was used to sleeping at someone's side. Where was Ellan? Where was Mama? Tonight, for the first time, he was alone.

"Mama?" Orlan scrambled from beneath his blankets and fell to the floor. He leapt up again instantly, mindless of the jolt. Where was the door? He could see nothing in the dark. The walls seemed so far away; he couldn't reach them. He twisted back suddenly. Which way must he go? Arms outstretched, he stumbled blindly. His fingers brushed smooth wood. The bed? No, a sort of table. Where was the door? He had to get out. "Mama!"

With a sudden throb of renewed grief, he realized that his mother was gone. She was not here; he had left her at Lammouthe, a hundred miles away, and he would never see her again. Vividly, he saw her face again, eyes shut, blonde curls limp on the pillow, lips faintly blue. Dead. His mother was dead.

He fell to the floor, howling his terror.

The door opened and candlelight shone upon him. His father was there.

Orlan clung to the wizard, sobbing wildly, refusing to answer the repeated question, "What's wrong? Can you tell me?" as Redmantyl took him up and carried him back to his chambers. He sat before the cavernous sitting-room fireplace. "What's wrong?"

"I want my mama!" the boy yelped. "I wanna go home! Please? I want my mama? Make Mama come back?"

"I can't," his father answered. "I'm sorry, but your mother can't be brought back. You must know that she was very ill and she is beyond that pain now. She is no longer here."

"Where has Mama gone then?"

"I cannot say. Somewhere."

Again, Orlan felt the pull of that gentle magic and he surrendered to the comfort his father offered. How strong the arms about him seemed; how truly safe he felt against the powerful rhythms of that thundering heart. "Ye think she is better, Father? Where she is?"

"I do," Redmantyl whispered. "As you are better here. This is your home now, Little One. You need not be affrighted, for I am here and I shall care for you. I promise."

Orlan knew that something was being done to him. He was beginning to forget his mother. He didn't want to forget her! If he did, Mama would truly be gone forever. But it hurt so much to think of her.

11

The pain cut him so that he wanted to cry out. He couldn't bear it. Here, it didn't hurt so much. Already, the memory of her was fading, lost in the stronger currents which soothed his mind. In his father's enchantment there was peace...

"Mama–!"

"Sleep now, my darling. Hush." Redmantyl kissed the child's brow and pressed his fingers to his temple; Orlan sighed and relaxed. "Sleep, and do not trouble to remember."

As Orlan slept, his father continued to whisper words that would ease and comfort, although the child would not understand if he heard them. The soft chant was interrupted by a tentative knock at the door, and Simon came in.

"M'Lord? I `eard the little one weepin'."

"He's had a bad dream," Redmantyl answered. "`Tis ended now. You may go."

"Yes, M'Lord." But Simon did not leave.

"What is it?" the wizard asked after a moment.

"M'Lord, the rags that child came in, I'd not like to think where `e's been all this time. Ye've never said a thing about `im `til `e came today."

"I didn't know of him," Redmantyl confessed. "If I had, I would have acknowledged him before."

"`Is mother–?"

"She is not important. A girl, a barmaid I knew many years ago. I had almost forgotten her. If there had not been a child–" he paused. "Well, I cannot go back and mend my faults of years ago. She is dead now and my son is here. You must be loyal to him, as you would to me."

"If I must," Simon replied. "`E's a pretty little lad."

"Yes, he is."

"Got a charmin' way to `im."

"That's from his mother. She was a pretty maid when I knew her. They called her Dafodylle."

"But `e's mostly yers, I expect." Orlan's hair was a froth of curls rather than long, smooth plaits but it was as silvery as his father's, and the little chin was dimpled where Redmantyl's was smooth beneath his tarnished gilt, short-clipped beard, but the line of the jaw was as strong and squared; the boy's mouth, a rosy curve half-hidden by a small fist, was soft and less resolute than his father's, but no child could have the self-discipline of an adult wizard. "`E'll be a credit t'ye, M'Lord, if we see to `e's proper brought up. Give a year, an' ye won't be able t'say `e's ever been anywheres but `ere and a rightly born little Lordling."

Redmantyl smiled. "You must assist me in that, Simon. I am especially unused to caring for little children." He tousled Orlan's curls. "Look. What a helpless, tiny thing it is, and it frightens me more than all rival magicians I've faced in battle and all the dangers to life and soul I've yet encountered. My son. What am I to do with him? The best wizards never know their children so they are not distracted by family bonds. I meant to— Do you know, half a dozen times I've thought of sending this one along to Maryesfont Abbey or my aunt at Tremontegne, or back to his horrible old nurse so that she may have charge of him."

"Ye won't."

"I couldn't. He's mine. He belongs here."

"That's as it should be," Simon agreed frankly. "Shall I see `im to `is bed, M'Lord?"

"No, I'll watch over him. See yourself to bed, Lad, and sleep well."

"An' ye, M'Lord." After Simon had gone, the wizard lifted the sleeping child and carried him to his bed.

tu

Orlan's memories of his mother faded quickly, for Redmantyl held him each night before sending him to bed and whispered soothing words that gave him untroubled sleep. He no longer woke in the middle of the night crying for her. He did not think of her for days at a time, and when he did he found that that unbearable ache which he thought would never end was, in fact, dulled. Forgetfulness claimed him. By the time Ellan arrived at end of the month, grumbling at the discomforts of a sea voyage at *her* age as she was brought ashore, the little boy looked upon his old nurse as almost a stranger rather than a comforting reminder of his former home. He'd began to believe that his life in Lammouthe had been an unpleasant dream. The castle was his true home. It seemed right to him that he should be here. He belonged in the wizard's house, for he belonged to the wizard.

Lord Redmantyl was the most wondrous part of Wizardes Cliff. Orlan had never seen any man so tall and so fair. Redmantyl knew everything; every question was answered and if the words were not always within his understanding, Orlan marveled even more. He was in awe of this mysterious, magical being, and his amazement and pride grew as he saw that his mother had not lied; *this* was his father!

In the remote past, Ellan had told him tales of little boys and girls taken up by Oberon, King of the Faerye. Orlan imagined himself such a child, but not an ordinary mortal stolen away from his rightful place. He was the Faerye-Lord's child, an elven prince who had been lost and was now brought home.

The halls and towers of Wizardes Cliff contained more than three hundred rooms; most were unused and covered with dusty cloths, but others were the most magical places Orlan had ever seen. The top-most room of the slender, sky-touching Daune Tower, where Redmantyl's apprentices had their lessons, was separated into little compartments by shelves and tables filled with books; Orlan could not yet read, but he studied the strange hieroglyphs, the bright illustrations of fabulous creatures, the detailed diagrams of spells, and he wished he could know what they meant. His father's sitting-room was filled with more huge, leather-bound and copper-clasped books, carved chests containing antique curiosities, and dark wood furniture covered by colorful carpets and tapestries, some which Redmantyl had carried back from Persia and Asia himself.

There were so many people in his father's house, more than he had known in all of Lammouthe. Lord Redmantyl kept messengers, guards and craftsmen and twenty lads and maidservants to serve in the laundry, scullery and Feast Hall. Servants bathed Orlan and dressed him, fed him, picked up after him, kept him out of mischief and well away from the edge of the cliffs. His father's Chatelaine Adyna was especially responsible for looking after him until Ellan arrived. Her sons, near his own age, Kyarde and Kaiberte, became his friends; they played tag with him on the maze of platforms, stairways and catwalks in the Great Tower and played games of catch on the smooth flagstones of the vast Summer Plaza with a rubber ball Redmantyl had brought back from his travels. His father's apprentices also joined them when they were free of their lessons: the younger, a pale, slight boy with masses of dark curls, was Godefroi Suanesbloode and the elder, taller and darker, was Olyr. These two were much older than Orlan and might have scorned his company if he hadn't been their master's child. As it was, Orlan was petted and pampered by everyone in the household. They called him Chyelde, which was the proper address for a Lordling's son, and no one ever told him to go away and not be troublesome.

The ship from Storm Port that had brought Ellan to Wizardes Cliff also brought bolts of woolen broadcloth and rich velvet of sooty gray, pressed lawn and linen of snowy white and silks of ivory and scarlet. Orlan stood restlessly while the household tailor fitted him for his new clothes: tunics with detached sleeves and scarlet sashes, a riding habit with a long cloak and knee-breeches—his father had promised that he might have a pony—pleated kirtles, and piles of shirts. Adyna and Simon and all the chambermaids were busy at their needles, leaving broad bands of embroidery at every hem and collar and sleeve border. Orlan, used to common brown, could not imagine anyone owning so many beautiful clothes; he marveled as he dressed each morning that they were his. His father had explained to him that by his dark gray and scarlet he would be known to all as Lord Redmantyl's child, just as the red ribbons tied about the servants' sleeves marked them as members of his household.

Orlan was taught the significance of the colorful garments of the Norman people. Just as Redmantyl's robes declared him a wizard of highest rank and Orlan's own sooty gray and scarlet marked him as the wizard's son, so Norman citizens wore colors which announced their castes unmistakably. It was a comfortable custom: all were immediately recognized for what they were and received precisely the amenities expected without social error or embarrassment.

Orlan began his education as a noble Chyelde. Noble-born Normans learned early to ride a pony, to shoot an arrow and wield a sword, to display refined table manners and to speak proper Norman instead of the vulgar tongues of the common folk; Lord Redmantyl's son received his first lessons in these important matters that same summer. A young nobleman must follow a strict code of conduct which directed his behavior in every circumstance. He must be able to present himself to each with the most elegant courtesy, and learned to recite the proper address for every rank he might be presented to, from the Duke, My Gracious Lord Dafythe, to the lesser nobles and gentry. He must always be kind and courteous with inferiors as befit one of his rank, but he must never forget his own place. As son to the Lord of the castle, he was given great privileges, but he also assumed heavy responsibilities. A nobleman was obliged by honor and long-standing tradition to offer aid to any person he found in need—commoners, maids, children, the elderly, the weak or helpless. To abuse his power over those he was sworn to protect was the worst crime a noble could commit.

The nobility could also read and write, and Orlan learned these skills too, from the books on his father's sitting-room shelves. Within a few weeks, he could form the letters of his name with an uneven but legible hand. His father also taught him the stories and history that were important to the Norman people.

Orlan gave earnest, wondering attention to every lesson, but he took particular interest in magic. He did not yet show any ability of his own, but he was fascinated by his father's work and Redmantyl was forced to answer his multitude of questions. As one who would be a poet learned the beauty of rhymes and images before a single song had been composed, so Orlan learned of a wizard's power before the faintest sparkles of his own talent were evident. Like a poet, Orlan marveled at words. He hung upon his father's shoulder and watched Lord Redmantyl write line after line of minuscule script; he could not read so well to understand the nature of this treatise, but he was desperately curious.

"What is it, Father?" He reached for the page, but Redmantyl stopped him before small fingers smeared the fresh ink.

"I write of bonding spells, such as your amulet."

"'Tis spelled?" Orlan touched the silver disk, which had hung at his throat since his father had placed it there six months before. "How does it work?"

"A spell is a matter of concentrating your will onto one thing and commanding it thusly," Redmantyl answered. "I think of a thing, and make it so. But thought alone does not last unless it is fixed upon the material world. A written spell may survive so long as its devices remain intact."

"Devices?"

"The markings there."

"Oh." He studied the worn engraving, but it meant less to him than the written words. "'Tis only lines and circles."

"Words and devices are not simple scratchings, Orlan. They mean a great deal. If you will know any magic, you will know this: a word has power. It is bound to the essence of the object or idea it represents, and the thing it names will answer if you are able to call. A written spell is an abbreviated form of writing. It represents the word and the object, and contains all their power. I am Lightmaster—the word means me. This is my sign." The wizard indicated a swirl like a small, curling *L* above the top point of the pentacle on Orlan's amulet. "All these signs have meanings. When you know their meanings, they have power that you may command. Here, the pentacle brings them together to form a spell which says: *Whosoever wears this is bonded to Yryd Lightmaster and may call upon him.* When your mother wore it, I felt her pain and illness. She wished me to come to her and I knew that I must. I write of this—as you are my child, you and I are already bonded by blood and I will know when you are troubled without the aid of any spell. But the amulet increases our bond. If you will be a magician, I shall teach you of spell casting."

"You'll teach me?" Orlan asked hopefully.

"When you are older. Did you learn to read in one afternoon?"

"No, Father."

"This reading is more difficult to master, and you are yet young. Apprentices must be at least sixteen."

"Godefroi is fourteen."

"Godefroi's talents do not yet require 'prenticing. He is here because his mother would have me receive him."

"Must you work very long to be a wizard?"

"Yes, I must. I was 'prenticed to my master, the Old Lord, for seven years, then I traveled for five years as a mage before I was tested in my knowledge and self-command and confirmed a full wizard. I must work now to maintain my place among the great." He dipped his pen and resumed his writing.

"Are many wizards so great as you?"

"Great wizards are rare, Orlan. No more than twenty live in all the world at one time, and fewer now. Arysbethe Darklingsuan, Alonz of Palefyt, Korbyn the Blind—these are the living wizards of power." He put the pen down. "But many have a lesser magic. They look into other minds, to know what they think and perhaps influence these thoughts, and they see things that happened long ago or far off, or will happen in the future. All magicians possess something of these abilities, but a mental magician possesses them alone. Training in the magic arts is lost on them. I have never heard of a mental magician becoming a wizard. They could not, you see."

"Why not?"

"They cannot command the material world—that is, all things that may be felt and seen around us. True wizards may command the material at their will."

"The little magicians can't do so too?"

"No. As wizards, they would be helpless."

"Why?"

"They cannot weave spells, and so could not wear mantles of power. A mantle is a thing heavily spelled to protect the one who wears it. If another wore my mantle, it would be a piece of cloth which gives no more protection than an ordinary robe. A wizard who cast no spells of protection would not remain a wizard long. He would be at the lowest ranks of wizardry were he able to survive at all. But such magic is feared so much as we of power possess."

"Why?"

"Magic makes us different. If you are a wizard, you may be respected and loved by those without magic, but you'll make them afraid if they see you use your power. They will see that you are not like them."

Orlan knew what it was to be different. At Lammouthe, the common folk had called him *elfling* for his odd, over-fair appearance and crossed themselves when he was near. None of the children would play with him. "But why for magic?" he wondered. He had seen his father's powers exercised, the glittering orbs and bursts of flame. A week ago, Redmantyl had filled this same room with a delightful whirl of thousands of wildly spinning spots of bright light that would pass right through his hands whenever he tried to capture one. "'Tis most wondrous, but it doesn't do anything."

"Of course it does, silly child." Redmantyl tousled the boy's curls.

"Magic is far more than pretty toys for the amusement of children. I have the substance of the universe at my command—storm and fire, the flesh of the earth itself. A wizard's power made this castle. She who was Layn Redmantyl raised the cliffs from the sea. I have influence in the forces of life and death. What mortal would not fear for that?

"For countless years, magicians were thought to serve pagan gods or Christian demons and so were tortured and killed for the least little flicker of power. Some did serve evil forces, for there are such forces, my small one, which will corrupt the mortal soul, but magic itself is not of evil design. Before Kyrnelys Magnus became premiere Wizard-Lord, wizards sought the protection of nobles against the hatred of the Church and ignorance of common folk. Because the Magnus crafted a spelled mantle to protect himself and formed the ranks of the magical to remove the malignant and the weak from us, magicians are prominent these days. We are friends to those noble families who championed us in days past, but fear remains in the clergy and the common folk."

"Where does magic come from then?"

"From the heart and the mind," the wizard said. "But why my heart should be so different from all others that I have this ability, I cannot say. I simply do. The magic is there and I must use it. It may be in you as well." He considered the boy for a moment, then took up a candle, though it was daylight, and set it down before his son.

"Orlan, I wish you to try this." He touched the wick with his fingertip, and a small spark appeared, setting it afire. "It is the first test of a magician's talent. You are very young, but you may already show some glimmerings." He quelled the flame, then took the boy's left hand and arranged the fingers gently, so that all but the thumb and forefinger were tucked against the palm. "Place your fingers so–" He led the small hand toward the blackened wick. "Like so. It must be the left hand, Orlan, for that hand is closer to your heart. The mind directs the power, but the heart is its source. Left hand, always." Orlan had let his thumb and forefinger droop from either side of the wick and Redmantyl brought them back into place. "Focus upon the space between your fingers, so that you think of nothing else. Concentrate, Orlan."

Orlan concentrated. His brow furrowed and his mouth worked into a frown with the effort. For an instant, he felt the same hot pulse of energy that he had experienced in the tower. A thrilling tingle ran through him, then it was gone before he could will it to flame. The magic was there, faint and unformed, without direction. He could not bring it out of his heart and command it. He did not know how. He was not yet ready to bear that power within him.

He squirmed in frustration. "I can't–"

"It was a grand attempt, Little One," his father answered. "You've nothing to be shamed for."

"`Twas fine then? Shall I be truly magical?"

"Yes, Orlan, I think you will."

Redmantyl went away to Pendaunzel at the beginning of September and upon his return brought Orlan up to the top-most room of the Daune Tower, high above the rest of the castle. The ceiling sloped beneath the pointed roof and two windows were set high upon the round wall, one on either side.

"I will show you something best seen from here," he explained as he lifted the little boy up to sit on the deep, narrow ledge of the westward window.

Orlan could see for miles, over the chasm between the castle and the barbican, past the front walls, to the full breadth of the large island which blurred against the blue-green water in the afternoon haze. Tiny cottages and barns dotted the patchwork of green forests, grassy meadows, and newly-shorn fields. A single road led down through the green, out of his sight. Orlan gripped the window bars, beyond the open casement, and rested his cheek on the cold iron. The wind, fierce around the tower's top, blustered past his nose and blew his hair back from his brow. "Miles and miles," he whispered.

"That is Greenwaters Island, Child," Redmantyl said. "I am its Lord and Aubrey—that is, protector of all its lands and people."

"`Tis yours?"

"I was given this land, as far as you can see, by the Emperor. Before this past year, Greenwaters Island was the fief of a noble Layn who lived to the south."

"Over there?" Orlan pointed in the correct direction, at a village on a distant peninsula. "`Tis there?"

"No, that is Dubbin-on-Pont. Keyfins is much larger and further away. You cannot see it from here. Perhaps when it is warmer we may ride down to Castle Kefesea. No one lives there now, for the old Layn has died and left no heirs. My Liege Lord Dafythe thought that the island should be bestowed on its surviving Lordling—myself. He petitioned the young Emperor on my behalf."

"Because you are the best of all wizards?"

"Yes, that's why."

The boy smiled up at him with new pride. "And shall I be Lord of

Greenwaters Island after you?"

Redmantyl answered, "No, Child, you won't be."

Orlan was immediately abashed. "Why?" he asked shyly, his eyes wide and fixed on his father's face. "Because of Mama?"

"No, not because of that," Redmantyl assured him. "I've had the matter of your birth settled, but this land is entailed to the title of Redmantyl. The most powerful wizard after me will also have Greenwaters Island."

The child was comforted that, whatever the reasons, he was not at fault. "But it won't be," he whispered.

"That is how young Kharles would settle it. I am not noble by birth myself and my title is not hereditary—that means I cannot pass it to my child. All I have must be given to another wizard one day."

"Why?"

"Young wizards must find their place among the ranks of the magical by challenging elder wizards as they grow to their powers. Once one has fixed his place he must defend against younger wizards to keep it, especially after he has passed his zenith. Do you know that word, *zenith*, Child?"

"No, Father."

"It means the height, the best he will ever be, the most strong. After that, he grows weaker. Oh, not all at once—" Redmantyl explained quickly at the boy's alarm. "It fades over many years. A wizard of power may hold his position and defeat all challengers for twenty, thirty, or more years past his zenith."

"Ye'll be most powerful for a long time then?"

"In all the tales I have heard of a Redmantyl's fall, the Lord or Layn was very old, well past their century. `Twas so when I defeated the Old Lord. He was one hundred and twelve and I nine and thirty, so you see I have many years before I will face a more powerful challenger." He rumpled Orlan's curls. "When I am one hundred, you will be five and sixty—and a wizard yourself, I do not doubt."

"What happened to—" Orlan began, then paused. "What'll happen then?"

Redmantyl was long silent before he made his reply. "Wizard-battle is a fierce thing, Orlan, even more cruel than a soldier's war. We fight not with swords and arrows, but with the will of one mind set against another. If one is determined to defeat at all costs, then the weaker must die. If I am not killed in my last battle, then I will have to leave this place and my title will go to the wizard who defeats me."

"Did ye kill him, Father?"

"Who? The Old Lord?"

"Did ye?"

Redmantyl lifted the boy down from the narrow ledge. "He was a cruel old man, and he would have killed me had I lost. He had hated me, always, since I came to him as a boy to be `prenticed and he saw that I was very talented and growing to my powers quickly."

"Ye didna—"

"No, not in our battle."

"I shouldn't like to hurt you," Orlan said solemnly. "Even for Wizardes Cliff."

His father looked amused. "If you and I meet, Orlan, I shall be a very old man and ready to leave my place. To be a wizard, you must battle someone, if not me."

"But why?"

"It is the way things are."

"I'd like to be a great Lord when I am grown, Father," Orlan told him. "But I shan't harm anyone if I fight them. I'll be a most kind wizard."

"A gentle wizard," Redmantyl said as he set Orlan on the floor. "That, Child, I should like to see."

tre

The warm summer weather lasted to the end of September, so Orlan went to Dubbs Beach with Olyr, Godefroi, Kyarde, and Kai. Redmantyl said that children ought not always play on stone floors; they needed green grass and trees, sand and brisk, salt water. Godefroi, raised on a semi-tropical island, had grown pale in his months at Wizardes Cliff, and Orlan had not been beyond crafted walls as much as he should. The boys were allowed a day free of lessons and mother's and wizard's watchful eyes. Olyr, the eldest, was led the little party down through the village Lyges and through the woods to the cove. There, they tossed their clothes over low branches at the edge of the sand and the older boys plunged readily into the waves, but Orlan hesitated. To him, so much water was meant to float ships, not small boys, and he could do no more than stand ankle-deep and jump back at every lapping wave until Kai coaxed him in. They dug moats in the damp sand and built sagging, wet mounds meant to be castles, then stomped them back into muck. They ran up the strip of hot sand, chasing gulls and pipers, pitching rocks, and yelping when they splashed each other. And at last, hair damp and shoulders pink from sunburn, they brushed the sand from their bare limbs, dressed, and started back to Wizardes Cliff.

Lyges was built on three terraces below the barbican gates, and the villagers were gathered on the green at the bottom of the hamlet that day to greet a colorful caravan. The boys, too, stopped to look. The visitors were a flamboyant company, dressed so colorfully as their painted wagons, in magenta, leaf-green and sunny yellow, in bold stripes and polka-dots, in yards of ribbon and in billowing breeches or in kirtles that were little more than inches of frill. One man in bright orange and blue with bells on his cap and shoes was juggling wooden balls. Three girls in gauzy skirts were spinning madly with slender-legged lads in golden, embroidered hose. Another young man blasted a horn that dripped with red ribbons and an older woman played a brightly painted lute, accompanied by a boy with a tambourine. This last trio were the only ones who looked somewhat familiar to Orlan and he based his confused impression of the outlandish group on them.

"`Tis like a band of minstrels."

"No," said Godefroi. "They're thespians."

"What?"

"They perform before audiences for their living. They act out tales," Olyr explained. "You've never seen such before?"

Orlan shook his head.

Another woman swung down from one of the wagons, smiled as she saw the boys at the edge of the commotion, and came toward them. Her jerkin, hose, and short cape were all bluish gray with a silvery sheen and her broad-brimmed hat was adorned with a tall feather dyed red. Her chestnut forelocks were worked into four long braids interwoven with silver cords.

"You are the Chatelaine's sons," she said to Kyarde and Kaiberte. "And you..." She looked at Orlan curiously. "You all belong to the castle?"

"Yes," Olyr answered.

"Then I will walk up with you." She took Olyr's arm, and they went up through the village. Orlan and Kaiberte walked slowly behind.

"Who is she?" the smaller boy whispered.

"She's the Headethesper," Kai answered. "They come here often." Godefroi turned back and urged them to step more swiftly, and they ran to catch up with the others on the highest terrace.

"Is someone up there?" Olyr yelled to the gate towers.

A guard peered over the parapet. "His Lordship's been waiting for ye, Lads. Are ye all well?"

"Yes," Olyr answered impatiently.

"Let us in!" Kyarde yelped.

"Who is that with ye?" the other guard on the wall asked. "It looks like the Headethesper."

"It is the Headethesper!" the woman answered. "The troupe is in Lyges, and I will ask My Lord Yryd for permission to enter the castle."

"Yryd?" Orlan whispered; Kai shrugged. The great gates swung open. As she passed through to the castle yard, the Headethesper shouted up friendly insults to the guards, and the guards shouted back in kind.

Redmantyl was wandering the gardens behind the chapel when Orlan ran to him through the sheltering trees.

"Did you have a pleasant day, my Little One?"

"Oh, yes, Father! `Twas wondrous fun! May we go again?"

"If the weather remains fair–" Then Redmantyl saw the woman, who had followed. "Tedora."

"Yryd."

He set his son down and went to her. They took each other's hands. The thesper reached up to brush her lips against Redmantyl's cheek.

"It's wonderful to see you again, My Lord."

"And you. Are you well, Tedora? Has the troupe returned?"

"They wait below for you to have them in." She smiled. "It's taken us all day to travel from Greenlet."

"Well, we shall have them in, certainly. I hoped I could expect you back this autumn." Redmantyl released her hands. "Kyarde, run back to the gate and have one of the guards bring the troupe."

"Yes, M'Lord." The boy turned and ran.

"Have you met all the children?" the wizard asked.

"I recall the Chatelaine's lads, yes, and I spoke to your elder 'prentice as we walked up, but we were not introduced."

"Then you will meet them now. Olyr arrived after you last left here in the spring, and this is Godefroi, who has come from St. Eduardes Isle. And this–" The wizard gestured. "This is Orlan, my son. Orlan, Lads, this is Tedora Headethesper. I am patron to her troupe and you will see them perform while they are my guests here."

"I am honored," Tedora said correctly, "Olyr, Godefroi, and you especially, Chyelde Orlan."

The small boy whispered a reply. His father kept an arm about the thesper's waist, a casual and friendly embrace, as they went through the barbican and the boys tried to keep up with their brisk pace.

"Would you have us perform tonight, Yryd?" Tedora asked.

"Not this night," he reminded her. "'Tis St. Matthieu's Eve."

The thesper nodded. "The Equinox. Wizard's Keep."

"I shan't be in the castle." At the steep steps up to the bridge, Redmantyl stopped and took Orlan's hand. "Olyr, wait here for Kyarde and walk with him. Godefroi, I bid you hold tightly to Kai." Orlan shut his eyes as they crossed the bridge; the great height made him dizzy.

Redmantyl continued: "Your troupe may rest this night, Tedora. I shall have a feast set for you. You'll be without host, but Adyna will see to your comforts. Tomorrow, you may prepare for a performance on the smallest plaza, for I shall return by the afternoon." The great doors were opened and they walked into the Daune Tower.

Redmantyl left after greeting the troupe, and Orlan stayed in his room until he was summoned to dinner. It troubled the boy that there should be so many strange people in the castle while his father was out. Redmantyl had gone out before, on Maryemas Eve; Orlan had been worried then, but not so much as he was now with all these noisy, colorful people in the corridors. Adyna had put some of the thespians in rooms near his and he could hear them laughing and calling out to each other in merry voices. He had been fascinated at first by the jongleur, the dancers and the sweet-voiced minstrel, but once they quit their performances their vivacity was overwhelming. Sometimes, he thought he could hear that Headethesper's voice, and that troubled him more than anything else. He thought of how his father had smiled and put his arm around her, and how she had said *Yryd* instead of *My Lord*, and he wished his father would come back and make that woman and her people leave.

Dinner was riotous, as all the troupe crowded about the long table in the Feast Hall. Adyna presided over the meal in Redmantyl's absence, but Tedora seemed more in command. She was the one to call for silence for the evening prayer and keep the babble down, although she could be as boisterous as any young lad or maid in her troupe. Orlan was lost in shyness at the uproar. He only dared speak to two people, a girl named Anyse and her father, a kindly, middle-aged actor named Jareth, and that was because they sat near him and tried so often to engage him in conversation. He asked to leave the table before he had cleared his plate.

"Are ye not feeling well?" Ellan asked. She had stationed herself behind his chair throughout the meal.

Orlan shook his head. "I wanna go now," he whispered.

Tedora, at the far end of the table, looked up. "I'll take him to his rooms."

"As ye wish, Lady." Ellan tugged her skirts in the barest, polite curtsey.

"Oh, I'm no Lady, Nurse," Tedora grinned. There were some laughs and cheerful, raucous remarks of agreement from the table. "Come along, Dearest." She rumpled the boy's curls. Orlan didn't want her to touch him, but he allowed her to lead him back to his chambers.

Tedora was much nicer when she wasn't in a crowd. Her voice was so much softer when she spoke to him alone; she asked when he had come to Wizardes Cliff and where he had been before then, and about his mother, but Orlan could only answer her questions with mumbles. She lifted him up onto his bed, felt his brow with a gentle hand, and told him that she thought he would be fine; a little rest would set him right. Then she went back to her dinner and Ellan came in to ready him for bed.

"Are ye feeling fit now?" She felt his forehead too. "Ye're not at all warm."

"She said I was only wearied," Orlan answered.

"Pro'bly right she is, too." The nurse laid out a nightshirt and helped him unlace the velvet tunic Adyna had insisted he wear to dinner. "A good night of sleep'll have ye as well as ye should be feeling on the morrow. Aye, she's a wild one, 'tis certain, but pleasant e'en so. Got a sensible head on her shoulders, an' age'll only better it." She pulled the nightshirt over the boy's head. "Oh, not a Lady yet, but she's planning for it, she is. Yer father takes a fancy to her, Child."

"Truly?"

"So far as I can see. Now, no more of this. Sleep, Little Orlan."

But he did not sleep well that night. Even when the members of the troupe were quiet, Orlan could feel them crowding all around him, whispering and chuckling softly and moving in the dark. Late at night, he heard the minstrel singing to her own son in her clear, soprano voice and softly striking the strings of her lute.

Lord Redmantyl returned the next morning, but he spent much of the day with the troupe. Orlan ventured out onto the roof of the Feast Hall and watched the thespers on the small courtyard below as they unfurled long cloths, unpacked bundles of clothes, and gathered in small, murmuring groups. Tedora yelled to them, giving orders and directions, and his father was always with her; sometimes his voice rose in laughter.

After dinner, Redmantyl brought Orlan downstairs.

"You're going to see a play tonight, Little One," he said.

A stage had been set on the courtyard between the Seayrifte Plaza and the narrow passageway to the Summer Plaza. Torches blazed on the walls and huge squares of black canvas hung across the southern side. There were few props—painted chairs, a baptismal font, an odd pile of lumber and canvas with a platform at the top, and a large, sheet-draped object at one corner—but Orlan looked around, wondering, as his father took him across. They sat on the Seayrifte Plaza just below the steps. All the servants, the off-duty guards, and the more prominent citizens of Lyges sat behind them, on benches and cushions. Orlan saw none of the thespians who had been rushing about all day.

"It'll be starting soon?" He looked up at his father.

"At any moment," Redmantyl answered softly. "Hush." And as Orlan began to squirm with impatience, a young maid in plain dress—

that girl, Anyse—walked out from the Bottom Hall and curtsied pertly.

"Our noble patron, Lord Redmantyl, his household, and welcome guests from Lyges," her voice rang out clearly. "We the members of Redmantyl's most kindly sustained thespian troupe thank you all for your favor and bid you attend the tale we perform tonight. 'Tis a sad but worthy story of a man of pride and temper and of his grievous sins. With no more apology nor delay, we humbly present our tale of times long passed and people long dead, of Oedipus, the tragic King." She bobbed again and exited.

Orlan watched the pageant with uncomprehending fascination. A man and a woman in purple robes and gold crowns stood by the baptismal font. The woman held a squirming baby. They spoke to each other of the baby, their son, of how he would be King of Angeland someday, as his father was King now. A man who was meant to be a priest, as he wore a long, white robe and a large gold cross, came to them and prepared for the christening, when another man in red and black—like Lord Redmantyl but with no mysterious markings on his mantle—appeared in a puff of smoke. The wizard, Merlin, warned the King and Queen that the baby would murder his father and wed his mother one day if he were to grow to manhood. The royal couple was horrified by this prediction; they demanded that the wizard repeat it, then they stepped to one side of the stage to discuss it between themselves. The King was shocked that his own son would murder him, but he had heard of such things happening before. The Queen could not believe her child would commit such horrible crimes. She said she did not believe Merlin's predictions, but her husband grew more fierce as he grew more afraid and at last he forced her to surrender the child. The King gave the baby to a servant and told him to kill it.

On another part of the stage, the servant ran up onto the platform meant to be a mountain top, set the crying baby down, and prepared to stab it through with a dramatically raised dagger. Orlan hid his face against his father's sleeve so he would not have to watch, when suddenly the red-cloaked wizard appeared and stopped the murder. He said he would take the child and care for it hereafter. The servant ran away, and the wizard picked up the screaming baby, told it that it was the child of a wicked, unworthy man who had sealed his own fate by his cruelty, and carried it into the Bottom Hall.

The play continued after the baby stopped crying. Anyse returned and told the audience that many years had passed and the infant Oedipus had grown into a fine young man. The King and Queen of

Angeland ruled well, but they had no other children. A dragon ran wild in the land, destroying villages and eating people; all of Angeland was in fear and the King had gone to fight the dragon himself. Then the old wizard and his apprentice came out and spoke together. The young man called the wizard "Father," and said that he must leave his home to seek his fortune in the world. Merlin agreed that it was time for Oedipus to go, but he warned the boy not to engage in any fights with strangers, as he was so hot-tempered and passionate that anger would only cause him sorrow. Oedipus promised that he would control himself. He changed into the armor of a knight and he went out in search of adventure. On his travels, he met an older man also in heavy armor at a crossroads. They argued, then engaged in an exciting sword fight and jumped back and forth across the courtyard, until the older man was killed. The young man went on to the magnificent city of London. There, he heard of the dragon and the missing King and he proclaimed that he would go on a quest to kill the beast, and find the King as well.

Oedipus went to the dragon's lair. The shrouded thing at the edge of the courtyard turned out to be a terrible monster with a long, green, scaly neck, huge claws, and red and orange ribbons like flame charging from its mouth. The young knight fought this dragon as it squirmed half-way out onto the courtyard with frightful roars; he used his sword and used some spells that the wizard had taught him, and at last the creature fell to the stone floor and died. When Oedipus returned to London, bearing one of the dragon's sharp claws as proof of his victory, the city rejoiced. They told him that the King had been found dead, murdered on the road, and the Queen was in mourning for her husband. Oedipus went to comfort her, and she came to love him as a handsome and brave young knight. She decided to marry the young man and make him King. There was a splendid wedding ceremony: music from lutes and horns and drums rang out gaily and the thespers went out into the audience and pulled some of them to their feet, up onto the stage. The Queen herself took Lord Redmantyl's hand and the wizard rose to join the dance. Colorful streamers flew everywhere.

Once this festival had ended and the audience returned reluctantly to their seats, the dancers collected the streamers and Anyse stepped forward to announce that more years had passed. Oedipus and the Queen ruled well together and had four children. They were very happy and the kingdom was safe and prosperous. Then, one day, a storm roared over all the country and would not go away.

King Oedipus and his Queen sat in their throne room, wondering what this storm could mean, when a messenger entered and told them that the wizard Merlin had returned from long years of travel and heard of their unholy marriage.

"What dost thou mean, *Unholy*?" the Queen demanded, but the messenger could only answer that he knew not. The wizard appeared in a puff of smoke, as before, and told Oedipus who his true parents were and how he had committed the most hideous crimes imaginable. The Queen was horrified and she ran into the darkness, screaming. The young man cried out his sins, how he had murdered his father at the crossroads and then married his mother to become King, then he heard from another messenger that the Queen had hung herself. Oedipus was screaming now too and he dropped to his knees on the stage and huddled like a small, crushed thing. He cried out that he could not bear this, that he could not live, and then he gripped his hands to his face. Blood flowed from his eyes and he fell forward as if dead. A maiden came to his side and gently led him away.

The audience cheered and applauded. The thespers stepped out to bow and thank them for their kindness. Orlan shuddered in Redmantyl's lap.

"Horrible," he whispered. "Is he dead, F-father?"

"No, Child. No one died. It is only a story. Come along, and you will see for yourself." Redmantyl carried the boy up onto the stage to the spot where Oedipus had fallen. Wet, reddish puddles stained the flagstones, but the fallen King was gone.

"Did they carry him away?" Orlan asked.

"He must have gone off to the Bottom Hall. We'll see." They went into the hall where the troupe had gathered.

"Excellent, Tedora! A grand performance." The wizard turned from the Queen to the old King. "Now there's the value of a university education, Jareth. Your headethesper's learned the best tales of all time in her years at Maryesfont, and she's adapted them for the eyes of common folk."

Orlan watched as these grand people stripped away their costumes, and he realized that all he had seen was only make-believe. The Queen, who had been so lovely with her long, golden hair and purple robes, and who had run to kill herself in her madness only minutes ago, was Tedora Headethesper once she pulled off her wig. The old King was Jareth, and he had not been hurt at all by the sword fight. And Oedipus turned out to be a young man with an engaging smile and a tin sword; his eyes looked perfectly fine even though Orlan had seen him tear them out. His name was Rymbaughe and after he had changed out of his kingly robes he took Orlan out to the courtyard to show him the dragon, a huge, elaborate puppet of painted cloth that was worked by poles from within.

"`Tis only play?" The boy examined the harmless monster, pushed back against the Seayriee Tower.

"Only play, Little One," Rymbaughe assured him. "That's why they call them plays. `Tis a great game of pretend. Why, I've died a dozen times and more since I joined the troupe and I've always been ready to spring right up and bow to the audience the minute the story's finished. Here." The sword he had used to kill the old King and slay the dragon was still tucked into his girte and he pulled it out. "See how the edges are blunted? I could get a nasty bruise with that, but it wouldn't hurt so much as a real sword."

Orlan took the hilt in his own hands; it was very light and he could swing it easily. "`Tis like the wood swords we have," he told Rymbaughe. "Kai, Kyarde, and me."

"You can play with it if you like," the young man said. "But promise to give it back before the troupe leaves."

The boy smiled at him. "Promise." He tucked the sword into his own girte and ran to shown his friends what the thesper had given him. Kyarde and Kaiberte wanted to play with it too, and the three boys raced out onto the dark Summer Plaza to take turns swinging it and chasing each other until Adyna called for them. Orlan lagged behind. When he reached the courtyard, Rymbaughe was surrounded by congratulatory yeoman farmers and village folk, and young maids who thought him handsome. Anyse was flirting with Olyr. Adyna was busy with her own sons and no one would tell the small boy what to do. Dragging the sword's blunt point on the stones, he slipped back into the Bottom Hall.

Even in the midst of this flamboyant troupe, Redmantyl stood out. Orlan easily found his tall, striking father at the center of the commotion, cradling the tiny actor who had played the infant Oedipus. The baby was crying again. Orlan watched as his father gently ran his fingertips over the baby's brow; the howling quieted to sobs, then to a placid gurgle.

"There." Redmantyl tickled the baby's nose. "Your Andemyon has grown well since he was last here, Tedora. He's a handsome little pup. And you've placed him on the stage so young."

Jareth laughed. "He's been our most convincing prop this last month, My Lord, as we've done our Oedipus and the Youth of Arthur. We've been accustomed to use wax dolls in the place of infants, but they are horribly dead in a performance and this little one always adds spirit to the play."

"We expect a stunning debut of our new Nativity tableau at Christmastide," Tedora added and recovered her baby. "He's usually very good about his roles and only cries enough to let the audience know he's there. I expect he'll be a great thesper or an insufferable, arrogant lout before he's able to walk."

"No, not this little one," Redmantyl said. "Loutishness won't be in him. How could it be, with such a scholar to guide him?" He turned to Jareth. "The best headethesper in all the Empire, my man, and you're lucky to have her among your troupe."

Jareth agreed. "We count our good fortune daily, My Lord. `Tis no simple task she sets herself. I can say so honestly, having been in the position once myself. Recall when she came to us, My Lord, Hybbarde's wife and not out of Maryesfont before in her life?"

"He knows this well enough," Tedora said.

"And I was most impressed." Redmantyl smiled at her, and saw Orlan. "Shouldn't you be upstairs, Child?"

"The others aren't," the boy answered.

"Where did you get that sword?" Jareth asked.

"Rymbaughe. He said I could have it." Orlan stepped away and stumbled on the tin blade.

"He knows better than to give our props away," Tedora said. "He's little more than a lad yet but he's no fool. Yryd."

"Give her the sword, Orlan, and go to bed," Redmantyl ordered gently.

"Ye'll not be coming upstairs?"

"Not `til later." The wizard took the tin sword from his son's hand and gave it to Tedora. "To bed, Little One. Simon or Ellan or one of the chamber-lasses will take you."

"Yes, Father." As he walked out to the lighted courtyard, he could hear Redmantyl and Tedora Headethesper laughing.

The guests from Lyges were leaving, escorted by the castle guards, but a number of people still filled the courtyard. There was no one to attend to Orlan now; Adyna had gone with Kyarde and Kai, and Bess walked with one of the young farmers out to the darkness of the Summer Plaza.

"You've seen the baby then?" The voice of one of the chambermaids carried to him as he crept around the edges of the stage and he looked up to see where she was and if she had seen him. Alfryda was sitting on the wide steps down to the Seayrifte Plaza with

Redmantyl's manservant, talking softly.

"Now I'd call `im the best of all masters," said Simon. "Been in `is service six years now, before we won this `ouse, and I'd call `im the sort what makes me think the Empire's in the right `ands after all. But I've seen a bit of this before and I can't `elp t'wondering. The way `e's been cosseting t'er, and then there's t'other little lad and `oo `is mother might've been. `Fryda, `oo's t'say if `e can claim that fair-`eaded babe as `is own too? `Tis no more difficult to `ave two sons as well as one."

"And His Lordship so handsome `n' all," Alfryda whispered.

"Ye think so, do ye?"

"Don't be daft, Lad. Ye'd do well to look as he does. An' it wouldna surprise me a bit. Could ye e'er tell how many–"

"`Fryda," Orlan interrupted. He was baffled by this conversation and he didn't see how it could be anything important. "Father said someone must take me up to bed."

She started at the sound of his voice, then smiled and glanced quickly at Simon. "I'll go with ye, Little One." Her voice was a little too cheerful as she offered a hand. "`Tis well after yer bedtime, an' ye should've been settled long ago. Er– A pleasant night t'ye, Simon."

"And ye. Sleep well, little Orlan."

Orlan walked with the maid through the Bottom Hall, to the stairs, and up. "`Fryda, what did ye mean before? Ye an' Simon. What baby?"

She frowned. "`Tis none of yer concern, Orlan."

"Ye were meaning the thesper-baby? And– Andemyon?"

"Hush!" Alfryda hissed. "Ye shouldna be listening to the talk of others, an' asking after such things. `Twas doubly rude." She would say nothing more until she surrendered him to Ellan and wished him a good night.

But Orlan could not sleep. Too many things troubled him: the sword Tedora had made him give up, Andemyon, the strange exchange between Simon and Alfryda, Ellan's words "Yer father fancies her," the cool hand on his brow, and the way Redmantyl smiled at the Headethesper. He needed to see his father before he could settle himself to fall asleep.

A light shone beyond the half-open door to Redmantyl's chambers. Orlan crossed the hallway eagerly, then paused at the ajar door; a woman was laughing softly in his father's sitting-room.

Orlan peeked in. That woman, Tedora, sat before the fireplace, stirring the red coals with a poker. Redmantyl was in his chair with

Tedora's small son cradled against his chest and blanketed by a fold of his red cloak.

"-his first performance," Redmantyl was speaking. "You truly intend him to be a thespian?"

"If he shows any such talent once he's old enough to walk the stageboards," Tedora answered. She looked at Redmantyl in a way that disturbed the boy at the doorway. "I'm glad for him, Yryd. I was afraid these last long months, alone, and this little one has been more help than he knows. He's given me something to work for. I'm glad for you too. You've been so kind, much more than a patron to me."

"And you've been more than an artistic investment," Redmantyl answered.

"Was she much to you?" Tedora asked.

"Who?"

She opened her mouth to reply and saw Orlan before he could slip back into the hallway. "Orlan. What is it, Little One?"

His father turned, gently so that he wouldn't wake the baby. "Will you come in, Orlan?"

"No. I–" The boy retreated shyly. "I didna want– I– G'night, Father." He turned and ran back to his own chambers.

Redmantyl spent most of his time with Tedora in the days that followed. They seemed happy when they were near each other. Orlan saw them walking about the castle hand in hand or talking in his father's sitting room about a number of things, mostly incomprehensible to him. They discussed Tedora's accounts for her troupe's expenses, how much they had made in the last four months and how much they would need from Redmantyl to keep their caravan and costumes in good condition. They talked of the new productions Tedora planned. Other times, they spoke of more personal things, of Andemyon and himself, of Tedora's late husband, of wizards who chose to marry. Orlan understood very little of what they said but he would eavesdrop frequently and try to comprehend what was happening.

Redmantyl also cared for little Andemyon. He cradled him and sang lullabies in a haunting baritone that comforted Orlan when he heard it, almost as much as it disturbed him. His father hadn't ever sung to him. The wizard also amused Andemyon with sparkling toys of light. The infant never cried when Redmantyl held him. Orlan didn't see the point of all this attention to a useless, mewling thing; even Adyna's toddler, Ren, was more interesting company for all her drooling and whining. The boy began to hear many references to "My

Lord's little one," and he knew now that they were not speaking of him.

Tedora and her troupe left Wizardes Cliff two days after Mykhaelemas. Orlan was glad to see them go; he thought that they might be staying forever.

"Father, is Andemyon my brother?"

Redmantyl looked surprised by the question. "No, Orlan, he's not. Tedora Headethesper was wed to another in her troupe, a drunkard. He died this last winter before Andemyon was born. Tedora and I have come to a closer understanding since then, but I am not her son's father."

"Ye treat him like he is."

Redmantyl glanced at the boy again. "He isn't, Orlan. I would tell you were it so."

Orlan met his eyes, and nodded.

"All right, then."

They walked on the Klyffesend path, a narrow walk along the top of the grassy, slanting plateau that led up to the Crouwne Tower, well away from the rest of the castle. Because of the tower's elevated position on the rocky outcropping, it seemed to rival the Daune Tower though it was only half as tall, and it served as a lighthouse to warn ships away from the cliffs. The path was open along most of its way, even though the land dropped sharply within ten yards on either side. Redmantyl held the boy's hand.

"Ye'll marry her?" Orlan asked.

"Tedora? No. She has her duties elsewhere. Tedora is the leader of her troupe and she must protect all who travel with her. She does not have to stay, but thespers are wanderers, Free Folk, Orlan. They choose to live as they do because our ways are too formal for them. Tedora may leave her troupe if she wishes but I don't believe she will, any more than I would leave this castle of my own choice. We might be happy together, but not here and not there. Not yet. If Tedora marries again, it will be among the thespians. I shall never wed."

"Why?"

"Wizards do not marry." A broad stone wall was erected as a measure of safety as the path drew near the edge of the cliff. Redmantyl sat down and Orlan climbed up beside him. "You must understand, Little One, that magic bears great responsibility. A magician must give everything to his craft, or be weakened by distraction and thus fail."

"How? Will other wizards kill ye?"

"If they could. They cannot now, for I am most powerful, above all, but it will not always be so. You know how wizards must battle."

Orlan nodded solemnly.

Redmantyl lifted the child into his lap and watched the pebbles beneath Orlan's feet skitter off the wall and rebound over the edge of the cliff. "To become a great wizard and keep your place for so long, your magic must be first, or it is nothing. A wedded wizard is always distracted from his craft by obligations to his house and wife, and as his magic fails he must weaken and fall prey to greater Forces. It was so with My Layn Arysbethe of St. Eduardes Isle, Godefroi's mother. She married a man of no magic and could not be both proper wife and true wizard. She cast him from her household long ago to save herself. If you have the talent, Child, you will see how it is."

Orlan knew that this was very important and he wanted to understand, but all he felt at his father's words was relief. Tedora would not come to live with them. "`Tis why ye didna marry Mama? And ye won't marry the thesper?"

"Yes," Redmantyl answered. "She has her own reasons for refusing me."

"If I become a wizard, I shan't ever marry?"

"You may if you wish to, but it will be at a great price to your power." He carried Orlan a few steps, then set him down on the path.

The Youth
1953

quar

Orlan's mount slowed to a trot, then stopped, as he approached the bank of the river, the boundary between the small island kept as the Duke's hunting park and the city of Storm Port. The Duke had not been down to hunt in nearly thirty years, so the park had become a wilderness occupied by gamekeepers and used by travelers from Greenwaters Island as the shortest route to the city. Orlan had ridden so from Wizardes Cliff. He was at the end of the miles-long, dusty road and the edge of the forest; the raised drawbridge and guard towers of Storm Port loomed over him from the opposite bank.

"Is anyone there?" he called out.

A voice made into a bellow by a megaphone replied from the guardspost above: "What d'ye want?"

"I wish to enter the city!"

"Name yourself!"

The young man scowled at this impudence. Why were city garrisoned soldiers so slow-witted? One would think the Northlands was at war and he a suspected spy for these precautions. "I am Orlan, son of Lord Redmantyl!" he shouted. He wore a long, dark gray cloak and he'd ridden most of the way with the hood pulled forward and the cape drawn close in the hopes that he would be mistaken for a mage. Now, he pushed back the hood to show his face, the face of a handsome youth beginning his adult years. His cheeks were still downy with childhood, but his chin was set firmly, almost with arrogance, and the glint of his silvery eyes showed his rapidly growing talents and his knowledge of them. The resemblance to his wizard father was now remarkable.

"Orlan?" Another voice, younger and undistorted by magnification, called from above. "Orlan, the bridge is coming down. Pull your horse back!"

"Kyarde?" Orlan wondered at the top of his voice.

"Yes! I'll be directly down!"

Orlan turned his horse and rode back into the shadows of the forest. Guards shouted from the towers and the great drawbridge chains creaked as the bridge slowly lowered, then fell into place with a bang. A cloud of dust spewed up and Orlan's horse shied and neighed fretfully; he soothed the beast with a pat on the neck and urged it forward.

At sixteen, Kyarde had gone to serve as squire to the Captain of the Guard at Storm Port. He was now a sturdy youth, his first beard in the rough style of the infantry, and his uniform—bronze helm and breastplate, leathern, studded tuille and gauntlets, and gisarme—after the style of a Roman soldier.

"Orlan, it's good to see you!"

"And you, my friend." Orlan offered his hand and the young guard reached up to take it. "Are you with the garrison now? When we last heard from your mother, I imagined you were still in the Captain's service."

"Captain Kerrith retired last winter and the new officer thought it unsuitable to have a boy in her attendance. That sort of thing may cause idle talk."

Orlan laughed. "You look like the guards at Wizardes Cliff."

"Our armor's a bit heavier." Kyarde knocked at his breastplate. "We are sometimes in danger here, from within. Thieves, smugglers, scoundrels– You know the sort."

"I've heard," Orlan said, although he had in truth heard very little.

"But it's not so bad at this post, as hardly anyone comes in through the Dukesgate. Most traffic goes through the Lyngate and the docks, as well." He grinned. "If you could but imagine how much trouble it is to raise and lower this bloody trap, you'd have gone `round."

"And missed seeing you again? No, I'd rather give you the trouble."

"Well, the truth is I'd rather have the trouble than miss you. I see so little of old friends."

"Do you like this work, Kyarde?"

"It suits me well enough, as I am still near my mother's home, but I'm going to join a regiment on the frontier when I am older. `Tis said that My Layn Margueryt may have need of fighting ranks soon."

A portly sergeant came down from the gatetower and barked at Kyarde. "Boy, be at your business." He bowed to Orlan. "Apologies, M'Lord, but orders are orders. Captain'd have a rolling fit if she heard of anyone leaving his post, even this one."

"I understand. We'll speak later, Kyarde, once you are free and I am able to find your mother's house."

"There's no trick to that," the young guard replied. "Mother's house is straight back on the Long Street, before the bazaar and below street. Shall I accompany you?" The sergeant looked vexed, but did not protest.

Orlan smiled. "No, Kyarde. I've ridden the length of Greenwaters Island alone, and I may ride a little further." He clicked to his horse and tried to guide it through the traffic on the main street.

When Redmantyl had asked him to ride to Storm Port for this business with Adyna, he had consented readily. Adyna had left Wizardes Cliff some years ago. After a plague at the castle had crippled her younger son and killed several of the servants, including Orlan's nurse Ellan, she had settled in Storm Port; financed by Redmantyl, so that her children would have a solid place for themselves, she kept a tavern. Orlan was to see to her accounts and copy her ledgers for examination. He was proud to be given so much responsibility and anxious to prove himself worthy of his father's trust.

He had traveled before, but always in company. Last summer, he had gone to the southern shore of Greenwaters Island with Mathias, his father's new apprentice, Andemyon, and his little servant, Jem. The great wizard had been petitioning the Duke to have the fief of Greenwaters Island made separate from his title of Lord Redmantyl so that his son could be heir to one if not the other. If the petition proved successful, Orlan would be Lord of Greenwaters Island one day and Castle Kefesea his home. With this possibility in mind, Orlan had planned to spend a full fortnight at Keyfins, in the abandoned castle of the last Layn, to see if it could be restored or was best torn down. He had played at Lordling in the ruined halls with his retinue of three and walked on the beaches below, but they were forced to return early when Andemyon had nearly drowned. That had been an accident—not Orlan's fault—but he felt responsible. This past month, he and his father had escorted Andemyon to Pendaunzel, for Tedora's son was to enter the Duke's service as a herald. They'd remained at court throughout April and were welcomed as favored guests of Duke Dafythe; they attended great feasts and dances every evening. Orlan was introduced to the most important people of the Northlands and he was honored in return as the son of a great Lord, with no stain of bastardy to his name. He was Lord Redmantyl's child; that was all, but it was more than sufficient. With so much attention paid to him, he did not even mind that Andemyon was so petted and fussed over by the courtiers and treated so kindly by the Duke himself. Orlan thought of returning to the great city one day, but this trip to Storm Port was nearly as exciting. He had worried during his journey along Greenwaters Island, but now that it was ended he was glad to be here, away from Wizardes Cliff.

He soon discovered that riding down the crowded street was like trying to ride through a deep stream; people pressed him on all sides, blocking every step. The horse balked and danced and finally refused to move. Orlan slipped down from his saddle, tugged at the bridle, and slowly coaxed his mount along the cobblestone walk. With each dogged step, he paused to look up and around.

Orlan was impressed, as he had been at his visit to Pendaunzel, by the elaborate splendor of the city. Storm Port was not so grand as the capital, with the tall stone and darkwood houses of its finest citizens, the polished copper roofs of the Council Halls, the splendid, sprawling palace in its green parkland. In Pendaunzel, the streets were lined with statues, marble and bronze figures of great warriors, chancellors, dukes, and their consorts. The fifty-foot tall figure of Eduarde Redlyon, armed for battle, sword drawn, face scarred but sternly handsome, frowned down over the city's marketplace; Orlan could almost believe that the nineteenth-century Emperor was truly that size in life. The few statues here were small and dotted with pigeon droppings and obscenities, and the tall buildings of stone, wood and plaster were all shops with private homes on the outhanging floors above. Orlan saw no grand residences and he knew that there was no castle. Storm Port was a city with no noble-born citizens; no Lordling was given to rule beyond the elected Mayor, nor could any claim it. Like any port, it was a city of merchants and mariners, a city of trade.

Like the Duke's city, Storm Port had a cathedral, a magnificent, huge, stone lacework of sky-scraping bell towers and spectacular flying buttresses; its gold-leafed dome and vaulted roofs gleamed like the promise of Heaven. Named for St. Khrystopher, patron and protector of travelers, it stood as the holy guardian of Storm Port, rising from the jumble of the lesser walls, above the colorful commotion of the marketplace ahead.

In Pendaunzel, it was impossible to go half a block without seeing at least three government officials, but Orlan had already traveled nearly half the length of Storm Port without seeing one customs clerk or bailiff. This was odd, for Pendaunzel was concerned with the government of all the Northlands, but even the smallest hamlet in the land, no matter its business, had its share of ducal officers. Surely there must be councilors to the Mayor, justices, a sheriff, but Orlan did not see them. Such folk were not out in public view. The people around him looked quite common, with swarthy faces and guild badges and stained, working ``s of linen and leather, the women in calico kerchiefs and the men with untrimmed beards. All wore brown: brown skirts and kirtles, brown tunics and jerkins, brown hose and leggings and ankle-laced boots, as if he had been caught in the middle of a turbulent, muddy sea. He saw a few well-dressed merchants and bright travelers, but these were nearly lost amid the tradesfolk, the drabs, the mariners, and the scurvy-looking characters who loitered in the doorways and glanced hopefully at his horse.

Cobblestones beneath his feet clattered, loose; others were missing completely, leaving muddy gaps. The city carried a strange, pungent smell of fish, sea salt, smoke, and sewers; Orlan crossed several short bridges over gutters, clogged and waiting for rain to clear them. Storm Port was not so carefully tended as the capital. Orlan had heard that it was the most Plague-stricken spot in the Northlands. He had heard tales of this vast, peopled city abandoned by all who were able to leave and left with beggars dying in the empty streets. Only last summer, carts had been sent from St. Khrystopher's to gather the scores of corpses and take them to the churchyard for quick burial. Bonfires burned in every courtyard and square to destroy the bedding of the victims. Innumerable rats were slaughtered. Sea water was brought up by the bucketful to clear the sewers. The disease abated at last, but after hundreds had died, as hundreds died whenever Plague descended. August, it was said, was the dangerous time, but Orlan planned to be gone before then. His business here would not take so long.

He found Adyna's alehouse, five steps down to a sunken cellar; an imported glassware shop above, six steps up, and upper levels jutted over the street. A sign hung over the tavern door, bearing a mighty elm with silvery-white leaves and one leaf pushed huge into the foreground, painted with careful, frosty detail. Every greenish vein stood out. Below, also in frosty white on a dark green background were words: *The Whitelm*. Orlan tied his horse's reins to a post, set a spell upon the knot, and went down.

The tavern was a musty, cool, ale-scented place with stone walls, damp floors, and a heavily-beamed, low ceiling to support the building above. There were no windows and all the lanterns were lit as if it were midnight instead of midday. Few customers visited at that hour, common merchants and tradesfolk who had abandoned their shops and market stalls for a brief refreshment and, at the bar in back, one heavy-set, middle-aged man with thinning hair and a reddish tint to his nose and cheeks. He wore the dusty gray tunic of a wealthy merchant; the dark blue and dull orange mantle and large copper badge of a city reeve lay on the stool nearest him. Adyna stood in the narrow space between the bar and shelves filled with glass tumblers, tin tankards, and row upon row of dimly glinting jugs of wines and liqueurs behind.

"Orlan!" She looked up, saw him, and beamed. "Come to me, my pet. Tell me, how are they all back at My Lord's house?"

"Well enough, Adyna. Father sends greetings." Orlan brushed the dust from his short tunic and breeches as he crossed the room.

"You look so handsome, Chyelde." She stepped around the bar to kiss his cheek. "You're the image of My Lord exactly, were you old enough for a beard."

The man at the bar grinned.

"Are you weary from your ride? Will you have some refreshment?" Before he could reply, she turned and took down a flask of sweet red wine, half-filled a tumbler, and added water and a dash of crushed mint. This was the sort of light spirit usually allowed children, all Orlan was permitted to drink at home. "Was your journey very rough?"

"No, not at all. I was lonely, as I rode with no one to talk to, but the weather was fine and the road smooth. At Father's advice, I rode in three days and lodged one night at Midkrosse and the second at Narby." The boy tasted his drink. "`Twas quite easy."

"The folk there are kind to travelers," Adyna said.

"They were kind to me, at the least. I cannot say how they might treat lesser guests. I was given rooms to myself and meals that would suit, and none would ask for more payment than was fair. They would not dare, or Father would pay them back in kind when he called for the harvest taxes."

Adyna's customer chuckled.

"I wish I could provide such comfort for you here," Adyna said. "The lodgings of my house are not so fine, but I may give you a room to yourself."

"I would not crowd you."

"Nonsense. Many have stayed in our house before. The thespers lodge with us two and three times a year, and Godefroi and Olyr have been here."

"Godefroi and Olyr? When?"

"Oh, two summers back, after all that trouble. Oh, I could see that something was wrong, but I never asked questions and they stayed a fortnight and earned their keep. Why, Godefroi painted the new board at the door."

"I noticed it as I entered," Orlan said.

"Lovely, isn't it? I didn't know the lad had such a fine hand with paints before he asked to do that."

"Godefroi always drew so well, portraits of Laurel and Igren. Do you know where they went from here, Adyna?"

She shook her head. "I couldn't say, Lad. They left with one of the carny troupes that comes in for festivals, but they weren't there when the troupe was around again at Fat Tuesday."

"You haven't heard where they've gone?"

"No, Lad, I've not heard a thing." She picked up the empty mug her customer had left and bent to the kegs beneath the bar to refill it. "'Tis a pity about Olyr."

"Yes."

"Still, you'll be a fine wizard yourself, Orlan, as your father," Adyna said wistfully.

"I hope to be."

"Now you've been 'prenticing how long?"

"Eight years. Father says that I might test and be confirmed a mage at Christmastide." Young magicians must take vows and keep to them strictly for the five years between apprenticeship and full wizardry: to avoid fermented drinks, red meats, and salt, to keep sleepless vigils and fasts, and to remain celibate. Orlan was troubled at the rigors of this testing, but he believed he had reached the levels of self-control and discipline necessary to avoid temptations. It was the only way he could become a wizard.

He sipped his wine. "Shall we attend to my father's business this afternoon, Adyna? I was given careful instructions as to your accounts."

"Oh, never mind that for now. There's time after working hours. I must see to you as a guest first. We have three rooms at back, one kept for Kyarde when he's off guard and 'tis empty now. We'll settle you there. Rennie!"

Adyna's daughter Ren, now a small, plump maid of fifteen, apron water-spotted from washing mugs and platters, came in from the back. She smiled shyly and curtsied. "Orlan, welcome."

"Lass, take Orlan's baggage to Kyarde's room."

"Adyna, I can carry my own bags as well as a little maid—"

"Nonsense, Chyelde," Adyna replied and blocked Orlan from retrieving his parcels before Ren dragged them away. "Will you stay with us long, Lad?"

"A fortnight or so. Father said I might stay a little beyond my business if you make me welcome. I've not been to Storm Port before."

"Never before?" the man at the bar spoke. "We must show you about our city then, Lad. `Tis the finest in all of the Northlands." He bowed his head and placed a broad hand at his breast. "Houarde Portreeve, at your service."

"He is reeve given to keep all custom houses in Storm Port, and master of many great ships, and also husband to our Layn Mayor," Adyna explained. "Syre, I am proud to have you meet Orlan Lightesblood, son to My Lord Redmantyl."

"Indeed?" Houarde looked more cheerful than before. "Why, `tis a great honor to meet the son of such a Lordling, Chyelde Orlande."

"Ta, Syre. But I am plainly Orlan. It is not a noble name."

"No less an honor, whatever your right name. I've heard much of the Red-Lord. A wizard, I believe?"

"Yes, Syre."

"Most powerful of all living," Adyna said. "More wine?"

"I'll have another, if you please." Houarde offered his empty mug.

"When does the tavern close?" Orlan asked.

"Oh, hours yet. We close earlier than most, for Ren's sake, but after sunset. You might sit here for so long, but I think you would entertain yourself better about the city. See the sights."

"The bazaar's not a step away," Houarde suggested.

"Yes!" Adyna agreed. "You might find some lovely trinkets, gifts to My Lord's household. That's the best of a port city—shiploads of goods from all over the world. Silks, tea, Cathay porcelain, the most beautiful tapestries. They say that if you cannot find your heart's desire in Storm Port then it does not exist elsewhere."

"In truth," Houarde smiled vigorously.

"It sounds wondrous. I'll go and explore then."

"I'll go with you," the Portreeve drained his mug. "As fine an ale as you serve, Keeper Adyna, there's nothing better than a walk in goodly company on a summer's day."

They left the tavern together. A ragged child, not yet Ren's age, was working frantically to untie Orlan's horse from the post. She looked up at Orlan and Houarde in despair.

The young man frowned at her and brought up a faint hint of fairy-sparkles; his father had taught him the merits of this trick. "Go now, Child," he said, and the girl, wide-eyed, fled to the safety of the crowds.

"Bloody little beggars," Houarde huffed. "You've got to watch them at every turn, Chyelde Orlan, or they'll steal the nails right off your toes. Hold tight to your purse while we walk."

"There's no need of that, Syre," Orlan assured him. The little moneybag tied at his waist featured an elaborate red and silver pentagram which appeared as no more than decoration, but the cutpurse who touched it would be in for a nasty surprise.

The uproar at the bazaar was deafening. Amid the throng of Storm Port folk, merchants in strange garments stood at colorful tents and open stalls shouting the merits of their wares, greater merchants examined whole booths of merchandise critically and muttered their offers of trade, suspicious characters slipped easily from purse to pocket to unguarded table, minstrels and carnival troupes performed for pennies, and small children sold bundles of country flowers for less. This was the heart of the city, the reason for its being. The advantages of a joined farmers' market and import bazaar open from first thaw to first snowfall—if the weather and the city's health permitted—drew merchants from all over the world and customers for any desired thing and forced Storm Port to grow to its present, enormous, ever-busy size.

The odor of the place was incredible. The perfume of a thousand scents from fresh hay to sandalwood to broken black tea leaves to cut lilac overpowered the prevailing stink. Orlan shielded his nose and mouth as he wandered from stall to stall, viewing small marvels. Merchants from the Far East showed him rockets, long-handled swords in decorative scabbards, painted kites featuring warriors, dragons and couples embracing in pink-flowered gardens. Portuguese merchants, in good standing with the reclusive Incans, displayed tiny pendants of gold and offered samples of a bittersweet mixture of cream and something called cacao; Houarde bought two large packets for a copper sixpence. And the merchants themselves were astonishing, for Orlan had heard much of the people of India and Cathay, of black Abyssinians and Italians, of blonde Norseman, but they all were so different from the people of his native land. He had always imagined them to be—well, not so much like himself, for his appearance was not ordinary—but like the people he saw each day. That the shape of their eyes, their noses, their lips should be so unfamiliar was not expected. That their tongues formed the words of the Norman language so peculiarly was a surprise. After a few baffling conversations, Orlan was comforted by the raucous tones of Storm Port's own peasantry. It was too early for a harvest market, but there were barrels of ale, pots of honey, jugs of cider and berry wine, freshly-caught fish strung into bundles and freshly-killed fowl, rabbits and deer stretched on wooden racks. Local smiths had left their shops to display pans and kettles of burnished copper and cups wrought of fine pewter and cheap tin. Pens filled with kids, lambs, and piglets blocked pathways amid the confusion.

Orlan examined rings and cloak-pins and fingered strings of pretty beads, but found nothing to interest him. He saw no appropriate gift for his host here in Storm Port nor for Ren, and certainly nothing worth buying for his father. He counted many pretty trinkets, but was offered few real bargains; too many people took in his riding habit, new boots, polished silver amulet, and his delicately modeled hands and long, free hair, and asked more from him than they would of others, more than Orlan was willing to pay. In spite of his youth and inexperience, he was not so naive to believe that these were the true values of things, and Houarde was always at his side to insult and bicker at the more outlandish offers.

"I'm sorry there's nothing to your pleasure, Chyelde," the Portreeve said as they walked away from another booth.

"It's not so much if I'm unable to find all things to my liking," Orlan answered, pausing to examine pairs of Florentine kid gloves. "But I had hoped– Here, what's that?" He leapt through a gap in the shuffling crowd to reach a canopied table of licorns—the horns of unicorns—displayed by a solid Dane in mariner garb. The finest, seven feet long and unbroken at the point, polished and set with gold along the spirals, rested in velvet wraps. Lesser, crumbled, specimens were scattered on the table, ready to be cut into smaller pieces or scraped for medicinal powder.

"Do you think such a thing might be suitable?" he asked Houarde, who had pushed his way through the mob after a floundering struggle. "They are so expensive." The Dane did not disagree.

"Perhaps," Houarde answered, "but well worth the price, I hear. That is, Chyelde, 'tis well known they hold powerful magic in healing all sorts of ills and, of course, the true horn will bead with dew near poisons. If you possess such a treasure, it may be the saving of all at your table."

"I'm not as sure of that," Orlan said. "Father keeps two such horns in our library, but only as a curiosity. He says that there is no magic to them. They are lovely, but I think I would waste my money to abandon it here."

Houarde looked surprised. "You've no fear of poison?"

"Who would poison me?"

"Now, I've heard tales of harm done to an innocent child to take revenge against the parent."

"Father has no enemies," Orlan laughed. "Besides, there are better guards from poison than these. A simple slip of paper will color at the presence of some vitriols. And too many noble princes have weighted their tables with licorns, toad stones, and snake's tongue and still died young. `Tis true that these will soothe a bellyache, but only so well as hartshorn or mint, which may be got for copper instead of gold. My father would not forgive me such extravagant folly." The mariner-merchant was frowning dangerously, and Orlan moved on. "He says that when he was a young mage, he traveled through Africa and India in quest of the sight of a one-horned beast, but saw none."

"Ah," Houarde said with some disappointment. "`Tis lucky you didn't toss any gold to that man. He looked a scurvy sort. True licorn or no, it did not come to him honestly, you may be sure."

They passed tables with colorfully labeled spice boxes—cinnamon, mustard-seed, pepper, saffron—and more tables laden with rolls of cloth: bright, shining satins and printed calicoes, bleached muslin and speckled tabby silks from India, painfully brilliant silks dyed in Cathay, the finest gold-spun Languedok samite, starched white linens and lace woven within the city walls, woolens rusty-red and butternut shorn from the backs of the Northlands sheep, Skottish, Cashmere, Angoran beasts and an unknown creature which the merchants called alpaca. At the edge of the bazaar, beyond this, were more strange animals in the living flesh: slender, nervous Arabian mares, caged turtledoves and nightingales, long-haired hound pups, white cats with bright blue eyes and black faces, and a small, shrieking monkey on a leash. All shied at Orlan's approach, which confounded Houarde.

"What manner of witchery is this?" the reeve wondered aloud. "Why, I've never seen such oddness from any natural animal of the Northlands. What d'you suppose `frighted them so, Chyelde?"

"Nothing I know," Orlan answered, himself distressed by the commotion. One of the pups was still yelping frantically. "Shall we go back to the Whitelm?"

"If it please you, Chyelde, but we've not seen half the wonders here."

The youth consented to return to the bazaar. With Houarde's direction, he passed more booths and tents, examined more cloths and trinkets and Eastern curiosities and at last discovered a table with ivory carvings. Houarde took up one of the largest pieces, a strange creature with round legs like trees, outsized ears, tusks polished to gleaming white, and a long trunk upraised. The eyes were bright, red stones.

"Here, what manner of beast is this?" he demanded of the merchant. "A sort of long-snouted pig?"

"No, Syre, oliphaunt."

"A fabulous monster, no doubt."

"No," said Orlan. "There are such beasts." He caressed the figure's carved back.

"Truly?" The Portreeve sounded skeptical.

"We have a tapestry from the Ind that shows oliphaunts, but they are very dark, not white. How much will you ask for this piece, goode merchant?"

The merchant, an aged Asian woman, smiled. "Thirty silver shillings, Norman coin, M'Lord."

Houarde frowned. "Thirty? For that bit of ivory?"

"The eyes, Syre, are rubies." She turned the figure so that one eye caught the sunlight and glittered fiercely.

"I'm sure it's well worth your price," Orlan said. "But I can't—"

"Eight and twenty?"

"No."

She frowned at Houarde. "Six and twenty and five silver pennies, as low as I dare to offer. It cost more than that to make, I assure you."

The youth shook his head. "It would be too large to carry home." He examined several of the smaller pieces. "What is this? A cat?"

"No, M'Lord, martikhore."

"Tiger," Orlan explained at Houarde's puzzlement. "Oh, look!" He took up the piece that had caught his eye, a delicate swan in flight.

"Eleven silver shillings, M'Lord."

"The eyes are not ruby," Houarde protested. "Any fool may see that. They're a sort of pale blue."

"Diamonds, Syre. See how cleverly it has been carved? Each feather of the wings, the feet, as fine as the swan's itself. It seems ready to fly from the young Lord's hands." She smiled brightly. "For you, as you are so handsome and fine a young Lordling, I will say eight shillings."

Houarde scowled. "A silly little chip."

"Three," Orlan said.

"M'Lord!"

"I rather like it, but not more than that."

"Seven, if it please you."

"Three would please me more, but I may offer three shillings and twenty pennies with comfort."

"Copper pennies?"

"I do not have so much silver about me."

"Six shillings."

Orlan put the swan down.

Their haggling continued, the merchant anxious to make her sale and Orlan willing to buy for the right price but always ready to walk away. At last, they were settled. The merchant sighed with resignation as the youth counted out his coins. "There is danger in dealing with handsome youths," she said. "I always make the fool for their smiles. Go, M'Lord, and enjoy."

As they walked away, Houarde took the carving and examined it critically. "A waste of good silver. Four bloody shillings. What did you want it for?"

"A gift."

"You talk it down well. Women will make themselves fools over you, Lad, which may save you much trouble over the years, and cause you more. But 'tis an amusement to watch such ancient merchants and alehouse keepers— Tell me, Chyelde, was Adyna your nursery maid? All the time I've spent in her tavern and never heard her coo over any lad before. Nurse-maid, was she?"

"No, Syre. She was my father's Chatelaine and as a mother to me when I was small."

"Your own mother's dead?"

"Yes," Orlan answered.

"And your father's never married again? Why, I understand from my wife, the Layn Mayor, that Lord Redmantyl's a handsome young wizard not yet sixty. Greenwaters Island's Lord, I think, would be a prize for any ambitious woman even so."

"Perhaps, but Father would not marry. He doesn't think it proper for wizards."

Houarde looked astounded at the idea, then shrugged. "Ah, well, wizards. Who can say?"

"He loved a woman once, a thesper, but she's been dead for many years." Orlan stepped suddenly into shadow and looked up at the towering cathedral facade, carving upon carving of feather-winged angels, placid-faced saints, grimacing gargoyles, owls and griffins, stags and satyrs, at once horrifying and beautiful. This was where Tedora had given her last performance. It occurred to Orlan that the room where he would sleep tonight must be where she had stayed in her illness. She had died there.

Redmantyl had become increasingly gloomy these past years. Orlan had only begun to realize how young his father must be when Redmantyl had lost the lightness of youth. He was now a man weary and uninterested; he kept to his books and spells and smiled little. He might laugh aloud at bold jests or tell hearty tales when prompted by good company, as those who gathered at the Duke's court, but no merriment warmed his eyes. In his own castle, he would pace the corridors at night or leave the house altogether without saying where he had gone. He would not shout, nor weep, cast great storms of anger, nor strike any of his household, but these would have been preferred to his grim silence.

Orlan was frightened at his father these days, as much as he loved him. He wished he might do something, but his desire to cheer the wizard remained unspoken and he was not invited to speak. He could offer no comfort; he was no comfort to Redmantyl.

He wanted so much to prove himself, to help if he could not soothe. He excelled in all his studies, prepared for his mage-vows, behaved as well as he could, and even accepted the business of this journey to please his father. He wondered now if he had done enough. Wizardes Cliff would never be as it had been in his childhood—for, truly, the days when the castle had been full of servants and apprentices and visiting thespers were far better than its present empty state—but he continued to try. Perhaps if he were very good...

He sensed someone nearby. Fingers brushed his waist and tugged at his pursestrings; a loud yelp of surprise erupted at his ear. Orlan turned to watch the fleeing figure, then looked around to see if the Portreeve enjoyed the trick. But Houarde had gone and taken the ivory swan with him.

cinq

The Mayor of Storm Port and her husband sat in their parlor. The windows were open to let in a cool evening breeze, but a red-hot bed of coals glowed in the fireplace. Seldom-used hunting dogs stretched out at their feet, panting, and a small serving-boy knelt on the hearth with dew-like beads of perspiration on his reddened face as he toasted bread and cheese on a long-handled iron fork.

"I met a lovely young lad at the Whitelm," the Portreeve said.

Ilset, Layn Mayor, looked up from her work and lifted an eyebrow delicately at this announcement. "Did you?" she asked.

"He's called Orlan," Houarde replied cheerfully. "And you'll never imagine, my Love—he's the Red Lord's son!"

"Lord Redmantyl?"

"Yes, that's the one. The same great wizard you always went on about when you were in that profession yourself. Remember?"

"Of course I remember," Ilset said, and forced herself to be patient. If Houarde had a point, he would reach it in his own time. "I didn't know there was a son."

"He's only a boy, not far past twenty, I'd say."

The common Norman folk had a time-honored saying: *Only the foolish and the dead make enemies of wizards.* Lord Redmantyl had few living enemies, lesser wizards who had met him in battle and could not forget the sting of defeat. Ilset had met Redmantyl, once, while a young magician herself and encouraged by the protection of Layn Dyrkhesse of Anglessey, an aged and powerful wizard who didn't think her at all a threat; Dyrkhesse knew all the power she possessed, and they trusted their friendship as long as they understood where they stood against each other, which was often the way with wizards who were not enemies. Ilset had been at Anglessey when they'd heard of the old Redmantyl's overthrow by a young wizard; as more news reached them, both were surprised to learn that the new Redmantyl was a youth not yet forty.

Such a thing was unheard of; Dyrkhesse exclaimed that the victory must have been accomplished by unfair means, poison or trickery. She named it the place of all honorable Wizard Lordlings, such as herself, to teach the upstart pup a lesson. Ilset, not yet established, had accompanied her to the Northlands.

They'd met the young Redmantyl in the fields beyond Lyges; he had heard of their challenge and stood waiting for them, unafraid. His fearlessness ought to have been a warning, but at the time the great wizard and her companion only saw a brash, arrogant young fool, an overconfident boy. Ilset learned afterwards that this same brash youth had defeated three well-established wizards in the five months since he had claimed his title. This Redmantyl had nothing to fear from them.

Ilset trembled now, though Houarde did not notice, at the memory of their swift defeat. Dyrkhesse had fallen in the first confrontation— there had been the faintest sparkle from the young Lord once their eyes locked in combat, then the elder wizard lay dead—and Ilset was left to fight alone. All her powers, all her spells, all her strength of will had been blasted at him and he had withstood it. She led herself like a mad thing into all the traps Redmantyl had cast for her, and her last sight before darkness claimed her was of this youth, silver-haired and silver-eyed, standing over her and smiling softly; he glittered with untapped powers. Ilset could not forget. She still had fierce, stabbing headaches; one was beginning at that moment.

She fingered a trinket, a small ivory carving that her husband had set down on the table at her elbow when he'd come in, and spoke with a disinterested tone. "Where is he staying?"

"At the Whitelm."

"I don't know the house well, but I believe it is not an inn?"

"No. The keeper, Adyna, was his father's chatelaine."

"It doesn't seem fitting that a noble child should be lodged within a tavern," Ilset said. "Houarde, shouldn't we extend an invitation to the youth? I believe he would be more accustomed to the comforts of our home."

"Excellent idea. Here, Boy," Houarde took the toasted bread offered by the small servant. He tore off a burnt crust and tossed it to the hopeful-looking dogs, then laughed at their scramble.

"You would certainly be of more use in showing him about. An alekeeper wouldn't know the best amusements available to a young visitor in our city, and we have an obligation to entertain such nobles. You might show him to your own haunts, perhaps? Or introduce him to suitable companions. Justice Hugobarde has a son of about that age..." The tip of Ilset's lacquered nail-shield caught on the swan's outstretched wing and snapped.

"Yes," Houarde tested the hot cheese with his teeth, lips drawn back.

"It might be wise to speak to the youth tomorrow, at your best opportunity," she suggested.

"I think I shall." He nibbled at the bread thoughtfully, then reached for the tankard of house-brewed ale at his feet. He nodded. "My Love, I'll find young Orlan in the morning."

The Whitelm was closed. The mugs and glassware had been washed and put away, the tables cleared, the fire banked. Adyna had gone to bed and Orlan sat and talked with Ren while she swept up. He had offered to help, but she refused him as sternly as her mother might; it wasn't his place. Boots clopping on the stairs outside made them both look up.

"We are shut for the night!" the girl called out, but the latch was lifted and Kyarde came in. He had shed his armor, gauntlets and guisarme and stood strangely bare and vulnerable in his short sleeves and kirtle.

"No matter to me, Ren," he said, smiling. "Is Mother here?"

"She's sleeping."

"As you should be, little sister. 'Tis late for you to be up with such work. But before you go, you must play at alekeeper and bring me a beer. Will you? The soldier's brew, if there's any left."

Ren set down her broom and disappeared behind the bar.

Kyarde took a seat at the nearest table. "'Twas troublesome at the gate after you passed this morning," he told his friend. "The sergeant kept his eyes close on me, as if he thought I meant to escape my post a few hours early."

"I'm sorry if it was my fault."

"No, no matter. The sergeant does nothing but bawl and shoot his sharp eyes about. I think he would carry tales to Captain Alyx, but she might have sent me to accompany you. She'd be more angry at a neglected noble than an empty gate-post."

"But to make so much fuss—"

"Oh, they'll all make a great fuss—our Captain, the council clerks, the officers of the city even to the Layn Mayor herself. They fret at every Lordling's visit, for we must make our noble visitors as comfortable here as if they'd never left their castles. I vow, Orlan, that once news of you gets about our best citizens will speed to make your acquaintance."

"I've met one, the Mayor's husband."

Kyarde laughed. "Yes, him! No surprise if you found him here."

Orlan grinned. "He is a drunkard then?"

"Most famously– But enough of that. I came to hear gossip, not to give it. Tell me of home, Orlan. How is everyone at Wizardes Cliff? My Lord?"

"He's well. More stern since Olyr and Godefroi and Laurel left, but little changed otherwise."

"You've heard from them?"

"Olyr and Godefroi, no, but Laurel's mother to a little boy. We saw her and the baby at Pendaunzel this spring, but Father was barely courteous when they met and would not speak to her husband at all. He was angry—still may be—that she would cast aside all her talents offer for a wealthy match. He is pleased with the little one, I believe, but 'tis difficult to know what Father truly thinks of anything. My cousin Igren– Do you know her, Kyarde? You were not at Wizardes Cliff when my cousins visited."

"I've heard that she is wondrous lovely."

"Pretty enough," Orlan said. "More pretty than Laurel, though not half so fierce. A gentle, dovesome maid. She is wed as well now, to the Earl of Oerykeshire. Father promises I may visit this summer, for I must travel a little before I begin my mage-journeys. 'Tis why I am sent here."

Ren returned with a mug of brown ale and set it before her brother. "The leavings from the bottom of the keg, Kyarde. You might find it bitter."

"Could you pour in a drop of water to soften it then?"

"There's none left."

"Then damn it."

"Would you like some drink, Orlan?" she offered. "There is still a little wine."

"No, Rennie, ta."

"Leave us, girl," Kyarde dismissed her brusquely. "'Tis late and you'd best be to your bed and sleep."

Ren wiped her hands on her skirt and sat quietly on a stool behind her brother, out of his immediate sight.

Kyarde sipped his beer. "Ugh." He tried a second pull, apparently no less bitter. "If you are going up to Oerykton, Orlan, you might visit Kai. St. Yzra's is only across the river in Yrfordeshire, not a five-mile walk."

"I've thought of it," Orlan admitted. "But cannot say if I would be glad to see Kai again." Kai's brother nodded. Kaiberte had been sent away to the Brothers of St. Yrza after his illness to be healed. He had recovered during his years away, but when he returned to Wizardes Cliff, he had changed. There was a tightened, strained look about his mouth. Although he did not limp and his hands seemed limber and capable and his back straight, his movements were careful and deliberate, as if he had to think before every act. At fifteen, he had asked to join the Brothers as a novice. Orlan had not seen him since.

"Is the thesper boy still at your father's house, Orlan?"

"No. What of him?"

"I only wondered."

"He's not with us any longer. Father's sent him to serve as herald to My Lord Dafythe. 'Tis a grand honor, and Andemyon needs a place to carry him through life. Father hoped he'd be magical and so might 'prentice, but the boy's no more talented than you are." Redmantyl had been disappointed, but Orlan was relieved; he could not have tolerated Andemyon being magical too.

He thought of the beach at Keyfins last summer, of bright sun on the sand, green water splashing at his bare calves, and seagulls crying. He thought of the brisk ocean breeze fluttering his unlaced shirt and the slippery rocks beneath his feet. He thought of Andemyon following him down from the old castle, always at a safe distance. He remembered the silence behind him.

"Father says he'll do well. Andemyon might be a great minister in sixty years' time if he is successful at courtly life and My Lord Dafythe is kind."

"The Duke won't live so long."

"No, but his son Ambris might, and Laurel and My Layn Margueryt certainly will. They'll be a help to him."

"He's a sweet little lad," Ren said.

He could not bear Andemyon so near, like an angel of vengeance, a solemn, unspeaking, beautiful thing with determined, clear blue eyes fixed on him, impossible to escape or ignore. He had climbed out to the end of the cool, slippery rocks that jutted from the beach at low tide, knowing that Andemyon was not far behind. He could hear the boy's fingers and feet scrabble against the mossy surface for holds, almost hear his soft breath in the sighs of the summer wind and the lapping waves. Then it was quiet.

Kyarde's voice broke into the memory. "I still think of the plays the thespers performed when we were children. Nothing so wonderful has been done by any troupe in Storm Port. 'Twas all Tedora's doing. Remember their show of the Holy Grail? Or the dragon that fought Oedipus and Arthur and St. George, for it was always that same creation of green cloth and sticks?"

"`Twas most grand," Ren added.

Her brother ignored this. "Recall, Orlan, `twas at Wizardes Cliff that the troupe first gave Andemyon a speaking role and he wept when Rymbaughe brought him out?"

"I remember," Orlan said. "Tedora tried to have him in other roles too, after that, but he was always so afraid, and then they could not have him on stage at all. He still weeps a good deal."

"Some, I think, are not fit for the grand style and must always live unseen and unknown."

"That's Andemyon exactly."

"He was never meant to be a thesper," Kyarde said. "`Tis a shame to see him so mously, not like his mother at all. Now *she* was one for a grand life."

"Yes," Orlan said.

"We miss Tedora terribly here, Mother especially so. The troupe isn't the same without her. They've no imagination for spectacle."

Orlan remembered the yellow hair and white shirt floating below the surface of the murky water like seaweed. He hadn't heard Andemyon slip. Had there been a splash? He did not remember jumping in, only the salty sting of cold water and the weight of the small body as he took it to his arms, the fingers that clutched his shirt sleeve as he dragged the boy to the shore. He recalled the sand vividly—white, dry, warm, growing dark and damp as it stuck to their sodden clothes. The child lay so still, bright curls limp about his pale face. Blue tainted his lips. Nothing moved—even the sea was still— and Orlan could not think what to do. He shook the little body, slapped his back, and whispered "please, don't die, don't die," but Andemyon wasn't breathing. He pressed his mouth to Andemyon's to force air in, until the boy finally spit water and turned away, coughing and gasping.

"When the thespians visit, they make a sort of pilgrimage to the cathedral and speak of that last Nativity performance as if it were the finest ever given," said Kyarde. "Have you been in St. Khrystopher's yet, Orlan?"

"No. I've only seen the outside."

"You must go over with Mother for Mass. I know that wizards are not so pious, but it will give you a fine time to look around. There's a crucifix over the vestry door with a painted, bleeding Christ that gave Rennie a bad fright when she first saw it."

The girl smiled and looked embarrassed. "I was a child then, Kyarde."

Her brother laughed. "You're little less a child now, and you'll still not go near."

"Well, it's a horrid thing. Nothing should suffer as that poor figure does."

"You'll never be a proper soldier, Rennie. Have you heard she wishes to join the Guard herself, Orlan?"

"No, I hadn't."

"Truly. She talks so of Mildred Shieldmaid and Alys Ladyeknight, and even more of Layn Margueryt."

"That's because My Layn Margueryt is living now," Ren retorted.

"But you'd never fight in her name, little lass. A girl afraid to face a red-daubed bit of wood– Could you stand to spear an enemy in battle, or would you cry at that as well?"

Ren blushed and stepped away quickly.

Andemyon was not going to die—he was sure of that—and Mathias ran to them over the sand hills and asked, "What happened?"

He had answered simply, "He fell," and, as they helped the wet, bedraggled child to his feet, Orlan looked up at the apprentice and saw that expression, the same expression that would be on his father's face when they returned home the next day. But neither asked for an explanation.

"Rennie, come along!" Kyarde urged his sister. "Don't cry. `Twas only in jest. Orlan, tell her."

Orlan found the girl in the corner behind the fireplace. "Rennie, Kyarde didn't mean to be cruel."

"Yes, he did."

"No. Boys are like that, you must understand. We don't think `til after we've caused some pain and then we are very sorry. Kyarde is sorry."

"I am, I swear."

Orlan held out a hand. "Come along then."

They had never asked him. He was always aware of his father watching him, even after Andemyon was gone, and he felt ashamed. Redmantyl never voiced a suspicion so that he could answer, could say that he had done nothing wrong this time. It was horrible to know that Father thought him responsible.

Ren dried her face with the corner of her apron.

"You mustn't be so tender, my sister," Kyarde said. "If you will be a soldier, you'll have to learn not to cry at every slight." He finished his beer with one gulp, made a sour face, and left the table. "I meant to visit for longer, Orlan, but I must to return to the garrison hall before the clocks strike midnight," he admitted.   "The sergeant is most exacting against guards who stay out 'til the morning hours, and no excuse to the Captain will do. Shall I see you tomorrow?"

"I'll be here," Orlan answered.

"I bid you good night then. And you, Ren."

"Night," the girl replied. Kyarde shut the great door behind him as he left, and Ren lifted her broom.

"Rennie, leave that 'til morning," Orlan told her impatiently. "Go to sleep, Little One, and pleasant night's dreams."

After Ren had gone, Orlan went to his room but he did not sleep. He thought of Tedora lying in this same bed, delirious, bleeding, drugged out of pain, dying, and of her son's yellow curls floating in the murky, green water. He wondered if it were true that ghosts walked.

syx

He had never liked Tedora, for he saw how his father loved her. He'd watched them together, observed the looks they exchanged, their secret smiles, the way they walked with their arms about each other. Countless times, he'd seen the Headethesper reach out to place a hand on his father's arm or caress his hair, or heard Redmantyl laugh at Tedora's teasing.

The wizard, Orlan concluded from castle gossip, had gained a reputation for casual dalliance in his youth. When he first courted the thesper, no one had expected their love-affair to continue exclusively for ten years—yet it did. No other woman interested Redmantyl. Whatever tales might be told of his romantic adventures were clearly from days long past; after Tedora, there was no one else. And if the thesper took more casual lovers in her travels, she did not flaunt them. At least, Orlan heard no rumors of her conduct outside Wizardes Cliff and he observed that his father did not seem jealous nor resentful of Tedora's life away from him. The wizard was able to wait for her eventual return without impatience.

Though they did not marry, the two had pledged to each other so much as their independent obligations allowed. Tedora was outspoken in her dislike for the entanglements of marriage and in her intention never to abandon the freedom she found with her troupe; her contempt for the life of a Lady of the Manor was well known. She might love Redmantyl, but she would not become Lady of Wizardes Cliff. Redmantyl did not ask; his magic took precedence before all else, even the attachments of family, wife and children. He had sworn never to jeopardize his place as supreme wizard-lordling for the sake of a lover, as all serious students of the craft learned to forsake such emotional distractions. This was wizardry's highest edict: *Magic must be first, or it becomes nothing.* Tedora's visits were their compromise. For a sennight or so they played at husband and wife, and parted again on affectionate terms.

No sounds were more dismal to Orlan than the tinkling of bells, the wind-muted music of lutes and pipes, and the burbling laughter that announced the arrival of the troupe. Although he knew that Tedora would not stay and become his stepmother, her visits were unbearable. He felt a heart-sinking sickness whenever the thespers playfully addressed her as *My Lady*.

Tedora meant to be amiable: she greeted Orlan with hugs and kisses and friendly, teasing remarks, as she met all the young folk in the castle. She must be aware of his dislike, but she appeared blithely determined to overlook it. It was Tedora's professed desire that everyone be happy and everything peaceable. Free Folk, she declared, traveled to bring amusement to the dull work-a-day lives of their hosts; at Wizardes Cliff, she was especially resolved that her visits be pleasant. She would allow no quarrel between herself and her lover's son to disrupt the atmosphere of merriment she worked so hard to maintain.

Yet her presence *was* a disruption. When Tedora visited, she was foremost in Redmantyl's attention. He neglected all responsibilities, save those inescapable duties of his wizardry. Orlan was forgotten. Usually, his father took time for him, personally supervised his education, governed his magical development, simply talked with him. Orlan's favorite hours had been those drowsy evenings spent playing chess or lying on the hearthrug reading from Redmantyl's latest piece of scholarship. Even when he had been too young to comprehend the significance of these writings, he had felt so proud to be permitted this glimpse of true wizardly work.

Sometimes, his father told him sensational tales of his adventures as a traveling mage and fledgling wizard. Redmantyl described his escape from the dungeons of a rival wizard in Malta, with Simon's assistance, or his quest for that ugly little jade figurine which sat on the chimneypiece: its powers were legendary and it had long been reputed lost in the Orient, but he had discovered it accidentally in another part of the world and learned in the most disconcerting circumstance that its magic was no more than legend. He spoke of how he had once rescued the Duke's own son from assassins in Venice. And he hinted of things more dangerous and strange, not suitable for a young boy's ears and therefore much more tantalizing: Redmantyl once referred to an infamous black stone which was no hoax, which he had destroyed, and mentioned a beautiful Lady revealed as a necromancer—but he would not say what had become of her. Orlan listened with wonder and delight. It seemed that his father had been everywhere, seen everything of interest and done everything worth doing. Redmantyl knew so much of the world. Would he ever be so resourceful, so wise, so brave? Would he ever have such thrilling adventures for himself?

This had been his privileged time; no other child spent such evenings in the wizard's company. He was, after all, Lord Redmantyl's son and this special indulgence was his by rights. But when Tedora arrived, his privilege disappeared. His place was usurped. The sitting-room door was shut.

Andemyon might be admitted within, but Orlan always hesitated before knocking. He knew he was not welcome. He felt himself excluded from the brief and private family circle his father and Tedora had created. When she was there, he ceased to be the acknowledged son of the household; at best, he was an awkward reminder of the wizard's careless past, at worst, an intrusion of present-day concerns that must call Redmantyl away from the Headethesper and her son.

Tedora had spoiled the first day of his apprenticeship. At fourteen, his years of uncertainty were ended. He had wanted so much to be magical, like his father, but there was so little evidence to fasten his hopes upon. His senses unfolded *out* at times, suddenly, unexpectedly, with painful new awareness: the tiniest sound roared in his ears; the unsought thoughts and emotions of the people around him exploded in his head. He saw the energies of both living beings and inanimate material. All things—human, beast, plant, stone, water, dust-grains— contained their own distinct flux of regularly pulsing vitality visible to the sensitive; it was this which the magical summoned to mastery. And magicians themselves shone brightest of all. Sometimes Redmantyl blazed with such electric intensity that Orlan had to shield his burning eyes. Though he was often unnerved by these unwanted perceptions, he looked to them as a promise for his future. Was this head-splitting sensitivity a sign that he was magical? His first blasts of emotion-released power were a terrifying display of unrestrained force, but again they fed his aspirations. Was this magic? He wanted to believe, yet he doubted. Redmantyl had told him again and again: *the essence of magic is self-control*, and he had no control over these outbursts. Throughout the winter before his birthday, he practiced in private to bring his undeveloped powers under his command. His efforts were not always successful, sometimes disastrous, and each failure more distressing than the last. It seemed to him that he would never be a true magician. Finally, Redmantyl had tested him and judged his powers suitable for training.

Apprenticeship was the confirmation of all his hopes. He had taken such care that morning to tie a bit of red ribbon about his arm, as the apprentices did; he had been so proud to prove himself and to be received into the mysteries of his father's craft.

Joy had ended with merry, loud voices from the narrow avenue below the Daune Tower gate. The castle was suddenly overwhelmed with thespers. Redmantyl immediately disappeared with Tedora, and Orlan was left to welcome the troupe. Once, however, he had performed the duties of host, greeted them, guided them to their rooms, showed them their stage in the Bottom Hall, he was disregarded. The servants rushed about in preparation for the visitors, and the visitors shouted and scrambled to set their stage. Even Rymbaughe, his one friend among the thespers, had been given the direction of the troupe in Tedora's absence and was preoccupied by the important business of organizing the others for the evening performance.

Orlan tried to behave as his father would and oversee the arrangements of the household, but his words were simply ignored. The thespers met his suggestions with a courteous smile and answered, "Yes, Chyelde, if you please," and went on as they chose. They would not dare laugh at him before his face; he was due a certain deference as their patron's son, but he knew that they regarded him as a presumptuous child. Like Andemyon and Ren, he was a hindrance underfoot who might be tripped over or accidentally crushed by fallen baggage. The little ones were removed from this danger and the thespers wished Orlan would remove himself as well. He'd retreated to his room.

When he emerged hours later for his first session as an apprentice and found little Andemyon waiting for him in the stairwell, he'd called out impatiently for his cousin Laurel, who was meant to be watching the child.

But Laurel listened to his complaint and replied: "Didn't you hear, Orlan? There'll be no lessons this sennight, at least so long as the troupe is here."

Olyr, with her, added: "You must know that My Lord wishes to spend his days with the Headethesper while he can, rather than stay in that dusty room."

It should have been his finest day, but once again he had been forgotten. Tedora came first. "Why does she have to come, and Father abandons everything for her?" he protested. "'Tisn't fair!"

"He loves her, Orlan. Aren't you grown enough to understand that?"

"Soon enough, Laurel."

Neither of them thought the canceled lessons a great disruption. They liked Tedora. They welcomed her visits as the return of wayward, young aunt or errant older sister and reveled at the thespers' rush and bustle. For them, it was a holiday. Olyr was in his last year and would take his mage-vows that summer; he studied alone and did not need Redmantyl's daily attention. And Laurel could never remain solemn, even in her own disappointments. His disappointment meant less.

"Orlan, it's no great matter," she told him. "There's little any of us will miss in a sennight, you least of all. Uncle Redmantyl would have taught you exercises to focus and direct your power. Olyr can show you the same if you must know them immediately."

"If you like," Olyr offered, and looked very pleased with himself and a little silly when Laurel smiled at him.

"There you are, Cos. Nothing's lost. The troupe will play the tale of St. Parsyfal in the Bottom Hall tonight and Rymbaughe said we might help set the stage. I imagine that new young thespian, the handsome one, will play Parsyfal. Coming, Lads?" She flew down the corridor, Olyr after her.

As Orlan followed, Andemyon at his heels, the walls thumped furiously as if a huge creature trapped within were trying to break free. This was the earliest manifestation of his adolescent magic and the most difficult to control. He did not try to suppress it then. At the time, he'd wished he could tear the castle down.

It was Tedora's fault; it was always her fault. If it were not for her, he would not be an embarrassment and an encumbrance. His father would not choose to forget him. Each time she came to Wizardes Cliff, Orlan sulked and fretted and wished in earnest that she would go away and never return. Then, one day, she was gone forever.

The news had come in February, four years past. He'd been seventeen. On that particular afternoon, his father was involved in the monitoring of Mathias's exercises in self-command, the most crucial part of instruction required for a novice apprentice. While he waited to be called to his own lessons, Orlan passed the time by using his magic to fling a rubber ball against the walls of the long, lowest corridor of the Shadu Hall.

Though he displayed a minor talent with the medium of light, which his father mastered so spectacularly, his principal ability lay in the control of material objects. He could move items much larger than a toy ball at will, but the game was meant to exercise precision, not motion. It was no easy feat to direct so small and swift-moving an object. He ought to be able to strike the ball at a specific point on its surface and send it at an exact angle and speed toward a chosen target. When it sprang back toward him, he ought to be able to seize and deflect it. Sometimes he could. More often, the ball shot away unpredictably and he had to employ all his concentration to anticipate the bounding trajectory. Once or twice, he had cast a hurried barrier for the ball to bounce off before it hit him. He practiced his mastery of this skill with most diligent and painstaking attention, for he felt himself erratic and knew he had to perfect his control. Although he was now an established third-year proficient, he still believed he must prove himself.

He had missed once and was cursing childishly when the guard at the bridgepost called down to him: "Chyelde Orlan!"

He went to the end of the corridor, to the icy, empty cavern of the Daune Tower gateway, the main entrance to the castle from the bridge. Frost hung on the walls and his breath fogged before his face. Malfe, the guard, was struggling with the machinery of ropes, cranks and pulleys above the great gate.

"There's thespers!" Malfe shouted down to him.

"The troupe?" he wondered. "Before Lententide?" But the portcullis lifted to admit only three thespians: Rymbaughe, Anyse, and Tedora's cousin Klyffaude, the handsome and dashing boy who had once played Parsyfal and made all the castle maids giggle and smile. Andemyon was with them, a pretty, golden-haired child of ten. They looked around hopefully, saw him below, and descended the wide stairway through the tower as Malfe came down the narrow steps against the curving wall.

"We would speak to My Lord Redmantyl," Rymbaughe said. "We've come a long way and it is most urgent."

"My Lord don't wish to be disturbed when he's at 'prenticing," Malfe answered solidly. "You must wait."

"I think it can be allowed," Orlan intervened, curious, "if it is truly important. I'll be responsible, Malfe. Tell Father so when you bid him come down."

"When I—"

"I must play host to the thespers, so you must go up to the lesson-room." He assumed his father's commanding frown. "Go now."

"Oh, very well." The guard turned to huff his way to the tower's top.

Orlan knew then that something was wrong: the thespers, usually so merry, kept a tight-lipped, forbidding silence as he escorted them into the Shadu Hall. He had never seen any member of the troupe so solemn. Andemyon, too, was strangely quiet. His face was like a painted doll's—expressionless, blank, pale except where the winter winds had tinted his nose and cheeks with red. The little boy didn't seem to know nor care where he was, and the adults led him gently.

All of them wore gauzy white cloaks beneath their winter capes. This was the traditional garment of mourning, though Orlan had not known this at the time. Both his mother and Ellan had died without such ceremonies as white mourning-cloaks and Masses for their departed souls.

The thespers dropped to one knee when Redmantyl entered the hall.

"Rymbaughe, Anyse, Klyffaude," the wizard greeted them, but his eyes cast about the corridor in search of one not there. "And Andemyon. Welcome, Little One. Is the troupe returned so early?"

"We would return, My Lord," Rymbaughe answered. "But you must hear our tidings. My Lord Redmantyl, our headethesper Tedora is dead."

The psychic bonds which linked all magicians were especially strong between Orlan and his father, as they shared common blood. Redmantyl was careful to veil his thoughts against his son's growing sensitivity; often, Orlan sensed no more than the surface of the wizard's mind, and he did not always understand the impressions he received. But he felt the effect of Rymbaughe's words. The shock fell like a hard, sudden blow. Wrenching sorrow stabbed through his own being so powerfully that he gasped aloud and pressed his hands to his own breast. Tears blurred his vision. He felt his father's anguish, but no flicker of pain showed on Redmantyl's face. A wizard never loses himself in emotional distraction.

"How did this happen?" Redmantyl asked steadily. "I did not know of it. She was not forty."

Rymbaughe told the tale: "She fell, My Lord, during our third Nativity performance at St. Khrystopher's. We wintered in Storm Port this year and the Bishop of Greenstephan paid our December lodgings in return for a Christmas show."

Although Tedora was one of the Free Folk, she was also the daughter of a Maryesfont dean and niece to the Abbey Pryor. Clergy acquaintances of her family overlooked her thesperish mode of life and granted that she was not so decadent as the majority of that disreputable and unorthodox lot. They hired her during holiday festivals; church plays made up a substantial part of the troupe's performances beyond Wizardes Cliff. Tedora had a reputation for spectacle without vulgar comedy, which the Bishop favored for display within cathedral doors.

This last Christmas, said Rymbaughe, she had not disappointed:

the Magi appeared in spangled robes, beast-heads represented the ox and ass at the manger, and angels flew above the last tableau. The smallest maids in the troupe were suspended by a rigging of thin cords that would not be seen in candlelight.

"'Twas a full spectacle, My Lord. One of her best. The city folk crowded in to see the show at Mass. The first two nights were wondrous, and the third night was going as splendidly 'til the moment when the angels were pulled up behind the Nativity. Then the cords caught—the girls would only rise a few feet from the floor and couldn't be drawn up any higher. Tedora climbed into the transept rafters to undo the tangle. We didn't think there was any true danger—'tis the sort of mishap we have a dozen times a year in the midst of a performance and our headethesper was always the first the put things right herself. She was working out the knots so swiftly as she could before the pageant was spoiled, when one cord suddenly snapped free while she still held it. The weight of the maids pulled her from the crossbeam before she could let go."

"Christmas was months ago," said Redmantyl. "She did not die then."

"No, My Lord. But the fall left her bones broken beyond mending. Her legs—she could never walk again even if she healed. Her backbone–" Rymbaughe gestured at the nape of his own neck. "There was no hope. We brought her to Adyna's and she kept abed these two months. There are such physics, My Lord, that kept her from the worst pain," he concluded. "She died in her sleep this Monday night, as is best if you can't go on stage, she would say."

Tedora had left a message; Klyffaude read it.

"*Yryd–*" He faltered instantly. Like most folk, the young thesper would not dare to call the great wizard by his given name and he stood embarrassed and speechless until Redmantyl urged him on. "Er-*Yryd, I greet thee as my most honored patron and beloved. I am grievously ill and may not survive. Therefore, I bid you grant me two requests, if you have truly loved me.*

"*First, I ask that you maintain your patronage of my troupe, for they are no less a worthy band of thespians without my guidance.*"

"My Lord," Rymbaughe interrupted. "Upon our headethesper's death I was chosen to lead the troupe. I have Tedora's token for you to keep or to bestow as you choose." He fumbled at his pockets, but Redmantyl held up a hand.

"I shall deal with that shortly. Klyffaude, continue."

Klyffaude read on: "*Second, I ask that you receive my son*

Andemyon and call him your own. I would have asked this of you long ago, but I could not leave him where I could not stay. Now, I must entrust him to your care and pray he finds his home among your house. Yryd, know I have loved you well and I regret only that I may not see you again. I bid you remember me. `Tis signed, M'Lord, Tedora Headethesper, Year of Our Just and Most Holy Savior, nineteen-hundred, nine and forty."

Once the reading was finished and Redmantyl agreed to continue his patronage of Rymbaughe Headethesper's troupe, he called upon the thespians to witness his reception of Tedora's son.

The laws of wardship had been reformed in the eighteenth century by the Emperor Adalemarde, when it came to her attention that hundreds of children in her empire needed proper care, even in such essentials as food and a safe bed. The old laws were inadequate; children were beaten, molested, neglected, and cheated out of rightful inheritances by the guardians appointed to protect them. The Sainted Ada's reforms directed all members of the clergy and nobility to provide for any children they found in need or were petitioned to take into their house by subjects of the parish or fief. The new laws rarely lapsed: breaking a solemn vow of guardance was not only a grave dishonor, it was an act of treason. The least punishment an offender could hope to receive was the forfeiture of lands and titles. Others were imprisoned or executed.

Redmantyl would not refuse Tedora's request. For Andemyon, he took this vow.

"I swear solemnly in the name of Kharles, Emperor of the Normans, and in the name of My Liege Lord Dafythe, Duke of the Northlands. As I am Lord of Greenwaters Island and premiere Lord Wizard, as I am an honorable man worthy of noble rank in all acts, I receive this child as ward of my house. I swear that Andemyon Thesperson will be provided for while in my care and given to a position befitting his interests at such a time as he is of an age to be responsible for himself. Andemyon, I welcome you as my own." He embraced the child, although it seemed to Orlan that his father held Andemyon a little longer than the ceremony required.

Redmantyl also called for six weeks of formal mourning, the customary period reserved for a husband or wife.

Wizardes Cliff mourned the Headethesper, but the days that followed were worst for Andemyon. Orlan was not bonded to the child as he was to his father; nevertheless, he sensed Andemyon's sorrow—not in overwhelming bursts, but in a subtle, gentle, faint tickling at the edges of his awareness, like soft patters of rain on the windows of a distant room. The child's sadness, his bafflement, his aching loneliness, washed through Orlan briefly, then faded again.

One night, he imagined he heard the little boy's sobs echoing in the corridors. This was impossible; Andemyon was too far away to be heard. Orlan had taken larger chambers at the top of the Magne Hall with Godefroi upon his apprenticeship; Andemyon was two floors below, in his old cubby across from Redmantyl's rooms. He shouldn't be able to hear—yet the sound haunted him. He could never care much for Andemyon and he felt no grief at Tedora's death, but he could not ignore that pain. Andemyon's sobs brought back memories of his own mother's death; he had cried in that same room ten years before. Tentatively, he went down.

Before he reached Andemyon's door, footsteps crossed the unlit corridor ahead and he heard his father whisper, "Hush, Little One." A stream of fire arced through the darkness and a candle flamed. Through the open doorway, he saw his father at the foot of the bed, cradling Andemyon.

"Hush, my darling." The wizard's voice was very soft. "I know. I grieve with you. I feel what it is to be without her. I cannot believe myself that a woman so vital as your mother could end so untimely, and for no better reason than a ridiculous accident."

He began to talk of Tedora, of his love for her. He spoke of things neither boy had guessed: of how he, a lone wanderer, injured, had been taken up by the hospitality of the troupe. Tedora had been little more than a girl in those days, recently flown from the cloisters of Maryesfont with a handsome young thesper whom she found she did not love after all. He was touched by her disappointment, and heartened by her determination not to succumb to regret; instead, she had turned her energies elsewhere—to the troupe which was not yet hers. So young a woman, and already the thespers looked to her as a mother. She'd befriended him as well, offered him haven from whatever harshness he met in his wizardly world. From the beginning, he trusted her more than he'd ever been able to trust anyone—but there was nothing more than playful flirtation between them. He would not damage their friendship by making it mere dalliance, and he had not believed then that they could ever have anything more important.

Of later, when he had achieved his title Redmantyl and could repay the troupe for their protection. His patronage, he could say now, had been primarily for her sake. He did not like to think of her and her little band of thespians aimless, homeless, rag-tag, perhaps going hungry for lack of work. He'd wanted to help her; he'd waited for her to ask for more. The women he had known before had wanted more from him—a reflection of his power, the mystical prestige of a magician lover, emotional guarantees he was unable to give. Tedora had accepted his favor, but proudly refused more from him than a thesper had a right to ask from her patron. Did she love him then? He didn't know. She answered his gallantries with laughter, suggesting that she would not receive him seriously as a suitor. He did not press her. Both were too guarded to offer their hearts readily.

Of the day they had acknowledged their love—a cautious laying-down of arms and shields in mutual, conditional surrender. He thought her the perfect mate for a wizard, one who possessed a will and way of her own and did not demand that he give over his duties to his magic for her. She had understood: though they discussed marriage, she would no more abandon her troupe than he would surrender his red robes and Wizardes Cliff.

He spoke of all he had admired in her: her fierce independence, her elfin, untamed nature, her irrepressible spirit, her wit born of bitter experience, her surprising strength for so small and waiflike a woman, her talent for storytelling.

"She had freedoms a wizard dare not dream of. We are so bound by duties we cannot escape, and her obligations were those she chose to take up because she loved them. You, Little One. Myself. Her troupe's performances. That was her passion, you know, the plays she wrote and directed for poor, blind folk with no imagination of life beyond their own livings. 'Twas a magic she possessed, unlike any form of wizardry. She could create any world she wished on a stage and make it seem true."

"Yes," the child in his arms whispered. "Mama told the most grand stories."

"'Twas a talent most wonderful to see."

Andemyon curled against the wizard, comforted, as Redmantyl told his heart. Orlan remained in the drafty hall, shivering in his gauzy mourning cloak, listening to every word. Throughout, he wondered: had his father spoken of Nann Dafodylle on those similar nights ten years before? Had Redmantyl mentioned his mother at all?

He recalled the comfort Redmantyl had offered in those horrible half-remembered days immediately after his own mother's death: no heart-easing words of his beloved, Redmantyl had not soothed Orlan's sorrow by sharing it, simply cradled him and whispered soft incantations to make him forget his grief. Orlan realized then that Redmantyl had not known what to say—not to a strange little boy, thrust upon him when he knew little about children and knew nothing at all about his own son.

When he tried to remember his mother, Orlan encountered a barrier of impenetrable blankness. His memory only went back so far; beyond his first days at Wizardes Cliff, there was nothing. The spells remained intact. He half-expected Redmantyl to wind Andemyon in the same glamour of soothing forgetfulness, but the wizard did not. Andemyon had been Redmantyl's from infancy; for *this* boy, he knew the words to bring true peace. He did not need to rely on enchantments.

"I see her in you," Redmantyl said to Andemyon. "Your hair is more fair, but your eyes are as blue. The likeness of her face is in yours." He ran his thumb over Andemyon's brow, tracing its shape. "My lovely child."

Andemyon looked up hopefully. "Am I yours truly?"

"Yes, of course you are," the wizard answered. "Your mother sent you to me so that we might care for each other. I have nothing of her now, save you."

He bent his head to the boy's fair curls. Silent minutes followed. The wizard's careful guard relaxed for an instant and Orlan caught the stream of thoughts which flew through Redmantyl's mind: *She is gone. My beloved. Why did I not know? Was our bond no greater than that? I should have sensed her pain these weeks. Could I have saved her? At least, I might have eased her suffering. I might have been with her at the end.*

When Redmantyl raised his head, droplets shone on his cheeks like stars in the candlelight. Orlan was horrified. He didn't think it possible his father could weep.

Redmantyl had had many lovers since Tedora's death: courtiers, noble guests, minstrels and bards who stopped at Wizardes Cliff, though none of the patronized troupe. At Pendaunzel, his father had disappeared from the great halls of the Duke's Manor for hours together. The courtiers assumed that it was the way of wizards to seek solitude rather than the hearty fellow-feeling of regular society; few observed that a Lady of the court would disappear for these same intervals, and not the same woman each time. When Redmantyl was visible, he was in dancing figures with pretty, giggling damosels, offering escort to Margueryt's lieutenants, seated in bowers with young ministers, or engaged in soft conversations with councilors' wives. Women of law and war as well as languid courtly flowers, all were too fond of the solemn wizard. Worse, travelers and noblewomen visited Wizardes Cliff and made little pretense of occupying the chambers they were first shown to. Orlan was baffled at seeing his father sport so carelessly with these women, then forget them. He knew that many—as Houarde Portreeve had rightly guessed—thought a handsome Wizard Lordling in the Duke's favor and in possession of a good-sized fief a remarkable marriage prize, and he knew as surely that his father would never marry. The trust he had given Tedora, the tenderness of his passion for her, were lost. Not one of these passing lovers was more than a moment's amusement. They were nothing, not a tenth together of what the Headethesper had been. It had always disturbed Orlan to see his father so in love, but it was unbearable to see his father not happy with one love.

So, Tedora was gone, but Andemyon became one of the household. While the thesper lived, Orlan had only had to endure her child for a week at each visit, but afterwards he was always there. In the weeks following the Headethesper's death, Redmantyl kept the little boy at his side. During the apprentices' lessons, Andemyon looked through the books on the Daune Tower shelves; Redmantyl taught him to read the arcane writings within. When he took Orlan and Mathias out for studies in stargazing, Andemyon went along too. The wizard showed the boy how to find Orion, the winter hunter, Aldebaran, the eye of the Springtide Bull, and the glittering cluster of the Pleiades in the night sky; he taught him to trace the paths of the planets across the firmament. Each night, he sat at the foot of Andemyon's bed until the child fell asleep.

All that remained of the wizard's love for Tedora was given to her son. He did not proclaim Andemyon his child before the household, but he no longer denied the gossip. In fact, his actions encouraged it. He gave Andemyon Orlan's outgrown gray tunics and let the little boy sit at his right at the L-shaped table in the Feast Hall. This spring at Pendaunzel, he had performed the ceremonies of formal adoption. So the matter was settled by law; the question of whether or not Andemyon was a true child of the wizard's blood was now moot. Redmantyl had even left the boy with a silver amulet exactly like Orlan's. Orlan found this intolerable.

Why didn't he like Andemyon? Orlan couldn't explain. He didn't fully understand himself. Redmantyl paid too much attention to the boy, true; it wasn't fair that he should teach a child with no magic so much of wizard-lore, but Orlan knew well that his father had always treated Andemyon specially. He always would. Redmantyl never neglected Orlan's lessons, as he had when Tedora was about, nor gave the little boy anything that Orlan knew to be exclusively his own by right as firstborn. Orlan could not feel usurped by this small intruder. He didn't want the petting and pampering Andemyon received; it would be babyish to ask for it. He could not protest the boy's presence. But he thought of all the affection his father bestowed upon this silent, meaningless child, of the little figure cradled in Redmantyl's arms, of his father promising Andemyon that he belonged to him, too. Andemyon, true child or no, was more to the wizard than any other. When Andemyon looked up at him with innocent blue eyes, Orlan was infuriated.

Perhaps if Andemyon had kept out of his way, Orlan might have been more tolerant. But this was impossible, for Andemyon adored him. The child had toddled after Orlan as soon as he was old enough to walk, rarely speaking, never coming near enough for Orlan to claim that he was bothersome, but always there. Orlan was gruff with the little boy. He tried to ignore him, but Andemyon would not go away. Once he came to Wizardes Cliff, he was forever at Orlan's heels, watching him intently, bearing his casual insults, loving him as any small boy would love his older brother. He hung on the arm of Orlan's chair when he read or wrote out his lessons, asking questions. He interrupted Orlan and Mathias and upset their games. Orlan couldn't escape; Andemyon wanted to be with him and do everything that he did.

"Please, Orlan, may I go too?"

How he'd hated the sound of that! Through the summer after Tedora's death, he suffered Andemyon's plea endlessly. Finally, he refused outright.

"No, Andemyon, you can't. Go away!"

Andemyon winced as if he'd been slapped.

Boys could be thoughtlessly cruel. Orlan hadn't meant any harm—he was very sorry at the end of the day—but once he had shouted, it was easy to go on. He enjoyed the burst of brute anger; there was strange satisfaction in seeing Andemyon's tears.

"I shan't be any trouble, Orlan. I promise."

"Certainly you'll be trouble. You're always trouble! You're too young to play with us, Baby."

"Always underfoot," added the apprentice Mathias.

"You spoil everything. Andemyon, leave us alone!" He shoved the little boy into Mathias, who shoved him back. "Go on! Go away,

Baby!"

"Get away, Brat!"

"We don't want you!"

He didn't think nor care what he did, and Mathias joined him simply for the sport.

Mathias was a wayward, undisciplined youth, the youngest son of the Duke's Exchequer. His ministerial father was anxious to find him a situation that would keep him out of mischief; he had served in turn as herald, squire, clerk, and scribe's apprentice at court, but each position found him lax in his duties. He was an embarrassment to his family reputation. As he showed a modest but explosive magic, his parents had petitioned Redmantyl to receive him into apprenticeship.

Mathias had arrived at Wizardes Cliff the autumn before, a scrawny boy of sixteen with a sullen, wary, watchful air and tangled hair which frequently fell over his face to be brushed back from dark eyes. Redmantyl had received reports of the youth's character before accepting him; the wizard expected a great deal of difficulty in teaching this new apprentice the arts of self-command, but Mathias was always scrupulously civil, even timid, before his master. He meekly performed every task set for him and obeyed each instruction with an obsequious manner which suggested he was plainly afraid of rousing the fearsome magician's wrath. Away from Redmantyl's supervision, however, his manner was quite altered.

Lonely after Kaiberte and Kyarde had gone away, Orlan made special efforts to befriend the new apprentice. He was fascinated by this odd boy, Pendaunzel-born, brought up at the Duke's court and acquainted with the highest dignitaries of the land. Mathias could tell backstairs tales concerning the most famous ministers and their families. He related pranks he had played during his brief months in Dafythe's service and told probably exaggerated stories of stealing away from his duties to run wild in the city. In turn, Mathias, a little younger than Orlan, was impressed by his advanced magical education and greater talents. He flattered Orlan as his master's son. They encouraged the worst in each other.

They hadn't meant to be cruel, but they'd hurt Andemyon just the same.

Amid the shouting and pushing and pinching, Andemyon tried to make his escape. Mathias stuck out a foot to trip the little boy and, while Andemyon's path was blocked, Orlan took out the chalk stick which apprentices regularly carried and drew a circle about the child— "to trap him. The imp can't follow us now."

"The circle holds you, Demy," said Mathias. "You can't step outside it 'til the magician breaks the spell and releases you."

This threat might have proved true if Orlan had actually cast a spell; as it was, the circle was no more than a curve of chalk dust on the stone pavement. But Andemyon didn't know that. Hesitantly, he extended a foot toward the rim of the circle, then drew it back as Orlan slashed a straight line before his outstretched toes.

"Back with you, Imp! Mathias, quickly! Help me form a pentacle."

Andemyon whirled as the apprentice darted in to make a second chalk slash past his ankle, then tripped himself and fell on his backside. He sat at the center of the false spell, trapped as if he were truly bound by enchantments, as they fixed their lines about him—five lines in all, crisscrossed and joined at the points to form a star within the circle.

"Where shall we send him?"

"To the out-most Netherworlds! We'll call upon the demons who left him and bid they take the imp back to where he belongs."

"Do you know the rites to conjure a demon?"

"A few, my lad. A few."

"Can you call upon the Dread Nalro Saitham, Master of Darkest Night?" asked Mathias, grinning.

"Host of the ninth and blackest Pit of Hell?" Orlan laughed. "Warden of Deep Waters and Cold Fires? Manifest of the Red-Eyed Cat and Toad-Spawned Cock? A most fearsome wretch. I shudder to think what *he* would do to this lost little hobgoblin."

"I dare not think we have the power to hold him 'til he has claimed his own."

"Perhaps not. We can but try."

Necromancy was a practice forbidden to proper magicians. The great, wise, and powerful abhorred those renegade and depraved who sought to wield vast powers through knowledge of the dark arts, and instead became enslaved; they despised even the mention of these lost ones. Young apprentices were warned against the lure of such seductive and soul-corrupting forces. Orlan and Mathias would never have made such jests in their master's hearing, but it was good fun to frighten a little boy.

They conducted their spurious ritual, chants made up of gibberish—"*amo, amat, amas, ito, itas, itam*"—and frightful-sounding phrases:

"Lord of Darkness, hear our plea;

Bear thy hell-spawn down to thee."

It was nonsense, but Andemyon didn't know any better. Legs tucked beneath him in his diminishing space, he watched with credulous belief as Mathias danced and capered about the circle, composing his awful, gleeful songs and shooting little spurts of fire from the points of the star. Orlan made the slab of stone beneath Andemyon tremble, as if their fictitious demon would erupt and snatch him away at any moment.

Godefroi came and put an end to it.

Godefroi was a strange, quiet, thoughtful youth, different from the other apprentices, precociously disciplined for a boy in his early twenties, poet rather than prankster, more interested in the esoteric nature of their profession than its outward manifestations of power. Of course, he had never possessed the raw psychical force Laurel, Olyr, Orlan, or even Mathias exhibited, but must he look inward to the source of their magic, to the reasons behind every lesson, to the complex codes of conduct which bound every aspect of Norman society, and always ask *why*? Godefroi was a dreamer of the highest ideals: he'd been brought up, as had Orlan and Mathias, as a Chyelde given by noble birth to champion the mistreated and helpless, but he was much more likely to act upon that ancient creed.

Orlan had never seen the elder apprentice so angry. Godefroi was usually so self-restrained that it was impossible to imagine him capable of rage, but their performance was more than his careful discipline could withstand. Their game ended abruptly; at a curt command— "Stop it!"—Orlan broke the circle and set Andemyon free. The little boy flew straight into the apprentice in his haste to escape and when Godefroi tried to take him by the arm, he yelped and struggled blindly. Godefroi released him and turned to the guilty pair.

"That was monstrous! You make a mock of the dark arts. 'Tis an abuse of right magic, and to torment a defenseless child! You can have no reason to treat him so."

Orlan and Mathias stood, silent and abashed, at the cutting words of reproach. They couldn't argue. Godefroi held no power over them—he was a slight youth, disdainful of violence and magically incapable of blasting them—but he was in the right. They felt the enormity of their offense against Andemyon. They'd misused their magic. They'd gone too far. How could they think to defend themselves before the righteous outrage in those usually tranquil, too-large brown eyes?

The last words were most terrible of all: "My Lord Redmantyl would be ashamed to see you both behave so."

Orlan was surprised, then irritated, when he saw that Mathias was about to weep. *Coward*, he thought. *At the threat of my father, you burst into tears so easily as little Andemyon.* Mathias might jest and bluster out of Redmantyl's hearing, but he was truly afraid of the wizard. Contempt shook Orlan from his own shame.

"I don't care," he answered in defiance. "It matters not at all to me what Father thinks if I upset his precious little pet! He may be angry as seven demons." But this was only bluff; he was as afraid as Mathias of incurring his father's displeasure, and Godefroi knew it.

"Shall I tell him then, Orlan?"

"You wouldn't tell."

Godefroi wouldn't tell. His sense of honor would not allow him to carry tales against his fellow apprentices, in spite of their behavior. But Orlan was not so sure of Andemyon's silence, for Andemyon had better reasons to speak. Mathias agreed that Redmantyl mustn't know of their bullying, so they'd redoubled their crime and hunted for Andemyon until they found him sobbing on the back stairs in the Treturret Hall.

"Andemyon, you're such a cry-baby. No one's harmed you." He pounced up the lowest steps.

Mathias glanced anxiously down the corridors at either side. "Orlan..."

Orlan ignored him. He no longer needed Mathias's encouragement; this, he did himself. "There's no reason for such carryings-on," he told the small boy as he advanced. "And no reason to carry tales." Andemyon tried to inch away, but Orlan chased him to the top step and trapped him on the landing. "You dare not, Brat. Understand me?"

"I won't tell," Andemyon whispered. "Honestly. I shan't carry tales to Father–"

"*My* father!" He flashed with unthinking temper, and *pushed*. The force of his anger struck; Andemyon flew backwards to the edge of the landing. He wobbled there for a surprised instant, back arched, fingers out, fighting for balance, grasping for a railing that did not exist. Their eyes met, Andemyon's puzzled, almost calm with incomprehension at this last betrayal. His lips moved, as if he meant to speak. Then he tumbled over.

Mathias cried out, but Orlan had already caught the little boy with a more controlled flex of magic and held him suspended in mid-air. The stone floor lay twelve feet below. Andemyon squeaked, arms waving and feet kicking frantically.

"Don't squirm, or I shall drop you whether I mean to or not." Orlan released the child briefly, then caught him up again before he could fall very far. "Be still!"

The wordless whirl of terrified thoughts that fluttered through Andemyon's mind echoed in his own. The rapid pulse of the child's heart throbbed in his own veins. How small this body was! So light. Orlan had levitated heavier objects in the course of his daily exercises. He felt the life-force of the little being he had captured. So fragile. So frightened. So helpless in his grasp. It was no effort to hold this insignificant creature in his power. At a whim, he could wind his will about Andemyon's essence and *squeeze* until the breath was crushed out of his lungs and that beating heart stilled and every riotous thought made silent. It would be so easy. He might simply loose his hold and let Andemyon fall.

"Promise, Andemyon, on pain of death, the proper punishment for all talebearers and traitors, that you will keep your silence."

Andemyon only whimpered, "Please."

Mathias, still standing below, spoke: "Orlan, stop. Let him go. Please?"

The apprentice was nearly as frightened as Andemyon. Orlan hadn't expected that. Shame struck him anew, more powerfully than it had at Godefroi's scolding. Gently, he set Andemyon down.

"I wouldn't have dropped him, Mathias," he answered as the little boy ran away. "'Twas only meant to frighten."

"I thought so," Mathias sounded uncertain, "but Andemyon didn't." Then he hissed: "Orlan, you pushed him. I *felt* it. You were so angry—you weren't playing."

"It was an accident! I wouldn't harm him. I didn't mean to—"

Yes, you did. Was this his own thought or Mathias's? Orlan didn't know, but he felt the words slice through him. It was true. He had gone beyond the thoughtless brutality of children's games this time; he'd wanted to hurt Andemyon. He'd thought of killing him.

"What if My Lord Redmantyl hears of this?" asked Mathias.

"Father won't know," Orlan answered with more confidence than he felt. "At least, I managed that. Andemyon won't dare go to him now. He won't say a thing."

Of course, Redmantyl did know. Andemyon had no need to speak; his wide-eyed alarm if Orlan drew too near, Godefroi's tensely suppressed disapproval, and Mathias's whipped-dog remorse told all the tale. Orlan concealed his guilt more successfully than his companion, but he knew that his father was fully aware of the part he had played in the mischief.

All passed, eventually. Godefroi forgave him; Mathias remained his friend; Andemyon followed him, as he had at Keyfins, but at a cautious distance. Redmantyl never mentioned his transgression. No punishment befell the guilty. No reprimand was spoken, but Orlan could not forget what he had done. He was responsible; there was no one else to blame. He was sorry he had behaved so badly, but he could not apologize. Who would believe him? Andemyon, perhaps, for Andemyon was still willing to love him more than he deserved, but no one else. He had damaged a fragile trust. It was declared in the lack of former boisterousness in his games with Mathias—they were always anxious lest they go too far—and in the seemingly casual way in which his father and the apprentices contrived that Andemyon should not be left alone near him.

It had been so that day at Keyfins. Just as Andemyon had drawn his first choking breath and Orlan knew certainly that the boy was not going to die, Mathias had run up to ask, "What happened?" As he answered, "He fell," there, again, was the same unspoken accusation: *You pushed him. You meant to hurt him.*

But hadn't he shown himself capable of doing just that? Could he blame them if they thought he had tried to drown his brother?

Often thereafter, Orlan felt his father's intense, searching gaze upon him, stripping away layers of defensive wards and leaving him more exposed than if he were naked. Those cool, colorless eyes pierced him to the soul. And within each glance lay the question, *What are you?* as if Redmantyl faced a stranger.

Orlan felt like a stranger. Under that soul-baring gaze, he was not the son of the household, not a noble-bred Chyelde, not Redmantyl's. His brutal, spiteful actions had proved him no better than a common churl. He had injured one he ought to protect. And he had done more than break the codes of noble conduct. His crime was greater than base cruelty; it was a lapse in wizardly discipline. He had slipped. He had misused his power. He had acted in unthinking fury. Worst of all, he had lost his father's highest regard. He sensed the great disappointment behind Redmantyl's silent gaze. He knew his father must wonder at his competence: was he fit to be a wizard if he could lose control of himself so completely?

It was the duty of all true wizards to cast the weak-willed, unrestrained, malign and degenerate from their ranks, and even to destroy them if they became dangerous. Orlan knew how few students of magic survived the rigorous tests of apprenticeship and magedom, how harshly they were judged before they were named full wizards and permitted to join that austere company. He knew what his father examined him for. The signs of his vulnerability were there: he was reckless. He was temperamental. Could he be a danger one day? Redmantyl was reluctant to consider his own child a potential renegade, but sentiment had no place in this profession. A wizard must not be guided by his affections; if Orlan revealed himself unfit, he would be expelled as readily as any other fallen magician. No mercy could be expected; if Orlan had doubted this before Olyr's fall, he was agonizingly aware of it now. The possibility of expulsion terrified him more than any threat of punishment, for it was not a punishment; he would simply be deemed unable to withstand the strictures of wizardly life, and asked to leave.

These past months, he had been so careful to exercise his self-command at all times. He must demonstrate by his best behavior that he could conduct himself as a proper nobleman. He wasn't a renegade! He was qualified to become a wizard. And still Redmantyl watched him dispassionately, judged him, and waited for his jealous rage to surface and his careful discipline to slip again.

He was glad to leave Wizardes Cliff. He'd hoped that this journey would free him from his memories and give him the opportunity to prove himself after all. By taking up this commission in Redmantyl's name, he'd hoped to regain some of the honor he had lost. He wanted to be good. His father must see that he could be trusted. But Storm Port altered nothing. He was far from his father's penetrating gaze and farther from Andemyon, but his shame was here. Tedora was here. If ghosts did walk, she haunted him through the night and reminded him of his lapse. He had not escaped.

Orlan was up early the next morning, but Ren and Adyna were up before him, rolling out kegs of ale, filling decanters, coaxing the coals in the great fireplace to blaze. They had already eaten their breakfast, but a pot of porridge bubbled sluggishly over the low fire and thick slices of ham fried on an iron skillet on the grate.

"It is poor fare, I know, but I hope you will find it acceptable," Adyna apologized even before he could wish her a good morning.

"Adyna, it is fine," he assured her. "I am grateful for any meal kindly offered."

"I meant to send Rennie to you with a tray but we did not think you awake."

"Nonsense. I may sit at a table as any ordinary folk would." He looked around the tavern. "Do you eat here?"

"Yes," but the alekeeper sounded ashamed to admit to this. Orlan wondered; Adyna had not always been so servile in her manner toward him. In his childhood, she had looked upon him as one of her own. Like Kyarde, he was scolded or petted as required, for he had been as dear to her and as much a nuisance. But it seemed that in the years since, her attitude had changed. Now that he was grown, she saw him as the young Lord, her master.

"As you sit here, then I shall join you here also." He took a seat at the table nearest the hearth. A platter of freshly-baked bread was set before him and he took up a bun and tore it open. "If you mean to serve me, Adyna, I would be glad for the butter plate and a bowl of that porridge."

"As you wish, my pet. Rennie!"

The girl was serving this breakfast when Houarde Portreeve walked down into the Whitelm.

"We are not open yet, Syre," Adyna curtsied. "I am sorry."

"As am I, Goode Keeper, but I've not come as a thirsty man. Chyelde Orlan, I wanted to speak to you."

"And I with you, Syre. You have something of mine."

"Yes, I know, that little bird-thing you paid so much for. `Tis safely at my home—you need not worry for it. I forgot I had it in my hand `til I saw it on the table long after dinner. I forgot completely, and I offer deep apologies for that. You may have the opportunity to fetch it this morning."

"Will you have some bread with us, Syre?" Adyna offered.

"No, ta, Adyna. I took my morning meal before starting my way here with my purpose, for there is a purpose, Chyelde. My Lady—that is, my good wife the Layn Mayor—extends a civil invitation to you. You're welcome to reside at the Mayor's Hall during your visit to our city. An honored and noble guest has such a right, you understand, to the best lodgings we may offer, and I would not be too proud to say that My Layn keeps the finest house—the best tables, quiet servants, even makes wines and ales of remark. Tell Goode Keeper Adyna, if it please you, and send word to your father if you think that proper. We'd be graced at your presence, Lad– er– Chyelde Orlan."

"I should be happy in the company of such distinguished hosts, Syre." Orlan turned to the hearth. "Adyna, would you have objection?"

"Me? Objection, Lad?"

"I am your guest and it would not be right for me to abandon the welcome of one house in favor of another. But perhaps you'll find me less troublesome if I do not crowd you and cause such a fuss. You may enjoy my visit more if I lodge elsewhere."

"You've been no trouble to me," Adyna protested. "`Tis an honor to have you. But the Mayor's Hall would be best for a young noble, I suppose."

"Then it is agreeable to you?"

"It's not my place to disagree."

Orlan sighed. "Very well then. Syre Portreeve, you may tell your wife, My Layn Mayor, I am honored to accept her most generous invitation. I shall be at your house tonight."

sen

That afternoon, servants carried Orlan's baggage from the Whitelm and the youth dressed for dinner in guest chambers at the back of the Mayor's Hall. The rooms were pleasant, large and well-aired, cool even on this hot day. A porcelain washing-bowl had been filled with fresh rosewater for his arrival.

Orlan stripped to his hose and bathed at the washing-stand, pausing now and again in his splashing at the view from the tall windows, for he could look down into the Mayor's private garden. Below, neat flowerbeds flanked pebbled paths, and white geese wandered, plucking at the lush, green grass and wading in shallow, stony pools. Trellises were staked for grapes, sweet peas, roses; rows of carrots, turnips, cabbages, and herbs sprouted at the kitchen door, and blossoming apple, cherry, and pear trees blocked the alleyway and stables outside the tended walls. This was another surprise; he had no idea that such places could exist within a city.

"'Tis lovely," he said as he stepped out of his hose and accepted the clean pair offered by the small boy sent to assist him.

"Aye, M'Lord," the boy, who seemed slightly in awe of him, agreed quickly without glancing up. As he unpacked Orlan's best summer clothes, he handled each silken shirt and pressed linen tunic with wonder and great care. "M'Layn Ilset plants and tends them all herself. She has me to help."

"Have you been here very long?"

"So long as I know, M'Lord."

"No, I'm not a Lord," Orlan corrected him. "Chyelde, if you please."

The boy nodded. "Which shirt shall ye wear, Chyelde?"

"That one, with the long ruffs."

Styles had changed little since Orlan's childhood, but the nobility always searched for things new and fashionable. At Pendaunzel, Orlan had observed that many courtiers had taken to slashing the outer seams of their tunic sleeves from shoulder to wrist and pulling through frills of colorful lace sewn onto the shirt sleeves beneath. Young squires and damosels of the court wore their tunics cut short, an inch or two above the knee rather than the calf-length of their elders, and they imitated the hairstyles of the Free Folk by weaving thin braids into their long plaits. Orlan's formal dress reflected these fashions, for his sleeves revealed rows of red and silver lace, and three long and slender braids tied with red ribbons fell over his left shoulder. He had taken great care with his appearance tonight; the last thing he wished was to appear as a country-bred noble, grown away from the Duke's court. As he smoothed his tunic and sash and turned in front of the mirror held by the small servant, he looked very courtly indeed and more than a little dandified.

"Good enough, do you think?"

"Oh, yes, M'Lord. Very fine."

"Now, will you tell me how I might find the feast hall?"

With the boy's directions, Orlan went along the correct corridors, around corners and up and down the short steps peculiar to a town home, and at last found the great stairway.

Houarde, waiting below, was not so impressed with his appearance. "Never seen such a thing in my life beyond a carnival," he laughed, then tugged at Orlan's ribbons. "Is that what your Lordlings wear now?"

"At My Lord Dafythe's court, yes, Syre."

"Well!" the Portreeve said in amazement, then recovered his courtesy, for his wife was staring at their guest with something more than surprise. "Chyelde, I am a fool and a knave for all that. When you came to this house, you were not presented to my wife, and wouldn't know her from any other woman. Let me repair my error, if it please you now. My Love, may I have you meet the Chyelde Orlan Lightesblood, son to My Lord Redmantyl. Chyelde, the Layn Mayor and Aubrey given to the protection of Storm Port, my wife, Ilset of Glaustonbury."

"I welcome you to our home," Ilset, recovered also, said with perfect grace. She was a handsome, plumping woman past sixty, her hair streaked with white and her face carefully powdered to conceal a large mole on her upper lip. Her garments were the mayoral robes of rich orange and green needlework, and she wore her chain of office and signet ring as if she greeted important guests. Orlan thought that there must be other Storm Port officials expected for dinner, but the hour was nearly upon them and the front hall empty of all but himself and his hosts. "May I correct my husband's judgments by telling you I think your garments very handsome, young Orlan? They are higher in fashion than we are accustomed to here."

"Gramercy, My Layn," Orlan responded. "I am honored to call

you my host." He knelt before her and placed his brow to the backs of her hands, the traditional gesture of respect.

"And I to call you my guest, Chyelde." This was the proper response. "But, up, young Orlan, and accompany me to the table." Ilset took the youth's arm and escorted him into the dining hall. Orlan was given the seat to her right; Houarde followed and took his place on the left. "When were you last at the Duke's court, Chyelde? I bid you tell us of the doings at Pendaunzel. Houarde, will you carve the roast?" Ilset seated herself at the head of the table and summoned the serving maids.

They talked of court over the meal, of Prince Margueryt, Dafythe's daughter, and of the Duke's dislike for her bloodthirsty eagerness for war with Spain. They discussed the probability of war. Dafythe had kept peace in the Northlands for fifty years and he was opposed to any confrontation now, but it was said that the Emperor Kharles, his nephew, was all for the glory days of battle, as well as seizing the Spanish lands to the south of the Northlands, and Margueryt was ready to lead her first campaign. Dafythe was now ninety-seven; he might keep the peace in his lifetime, but that could not go on for too many more years. Orlan spoke of the Duke's illegitimate son, Ambris the Just, Earl of Eadeshire, who had been given the grand position of Lord High Chancellor and had returned to Pendaunzel with his new, young wife and infant son. There was a great scandal with Prince Katheryne of Eirelande, Dafythe's orphaned niece, who had lately conducted an unfortunate romance with a common bowman, and there was gossip involving courtiers, their romances and political intrigues. Orlan occasionally showed his ignorance, taking this Councillor for the wife of that Earl or confusing Lord Roodebroke with Lord Rafenshighte, but Ilset and Houarde were more ignorant and did not see his mistakes. The Mayor listened to all of Orlan's tales, true and apocryphal, but Houarde declared after a short tax on his attention that he'd never been one for such "fol-de-rummy."

"Houarde," his wife said.

The Portreeve, abashed, and wiped his fingers on his kirtle. "By your pardon, Lad, I mean no offense. For nobles, 'tis a thing to cosset to Kings and Dukes and such-like. Now, I'm a simple merchant man. My grandfather ran a customs house and did well, and my father took his earnings to do better still at the shipyards, but we're never fit for courtly gadding and primping for all that. Ilset's born no better'n me, I think. She carries herself as Layn Aubrey of the city, and though I'd be the first to say that gives her as much a right to cosset at court as you,

Chyelde, she'd be no more fit for it than I.

"Oh, we've been to Pendaunzel, twice a year if the Duke calls a Mayor's Council so often, but 'tis business for My Lady and I find ways of amusing myself in the city. We'd be unfit for more, you know. Can you see such as us done up and dancing about My Gracious Lord Dafythe with the Earl of This-n-That and Lord and Lady Nonesuch, my dear?"

Ilset's reply was a tight smile.

Dinner itself was magnificent, to suit the Mayor's noble guest. The best silver, polished, and finest crystal had been set out on damask, and the kitchen servants brought out delightful dishes one after another: after the roast haunch, a sharp, onion broth, then baked mackerel and apples, then ducks in honeyed sauce, then fresh strawberries, the first from Ilset's garden, with sweet cream whipped to a froth and the cacao Houarde had bought, then a round of cheese and tankards of cold beer. The Mayor's household was ready to please Orlan in matters of comfort. Maid-heralds in orange livery, stiff tabards bearing the city seal, stood at either end of the table with large painted fans, keeping the dining hall cool and the flies away from the food, and Ilset herself saw that each dish was to his taste and his goblet was always filled with honeyed pink wine. When he could not accept another bite of the treats his hosts offered, Houarde suggested a walk.

"What could be more fitting than a stroll to catch our breath after such a feast?" he asked as he brushed the leavings from his lap. "I can think of no better pursuit, and I may show you the sights of our city, if 'tis your pleasure, Chyelde Orlan."

"I'd be glad to walk with you, Syre."

"Will you join us, Ilset?"

"I would," Ilset replied pleasantly, "but I must seek Justice Hugobarde this night for his counsel. You must walk with our guest alone. Chyelde, I bid you go and enjoy, and do not stay out too late."

It was a fine summer night not long after sunset. The sky was a deep lavender and the streets not so crowded as they had been short hours before; the bazaar was abandoned except for beggars shuffling through the refuse and the last merchants left packing their wares and shutting up their booths. The windows of St. Khrystopher's glittered in a dozen bright colors like gemstones from the thousands of candles within and the sounds of Evensong haunted the empty square.

Once they crossed the marketplace, Houarde led him directly to the Whitelm. The tavern was crowded with all those who could not visit at earlier hours; weary merchants pressed the room from wall to wall and roared their demands for refreshment. Ren scrambled between the tables, skillfully balancing full trays, spilling little and smiling vaguely at the drunkards' jokes. Adyna was busy at the bar, filling mug after mug and emptying full kegs swiftly. Neither noticed Orlan's entrance, but the patrons nearest the door recognized Houarde and stepped back to give the Mayor's well-known husband a path to his favorite seat.

There was only one unattended stool at the bar; Houarde scowled at the crowd around him, but none moved. "Disrespectful— Here, Chyelde," he offered the unoccupied seat to Orlan, then bawled over the general commotion to draw Adyna's attention. "Alekeep!"

Adyna turned and forgot her lesser patrons. With a pleased smile, she pushed her straggling forelocks back beneath her kerchief. "A good evening to you, Syre. Welcome, Orlan. What would you have?"

"Two of your finest lights, Goode Adyna."

She shook her head. "A light ale, Syre, and pinked brandywine."

"That watery sop?" Houarde snorted in contempt at the suggestion. "Why, the lad's no infant suited for such candies. How old are you, Chyelde Orlan?"

"Two and twenty."

"There, Adyna!" the Portreeve cried in triumph. "Orlan's no longer the little one you once tendered. He's a man now and fit for the refreshments of grown folk. An ale for the youth."

"Brandy," Adyna said. "Orlan's not tasted ale yet, and shouldn't."

Houarde turned to Orlan. "Chyelde?"

"Father doesn't let me have strong drink at home. I would like the wine if you please, Adyna."

"As you say." She took down the decanter and a crystal goblet. She owned few such treasures and would not permit their use except at the most special occasions. The goblet was filled with care and set before him.

Orlan took up the wine, and drank. The sour-sweet taste of the stuff was stronger than he had expected; he swallowed. His eyes watered and he sputtered at the fiery sensation in his throat. "Imps and monkeys!"

"Here, Chyelde, not so fast!" Houarde chuckled. "You'll only lose it if you try to gulp it down so."

Adyna set down a tumbler of water. "Sip that slowly, Lad, 'til your stomach has settled, then take the wine at the same sipping pace. I'm sorry. I would have thought you'd know not to quaff a full goblet of brandy at once."

"I thought it would be the same as the pinked stuff, only more fulsome," Orlan said after following Adyna's advice. "It burns."

Houarde roared with laughter. "Aye, it'll burn you, Chyelde, if you think it to be the watery broth of children." He pushed the goblet at the boy. "Drink, my lad, and bless you for it. We'll see you a man yet."

Orlan drank again, taking his wine in small sips. A bright, burning shot from his lips to his stomach, then spread to the tips of his toes and fingers with a warm tingle; it was a strange, but not entirely unpleasant, experience. He began to feel as if the bubbles of the wine had rushed to fill his head. He floated in them. "Oh, this is wonderful."

"Will you have more?" Adyna offered the decanter a second time.

He glanced to Houarde. "Shall I?"

"I would, certainly. Are you fit for another?"

"Yes. Yes, Adyna, if you please." He held the goblet steady while the alekeeper refilled it. The ruby-red liquid glowed within the prisms of the crystal, inviting him. Orlan tasted, and relished the sparkling fire.

"It is to your liking?" Adyna asked.

"Yes, very much. It's not at all as I thought it would be." He smiled. "You must tell me, and honestly, is this how it is with grown folk?"

"You've been about grown folk all your life," she answered gently.

"But I've not been one." Orlan sipped his wine. "I feel changed, not as a child any longer. So–" he struggled for the appropriate words. "I feel so newly-made, as if there had never been anything before today. Do you know?" But it seemed to him from the amused expressions on Adyna's and Houarde's faces that, even if they had known the precise moment of their own maturity, they did not remember. "When I came of age I was told that I had become a man, but I never felt so. One day alone cannot truly make you a man, for that change must come before or after. I think I have arrived at it today."

"And only one goblet," Houarde chuckled. "Your tongue's loosened a good bit, Chyelde."

Orlan laughed. "Yes! I could go on talking all night." The wine glass was empty again. "Adyna, may I have more?"

"If you wish," she replied cautiously.

"I do. This brandy is marvelous stuff. It makes one feel–" When he tried to take up the goblet, his fingers did not grip as they ought; the slender stem of the crystal slipped from his grasp and Adyna reached out to catch it.

"Orlan!"

"I'm sorry." The bubbles which had sent him floating burst in that clumsy instant, and he was left on too solid ground. His awareness, always open to a multitude of perceptions, had been flung wide. The room was too bright and too loud. The wine had excited his nerves, setting him a-tremble. It was too much at once; Orlan was not able to cope with so many strange, new sensations. "I'm sorry, Adyna. I did not mean–" He brought his head down to rest on his hands.

"Chyelde? Orlan?" Adyna touched him gently. "What's wrong?"

"I don't know. I feel..." he brushed his hair from his eyes, "...so odd."

Adyna and Houarde exchanged an understanding glance.

"'Tis time, I think, to see yourself safely abed, Lad," said the alekeeper. "That's more than enough for a first night. He's not up to such carousing, Syre."

"You're right, Goode Adyna." Houarde paid for their drinks. "We'll bid you pleasant night and be on our way."

"Good night, Syre. Sleep well, Orlan."

"Yes, pleasant night," he replied as Houarde led him out to the street.

They had gone ten steps before he realized that they were walking in the wrong direction. The path to the Mayor's Hall should take them back across the bazaar, but Houarde was leading him down the Long Street, toward the Dukesgate at the south end of the city.

"I thought we were going back."

"Nonsense, Lad!" Houarde chuckled. "The sun's barely set. If Keeper Adyna refuses us, other tavernkeeps are willing to take my money." They reached a narrow side street and Houarde yanked Orlan's arm; the boy could only follow. "There's a fine place here, only a short step along."

They turned again, into another narrow street which ended at a courtyard. The stink of the city was stronger here, trapped by the close buildings, and Orlan pressed his hand over his nose as Houarde led him into an alleyway between two buildings and down a short flight of steps. The tavern was similar to the Whitelm, crowded, noisy, cool between stone walls, but Orlan knew no one here.

"Ale!" Houarde roared gleefully from the doorway, then addressed Orlan with deference as he led him to a table. "An ale for you, Chyelde?"

"No, ta."

"Still feeling that brandy you gulped in one breath, eh?"

"I do not wish to drink more, Syre."

"Now Goode Keeper Adyna's not here to frown at you. A lad your age, and no more than two sips of wine in one night? `Tis outrageous. An insult to every honest alehouse in this city. Here, Chyelde, you must have some cup to hold in your hands, or you'll offend my dear friend." He waved at the barkeeper. "Mightn't you take brandy, perhaps, if you've no taste for ale?"

"Very well, more brandy." He accepted the goblet, but drank little. The noise and confusion of the place rang in his ears. His stomach churned at the incredible stench and his head still spun from the wine at the Whitelm. If he wanted any drink, he wanted cool water to clear himself, not more unsettling wine. He did no more than touch his mouth to the goblet's rim from time to time and try to listen to Houarde's chatter. Was the man never silent?

"Keeper Adyna cannot know the needs of lads your age," Houarde was saying. "How she pets you as if you were her own little chick! Oh, she is a good woman. She's a fine woman, but she's forgotten how it is to be young and ready to see life for yourself. You must drink, Chyelde, and try all you will. The pleasures of life are best for the young." He drained his mug and beckoned for another. "We are given— how? One hundred years if we are blessed in good health. Twenty of that is spent as children and fifty spent as old. We must make the best of the middling years before they pass and enjoy while we may."

"There are duties beyond drink, Syre."

"But none so important. `Tis the duty of all good youths, whatever their birth, to take pleasure while they may. Young men in particular, you understand, for there is much to be offered them in the way of new and pleasant experience. By the Saints, what's a life without experience? We might so well be dead in our graves. Drink up, my lad, drink up! Soon enough, you'll be given in marriage to some maid, pretty or no, who may help your position. Your nobility, particular, is accustomed to wed young, for you've no need to get a living beforehand and little reason to grow fond of the Lady chosen for you."

"I don't believe my rank is so great to make me a marriage prize to anyone," Orlan said. "Father wouldn't be so ambitious to try and catch a well-placed bride for me. Wizards do not marry."

"Any noble's a prize to any other," Houarde answered. "A handsome lad as you are, you'll be caught soon enough." He gulped his ale and patted his belly for a belch. "The weight of a grown man's world will settle on you before you are ready to bear its burdens. May it never sour your heart's choler as it has mine. I can't run up stairs without it skipping its beat these days. More brandywine, Chyelde?"

"No, gramercies, Syre. I have not finished this."

"No excuse!" He called for the alekeeper and Orlan's barely-touched goblet was filled to the rim again. "Now Ilset and I were never blessed with such troubles as little ones underfoot. I cannot say why, but we have none. Still, there's much to be done as the husband of such a woman. Her business is mine, you might say. I love her well, make no mistake on that, but you are never so free with one woman as you may be with many. It'll be on you soon enough, Lad, so you must enjoy yourself now."

Orlan sipped his wine; the warmth of it spread through him, comforting, but the feeling soon dissipated and left him numbed and befuddled. Married, he thought. He might be married. Many youths of his age and rank were wed and already fathers. And, as vain as it was to think so, he would be worth catching in marriage, especially if the Duke declared him the rightful heir to the Lord of Greenwaters Island. At Pendaunzel, maids too young for his father had insisted on making his acquaintance; they were already calculating his worth. But all of them were silly creatures, empty-headed, flirtatious and disturbingly greedy for maidens so young. If all girls were like that, he would be happier left as a lone wizard. He did not want to be alone for all his life, but what alternative was there?

"Here, Lads!" Houarde shouted suddenly. Orlan looked up to see four young men, all near his own age, approaching from the doorway. They were a long-legged and spotty group, well-dressed in garments appropriate to the grown children of wealthy merchants: dull blue kirtles, short tunics, and family emblems—something between guild badges and coats of arms—embroidered on their shirt sleeves or breasts. All wore their hair cut short and curled under at their shoulders.

"How fares the old Portreeve?" one lad with a sharp, clever face asked and patted Houarde's shoulder roughly.

"As well as my old bones can be expected," the man replied cheerily. "Reynalde, Lads, I called you over in particular to acquaint you with a guest of my house—or Her Layn Mayorship's Hall, 'twould be more right. Lad, this is Orlan, Lord Redmantyl's son."

"Lord Redmantyl?" the youth echoed.

"Aye, Lord Redmantyl, you ignorant pup! God save you, Lad, you never learned a proper thing for all your years with the Sisters."

"And a good bit of luck, I thought," Reynalde said, and earned

Houarde's approving chuckle and shouts of agreement from his companions.

"My father is premiere wizard and Lord of Greenwaters Island," Orlan explained once the riot had faded.

"Yes?" The boy looked mildly interested, and began to study Orlan's clothes. "And you're a wizard yourself?"

"No, not yet," Orlan answered, flattered. "I'm 'prenticing under my father. I have five years before I'm a true wizard."

One of the boys groaned. "So much education!"

"Here, can you do something magical?" another asked.

Orlan reached out with his left hand, fingers fully extended, then turned them to a beckoning gesture as he spoke a spell of motion. The nearest table slid forward. It was impossible to keep his concentration for long, but before the spell collapsed the patrons at that table gripped their mugs and moved away quickly. Houarde and the boys were wide-eyed, and the barkeeper annoyed and a little frightened.

"H-here, no more of that, m'lad. No more of that."

Reynalde grinned boldly. "I've never met a wizard before."

"Reynalde's the youngest of my dear friend, Ozualte Spicemerchant," Houarde said. "They're a wealthy family and near as fine as you, I may say."

"Your servant, M'Lord," the boy made a low bow.

"Gramercies, young Syre," Orlan replied.

"Oh, there'll be differences 'twixt merchants and nobles, particularly the Wizard Lordlings like yourself, but I can think of no reason why you can't get on as friends while Orlan's here," Houarde continued.

"We'd be honored to welcome your young friend to join us, if it is his pleasure to do so."

"Well, Orlan?"

"Not this night," Orlan answered. "Please, Syre, I wish to leave." He smiled in apology. "I've had enough drink this evening, more than my fill."

"We've all done that before, eh, Lads?" Houarde said. "'Tis no shame."

"Perhaps another time," Reynalde suggested. "A good evening to you, My Lord, Houarde." The boys left the tavern without calling for a single drink.

"They're all fine lads," Houarde said once they had gone. "I ran with their fathers and we had our share of sport then! Ah, but that was years past when my health was better. Help you up, Chyelde Orlan?"

Orlan undressed for bed. After this long, hot, baffling evening, it was relief to toss aside his damp shirt and peel away his close-fitting hose. He ignored the nightshirt left by the small servant and settled at the center of the bed, legs folded beneath himself and hands turned up on his bare knees. The curtains were down, the candles out, his eyes shut. In warmth and darkness, Orlan tried to meditate. The wine had confused his senses. Though his awareness was wide open, the impressions he received were not so lucid as usual. Every sensation had a jarring edge—bright, hard, blaring. He would be overwhelmed if he did not regain control and clear his fuddled head.

Meditation was the first exercise of self-command, and the most important. To meditate, he must find a comfortable and quiet place where he would not be interrupted, relax, and think through the workings of his mind and his body, the breath drawing in and out of his lungs, the rhythm of his heart, the pathways of his nerves from the core of his being to the tips of his fingers and toes as the magic coursed along them. In this state, he *felt* the source of the power he possessed and understood that it was fully part of him. The magic was wound into his substance. As he controlled his breath, his heartbeat, the sensations of his flesh, so he could control this primal energy. It was his if he would own it and master it.

Self-discipline had never been simple for Orlan. From the first days of apprenticeship, his lessons had been difficult. As a novice, he'd often stood bare to the waist in the Daune Tower while Godefroi circled and, at his father's instructions, brushed him with a handful of nettles. The touch had burned; the skin on his back, his chest, his arms still tingled at the memory. He had to bite into his lips to keep from crying out. Tears had streamed down his face. And after each session, his father had soothed the stinging rash with a balm and explained:

"You must overcome pain and fear, for these are the most base of human influences. And after these, hunger and anger, lust, greed, jealousy, weariness, and the infirmity of will that desires drunkenness. Even love may be dangerous if you offer your heart without caution. A wizard must not need, for we are deceived through our unchecked desires. We become weak. The essence of magic is self-control—remember that! You cannot direct the external world if you are unable to command yourself. When you command your body, you command your magic. Magic begins at the heart, and the heart is flesh. Begin with it."

The lesson was harsh, but Orlan knew he must endure it to subdue the pain. Though he felt the sting, he refused to acknowledge it. He would not display his distress. He would not cry out, would not wince, would not weep. No sign of weakness would disgrace him before his father; this resolution gave Orlan the courage to persevere when he might otherwise have collapsed. In time, endurance became easier. When he ceased to fear the trial, he conquered it. Other trials were approached by the same means. Eventually, he learned to overpower his hunger and his need to sleep for two and three days at once. He was less successful with his emotions, but he tried to suppress what he could not banish. He attended Redmantyl's lectures against playful dalliance with the local maids to satisfy his curiosity and lusts; Orlan was troubled at the idea that he might have lusts and he dreaded the time when they must awaken and provide new distractions to test his strength of will. Desire still slept within him. His sexual thoughts were only the most vague and fanciful imaginings. He did not possess Andemyon's startling beauty, but many maidens at Pendaunzel—and one or two noblemen of the court as well—had told him he was a handsome boy and he was inclined to believe them. Yet he was not tempted. He did not know what temptation was.

Olyr, while a mage, had told him that temptation was best conquered by being avoided: he would never miss the taste of mead so long as he kept away from taverns, nor sweets so long as he did not walk near a baker's shop. Orlan had lived all his life so—chaste, inexperienced, untouched by enticements of the flesh or spirit. He had endured small tests of his control, but no true hardship. He had never been taken to his limits; his father always supervised his lessons and ended each exercise before his will was broken.

"My apprenticeship was a good deal more difficult," the wizard had once confessed. "He who was Redmantyl before would beat me to kill my spirit and destroy me if he could. He was bound to teach me, but he did not make my education comfortable. I wept and screamed for him to stop, but as he would not I learned to withstand his cruelty. It made me strong, far stronger than he could hope to be."

Orlan sometimes thought that he might be stronger if his exercises were more harsh; he might be a better magician if he were beaten down and able to rise against killing forces. Strict abstinence would take him successfully through his mage years, but it would not strengthen him as much as a wizard ought to be. He needed to face a challenge that he might overcome only with the greatest struggle and weld his will in flame, but he could not bear to inflict the most rigorous tests upon himself. Redmantyl had survived a baptism of fire and emerged supreme; Orlan had never been burned.

He had come to Storm Port a young magician, vows not yet taken, world not yet known, will not yet tested.

He lay in a heavy sleep that night, dreaming strange dreams, and he was ill the next day. The dull throbbing behind his eyes made him wince at the mid-morning sunlight, and all the water in the pitcher at his bedside could not satisfy the dry craving in his throat. He was slow at dressing; his fingers were not at all nimble in lacing his tunic and working his braids—both were loose and sloppy—and he was about to abandon the attempt and return to bed when there was a knock at the chamber door.

Ilset ventured in. "Pardon if I disturb you, Chyelde, but breakfast has been lain downstairs, and we wait for you," she said. "Are you well? Do you wish a tray sent up?"

"No, My Layn," Orlan answered. "I am perhaps a little ill, but I think I may eat downstairs, if I eat at all."

"I see," she smiled with some compassion. "Houarde took you to visit his favorite alehouses last night?"

"Yes, My Layn. But you must not blame him. I was foolish myself."

"Foolish? No, Chyelde. You have only been a young visitor to a new city, and I do not hold Houarde responsible for more than keeping you out after he must have seen you had taken your fill. Shall I have cool water and perhaps some fresh fruit set at your place at the table? No more will be appetizing to one in your present state. And, if 'tis your pleasure, I have brewed tonics from herbs in my garden that both Houarde and I have found relieve the headache."

Orlan smiled. "My Layn, the smallest relief will be welcome. Oh, and—" He took up the tunic thrown over the chest at the foot of his bed, where it had been discarded the night before. "I do not recall spilling my wine but there, you see, I've stained this. 'Twas nearly new, and now 'tis ruined."

Ilset's reply was no less sympathetic. "Don't fret for it, Chyelde. It may still be saved. Perhaps the laundry-lasses can bring the stain out."

"Gramercy, My Layn. You've been kind."

"You are my honored guest, Chyelde, and you mustn't fret for anything here. 'Tis only important that you enjoy your visit. You do enjoy yourself?"

"Yes, My Layn."

He did enjoy his visit here. It was summer, so Free Folk came to the city in multitudes; bards and minstrels, street-thespians and carnival troupes with trained animals, conjuring tricksters, and pinwheel games of chance became so commonplace that they did not draw the city folk as they would the villagers of Lyges. Storm Port was a city of music and merchants' shouts, of pungent scents of sewage and spice. It was a city made up of the press of bodies on the cobblestone streets and mysteries down every alleyway. Houarde had proudly informed him that there were more than 100,000 people in Storm Port; the city rivaled Pendaunzel and was not so much smaller than London or Paris.

Although many people the world over visited Storm Port—some even stayed to make it their home—Storm Port's people were not travelers themselves. All the world, its riches and its marvels would come to them; why should they move to meet it? Houarde, not Ilset, was the best reflection of the spirit of Storm Port, for he had been born in the city and never left it long nor willingly in his fifty-seven years. New York and Pendaunzel were the breadth of his experience and he disdained both as pale comparisons to his home.

Ilset, on the other hand, was not a native; she had been born in Devonshire, lived in Gallys, and taken pilgrimage to Rome and Jerusalem before settling here. She was well-traveled, well-educated, and more worldly than her townspeople, and she was admired throughout Storm Port. The citizens of the city and its environs were called upon to choose their Mayor, as thespians voted among themselves for a leader, and Ilset had been thrice chosen in popular election. She was a careful administrator, governing her household and her city with the same deliberate efficiency. Her manner was always pleasant and her voice polite and gentle to the ears. She fussed over Orlan nearly as much as Adyna in seeking to provide for his comfort and entertainment. Whatever he fancied was immediately called for, and he was encouraged to ask for more.

The upkeep of the Mayor's Hall and neighboring houses was not conducted as it would be at Wizardes Cliff, for the filth of the city was inescapable. The gutters on the main streets were as clogged as they had been on the day of Orlan's arrival, if not more so, but he was the only one who seemed bothered by the stench. Storm Port's people were used to it. Orlan wore his riding boots whenever he ventured into the street and left them at the door to Mayor's Hall before going in; his better shoes were saved for the house. He also bought a rose-petal pomander at the bazaar to carry with him out of doors. Indoors, Ilset used scented rushes from the nearby marsh for the same purpose, but tended her house little beyond sweeping and dusting. More effort was useless. Windows at the front of the Hall were kept shut except to throw out the garbage and empty chamber pots. By comparison, Wizardes Cliff seemed as clean as freshly bleached linens. The prevalent scents of the castle were salty sea air and thriving lichens.

Guests were frequently at the Mayor's Hall—Captain Alyx, the Sheriff, Justice Hugobarde and his wife, the Bishop of Greenstephan, Houarde's merchant friends and their hopeful daughters—and the meals became more opulent as the summer deepened. There had been no rainfall for weeks; the countryside was stricken with drought and the streets of Storm Port were dust-dry. A dry autumn, a poor harvest, and a hungry winter were expected, and everything that could not be preserved must be eaten quickly.

In the evenings, before or after dinner, Ilset gathered her guests in the great hall at the back of the house, where a fire blazed even on the warmest nights but tall windows were open to the garden, cold beer was poured generously, and music played, for Ilset had her patronized minstrels. She was fond of the soothing sounds of pipe and lute and lyre. Houarde preferred loud songs—the more bawdy and easy to shout along with, the better. After his wife's pleasant interludes, he would leave to seek his own amusements. Orlan found Ilset's tastes pleasing, but he heard little of the songs he was most familiar with, the bards' tales of spectacular adventure and of great love and greater loss. Such ballads were long, longer than many people were accustomed to sit and listen; Ilset's minstrels played more brief and sprightly melodies, but even at the end of these some of her guests looked impatient.

Like Houarde, all Storm Port sought to enjoy themselves, although not always with the Portreeve's single-mindedness. The hunt was popular. Orlan observed this pursuit one morning. He did not join the riders, for the thought of killing anything was abhorrent to him, but instead watched their antics from the guard towers overlooking the Duke's Park. He soon saw that the so-called hunt was more an opportunity for the better-born city folk to shout, chase the hounds, and tear about on horseback than to catch deer. They returned from the chase empty-handed. Orlan had never seen such carryings-on before, but he found them wonderfully amusing and he revised his first opinion of the bloody game; it might, after all, be fun, more fun than the entertainments he sought at home.

Most of the people Orlan met were completely illiterate. This lack was not so surprising in the common folk—for most commoners never learned more letters than they needed to spell their names and many tavern keepers could not read the signs over their own doors—but Houarde and his friends of the merchant caste were similarly lacking. More strange still, they did not think their ignorance an encumbrance; instead, Orlan's education was considered inflated and effeminate. No one his age, except university students who were rarely seen in Storm Port, had lessons. Storm Port 's merchants had their livelihood to think of; the things that the clergy and wizards and learned scholars chose to write in books were of no concern to them. Literacy in the native language was admired, for that had its practical purposes, but Latin was a mystery best left to Church folk and Greek was considered decadent. Mathematics higher than finger calculations were as marvelous as magic itself. Orlan was looked upon as a wonder of occult ability as much for his years of study as for his magic, and he began to conceal this.

As much as he enjoyed being an important and noble visitor to Storm Port, he was anxious not to be too outstanding. He wanted to fit in among the city folk as much as his rank, his talents, and his fair appearance would permit. Redmantyl had said that dumb beasts were nervous in the presence of magic, but Orlan had not fully understood this until now. Horses reared in the streets if he drew too close. The Mayor's dogs whined, cringed, and fled with their tails tucked beneath them, and the geese in the garden shrieked and flapped their wings. Cats hissed. He knew now how carefully his own mount had been trained to tolerate him and he tried to avoid all other animals. And animals were not the only ones to fear his powers. All except Ilset were unnerved when they saw him create a flame with a flick of his fingers and Orlan quickly learned to conceal this ability too. His father had been correct; magic was not meant for careless display.

In spite of these unfamiliar customs and the knowledge that he was considered weird, Orlan enjoyed the adventure of Storm Port. The differences between himself and his hosts unsettled him, but they also fascinated. That was the purpose of travel—was it not?—to learn the ways of folk in other lands, and surely Storm Port was as much a foreign land to his understanding as Spain or India. Here, he had his first taste of the experience and he delighted in it.

He wondered if Lammouthe had been like this. His memory of that time remained indistinct: Orlan vaguely recalled close-set buildings and narrow, cobblestone streets, rather like Lyges but more level and more crowded, noisy, and dirty. He remembered the stink of the dockyards and his awe at the tall-masted ships. Did he remember his mother? He could recall neither a face nor a voice but there had once been a presence which comforted him. He thought he remembered someone holding him when he was small and frightened, but that might be an early memory of his father.

His first vivid, visual impression was of Redmantyl standing over him in the morning sunlight, so tall and red and bright that the wizard had been burned into Orlan's memory. Indeed, Orlan marked his life from that moment, when all the light and strength and wondrous magic of the world had stepped into his childish awareness. He believed he had known he belonged to that man, even before he knew who Lord Redmantyl was. Before that, there was nothing.

That summer, he began to test the unyielding barrier which kept him from his childhood—his father's spell, placed upon him years ago. Until now, he had accepted it: who would wish to look back on dirt and poverty and misery when he lived in an ivory castle of magic? Orlan had not tried to remember, but his visit to Storm Port made him attempt to recall a past which had been kept from him. He wanted to know about his mother and the life he had known with her at Lammouthe. Could the spell be broken? He was a magician of some skill himself. Surely he could undo this. He must know: what had he been before his father had brought him to Wizardes Cliff?

heyghte

June began with the feasts of Whitsuntide. On Friday afternoon, the prominent city folk celebrated with the traditional procession down the Greenway and gathered on the Town Square that evening. Houarde went out immediately after Evensong, but Ilset returned to the Mayor's Hall to change from her heavy, ceremonial robes to lighter, festive garb. Orlan waited for her below.

"You must be my escort tonight, Dear Chyelde," she said when she descended. "My Houarde, I am afraid, is never of use at these public festivals. He forgets our office."

"You do not join the celebration, My Layn?"

Ilset shook her head with delicate regret. "I have spent many years among these Norledans—I consider them my people—and yet they are not like the English of my home. Their ways are strange to me." She took his arm. "But I would not be shamed to be seen with a presentable noble youth of any country."

They went out together. The orange-garbed heralds lighted them down the Mayor's Parade in the deepening twilight, but Ilset dismissed the girls once they reached the Square.

Here, the citizens of Storm Port assembled every seven years to elect their Mayor and Council, but tonight, they played. The best-born folk of the city lived in the great houses around the Square and along the Parade and Greenway; now, they joined their children, their guests, their servants, to reenact a joyous ceremony. Sunday was the true holiday; Friday was for festival. Age-old rituals, their purpose long forgotten, were performed and songs made nonsensical by time were sung anew. Motley clowns and swordbearers from the procession went among the merchant folk. White cloths painted with blood-red crosses hung upon every door and long, wilting tendrils of ivy hung from every eave. Torches blazed around the paved courtyard, makeshift tables crowded the porch of the Council Hall, and a maypole stood at the center of the Square, though May Day had passed weeks ago. Lawmakers and laundry-maids, they forgot themselves in the revelry and became people who sought a time when their games had a purpose. Only Ilset remained untouched. She acknowledged every greeting, but her words never took a tone of gaiety and her eyes were always elsewhere in the crowd.

"Do you seek your husband, My Layn?" Orlan, at her side, wondered. He looked about and found Houarde at the beer kegs behind the tables, already laughing too loudly.

"No, I was thinking of some goodly youths I would have you meet. The Spicemerchant, there—his son among them," she answered. "But the boy does not seem to be here. He must be off with his own amusements, as lads will." She smiled. "You may go too, if you wish, Chyelde. I would not keep you against youthful inclination."

The Spicemerchant had seen the Mayor gesture in his direction and he approached, wife at his elbow and daughters trailing reluctantly. The couple greeted the Mayor and her young guest warmly. The maids muttered something like "An honor, M'Lord" as they were presented and Orlan responded with the proper courtesies. He had met this family before, at Ilset's table; the Spicedaughters had been pushed at him then too. Drusilla, the elder, was near thirty and looked older for her solemn face and smooth-combed plaits. Her sister Julia was perhaps twenty-five and rather pretty, with large, dark eyes that snapped with resentment as her mother dragged her forward. She wore a white gown and hood with bright blue and red taudries wound about her as a bodice, the garb of a Whitsuntide dancer.

As they conversed, the music of drum and pipe rose from the center of the Square. Julia's friends, also in holiday garb of white, red, and blue, called to her to join them and she twisted as if she ached to follow, but her mother's hand remained firmly on her arm.

There was a problem; the four male dancers had disappeared. All eight lads and maids were by tradition children born on Whitsunday, but such people were rare and the number was more often made up of any with good birth or nimble feet available.

"'Tis a lack of suitable boys," the merchant's wife explained. "Our Reynalde, the others—I cannot think where they've got to."

Ilset nodded indulgently.

"Will you accompany my daughter, My Lord?" the woman persisted.

"No, gramercy. I think you will find me a poor partner." Orlan addressed the restless maid.

Dame Spicemerchant looked skeptical, as if Orlan had insulted her, but she allowed her daughter to slip away and join the maypole-ring with youths chosen from the crowd, servants and city guards. Orlan did not mean to be discourteous; he had told the truth. He did not like to dance; he did not know how. He had always sat through the Pendaunzel balls, for he would rather be taken as shy or aloof than known as clumsy.

Orlan had joined a maypole once, at Simon and Alfryda's wedding. Alfryda had wanted all the apprentices to dance; it was customary for six lads and six maids to accompany the bride and groom—*milk white and rose red and none that's known a kiss*, according to the old wedding song—but Godefroi and Orlan had been raised away from courtly graces and Mathias always avoided dances. Not one of them knew a step. She'd tried to teach them, but in the end only Orlan had consented. He'd paced around the Lyges churchyard green in stiff-kneed, jolting steps, face red and feet dragging at the smiles of the villagers who had gathered to watch. Godefroi had refused outright.

"It wouldn't be fitting," he explained afterwards. "Wizards aren't meant to prance about. 'Tis silly and undignified, and all for a meaningless ritual. Peasant-folk will perform their fertility rites at every wedding because they have always done so. Were you to ask, they could not say why, for there's truly no reason. Maypoles and flower petals and rolled eggs—do you think such toys could bring about the birth of a child even if a proper magician used them? No. 'Tis all useless tricks."

Orlan agreed. These were wealthy merchants, not the peasants of Lyges, but this was the same situation. As he spoke with Ilset and the Spicemerchants, he watched the dancers weaving ribbons about the pole; one lad tripped, and a roar of laughter erupted. Such celebratory games might be pretty fun for ordinary young people, but not for him. It wasn't a wizardly thing to do.

Orlan had begun his apprenticeship at fourteen. Most magical children began when they reached the age of puberty and their magic became apparent, but he had to take command of his awakening powers prematurely. Before he had been thirteen, the castle stones thumped at the unintentional release of his first energies. The empty corridors rumbled with the thunder of a thousand unseen iron-shod feet and the walls shook against invisible pounding fists at all hours of the day and night. Tapestries fluttered as if in a great wind and small objects leapt merrily from shelves to smash themselves on the floor. When Orlan became excited or angry, the air around him shimmered with his unrestrained emotion. He often woke to find smoldering spots on his bed-linens, as if sparks had landed about him in his sleep, and sometimes he turned in the early hours to see his cousin Laurel watching him from the chamber doorway with an anxious frown. She had set her own bed afire once and she feared for his safety. Orlan was not ashamed to admit he was frightened too. He felt helpless against his growing powers.

Tales were told of premature magicians: Orlan had heard of a lad of twelve who had been confirmed a mage by the Wizard of Palefyt only months after entering apprenticeship and of a little maid who had brought fire and destruction to the village of Lyngryn. Redmantyl, however, did not give credence to these tales and warned his son against the hope of being an improbable prodigy. If such creatures existed, they were not necessarily magicians and their violent, youthful manifestations were not signs of true magic. Redmantyl explained that the possession of *telekinetics*—as he named these powers—were not in themselves sufficient proof of wizardry. Far too many adolescents burst forth with ill-contained power but few were able to keep it past the initial explosion. Control was the crucial thing. With it, magic could be maintained and employed by adult wizards. Without it, the power was burned away by childish rages and lost.

The gift could not be taken lightly. A child of magic must work to see his talent grow to greater power. If it were at all possible for Orlan to take control of himself, he must do so soon. His first magics were too disruptive to be allowed to run unchecked until he reached the proper age of apprenticeship. He must be introduced to the disciplines of wizardry.

Upon Orlan's birthday, Redmantyl brought the boy up the top-most room of the Daune Tower.

They arrived amidst a great commotion. The wizard had left his apprentices at their levitation exercises while he had gone downstairs to fetch his son. In his absence, they had gone from silent concentration to a more rigorous game. Chalky clay balls flew everywhere, rebounding off the walls and tables, repulsed by a quick gesture, or sometimes missed and smearing an arm or face or jerkin with whitish dust. The apprentices, boy and girl, scrambled about the room, laughing and shouting. Shelves, tables, and chairs seemed to scramble too; misty, ill-formed furniture appeared and disappeared as the youth cast frantic spells to hide from his opponent. The maid yelped as a spray of balls dropped from above; she twisted to return the volley, but the balls melted into nothing around her. Solid missiles shot at her from another direction. She turned again; blue-green light shot from her fingertips. Her adversary ducked behind a solid chair. Clay spattered on wood.

"Laurel, Godefroi," the wizard spoke. "Stop."

The game ceased abruptly. Clay balls in flight or rolling madly stopped and knocked on the floor. The illusive furniture faded.

"This was not the work I left you at."

"I'm sorry, Uncle," the maid answered. "I was the one to start, to tease Godefroi."

Laurel was Redmantyl's niece, his cousin Tomasin's daughter, a tall, vigorous girl with silvery hair and the characteristic, colorless irises of the family. She had come to Wizardes Cliff from New York the year before. Redmantyl had hoped that his niece might be magical and he'd petitioned Kaiese, Tomasin's sister, to send the girl to him until, at last, Kaiese consented. The Lady feared and mistrusted magic; she bore a deep dislike for her powerful cousin, but she was more distressed when his hopes proved true and Laurel's talents grew too great to be suppressed any longer. Lord Redmantyl said that Laurel was the most promising young magician he'd ever seen.

Godefroi had grown into a slender, pensive, talented young man. He had no power to match the brute physical force of Olyr nor anything like Laurel's brilliance, only possessed the gentle, subtle art of illusion. This particular talent was usually held in disrepute by greater wizards, for it was considered little more than a mental magic and its influence solely a product of the mind. Haryet Stonekraft, the Redmantyl who had raised the stones of Wizardes Cliff, had been a master of illusionary spells, but few were so remarkable. Godefroi's spells were ghostly and insubstantial; they could confuse and obscure the real material around them, but they fooled no one.

As Laurel and Godefroi began their lessons at the same time, they had some exercises in common in spite of their unequal and vastly different mastered media. Redmantyl tried to teach them together, but the two never remained studious for long.

While the pair picked up their mess, Laurel chattered to Orlan about the wondrous secrets of magic: the arcane spells he would read, the obscure chants he would hear, the ceremonies of Wizard's Keep.

Redmantyl frowned at this last. "Laurel, what do you know of that?"

"Only that there are such things, Uncle," she answered regretfully. Apprentices were permitted to hear little of Wizard's Keep; only full wizards had knowledge of those nights and what they entailed. "I see they are related to the seasons and the holy-days—the Equinoxes, All Hallows, May Night–"

"Enough. Don't make an arrogant display of your little learning,

Maiden," Redmantyl chided. "Leave that 'til you are older and sure of what you know. Go now, Children."

Once they were gone, the wizard began by placing a candle on a table. "You are familiar with this."

Orlan smiled. He had been practicing for weeks on the candles in his rooms. He frowned in concentration, breathed deeply, then pulled his hand away at the spark between his fingertips. The candle was burning. His father looked pleased, but not surprised.

Then they tried another test: the wizard took up a small box and brought out a handful of cheap, tin spoons with flimsy-looking handles.

"For many masters of the physical medium, this is the first unintended display of power." Redmantyl took the boy's right hand and placed it palm down on the table top, fingers curving slightly over the surface. He picked up one utensil and placed the handle between Orlan's middle and ring fingers. "Gently touch the bowl of the spoon with your left hand. Gently," he emphasized. "Take care not to bend it in your grasp, for you could do so. Focus, and push."

Orlan caressed the rounded end of the spoon, thumb against the concave surface and fingers against the outer curve, until the metal was warmed. A thrilling tingle ran through him and the spoon suddenly twisted away in a half-turn against itself. He laughed.

"That was simple!"

"Yes, I thought it might be. Now, Orlan," Redmantyl said. "Straighten it."

"Straighten?"

"Straighten. You must pull instead of push. Try."

Orlan tried. Again, he caressed the metal, but there was no surge of power, only a dull pain at his temple and a ringing in his ears. The spoon remained bent double. "I can't!"

"Concentrate!" the wizard commanded. Orlan did not turn his attention away. He could not. It seemed that his father had engulfed him in his own vast powers, forcing him to concentrate with an intensity he could hardly bear. He was unable to stop himself from bringing all his energies onto one tiny spot, a point that expanded and overwhelmed until he could think of nothing else. There was only the glinting curve of the spoon handle, the buzzing in his head, and Redmantyl's irresistible voice:

"It's only a bit of tin, Orlan. Only material. It is in your power if you will command it! Do not fall to distraction. Your emotions will conquer your mind if you allow. You must place yourself beyond their influence. You are afraid and frustrated and you block your power.

You lose your focus." The tower trembled—or he trembled—and light burst within his brain as if it would explode. "Orlan, be unafraid. Clear your mind. Concentrate!"

Orlan made the effort to clear his mind. Self-imposed barriers fell into place, closing away the blinding, white pain, the terror, the tremors through his limbs, his father's shining eyes. He could not be afraid. He could not think of failure. Without distraction, he could see the glinting curve, feel its density, know its substance and its metallic energies—and *pull*!

He cried out at the force that shot along his left arm. Tears blurred his vision and his head drooped. He gasped to catch his breath. The spoon lay between his limp fingers, crimped in the middle but pulled straight. He brought his hands to his temples; the fire in his head had gone.

Redmantyl reached across the table and lifted Orlan's chin; he studied the boy's eyes. "Your head is cleared now?"

"Yes, Father. But it hurt!"

"I could see that it did. You employed far more power than the task required, but you directed it improperly. It remained trapped within you. You were about to give yourself a headache that would last all day. Tell me, Child, are you afraid of your power?"

"Yes," he confessed. "When it is so violent and I don't know why I should do such things. I don't mean to, Father. I– I am afraid of what I may do. I can't yet make my magic behave as I wish." Orlan picked up the spoon; it was still warm.

"It will be a very useful thing once you have command," his father assured him. "You will wonder how such simple tricks could tax you so."

There were other tests, but none so difficult after that. He had power; he possessed a promising force in the physical medium and a lesser talent for light. With training, he would be a great wizard. His first lesson, that same afternoon, was the litany of magic.

"Listen, my child," Redmantyl said. "Learn of the marvelous gift you possess. The source of the magic is at the heart. Have you noticed how terribly it beats when your power bursts forth? That power begins here–" he pressed his fingertips to his breast. "Forceful, but mindless, for a heart may desire but it cannot think. Magic rises with the heart's beat and strikes out. You cannot direct it, nor summon it nor stop it. The magic begins at the heart, but it is commanded by the mind. Its limits are the limits of your knowledge and your discipline. Spell-casting will give you greater employment of your power—the precise direction of a thought brought from the mind to the material world through written and spoken words. Remember this well, Orlan: *the magic begins at the heart; it is directed by the mind; and it is brought to use by the hand and tongue in spells.*"

His apprenticeship was delayed for the thespers' visit—that was Tedora's fault; it was always her fault—but once they had gone Orlan began his lessons in earnest. He gave himself to the craft. He bent and unbent the tin spoons until they snapped and he learned to direct the knockings in the walls, summon or banish them at will. The castle became quiet again. He fasted. He meditated. He endured the stinging nettles. When he slipped from his self-discipline, he was rebuked with a slap and a warning—"Orlan, be still! For your life!"—and when he kept himself well, he was rewarded with a kiss. As he conquered the weaknesses of his body and mind, the slaps came less frequently, but so did the kisses. By his eighteenth year, he received no rewards nor punishments except those his own pride and shame provided. He felt each error as an unpardonable sin.

Orlan studied mathematics and long-dead languages, for a proper, modern wizard must know the complex art of spell-crafting if he would guard himself against his enemies' devices. He was familiar with the contents of his father's libraries, but he had hitherto found these magical books, painted crimson and coal black, bone-white and bright gold, mysterious and unintelligible. Orlan had read them without seeing any purpose to the exercise; he thought them gibberish. But with more intense education, the words made sense: each syllable was a symbol. A runic verse that had seemed nonsensical could be a recipe for a potion, the incantation of an occult rite, a reference to spells cast long before by legendary magicians of a near-forgotten era. And more recent spells were often algebraic formulas to be solved; numbers too had colors and connotations. Spells were encoded thoughts. Without understanding, the words had no effect; with knowledge of the meaning behind each written device, they merged with his own powers. They became a part of him. He studied alchemy and pharmacology. Magic might be found in base metals and even sea water. All the leaves and roots in the garden had properties for healing and sleeping and easing pain, and he gathered them to be crushed and boiled into potions to stock the Daune Tower shelves. He learned to make love philtres and poisons too, but his father always destroyed these once the lessons were finished.

In preparation for his mage-vows and lifelong discipline, Orlan learned what was fitting for wizards. As a mage, he must abandon all distractions: drink befuddled the mind, bloody meats made one choleric, sugar excited the nerves, salt dulled the wits and made one phlegmatic. Lust disturbed the senses with desire. Unchecked emotions impaired judgment. All left a magician vulnerable. His self-command must become absolute and inviolate. Once a mage had proved himself, he was free within the limits of his own rigid discipline and the accepted standards of wizardly behavior. Grown wizards could love, could drink wine and ale, could eat as much roast beef as they chose, provided they didn't disgrace themselves in overindulgence and weaken their will.

Dancing was not forbidden; Redmantyl danced, and very well, when he was called to a courtly figure. But holiday festivals were improper for wizards, for such dances were part of the religious practices of peasants, merchants, nobles, and their Church. Orlan might join the magicless folk upon social occasions, but never in even the most benign and disguised forms of worship. To do so was more than an impropriety; it was a betrayal of wizardry, an infraction of an unspoken law as solemn as a mage-vow. Orlan didn't understand the distinction—dances were dances, songs were songs, and games were games—but his father warned him against religion: faith clouded perception as surely as love or wine.

Was this atheism? No! Redmantyl was most adamant. Gods existed, but what he believed of Them was, for the present, unexplained. He only said that wizards ought not serve any gods. Magicians had private ceremonies on the nights of Wizard's Keep; Orlan would learn of this one day, when he was fully prepared to assume such grave responsibilities.

At the eve of his magedom Orlan felt as if he understood all save the motives. He memorized all that Redmantyl told him he must know to be a competent wizard, but he didn't always comprehend the importance of particular rites. Godefroi had named these rituals meaningless too, though not when his master might hear; some of their education he thought purposeful—the strict self-discipline, the extensive literacy—but he claimed that the rest was wound into so much bunk that it was impossible to know the trappings from the substance. Orlan didn't know what was truth and what was nonsense, but he gave careful attention to every word. He intended to be a great wizard, like his father.

His father must be proud of him, see that he had learned from him, had followed him. To be like Lord Redmantyl was the most splendid thing. Redmantyl expected it; Orlan did not dare disappoint. Others stood before him in the wizard's favor—Tedora, Andemyon, Laurel— but he had his own place if he would work to prove himself worthy. Orlan might question the significance of his studies, but he knew that he liked being magical and magic was most important to his father. It was therefore crucial.

Each night in meditation, Orlan tested the spells his father had imposed upon his mind. Though he believed that this barrier had been placed over his earliest memories for his good, he was impatient to remove it through his skill as a magician. It was provoking to sense that there were areas of his own mind inaccessible to him. He sought a way in. Whatever his father had thought best for him as a child, he was a man now. He had the right to choose. He was prepared to confront the circumstances of that earlier time. How miserable could his childhood have been that Lord Redmantyl must close and lock it so securely against his prying?

Perhaps, he told himself, he was meant to dissolve the barrier. The enchantment placed upon him might be a test of his abilities: it had been left for him to disperse once he was sufficiently adept to cast effective counterspells and sufficiently mature to face what lay concealed beyond. Orlan nearly believed it; more likely, Redmantyl had simply forgotten that the spells were there. He didn't care. He was ready to undo this spellcraft. If he were truly meant as a grown wizard to command all aspects of his flesh and spirit, then he was meant to command the workings of his own brain. His memories, more than all else, were his own.

That Friday night, Orlan returned to the Mayor's Hall weary and threw himself on the bed. He was in no mood to enter a full trance, but the entertainments of the festival had left him disquieted. He must calm his nerves before he slept. Instead of sitting upright in the appropriate posture for meditation, he turned flat on his back. This was as comfortable; eyes shut, arms lightly across his chest, breath drawing in and out in slow, even measures, he was able to relax and cast his awareness toward the barrier. He saw it as a blank blot on the active flux of energy which carried his thoughts. Not a hole—rather, a stain concealing the pulsating fabric of his mind. He felt its borders, examined them for weaknesses he might work upon. The edges were blurred and softened; he had tugged and teased at them through several long sessions, painstakingly extracting fragile strands and cleansing the stain. Clear images emerged. Smells. Sounds. Emotions of the child he had been. Slowly, he regained what had been lost.

What did he remember? He recounted the threads of Lammouthe memory he had gathered: the cold cobblestones of a courtyard where he had played alone; shabby buildings that towered over him—he had been so small; a little, jointed wooden doll—a soldier?—with its blue paint chipped; a bath in a wooden tub in the yard behind a house, his home; the large, rough hands of the nurse Ellan as she forced spoonfuls of molasses-thick porridge into him; children in common, ragged garb shouting names; a woolen, white blanket; piled boxes and barrels on the wharf where he had hidden to watch the tall ships; the sound of a door scraping floorboards and a dancing glow of candlelight. So much. So little of importance. Where was his mother? What did he remember of her?

A new thread revealed itself: gentle nudging, waking him, urging him from the bed. Ellan's broad hand gripping his as she led him to the other room. The floorboards creaked. A man stood at the doorway—no, not his father.

Suddenly, he heard a voice, laughing: "No, my pet, your father's much more handsome than *that* one! He's like yourself, white hair and white eyes. Oh, ye'll see him someday." The face was not yet distinct, a blur surrounded by clipped, curled masses of fair hair. A hand, plump fingers, broken nails, caressed the amulet hung about her neck. "He'll come back. He hasn't forgotten me."

He had the counterspell! *Mother, bed, floorboard, father, amulet*—a pattern of thoughts in sequence accidentally encountered, but they provided the way in! It was incomplete, but it was enough. Eagerly, Orlan pressed on. The dark area dissolved as he caught at these thin threads, repeated them, freed them. The barrier was breaking! More memories flooded his senses, more and more. Knowledge filled him.

He lay curled beside his mother, rested against her breast, breathed the scent of her: sweet, warm summer-sweat that had not yet staled, beer, the gingery perfume of a sachet in her bodice. Mama told her tale of the magician who had once been her lover. He had come to her from over the seas, a traveler who had stopped at the inn where she worked as a chambermaid, a man like no other she had ever seen, so fair, so pleasing, so wondrous strange. He had filled a room with sparkling lights for her amusement. Orlan listened to this story often, like a bedtime fairytale that must be repeated exactly with each retelling. No details must be changed and nothing left out. Mama's story never changed. He had always asked: what happened to my father? Mama answered: the wizard was gone on his quest, but he had given her this special spell she wore to call upon him. And he'd left her a child, a little boy who had the look of his mysterious, magical father. Orlan would be like him someday. Orlan was her treasure; she could not think of losing him. Where was his father now? Mama said that he was on the other side of the world on such adventures as she could barely imagine, but one day he would come to Lammouthe again. He would receive her son as his own and he would take them away from this place. Everything would be wonderful when the wizard returned for them.

He heard Mama weeping. Sometimes she drank in the tavern below and it made her sad and sick. Sometimes a man she had liked had left her alone again—none of them stayed very long. Sometimes Mama was ill. Ellan tended her, whispering so that he wouldn't hear even though Mama moaned and screamed and whimpered. When she took to her bed, he had to be very quiet and not disturb her. She had wept so the night before she died.

He stood in the stairwell. Ellan was speaking on the landing above, words he had overheard but not understood at the time: "'Twas her third, M'Lord, since the little lad..."

Then he saw Mama's face. No blurring, comfortable haze cushioned the image. She was before him with cutting clarity: a delicate, fading beauty, a young woman ravaged by pain and illness, then made still. Yellow curls lay limp on the fever-damp pillow. Her lips were dry and torn. Her eyes were open, unseeing. And there was red—so much red! Tinted water in a basin on the floor. Blood on the bed sheets.

"She was never one to be patient lying in for a child that had no father by name. She'd lost the other two right enough and she said she'd be safe for this..."

Mama had cried all night.

Waves of pain coursed through him; Orlan sobbed out loud, engulfed by long-forgotten grief. Everything returned to him afresh, as if the years between had never been. He was eight years old, stunned, suddenly torn from all he had ever known. Mama was gone. The enchantment had been woven that day; at his first tears, Lord Redmantyl had taken him into his arms and eased him with tender oblivion. But that nepenthe had vanished. The spells were broken. And he wept at more than his mother's death.

He knew now. He understood.

On Saturday, Houarde went to confession to prepare for Whitsunday Mass. Religion was bound about his life; Storm Port's people prayed frequently, from morning matins to thanksgiving at every meal, to Evensong and rosaries before retiring each night. They attended Mass at the cathedral regularly, and feasts and celebrations for Saints seemed daily. Orlan had observed, however, that they showed generally less feeling than he had ever put into his own obscure faith. Often, they had none at all. Houarde would cross himself and swear by the Virgin and all the Saints in Heaven, but he spoke the oaths as easily as a blessing set on a sneeze. His sins and the confession of them weighed lightly on his mind. As soon as he left St. Khrystopher's, he led Orlan through the usual round of alehouses. The taverns were the favored places of many merchants, the great and the lesser, especially now that one could only hope to find relief from the summer's heat between the stone walls of a basement.

Orlan was still shaken by the bursts of grief he had suffered the night before, but he employed such disciplines as he possessed to conceal his tremulous emotional state and send him through the routine rounds of taverns with his friend. He did not wish to sit alone and brood over his newly recovered knowledge of the past. This was not the time to think of it.

Houarde usually provided diversion. Nobility was rare in Storm Port and magicians less familiar; Orlan was a novelty, and the Portreeve was ready to show off his young companion and introduce him to anyone they might meet for the treat of a good ale. This night, Houarde presented an enormous man who carried himself as if he were Emperor for all he wore a merchant's tunic. The device on his breast was elaborately embroidered and his rings and the chain about his throat gold and set with precious stones. Orlan knew that he would be a friend from Houarde's younger and wilder days.

"Young Orlan," said Houarde. "This is my dearest old friend, Leobolde Goldesmith. They say he's one of the richest merchants in Storm Port, if not all of the Northlands, and I've heard him called *Midas* many a time."

Orlan smiled to acknowledge the jest. "Your servant, Syre."

The Goldesmith grunted a response and stared unblinking at the youth, then he spoke to the Portreeve, "Your friend, Houarde?"

"He's a guest in our house—My Lord Redmantyl's son and here on his father's business." At this information, the great merchant unbent himself to reconsider Orlan and offer a slight bow. "Join us in mugs, Leo?"

The Goldesmith was willing to stop with them, even pay for the drink, but he complained about his ale as soon as he tasted it. "Bitter."

"Aye, not the best water's used for our brews this summer, nor the best malted barley," Houarde agreed. "That must be saved for the winter, so my wife will say. At any rate, the stuff here is never so fine an ale as is served at the Whitelm, but of course you won't go into that house." The Portreeve laughed at his own sly joke, incomprehensible to Orlan. The Goldesmith scowled and drained his mug.

"Why won't you go into the Whitelm, Syre?" Orlan asked. He'd been in many taverns here, but he could see little difference between one and another. The Whitelm, the Greenglof, the Toureshade, the Phoenician—what did it matter, so long as they sold the same drink at a similar price? Of course, he preferred the Whitelm and considered Adyna the most pleasant of alekeepers, for she was a friend, but he did not expect other tavern patrons make this distinction. If they were like Houarde, then they must think every alekeep a dear friend.

"Oh, he's shy at Keeper Adyna," Houarde explained with another chuckle. "'Twas well known not so many years ago that he and she were closer than they are now and the little lass must be discomfiting to see, eh, Leobolde?"

The Goldesmith nodded reluctantly.

Orlan was amazed. "Rennie is your daughter?"

"Likely," the man grunted.

"And Kyarde and Kai?"

"Who?"

"Adyna's sons. The elder is–" he stopped at the shouts of "Hallo!" and "Greetings!" and turned to find the young men he had met on his first night's carousing with Houarde coming down from the doorway.

"Lads!" Houarde called back. "Here! Stop yourselves with us!" As they approached, he went on: "What brings you here, my lads? This is not one of your favorite burrows, I know."

"No," Reynalde, the boy Orlan had spoken to, answered. "But where our wanderings take us, we'll go."

"'Tis all in fun, Syre," another boy, dark and ruggedly handsome, added. "And we're hiding from Father, since we cut from the procession last night. I'm damned if I'll dress myself as a blessed Dominican novice and prance up and down the Greenway."

Houarde laughed. "No one here would blame you! More than once when I was called out at holidays I wished I might do the same. Oh, they're lads as we once were, eh, Leobolde?"

The Goldesmith did not disagree.

"We did not expect to see you out so late, Syre," a third youth said.

"I have naught to do on the morrow save sit myself through Mass," the Portreeve answered. "'Tis simple to sleep then if the choir does not caterwaul too much."

Even the Goldesmith found this amusing.

"Now, I have been lax in my courtesy again, for I meant to have you all know each other. You met Reynalde Spiceson the other night, recall, Chyelde?"

"Yes, I remember."

"Greetings, My Lord." Reynalde bowed like a skilled thesper.

"Will you meet the rest now?" Houarde waved at the other youths. "The ginger-head trying his first beard—and not showing a full crop as yet, I can add, eh?—is Jepatha, Justice Hugobarde's son, and that's his cousin Goduin from Kallaykirke, who we had as a 'prenticing clerk to Her Mayorship 'til he left us. And here's Eduarde Sheriffson," the dark, rugged boy, who took Orlan in with an appraising glance, "and..." Houarde peered at the fifth boy, a little younger than the others and not so well dressed. "Who're you? I've not seen you about before this."

"Syre, this is a– er– friend we met at portside yesterday," Jepatha explained. "Tades, is it?"

"Aye, Syre, the lad's named Tades," Goduin chimed. "He's not been in Storm Port before, so we thought we'd take him around."

Tades bobbed his head and tugged at his clipped bangs. "M'Lord." The boys exchanged quick grins. An older man in the shabby dress of a weathered merchant mariner, unshaven and besotted, stood at the bar behind them and flashed another grin. Houarde did not notice him and the youths did not acknowledge him as one of their company.

"Well, as you're so kind to one stranger this evening, you'll be as kindly to another," the Portreeve suggested.

"We thought that ourselves," Reynalde said. "'Twould be an honor if you'd join us, both of you."

"No, Lads," Houarde shook his head. "I'm too old for such sport. Not so lively as I used to be, you see. But Orlan here– Chyelde, will you go? I vow they'll show you a better time than I could."

"If you don't mind, Syre."

"No, of course. I have such dull things to discuss with my friend Leobolde. Go, Chyelde, and have your fun. I'll leave the front door unlatched for you." He ordered another drink.

Orlan did not want to say so aloud, but he was glad to leave. There was no release here. Houarde was a bore, uncivil and slightly distasteful to sit beside after he'd taken a few drinks, and the

Goldesmith was a frightful man; between his prideful manner and his cold, serpentine eyes, he convinced Orlan that he was no one for a decent lad to know. These youths, on the other hand, were lightsome and charming, full of laughter and pranks, and Orlan found them appealing. He wondered what it was like to play as they did, to be one of them. It might be improper, undignified, unwizardly, but he didn't care. He would not be in Storm Port much longer and this opportunity would never come again. He wanted to have fun tonight. He wanted to run.

nyne

They ran down side streets, leaping the gutters and darting into tangled alleys off the broad, paved ways and through the maze only a native-born citizen of Storm Port could unravel. Orlan followed, though he did not understand their path.

"Where do we go?" he asked once breathless and completely lost.

"Here." Jepatha took his arm and yanked him toward a nearby tavern; the sign over the door was cut in the shape of a bell-capped jongleur's head and painted with an enormous, manic grin.

Within, the place was no different from the other taverns Orlan had visited that week. A tall fire blazed at one end of the room and the damp, stone floor was made even more damp by spilled mugs. Lads and maids who were far too young to taste the ales they served scurried between tables and benches, dodging the kicks and jests of their customers. But the room was filled with members of a younger group than Orlan had seen before. Young guardians, colorful Free Folk with their lutes and hurdy-gurdies, apprentices to the nearby shops, and even maidens of good birth, girls Orlan had met at the Mayor's Hall, crowded the tables. Some had gathered for a contest of darts near the fireplace and others knelt at the front wall to throw dice. The noise was as much song and laughter as shouts for more drink. As Orlan and the boys had come without Houarde, no pathway was immediately made open for them, and the youth followed his companions in shoving his way through the crowd until they reached a table far at the back occupied by a lone man, too drunk to lift his head. Jepatha and Eduarde dumped him from his stool and dragged him into a corner.

A serving woman, older than most, approached. "Here, Lads, that's not the best way to treat `im," she scolded like a nursery-maid.

Jepatha only laughed. "We would send him home, but I doubt he'll walk so far. He may sleep more comfortably there than in the gutters."

"Still, `twasn't kind. Great, grown boys as ye ought to be better behaved. Are ye not nearly men yourselves?"

"You'd know that for yourself, Polly, my pet," Reynalde pulled her down to sit on his knee and patted her hip familiarly. "Here y'go, and tell me."

"I've got work t'do, Love," she protested, but she slipped one arm about his neck and let her wooden serving tray drop to the table as she spoke. "An' ye know the old man smacked me down once already for doin' other business when he was paying for me spillin' `is swill." She flashed a rude grin at the beefy red-faced man at the bar. "Oh, an' he pays f' more'n that, but he's bleedin' right selfish. Here, let go." She slapped Reynalde's hand lightly and twisted in his lap until he released her. "Now, what'll the lot of ye have—and none of yer filthiness." She smiled at the boys and singled out Orlan as an unfamiliar face. "Hello? Who's this?"

"A Lordling," one of the group answered, "named Orlande."

"Orlan," Orlan corrected.

"An' what'll ye be drinking, my pretty lad?"

The boys sniggered and nudged and kicked each other beneath the table. "Wine, if you please," Orlan answered, ignoring them.

She shook her head. "Not here, Pet. `Tis sour for your tastes, `less you like a strong vinegar."

"Ale then."

"Ales around, Poll," Eduarde ordered. "The first is mine, to welcome our guest."

The alemaid nodded and was gone but she returned soon, her tray full, and swiftly set the mugs around. Orlan lifted his to drink, then paused. The liquid, now just beneath his nose, smelled of overripe wheat; indeed, he could see tiny, malted fragments floating in what looked like a dark, unfrothed, clouded beer. The drink was not as cold as beer, however, and the mug was warm between his hands. He hesitated, but the other boys had tasted theirs and appeared no worse for it, and Orlan followed their example.

A fire rose in his throat, his chest, behind his eyes. His stomach lurched in revolt at the bitter, grainy brew and he resisted the urge to spit over the table. "Ugh! How can you stand this stuff? Houarde Portreeve swallows great gallons each day, and I think now he must be mad."

"There's no trick, if you do not think on it too much," Eduarde answered, then shut his eyes tightly and gulped down half the mug at once. "Imagine brandywine in cinnamon."

"And Houarde Portreeve is mad," Reynalde smiled.

"Oh, that one!" Polly giggled.

"I believe he imagines himself a great boy still, playing at games he should have set aside long ago," said Jepatha. "`Tis sad in its way. I do not wish to be as he is in thirty years' time, as if I were still a youth who could drink through the night, run the streets, and bed maids as I choose, with no ill effect. No, by then, I shall be like my father. He's a respectable man, for all he ran wild as mad dogs in his day."

"I plan to be Lord Mayor myself," Reynalde announced, and was met by shouts of laughter. "Yes, I do. M'Layn Ilset's the one to admire."

"For all she's never liked the pack of us," Eduarde told Orlan. "Not since we were old enough to leave the nursery."

"Yet I must admire her," Reynalde persisted. "My Layn Ilset cares for all in this city as a mother might, from the drabs and beggar's brats to noble guests such as yourself, Chyelde. Why, she bade us seek you so that we might befriend and amuse you in your visit. She is much beloved here."

"And her efforts are finer still, when she is caught in marriage with what we must think of as a man like an old bawd," Jepatha said.

"Why do you befriend him then?" Orlan asked.

"The Portreeve? `Tis an amusement."

"As well as a warning," Eduarde added. "After all, `tis only sport we play at here. God save our souls if we would have no more for all our lives!"

The others took this as a sort of oath and lifted their mugs. "Save our souls," they echoed, and drank deeply. Reynalde and Goduin sent Polly to fill theirs again.

"All of us, save poor Tades here," Eduarde gestured at the young mariner, "shall be as wealthy and nearly as well-placed as any Lordling when we come to our own. What will be your fate, I wonder, Lad?"

"I dunna know," said Tades.

"Probably, you shall come to an end as the old scoundrel here, drowning in salt-water and piss-beer if you do not take care, eh?"

"Ye don't take on so against a mariner's lot," the older mariner, standing against the nearest wall, spoke. Orlan turned, surprised to find that he had followed them. "There's more to it than ye well-born lads wi' pretty manners and fine clothes can know."

Goduin grinned. "Tell us, then."

"Nor're ye meant to know," the man replied. "Pretty pups as y'selves, what d'ye know of anything? What d'ye know save how t'throw yer money about?"

"You'll take up whatever we throw it at," Reynalde said. "How many ales have we paid up for you since last night?"

The mariner shrugged. "I've got little money and better to do wi' it." He flashed a smile at the maid. "Ye pups know naught of what's to be got."

Eduarde laughed. "Why, you're as pleased with yourself in your poverty as any great Lord in wealth and power. `Tis an odd sort of snobbery."

"`Tis the only sort he may claim, the old dog," Reynalde said. "What else will he have to be proud of? He has no money, no hope of living better than he does now. Even his travels are no adventure of merit, for 'tis understood that one port in the world is exactly like all the others. Many better off have seen far more."

"Y'self?" The man looked doubtful.

"No," Reynalde admitted. "But Orlan has, certainly." He turned to the young nobleman, who was still trying to down his ale. "You have traveled much, haven't you, Chyelde? You've seen many great things you could tell tale of if you wished?"

"No, I've hardly traveled at all," Orlan answered reluctantly. "I have left my Father's house only a few times since childhood."

The mariner snorted. "Pups." And he stepped into the shadows.

"Who is that?" Orlan wondered.

"I don't know, precisely," Jepatha answered, laughing. "He followed us when we met Tades at the Phoenician yesterday and we've never found the courage to tell him to go away."

The jangling sound of a hurdy-gurdy struck up in one corner and a tenor voice rose in song:

> "Oh, in the dockyards of Lammouthe,
> Does a fair alemaid dwell.
> Young dogs call her Maggie.
> They all know her well.
> For beer and a sixpence,
> She's yours for the night
> But keep hold of your pockets
> When you wake to the light!
> Oo-oh, keep close count of your coppers
> When you wake to the light!"

Orlan didn't need to hear more to know that the song was bawdy to the point of obscenity; songs about alemaids and mariners invariably were. Soon, everyone in the tavern was pounding the tables, stamping their feet to the rhythm of the music, and shouting out the adventures of the famous Maggie as she bedded this mariner to exhaustion, then drank that one under the table and stole his purse, and so on, with the usual rough innuendo about ships sailing into harbor, tall masts, and sheets stiff with the breeze. When the raucous beat went on without words, a dark-haired maid, in dress identical to that of Orlan's friends, climbed up to dance on a table top. The alekeeper roared at her to get down, but she continued her dance, hands at her hips and feet nimble, encouraged by the shouts of nearly all the tavern, including the boys at Orlan's table. At last, her blushing companion, a young guard out of uniform, pulled her down, shrieking and laughing and thumping her fists playfully on his head and chest.

Reynalde was on his feet. "Here, you! Stop that! Let her down."

But the maid scowled at him instead. "Keep to your own business, Brat. I'll tell Mother I saw you here."

"She'll know you were here as well," the youth retorted. "And guess with whom."

She slid from the guard's arms, then led him by the hand to their table. "I only wanted to see what the sport was here, for you have spoken of it often, and this fine lad was so courteous to escort me." She patted her companion's arm. "He thinks it an indecent place for a maid alone. What base purpose brings you here, Reynalde the Fox?"

"The usual. Here, Chyelde Orlan, may I present my sister, Julia."

"We've met," Orlan said. "An honor, Damosel."

"M'Lord," she replied with something like a bow. "You know of this, Reynalde. Mother's been a-fluttered since the young Lord came to visit My Layn Ilset. She's pushed me at him, or Druse as an alternative, at the Mayor's all this last fortnight. It must be something to marry a Lordling, but I prefer a man of darker hues. I mean no offense to you, M'Lord."

"I'm not offended."

She smiled, and the young guard immediately looked suspicious and jealous. "I am surprised that you'd be here, and in such company. My brother and his friends will set about your corruption, you know."

"He may see for it himself if he chooses, as we all do," Jepatha answered. "We'll only point out the ways."

"La! Brute boys and their games," Julia said scornfully. "You mustn't let them lead you astray, M'Lord." She touched Orlan's hair.

"Julia." The guard's face grew dark and darker still at each teasing word.

"Oh, very well. We'll go now." She turned to the table. "I bid you good night, Fox, Jep, Eddie, Goduin. Have a care with them, M'Lord." She went away with her guardian.

"Fine lad, fah!" Reynalde said after them. "She wastes herself on a guard, and he's not the first she's taken a fancy to. Father and Mother are angry for that, for they want Julia, Drusilla, and myself to make good matches. I cannot blame them too much. It is a poor choice."

"Poor how?" Jepatha inquired. "Guards will make good husbands and wives, I am told. They are generally honest in their habits and if you later find yourself unhappy, they may be sent to the frontier. Julia would not be so well-off with a more wealthy man. Didn't your father once speak to you on the merits of the Dam'sel Julia, Eduarde?"

Eduarde slapped the back of his head in reply.

"I have a friend, a guard here," Orlan said. "Perhaps you know him?"

"Perhaps," Reynalde answered. "I know many. But you cannot befriend the guards, Chyelde. Soldiers are common folk of the lowest sort and so tied to their duties that they've forgotten their fun. You saw the way that brute stood over her, like a miser protecting his precious treasure. And my sister, you may know, is no dainty flower. I could not trust such a man as that. They always want to arrest someone just when the sport begins."

"And they carry tales," Eduarde said. "If we so much as speak kindly to one of the garrison, he'll fly straight to Captain Alyx with tales of all he's heard of us and the rumors go right to the ear of Her Mayorship."

"Shut your gaping gob, Eduarde." Reynalde shoved his friend's face. "'Tisn't true. We've never yet been called on any charge, have we?"

"Well, with my father to keep the peace and Jep's to see to justice, it's not bloody likely we ever will."

"But we'll ask this boy to join us, if you like, if he is your friend," Goduin offered.

"No, it isn't so important. He was my father's ward and we were raised together in the same house, and that's all."

"That's as well," said Jepatha.

Orlan did not reply. The first disruption of his stomach at the taste of the ale had not been settled by more drink. Instead, each tentative sip had increased his discomfort until he could not bear it another moment. He had to leave this room, and quickly. Legs quaking, he rose from his seat. "I beg your pardon, but I must—" No, it was too late to try and reach the tavern door. Bile rose in his throat and his face, usually a creamy tone, went as white as alabaster. His friends looked alarmed.

"Here, what's wrong?" Eduarde asked, then understanding

brightened his expression. "Oh. There's a slopping jar, M'Lord, there, at the back door. Go on! Quick!" He shoved him toward it.

Orlan returned to the table a few minutes later.

"Are you not well, Orlan?" Jepatha asked. "Do you wish to leave?"

"No, I'm passably well now. `Twas that horrid ale." There was still a little of this brown slop in his mug and he pushed it away. "Is there nowhere we could go to have better? Anything drinkable would be agreeable."

"Plenty of houses offer fine wines and honey-meads, but they do have a price," Reynalde offered.

"No matter." Orlan wiped his mouth on his shirt sleeve. "I'll pay."

Smiles turned from one face to another around him. "Very well, then." Reynalde took his arm. "I know a very good house not a far walk from here and their wines are brought from the best groves of France and Tuscany, not the local sopyards. I'll wager Tades has never had such stuff before."

"No," Tades admitted.

"And we do not see it often enough. To the Salamander!" They shoved their mugs away, as Orlan had done.

"Polly!" Goduin yelled. But there was no sign of the maid. "Now where's she got to?"

"No matter." Eduarde dropped some money on the table.

"Here, may I–" Orlan touched at his own pouch.

"No, M'Lord. You'll empty your purse easily enough at the next house. I did promise to pay for this one and if Poll doesn't find it, another will. The loss is to her for abandoning her service and better a luckless little maid finds it before that old bear does." He put his tongue out at the barkeeper, whose back was turned. "Shall we go?"

The streets had cooled in the evening hours and a strong wind gusted through even the most narrow passages. Orlan shut his eyes and stood at the tavern door, breathing deeply; his head was beginning to clear.

"Pray God for rain," Eduarde murmured and crossed himself. "This sty needs it. Now which is the swiftest way to the Salamander from here?"

"Turn right ahead and across Lyngate Street before the gates," Reynalde answered. "Not a far jaunt at all, M'Lord. Come along, Tades, this way." They began to follow him, slowly.

Goduin had not moved. "Hold a moment, Lads!" he shouted after them. "I can go no further with this burden. Where's the gutter?"

"None about!" Jepatha shouted back. "But the alley's just there, and will do as well."

"And it's a saving now, with all that ale racing through," his cousin laughed and toddled toward the dark corridor beside the alehouse, then stopped at the sounds of flurried commotion within. He danced backwards quickly, laughter redoubled.

Reynalde and Jepatha exchanged a curious glance. "What is it now?" the former demanded, and both went to see; one glance into the alleyway brought them down in giggles. Orlan stepped forward, wondering, then he saw them—a glimpse of pale, bare flesh in motion, skirts lifted and hose sagging at ankles, the scruffy mariner and Polly, either not aware or not caring that they were seen—and he looked away, blushing.

"If there were a bucket of water about," Eduarde, who had followed, laughed and walked small circles in the street as if searching for one.

"No," Reynalde sniffled and smiled. "'Tis best not to disturb them. Think, my lad, if it were you–"

"Me? And that lifeless drab?" the youth snorted his disgust. "No, not that one. Have you heard, Reynalde? They say that the whores of Storm Port are nearly so lux'ous as the brothel-mates of the East, only they bear more meat to their frames. I cannot say this is true myself, for I've never seen such Orient creatures and our whores are a greasy sort. In 'haps you may tell the truth of it, Tades?"

"I wouldna know," the boy muttered his answer.

"Then I suppose I must be content with what is at hand. And you, Chyelde Orlan? What maids might be found where you live?"

"None of interest," Orlan replied. "Only the daughters of farmers and tradesfolk and our own serving-maids."

The others chuckled. "You think nothing of serving-maids?"

"Must be a dull sort at your home then."

"My father has a talent for engaging the most comely maids in our service," Eduarde said. "I recall one—Maudlin, her name—my first taste of love's delight."

"Bess was the name of mine," Reynalde said. "But if I'd been wiser then she would have been my last in the house. Housemaids are such fools. They will expect you to marry 'em over one tumble and bawl 'til you promise all you may lie to quickly. No, a whore is better."

"And they know to fend against childbirth, which no house wench may do."

Reynalde laughed. "Eddie, you–?"

"My mother's gentyl was abed with a child this winter," he admitted. "She said it was mine, but in truth she might've been bellied by three others I know of and perhaps more. The brat died in its first hours, so no matter. I've learned that if I seek sport among the household, I must look elsewhere than the maids."

"Orlan, there's no maid worth speaking of in your own house?"

"None," he confessed. "I never–" The young mariner gave him a shy look of sympathy and the others did not laugh as much as he had expected.

"No worry," Jepatha said easily. "You're young yet and comely enough to have your choice. Why waste a good youth's love on a half-drunken, sleepy slut? Had I the wisdom before, I might have waited for a better first, but there's no use to fret on that now and no good to await myself again. I'm already spoiled for more than a pleasant drab."

"And he's ruined me by the same means," Goduin chimed.

"Yes, there's a truth. My cos never so much as kissed a girl before he came here and we brought him to the houses of pleasure."

"Are there such places here?" The boys would insist Orlan accompany them on their quest for sport tonight, but he was not prepared for this. He did not want to view the transactions of a brothel; the thought of so many wretched women in this city who would sell themselves for pennies was more disturbing than titillating. Could he refuse?

"Yes, Lad, a dozen at the least," Reynalde answered. "I've not visited them all, you must understand. Some are not fit for any decent youth. But others..." he laughed. "And the women there! There's one along our way tonight, we may show you, Orlan. We'll show you women as you never thought women could be."

"Women," Eduarde said in solemn tones, as if he spoke of some wondrous marvel. "Men are men. Some are more fetching than others, some smaller, some more brutish, but in essentials all the same. But women..." He waved at the alleyway behind them. "Look at them—the soft, lazy sluts, and those as fierce as fire and firm as stone goddesses, and others, again, who are like men in thought and deed and only a little changed from us in form. All women! Like snowflakes, my friends."

Jepatha kicked him. "Hush your besotted prattle, Eddie."

"Sotted? Perhaps so. But think on it, Jep. Is it simple to comprehend that that whorespawn and the Mayor Ilset– No, more incredible than that—that she and My Layn Margueryt are the same sort of creature?" It was an improbable thought, and he laughed with the others. "Picture, if you will, the Shieldmaid Prince of Gossunge strumping away with that low fellow, or our sweet, slaggish Poll leading legions against Spain." The picture was more absurd and the boys giggled, chuckled, hooted in derision.

"You've met her, haven't you, Lord Orlande?" Goduin asked, sitting on the curbstone and wiping the tears from his face.

"Prince Margueryt? Yes– And I'm not a Lordling myself."

"Near enough," Reynalde said.

"What of the Prince?" This question was from the young mariner.

"She is my kinswomen by marriage so I have spoken to her as a cousin, without tossing *M'Layn* in at every breath. But I must feel some awe at her, for she is like no one I've met, woman or man. To believe she is the same sort of creature as the alemaid? No, `tis effort enough to think her the same as any mortal. She is strange, fierce, beyond mortal passions. She is like–" His smile flashed at the thought. "You will laugh, but I would say she is like a saint of the old days."

The others did not laugh. Orlan thought that perhaps they would have liked to hear that the Duke's daughter was really no different from the tavern maid at heart—or at least like them—but that was not true.

"I think she is the way St. Parsyfal might've been on his quest for the Sangrael, or St. George in his fight with the dragon. It is her quest to drive the Spaniards from our borders and as you speak to her you believe that she is indeed given for that single purpose."

"Father says she'll be the saving Grace of the Northlands," Jepatha said. "Oh, he has no dislike for the old Duke, but Margueryt'll bring the Empire to its glory of old."

"They say she's like the Redlyon himself," Tades offered.

"They say that," Orlan agreed, "even My Lord Dafythe, and he should know his own father and daughter more well than any. But I don't think King Eduarde could be called saintly by anyone."

Eduarde, named for the dead Emperor, smiled at this. Eduarde Redlyon was too famous for his bloody cruelty, his numerous illegitimate children and his love of drink and sport to be honored as more than a spectacular warrior-king. He was much admired, but not revered. Margueryt was all that their culture embodied as the perfect ruler: just, fierce, pious, noble, proud, popular with all folk, brave and renown for skill in battle. Not one of these boys was more likely to lead armies than the alemaid they teased, but they dreamed of it. Glorious warfare was the pride of the Norman Empire.

"Forget the Salamander." Jepatha slapped his cousin's arm. "Let's go to the Bag o' Nails. You'll like that, Orlan. The girls there..." The sentence trailed away suggestively. "We'll find you one more lively than our Poll."

"More pretty too," Goduin added. "Come along, Lads!"

The other boys ran to keep apace with him. Orlan followed reluctantly.

But his diffidence faded quickly as he came to enjoy Storm Port more with every day. His new friends were exciting, far more than the older folk he had first met in the city. Ilset and her Council were kind, but complacent and dull to the passions of youth. Houarde might sport as a young lad if his maltreated heart did not prevent him, but in drunkenness he was stupid, loud, and vulgar; Reynalde and Eduarde were brilliant with drink, never so besotted. If they stumbled in the streets or vomited, they did so cheerfully and forgot it so that they would not spoil their evening's fun. They were better educated than their elders, for all their pretended ignorance. Wealthy merchant families sent their children away to be educated by the Church: Reynalde, his sisters, and Eduarde had spent most of their childhood in the Abbey at Maryesfont, Goduin with the Sisters of St. Samandra, and Jepatha in the house of the Bishop of Guylliamesburghe. None of them shared their fathers' contempt for learning. They joked about the bore of lessons, but they were impressed by Orlan's knowledge. He talked with them as he had talked to no one since his arrival in Storm Port, for they did not think him odd for being different. They liked him for it.

He was flattered by his friends' attentions. They respected his position as a nobleman and the son of a powerful Lord. Although all obeisance had been dropped soon after his introduction and Orlan was no more consciously complimented than Tades, the local boys knew that he held a much higher rank and far more wealth than theirs. He would one day be master of an island a thousand times larger than their city. They wanted to hear about his home. They were as fascinated by his tales of Pendaunzel, the Duke, and Prince Margueryt as Ilset had been. None except Tades had travelled far, but Orlan believed he had seen more interesting places than the others. Wizardes Cliff seemed wonderful when he talked of his life there. His friends did not fear his magic, but were curious at the craft and amused by his least tricks and spells, all he dared display. They thought him a young man of remarkable talents instead of one of many talented children in a great wizard's house. Their garments were altered in imitation of his own, more fashionable clothes; kirtles were cut short and ill-woven braids attempted. Even Reynalde's sisters followed this style although Orlan only met them infrequently. Both young women might drink with the boys and Julia ran with them once or twice, but their interests were not the same; Julia's mind was foremost on her young guard and Drusilla was unhappy in her home city and impatient to return to Maryesfont.

At night, they played. His friends taught him. Persuaded by their affable encouragement, he found peaks of wildness he had not expected, nor believed possible. Each new experience fed his sensitive perceptions and left him enervated, exhilarated. He was alive!

Under cloudless skies at twilight and a bright moon rising, they rode out of the Narnegate, along the river through forests and fields on "the hunt," but with no pretense at all of hunting; they never took dogs and not one of them owned a bow. On other nights, they showed him the taverns near the docks, nestled in back streets in the southwest quarter of the city where the younger folk found amusement, and Orlan grew accustomed to bitter ale and learned to drink a good deal without getting sick. He ran the streets with them every night in pursuit of fresh games: they teased beggars with the promise of coins. They pelted shop windows and statues with whatever foul-smelling stuff might be at hand. They hooted, shrieked like fighting cats, bayed like hounds to stir sleeping neighborhoods, then fled the city guards. Sometimes they followed women walking the night streets alone, but kept themselves at a safe distance and left before too long. Orlan had been troubled at this sport at first, for he was bound by his honor to assist a woman in danger, even from his friends, but these boys were not so brutal. They could not take their own virtue, as slight as it was, so lightly. It was vulgar, common, to commit a harmful crime and they were the sons of the Sheriff and Justice and prominent citizens in their own right as all but Goduin had come of age. They held some sense of responsibility, and they were not foolish enough to risk prison and disfigurement. The boys played their pranks, but only in the spirit of fun. They meant no more harm than when they taunted each other; it was all the same light-hearted, rough jest, and Orlan joined them with increasing enthusiasm.

He met many girls on his adventures, merchants' daughters of marriageable age and prostitutes who would consider themselves honored to be bedded by a nobleman, but he had not yet favored any. The well-born maids were either mercenary—Orlan believed that some would seduce any available noble past the age of sixteen if they thought they could gain by it—or they were pushed so by their families that they looked as if they would spit in his face if he gave any encouragement to their sullen flirtations.

And he could not involve himself with the whores. Women, even young and pretty, who worked in brothels were too lazy to rouse him. Orlan believed, as he had been taught, that the hierarchy of the Empire was flexible; everyone was born to a certain place, but any could be elevated through their own merit. Prostitutes, therefore, were people who could do nothing else; they had nothing but their bodies to live off, as thieves had nothing but ruthlessness and beggars nothing at all. If these were women of any capability, they would have some more honest profession.

The tavern drabs, however, were distressing to him. He saw how they lived: waiting on tables paid little beyond bed and bread and small serving maids and lads with no more than a handsome face or base shrewdness discovered early that they could turn their work to something more profitable. A crowded alehouse offered opportunities to meet all sorts of prospective patrons, even merchants of wealth who might be willing to settle some comfortable arrangement on the especially beautiful or clever. If no such patron arrived, the luckless continued to serve ale and earn what they could. Orlan learned that no tavern-maid past the age of twenty made her living simply as a servant. As he watched these women, more memories flooded him—he thought of another tavern and a woman who had waited through her life for that special suitor to return and carry her away. He didn't want to remember her. Now that he had burst through the barrier and regained his lost knowledge, he was determined to forget it again.

He rarely saw Houarde and Ilset, for he left the house before dinner each night and returned after they had gone to bed. Neither seemed to mind; they agreed that he was here to enjoy himself and, in truth, Orlan was glad not to provide company for them when he had more suitable friends and entertainment. He intended to write to his father to say that he wanted to stay in Storm Port another month, but could not find time. There was so much to do, so much to learn. He stayed out all night and slept late in the day.

Kyarde found him one night in the middle of the deserted Square before the Council Hall. Orlan wandered, dazed, unsure on his feet, and he whirled with alarm as Kyarde approached.

"Orlan?"

"Where did they all go?"

"Who?"

"The boys! We were drinking at that Orient tavern—the Jade

Dragon."

"I know of the place." But Kyarde would not go into it except to make an arrest; he had heard tales of the mysteries of the East that might be bought there, unobtainable on the open markets. "That's ten streets away."

"How–" Orlan stumbled and fell to his knees, then crawled to the gutter to vomit. When he finished, Kyarde took him by the shoulders and they sat on the cobblestones, Orlan with his head between his hands. "How did I get here?"

"I cannot say. Do you recall walking here at all?"

"No." He looked up. "Here? Where?"

The young guard sighed at the vacant look in his friend's eyes. Orlan had no idea where he was and little idea whom he was talking to. "You must stop this, Orlan. It's too much."

"But I'm having fun! More fun than I've ever had, and I don't want to stop."

"What would your father say if he heard of such doings? I know how you've been running wild."

"Father be damned! I should have him care as little for my amusements as I do for his." He sank back on the street, shining hair spilling on the dark stones like rain in moonlight. "His lovers, his Faerye-lord toys, his precious little pet. *His* life is not so blameless. Do you know who my mother was? He never told me. He made me forget her. But I know! Oh, gods, I know. Is it worse that it was so, or that he hid it from me? Magical self-discipline—What a hypocrite he is! Liar!"

"Orlan–"

"Oh, look at the stars! How bright they are. Do you know that I can name them all?"

"No," Kyarde began to babble too, as he tried to follow the outpouring of angry words. "Can you?"

"'Tis the training of all magicians. On nights without cloud nor moon– How bright stars can be on a winter night! So close that you can reach up to touch them. Father took us to the top of the Kroune Tower. He would take Andemyon along. Demy may name all the lights in the firmament as well as any wizard."

"He's a bright little lad, for all his meekness."

"Father's favorite. He loved her, you know. He doesn't have to be ashamed that her child was born. I didn't mean to hurt him. It was an accident!"

"Of course you didn't," said the young guard.

"Yes, I did. The stars draw too close! See them? Dazzle-bright, cold, cold spots in blackness. They smother me. Magic is a curse. I feel too much." His hands covered his eyes. "I can't shut it out. Is it so difficult for all magicians to master themselves?" Tears escaped the wells of his palms and trickled down his wrists. "Why can't I be a boy like the other boys and simply have my fun? Because I'm not. I'm different. Magician."

The torrent was subsiding. Kyarde helped Orlan to his feet. "Are you able to stand?"

"I think so." Orlan clutched his shoulder. "Where's the Mayor's Hall?"

"Not far. `Tis there, at the end of the street. See the lighted torch at the corner? Come along." He took Orlan's arm and led him gently, taking great care at every step that Orlan should not stumble.

Kyarde rapped at the door of the Hall, and was surprised when the Mayor herself answered. "My Layn." He bowed quickly and lost his hold on Orlan, who caught the doorpost before he slipped to his knees.

A tiny frown creased Ilset's brow at this unexpected disturbance. "Chyelde, are you well?"

"Perfectly fine!" Orlan insisted. "Why must there be such a fuss over my comings and goings? I'm not a child." He slumped against the open door and rested his head on his arms.

Ilset turned to the discomfited young guard with a soothing smile. "I am glad to see him returned safely. Has he been with you all this time?"

"No, My Layn," Kyarde answered. "I found him and thought it best to bring him here."

"Gramercies for that, Guardian." She nudged Orlan, at her feet, with a cautious slipper toe. "Lad, are you awake?"

"Yes," but he did not lift his head.

"You must be quite weary from your adventures, Chyelde. Take my hand. Yes, there, and we shall see you to your bed." She summoned the drowsy porter to escort her guest to his chambers. "And, you, Lad," the Mayor brought Kyarde to her attention as Orlan was taken upstairs. "May I reward you for your help?" She reached for her purse.

"I-I could not," Kyarde protested quickly. "Ta, My Layn. I am grateful for your kindness, but Orlan is my friend."

"Oh, take it." She pressed the silver into his hand. "I don't think the guards are paid well and it is not so much to disdain but the price of a good ale or two at my treat. If you see Chyelde Orlan again, you might treat him too, but take care. Nobles, they say, are apt to misbehave when we common-born folk are able to keep our heads. I imagine that this unpleasantness is usual to all youths of rank and so will pass once he tires of the sport. Nevertheless, you and I must see that he stays out of danger and that his father does not hear, or we may be blamed."

"Yes, My Layn," he answered, baffled by this unexpected confidence. "A pleasant night rest to you."

"And you, Guardian." She shut the door.

ten

Orlan was expected that morning at the Whitelm but he did not arrive until long after the cathedral bells chimed noon. He was dressed in his riding habit, tunic short and breeches close-fitting to the knee and tucked into his boot tops, apparel not ordinarily worn off horseback. Breeches were worn by foresters, heralds, and the occasional wandering entertainer, not well-born folk within a city. But Orlan was a tall youth, slender-flanked and long-legged, so the effect was not unattractive.

He tossed his hair from his eyes, revealing an odd, tired look in the colorless depths. "Sorry to be so late, Adyna. I overslept."

"No matter." She shrugged at the apology. "Are you leaving us so soon?"

"No, not yet. I shall stay through this sennight, `til Midsummer is past."

"Are you well, my lad? Kyarde told me he found you sotted on the Square last night."

"Kyarde says too much beyond his own business. I am fine, Adyna." He flashed a charming smile. "Hasn't a youth a right to overindulge once? I was foolish—I admit so—but I am in no danger of worse than an aching head. No more of your mother-hen cluckings, I beg."

"If it please you," she answered.

"It pleases me very much."

Ren came in, drying her hands on her apron. "I thought that was your voice, Orlan." She smiled. "You haven't come to see us in so long."

"I know, and I offer my apologies," he replied. "I meant to come by days ago, Little One. You mustn't be cross that I forgot."

"I'm not, Orlan," she answered. "Honestly."

Orlan had not realized until this moment how much Storm Port had taught him. He understood that this little girl was in love with him; he had not seen this before, although it now seemed more than obvious in her shyness, her soft-toned voice, her reluctance to meet his eyes. He had seen the same emotion imitated by older maids, but Ren did not have that artifice. How naive he had been not to see before!

"Rennie, here." He pulled at the ribbons which tied the gold arabesque pomander to his tunic. The cachet of dried rose petals within still held their fragrance. "I have a gift for you. See?" He held it out. "I have worn it myself these past weeks, but I shan't need it at home and I am a little more used to the smells of the city than I was. I'd be pleased if you would keep this."

"I will, Orlan." She took the offered gift and tied the ribbons at her waist. "'Tis so lovely." The pomander glittered, an absurdly huge and expensive bauble, in the folds of a small alemaid's brown skirt.

"Do you like it, then?"

"Oh, yes, very much." Her eyes were actually shining. For that, if for no better reason, he wanted to protect her.

"Come here, Rennie. Talk with me." The girl pinked as she took a seat at the empty table nearest him. "Do you know, I have thought much of Kyarde's teasing of you the night I stayed here, how he laughed at your admiration for My Layn Margueryt." In fact, Orlan had not thought of it at all between that time and this.

"I recall," Ren said softly.

"If that is true, it is nothing for your brother to laugh over. You may become a soldier as well as any fit youth in the Empire. I've thought that I might speak with the Mayor herself of you, and she would speak with Alyx, for the Captain often sits at the Mayor's table."

"You would tell Kyarde's captain of me?" She shied at the thought.

"Yes, and why not, my girl? Do you think yourself unworthy?"

"I'm only an alemaid, Orlan."

"You are a brave child, and my friend. If it is your wish, I shall ask My Layn Ilset to recommend you to Alyx's service. Think of that, Rennie!"

"In truth?"

"'Pon my honor as a nobleman and future wizard, it is the truth."

Tears filled her eyes. "I– Orlan, I–"

"Hush, Pet." He took the hem of her apron and blotted her damp face. "None of that. A brave lass doesn't weep."

"What of Mother? How may I leave her?"

"There are a dozen children who would be glad for a place in this house. But it is not for you. I tell you, Rennie, for you do not know all that may happen in this city, especially to a pretty maid as you are. I shall speak to the Mayor and if all goes well I promise I'll buy you a silken sash, a properly blue one as Captain Alyx herself wears."

"Gramercy!" She reached up as if to embrace him, then hesitated, blushed deeply, and fled to the back rooms.

Orlan smiled, then looked up to find that Adyna had returned and was scowling her disapproval. He blushed too, wondering how much of the conversation she had overheard and thinking that she misunderstood his intentions. He'd only meant to be kind, to help Ren, but Adyna must know even better than he that the seduction of many maids began with grand promises and pretty gifts. "Adyna–"

But Adyna's worries lay elsewhere. "You mustn't keep her dreaming after such fancies, Orlan," she said. "The girl is no warrior-maid. And she's far too young to leave me."

"Kyarde was sixteen when you sent him here alone in similar service. Ren will be as near you as he is now and you know she must have some other profession than alemaid for her life. I fear for her, Adyna. You know what becomes of little alemaids once they are grown."

"I know," she admitted. "I was one such myself."

"You met Leobolde Goldesmith then?"

"How do you know of him?"

"I met him once. He is Houarde Portreeve's friend."

She frowned. "He's a wicked man, Orlan. I was a foolish maid and he deceived me with promises of better. No more of him, I beg you!"

"As you wish. Shall we see to business now? It has waited too long."

But little was accomplished that day, for the afternoon patrons began to arrive as soon as the two turned their attention to the figures in Adyna's books, and the alekeeper was called back to her work. Orlan left.

Ilset returned from her garden accompanied by the small servant-boy and her orange-garbed heralds, all covered by large aprons. "I shall have to send you out to the river," she spoke as they entered the parlor. "It is not as good as our well water, but we cannot spare the best for plants and they will die if they have nothing–" She stopped, seeing Orlan seated by the quelled fire. "Chyelde? I thought you had gone out on your business."

"I wasn't out very long." He rose. "Pardon, I beg you, My Layn. I did not mean to interrupt. I saw you working from my window and I thought to ask–"

Ilset raised a hand. "Yes. In a moment." She turned to the servants. "Take buckets from the scullery, and be quick." The heralds and boy darted away and Mayor gave attention to her guest. "What is it you wish, Chyelde Orlan?"

"I would send a message to my father, explaining that I have been detained here and need to stay longer than anticipated. There is no writing paper in my room and I thought you might have some."

"Yes, in my office." Orlan followed her to a room at the front of the Hall, small and closed, lined with bookshelves. Ilset offered a pulped, pressed sheet with a distinctive watermark from a silver tray. "I would give you use of my writing desk, but I have my own responsibilities to attend to. We expect a rough winter ahead, you know, and this city must have enough food for all."

"I've heard of the trouble. The drought."

"It will be death to the crops. Our farm-folk cannot send for water so easily as I may." She found a sharpened pen and dipped it into the ink bottle. "I bid you write your message, Chyelde. My herald will be sent this very day."

Orlan wrote two terse sentences: *Father, I wish to stay in Storm Port until the end of June. I have not yet finished my business.* Ilset arranged the books on her desk, forming small stacks here and there, but she did not attend to her accounts. She watched the youth, seated on a sturdy chair, head on his arm as he pressed quill to paper. He glanced up suddenly into her intent gaze.

"My Layn?"

"Apologies, Chyelde. I did not mean to stare. I had not thought on it before, but I see now that you look much like your father. As I recall him, he was little more than a boy himself."

Orlan was surprised; Ilset had never mentioned Lord Redmantyl before. "You've met him?"

"Oh, yes, many years ago. I was a wizard once, did you know?"

"I might have guessed so, My Layn. You've shown often an understanding of magic that– er– those without talent do not." He waved the paper slowly to allow the ink to dry. "Tell me, if you will, what happened? Why did you leave?"

"I was defeated in wizard-battle by your father, when he was young and conquered all who challenged his supremacy. The memory is unpleasant. Do not ask more, Chyelde. I've no powers now, not enough to signify."

"I didn't know that that could be done."

"Nor did I, until it had happened. I am fortunate that he did not think me a threat, for I was permitted to live. Others, more powerful, did not fare so well."

"Have you–" Orlan paused. "Has my father killed many wizards?"

"The Old Lord, certainly," Ilset replied. "And my mentor and friend, Layn Dyrkhesse. I saw her fall myself. Others I have heard of, but cannot account for those tales. I am glad, truly, to be out of such a perilous profession."

"You think magic evil, My Layn?"

"No," she shook her head. "But its misuse may tempt the good to evil. Shall I show you?" Ilset brought down a large, leatherbound book from a case atop her shelves and undid two heavy copper clasps each locked with its own key. There was no title on the book's cover nor spine. Within, the text was modern Norman. "It is a translation from the Latin," she explained. "Copied by an acquaintance at Maryebridge, though it was not so easy to obtain. The Sisters keep close guard of the original."

Orlan read the frontispiece with a delicate shudder. "*Necromantia Perdyte*?"

Ilset lifted one eyebrow at this response. "Surely your father keeps such books?"

"Yes, but he won't let me see them. I found one once—the same title, I think—but he took it away before I could begin to read. He said it was too dangerous for me."

The Mayor laughed. "My master once told me the same—this forbidden lore is too dangerous, especially for an innocent apprentice. Yet it is safe for myself. My magic has fled me and I work no harm to study arts I cannot perform. I keep this merely as a curiosity.

"But if this book were in other hands-! Ah, Chyelde, magic bestows a great deal of power on mortal souls not fit to command it. Even the greatest wizards are no more than human. See what is offered here to seduce the magical."

She showed him certain pages. Orlan read fantastic accounts of sorcerers who reanimated whole corpses or dismembered limbs to work their bidding and of murdered necromancers who returned to their bodies months after death to take revenge. He read spells to destroy unwary enemies with madness or to cast glamours of love over a desired one. He read that on sacred nights a willing magician might invite the return of expelled, lost gods and receive rewards beyond mortal conception. He read a spell to recall the newly dead to life.

The dead to life.

"I fear I cannot show you all that is written here, Chyelde," said Ilset. "A young magician such as yourself is not of an age to refuse the temptations within. Imagine what a wizard of power might do if he did not seek to master himself and employed such dark arts!"

139

"Yes," Orlan breathed, though he scarcely heard her words. The spell remained before him. A simple rite. In a moment, he had committed the lines to memory: an incantation was spoken over the body before it began to cool—*blood to my blood, life to my life, soul to my soul, I give myself to thee*—and the magician placed his left hand over the still heart and spilled his blood. So simple.

"The effect would be catastrophic," Ilset continued. "No, I am glad to be rid of my magic and I fear much for those who possess it. Have care, my lad, when you come to your powers. You may fall to temptations you do not foresee."

"I won't, My Layn," Orlan answered. Carefully, he closed the book. "I have been trained for many years to keep my self-control. I would not abuse my power, any more than my father would."

She smiled gently. "You are so virtuous, Chyelde. You cannot know what evil is. Have you finished your message?"

Orlan folded the paper in half, then folded it again. He sealed it with a written spell. "There."

He had read that book before, years ago, discovered it in an unlocked closet on the lowest floor of the Spelle Tower library. It had been pushed into a dark corner where it was not likely to be found by casual search. Redmantyl had probably thought that best; a locked cabinet or an outright warning would have drawn undesired attention to the hidden object and stirred the curiosity of any one of the young people in the castle. Orlan had stumbled upon it by chance. He saw immediately what it was: a collection of necromantic secrets—not the sort of lore an apprentice received as part of his education, nor even the sort a right-thinking wizard dared to employ. He knew he was not meant to read it, but forbidden texts are the most intriguing. Horripilated, he had turned through the same pages Ilset had shown him.

He hadn't seen that particular spell; his father had shut up the book before he'd read so far. But it had been there. If the copy he had seen today contained that page, so must the copy he had discovered long ago. Redmantyl must have known what secrets that book held. He hadn't wanted Orlan to see.

Orlan remembered the nights immediately after his mother's death when he'd screamed for her and his father had taken him into his arms and wound him in soothing enchantments. Lord Redmantyl hadn't known what to say to comfort that little boy, so new and strange to him. But before that, the wizard had spoken once—the day Mama had died.

Orlan heard the words again: *I cannot recall one who is past healing....
No wizard who has ever lived had power for that!* Yet Redmantyl did
possess the power. He must have known how to use it even as he stood
at Nann Dafodylle's bedside and claimed her sobbing child. Her body
was not yet cold. A simple spell. He might have brought her back.

Why hadn't he? There must be a reason! Was the wizard reluctant
to use such a spell because it was by definition necromancy? Surely, if
no evil was intended in restoring a life, no evil was done. Did
Redmantyl fear the risk to himself so much that he had allowed a
woman to die when he might save her?

The distinction between right magic and sorcery was not always
clear. The apprentices frequently whispered of the abominations of
near-mythical necromancers to try to frighten each other. The litany of
terror was well-known: demon-slaves and incubi summoned to satisfy
unearthly pleasures, vengeful curses of death and destruction, ghastly
displays of occult influence to deceive, ensnare and terrify lesser
beings. Certainly, these were evil. Other devices of the sorcerer's art,
however, were not so easily defined. Orlan had heard of spellcrafts too
fabulous to be true, of magicians who grew homunculi in bottles or
made roses sing, who divined the future through crystals and silvered
mirrors or conjured the spirits of ancient masters to retrieve lost arcana.
These tricks might be employed for sinister ends, but they were not
essentially harmful. Why did wizards not test them to see if they might
be worked? Why couldn't they be known to students such as himself?
Orlan had asked, and his father answered bluntly: "Such arts must not
be attempted. They are a corruption of nature."

As an unskilled novice, Orlan must content himself with this
answer. Now, he found it unsatisfactory. True, necromancy was a
subversion of nature. But what magic was not? All of it extended
human will over the natural flux of energy which made up the universe.
Magicians wrested clouds from the sky and made rain fall where none
might if nature were given its course. Masters of the material reshaped
masses of earth and rock; indeed, the island which Wizardes Cliff was
built upon was as artificial as the castle, torn from the sea at the whim
of an elder Redmantyl. Even his father's modest toys of light
transformed the elemental energy of electricity. Why shrink at other
crafts no less unnatural?

The practices of modern magic were often as feared, mistrusted,
and named as unholy by common folk as the sorcery of legend, and not
entirely through ignorance and superstition. Right magic might be used
for destructive purposes, yet proper wizards did not forbid its exercise

because of that possibility. Orlan considered that the difference between good and evil lay in the intent of the magician, not the particulars of the spell cast. Squeamishness alone made wizards shun certain magic and name it wrong when they might embrace some of the so-called forbidden dark arts and gain the merits of that knowledge without danger. Ilset was wrong. Few of the great were seduced into corruption. The weak-willed and degenerate were the most dangerous magicians. For this reason, the codes of the established ranks of wizardry were unmercifully harsh in the endeavor to banish the dissolute and the exterminate the renegade. Lord Redmantyl himself destroyed weaker magicians and expelled fallen mages without mercy. Only the strongest were allowed to survive. Misuse of power might occur, but the highest levels were masters of such self-command that the temptations of necromancy did not sway them. His father, supreme of all living magicians, held the potential for a diabolic necromancer. Orlan had seen it. The wizard's rage unleashed was terrifying. Yet he did not succumb. His will was too strong.

His hesitation to intervene for Nann Dafodylle was strangely inconsistent. That man was impervious to corruption—Orlan did not doubt. Redmantyl had such iron resolve. He wielded such powers. Why should he not claim equal mastery over the forces of life and death?

She might be alive today.

That night, Orlan went to the Bag o' Nails. The boys had brought him there before and left him to seek his own amusement while they pursued theirs. Tonight was not different. Eduarde, Goduin, and Reynalde soon disappeared upstairs and Tades and Jepatha took a table in a corner with a pretty girl who knew the latter youth well. Orlan wandered the lower hall until he met a weary-looking drab, belly bulging beneath her loose-laced jerkin.

"What's your name?"

"Tess, an' it please ye, M'Lord." She studied him appreciatively from boots to silver curls. "Will ye come up wi' me?"

"I'd sooner stay down here."

They sat together in a closeted cubby and drank themselves to dizziness. Orlan told a string of outright lies about himself and didn't care if she believed him or not. She made sounds of amazement at the proper moments and that was sufficient encouragement. He thought this woman pleasant enough to pass time with, but not attractive. Her nose was large and sharp and her hair greasy and unkempt. As he spoke, a flea crawled along the upper edge of her eyebrow. He suppressed a shudder. No vermin troubled him; little insects disliked magic as heartily as the larger beasts. He could not imagine how common people endured such creatures on their skin.

"Have you been here long?" he asked.

"Two year now, M'Lord. I came from Puddensby in search of a place. Had one too, as maid in a great house, but 'twas no different from this and not so well-paid. I've got specially good since–" She patted her belly.

"Will you keep it?"

"Keep a babe in this house? What twad! I'll send it out, right off, the minute it's born."

"No– I meant that there are physics a woman will take–"

"Oh. No! 'Tis worse a cure than the illness, they say. I wouldna dare."

"You're wise in that, Goode Tess. My mother died of it."

"What, a Lady?"

Orlan did not correct this mistake. "She wanted no other children after me," he answered. "She was always sick and miserable, I remember. Died when I was eight."

"'Tis pity."

"'Tis," Orlan agreed. He understood about his mother now, why they had lived above the tavern in Lammouthe, who the men were that came in the night, and what self-induced remedy had killed her. He knew why she wept.

He understood, too, that when his father told him to avoid entanglements with common women, the wizard had spoken from experience. He was the proof of that. After all, hadn't Redmantyl dallied with a pretty alemaid, then paid for that momentary pleasure with the unexpected responsibility of a child? Orlan knew why his father could tell him so little of his mother: they had not known each other, had only the briefest acquaintance at his conception and had not seen each other after. She had been nothing to him, a hopeful tavern drab to be plied with promises. He would not have thought of her again if Orlan had not been born. It had been the one magical moment of her life, sufficient to keep her waiting for her lover's return and to keep her from aborting his child, but she had never known wizard's name.

Was that indifference reason enough to let her die when so little effort might restore her?

With the exception of Tedora, Redmantyl did not respect the women he took as lovers. He disliked those he found desirable and, more, disapproved of any man or woman who distracted wizardly disciplines. Apparently, love was less dangerous to a magician than lust. Also, Tedora did not need him as other women had. She did not demand more than his profession allowed him to give.

If Mama had lived, his father would have been obliged to aid her— more than take responsibility for their child, take her out of the miserable life she had endured while waiting for his return. His honor as a nobleman demanded that he not leave her there. Marry her? No, he wouldn't. But he must see that she was cared for. Had he hesitated for that? Was it easier to let her slip away rather than trouble himself with the hindrances which must follow her recall?

"Tell me, can you–?" He paused delicately.

"Can I–? Oh, with child? Right up 'til my time, they say, an' that's months off." She laughed. "You won't hurt me, Pet."

She slipped an arm about his waist and leaned close to breathe in his face; Orlan turned his head slightly so he wouldn't have to kiss her. Instead, her mouth brushed his throat and fingers fumbled lower. He heard a *chink!* of coins against his thigh, and the girl jerked away from him with a shriek.

Orlan blinked, startled. "What?" He looked down, and noticed that the purse strings at his girte had been undone. "You–?"

"What'd ye do?" she wailed. "What for God are ye?"

"What am I?" he laughed. "You're a little thief!"

"Demon!"

Half the brothel inmates and their clientele came out to watch and join in the commotion that followed, and Orlan was tossed into the street. His friends followed with shouted declarations that none would stay where not all were welcome, but they also left without paying.

"I've never heard a woman scream so," Jepatha sniggered as they wandered down Lyngate Street. "What did you do to her?"

"Not a bloody thing! The wreckage tried to rob me."

"They'll do that if you aren't watchful." Eduarde threw an arm about him. "You can't trust such creatures, M'Lord, with your purse nor your heart."

"But who can keep a-watch all the time?" Jepatha answered. "'Tis best if you keep your clothes laced as well as you can. You'll be hindered, but you'll leave with all you came with."

"I've heard tales of unsuspecting lads who woke to find themselves stripped as bare as market bunnies after a night of love," Reynalde giggled. "Imagine—you must walk home in the cruel dawn's light, all tender parts to the breeze–"

Eduarde slapped him to be silent, for a young woman walked not far ahead of them. The boys darted into the darkness of the shop doorways on either side of the street, but they were too loud, laughing and whispering as they scrambled; she heard them and turned.

"I know you're there, so you might come out." It was Julia.

"What are you doing?" Reynalde called out.

"No concern of yours," she answered, but explained shortly. "'Tis the fault of that brute guard I played a fool for—damn his 'pertinence! I would go to the Jongleur again, but *he* said if I would go, I must see myself there and back without his company."

"Are you going or coming?" Eduarde asked.

"Going. I'll walk where I please, and alone if I must."

"You ought not, Dam'sel," said Orlan. "'Tisn't safe for a lone maid to walk out so late."

Julia gave him a smile. "I'm not afraid. Who would harm me?" She shot a meaningful look at her brother and his fellows.

"But you would not object if we went with you?" Orlan glanced back at the boys. "Shall we go to the Jongleur? 'Tis barely past sundown and we may find some sport there."

"'Twould be far more merry than standing in this street all night," Jepatha said. "If you allow, Julia."

Julia did allow, but her thoughts remained on her argument with her guardsman-lover and the upstart treachery of peasants who thought themselves as fine as their betters. Some of the wretches, she proclaimed as she walked ahead of her slightly sotted companions, thought themselves so fine as noblemen.

"Tell me of your family, My Lord," she turned to Orlan, who was trying to keep Reynalde on his feet without losing his own. "You are the only nobleman I know. I've heard that your father is a great wizard, but I cannot credit all the tales they tell as truth. 'Tis too fantastic!"

"'Tis likely all true, whatever it is," Orlan answered.

"It can't be! The furies of light? The storms that covered all of the Northlands? They say he's killed all other wizards in battle."

"I cannot answer for that—'twas before I came. But I do not doubt it. Father can do such things when he is angry. I've seen him."

Julia shivered with pretty exaggeration. "It must be horrible. I shouldn't like to see for myself."

"I would," Eduarde laughed.

"You wouldn't, my lad," Orlan said. "You'd be blasted to pieces."

Reynalde giggled. "I'd see *that*!" He stumbled on a loose cobblestone and grabbed Orlan's shoulder. Goduin rushed to catch him from the other side.

"Are you well, Fox?"

"Well enough," the boy insisted. "'Twas the rotten wine. Devil's guess what grapes they press at that infernal place."

"What place?" his sister asked; the lads only sniggered and left her to seek her own answer. "Boys," she said in disgust. "They'll ruin you, M'Lord."

"No, not them," Orlan answered. As they went on, he began to sing. The others hummed with him sporadically, for the melody was well-known—minstrels had used it for centuries—but his lyrics were unfamiliar:

> *"A song for love lost, I sing to thee,*
> *My pretty lad, though you may not hear,*
> *For I gaze after thy parting smiles*
> *And brush away a lonely tear.*
> *One kiss and you leave...*

Half the notes struck falsely, but Orlan's friends applauded the effort.

"A pretty song," Julia said when he had finished. "But I've not heard such words. Are they yours?"

"They were written by a thesper I once knew." The boys burst into uproarious laughter. "No, my father's love and none of mine. I am always sad when I think on it."

"Why?"

"'Tis a sad song of an abandoned maid."

Orlan could not sing well; Andemyon could. The little boy had sung that song at the celebration of Olyr's return. Olyr had spent four years as a mage, traveling about as young magicians must, to Africa, Asia, and the golden cities of the Incas to discover their lore, and he'd returned to the house of his former master to make arrangements for his final testing. In his years away, he had changed from a lanky, tongue-tied boy to a travel-weary and lean youth. They called him Nightehauk. He'd looked so wizardly in the black tunic, cloak, and browband of a mage, his short-clipped black beard framing his mouth after the style of Redmantyl's tarnished silver. So empowered, so promising a magician, capable even of becoming one of the great. Lord Redmantyl had been so proud.

The tables in the Feast Hall were laden with delicacies and fine dishes, as many as Redmantyl could make available: roast haunch of venison, dressed squab, baked fish on beds of romaine, lamb pie, puddings, a full wheel of cheese, oat cakes, maple-sugar candies, a dozen loaves of steaming, fresh bread, baked apples in spice, buttermilk, pitchers of cider, red wine, and cooled mulberry tea. A pair of wandering minstrels had been visiting Lyges and Redmantyl had invited them to play and to be paid by welcome at the table.

Olyr, as a mage, avoided fermented drinks, bloodied meats, and sugared morsels, but he ate his fill as he entertained the company with his adventures and sang along to the more sprightly tunes. Although he was of common birth, he swallowed each morsel before speaking and, rather than wipe his fingers on his clothes or the table cloth, genteelly licked them clean, as he had learned at the same table years before. When all had fed to their satisfaction, the remainder of the meal was carried away to the kitchens and the minstrels settled in a corner to tune their lute and pipes. Redmantyl bid a few of the maids stay for a dance, but the boys were too shy and awkward to ask them.

Olyr sat in conversation with Redmantyl. "My Lord, tell me of Laurel," he whispered discreetly; all the household knew the meaning behind his request. "I asked after her in New York but the Mayor— your cousin Kaiese's husband by no coincidence, I am sure—told me I must leave before I learned of my friend's fate. Have you heard from her? Is she well?"

Redmantyl answered, "Olyr, she is married."

The young mage's face turned pale and he fell silent. Then, he said, "My Lord, tell me all," and after Redmantyl said all he wished to hear he rose and crossed the hall to where one pretty maid sat teasing Godefroi. "Pardon, Maiden, will you step with me in a dance?"

She took his hand, and they went out to join Alfryda and Simon, now Redmantyl's steward and chatelaine respectively, in a dancing figure at the center of the hall. Andemyon, encouraged by the minstrels, summoned all his bravery and sang in a sweet, trilling soprano. Tedora's lyrics were the only ones he knew to suit the ancient melody.

> *"A song for love lost, I sing to thee,*
> *My pretty lad, though you may not hear,*
> *For I gaze after thy parting smiles*
> *And brush away a lonely tear.*
> *One kiss and you leave ere dawn's first light,*
> *And cast me cold on the morrow.*

> *Thy fair promise hath led my heart astray,*
> *And filled it with naught but sorrow."*

Orlan had seen the maid about the castle before that evening, but he did not know her well. Her name was Nel and she was daughter to the Lyges butcher. She lived with her family in the village, but Simon called her up when extra help was needed.

Olyr took Nel's right hand and Alfryda's left; with Simon, they formed a circle and began to pace clockwise in time to the music. The four stepped together, then apart, each turning with their hands raised; Alfryda laughed when Simon tripped on his long aqua robe. Side by side, they skipped the length of the hall, then turned back in whirling pairs. Orlan could hear bits of conversation when Olyr and Nel spun near:

"...for work? You think this work then, Goode Maid?"

"Oh, no," she giggled. "If 'twere so, I'd gone to service before this. I remember you from the old days, 'Prentice Olyr, when M'Lord sent you on errands to my father's shop. Do you remember?"

"Of course. I am no longer 'prentice, but I am still simply Olyr." They skipped away in quick little steps, hand in hand, then spun back again. "My vows? Oh, some are more easy to keep than others.... Do you know, I've come to dream of good roasted beef, crisp at the skin and pink at the bone. I'm everlastingly sick of pale fish and fowl!"

At the top of the hall, they rejoined the circle with Simon and Alfryda and the dance began anew.

> *"A flood of tears could not soften thy hard love.*
> *Where ere you go, I must here remain,*
> *So leave me this day, a sad, sad maid,*
> *To await thy returning again."*

On and on, throughout the evening, they danced. And when the last of the wine and tea had gone and the music lagged, Redmantyl sent the sleepy boys to bed. Olyr walked out to see Nel safely home.

Orlan had surrendered his hopes of becoming Lord Redmantyl when his cousin Laurel came to Wizardes Cliff. She had crashed like a comet into the quiet house, a brilliant, unrestrained force to dazzle lesser beings. Laurel was faster, more clever, better at games, and far more talented than any of them. The apprentices had often talked among themselves of great power, what it must be to wield it, what they would be when they achieved their proper places among the ranks of grown wizards. Godefroi did not entertain thoughts of becoming Redmantyl—he knew the limits of his magic—but Olyr had his aspirations and Orlan had hoped from his childhood. Laurel showed them what a true young Redmantyl must be like. From the beginning of her apprenticeship, she had received a special place in Redmantyl's attention. Orlan could not resent her; that would have been as unthinkable as resenting his father's power and place, and Laurel was so much like the wizard. The boy thought of her as one of his own blood, an elder sister, sometimes adored and sometimes vexatious, but never an ordinary maid. Laurel was made of overwhelming energies and shining talents, a keen, steel-edged will and a temper as quick as a lightning bolt. She held the promise of a spectacular wizard.

Godefroi and Olyr fell in love with her immediately. Orlan recalled how they had gaped at her and followed her about like heartsick courtiers from her first days in the household; he thought they looked silly and he wondered how Laurel could tolerate them when they behaved so foolishly. But it had been no secret that his cousin enjoyed their attentions, especially Olyr's; Orlan had caught them kissing more than once before the elder apprentice had taken his mage-vows and gone away. Redmantyl tried to discourage the adolescent romance for the good of both. Young magicians about to take severe vows of abstinence ought not have the opportunity to regret those vows before they were spoken.

Laurel stayed at Wizardes Cliff for four years, until her aunt Kaiese abruptly called her back to New York. Kaiese thought magic a thing of evil purpose, Redmantyl explained; she could not abide her sister's child as a magician in her house, but evidently found it intolerable that Laurel should become a wizard. Her own daughters had been brought up to fear magic. When Orlan met them, he thought them meek, pretty girls—Igren was especially gentle and beautiful—and unable to use whatever talents they possessed.

Surprisingly, the wizard did not contest his cousin's summons. Laurel went back to New York—Orlan guessed because she was near twenty-one and his father was confident she would return once she attained the right to act for herself without the hindrance of a guardian. But Laurel came of age and still did not resume her apprenticeship. Month after month, she was absent, yet Redmantyl did not quit his hopes of her return until she wrote to announce her betrothal and invite them to the wedding. They did not attend. Redmantyl barely acknowledged the marriage. He blamed his niece's husband and rarely spoke of her thereafter. It pained him to think of that shining power lost.

And if Redmantyl had been crushed by the loss of his finest pupil, Godefroi and Olyr were heartbroken at the defection of their first love. They evidently thought much more of her than she had thought of either of them. When Laurel's betrothal announcement was read, Godefroi wept openly. After Olyr heard the news at his homecoming feast, he was no less devastated. He did not weep as Godefroi had; years of apprenticeship and magedom had taught him not to show the depth of his injury, but Orlan knew. There was no psychical bond between them, but Orlan had lived in the same house with this youth for seven years and knew him well enough to know what he felt.

That night, the young mage and Godefroi sat up for hours and talked of Laurel in the most honored terms, lamenting her marriage as if it were her death. Godefroi gave Olyr a sketch he had made of Laurel, carefully drawn from memory.

"I shall carry it with me always," the mage said as he folded the gift and tucked it into his tunic breast. "There, near my heart." He was solemn throughout his visit, and he departed melancholy.

Orlan felt his friends' sorrow, for he knew how they loved Laurel, but he thought it a hopeless cause. It was a waste of time to moon over a maid, and more foolish still when there was no chance of winning her love. Laurel was gone. He had seen her at Pendaunzel; she was more calm and dignified, as married women must be, but she was happy. She did not explain her reasons for leaving her magic, but Orlan imagined she chose to do so for love. Her husband obviously adored her, and she was proud of her small, silver-curled son. If she regretted her choice, he did not sense it. Orlan felt the absence of his bright cousin as much as anyone, but he could not believe her marriage a tragedy. She had made her decision and no one could alter it, not his father, not Godefroi, not Olyr.

Olyr's visit might have passed as inconsequential; it had been pleasant to see an old friend, exciting to hear of his travels and the difficulties of mage life, sad to know his pain, but the event was nothing in itself. Orlan would have forgotten the homecoming feast if it had not contained all the elements of the disaster that befell Wizardes Cliff a year later. Had he seen it then? Had there been any sort of premonition as he listened to Andemyon's pretty, sad song and watched Nel and Olyr turn together in their dance? No, not then. Now, the details stood out with vivid clarity; the beginnings had been there for all to see if they would only look. No one saw. But it had begun that night.

Thunder over the castle woke him another morning a year later. He went to the dressing-room window and pushed open the casement. The sky was black. Dark clouds gathered overhead, engulfing the slender top of the Daune Tower and descending ominously toward the roof of the Magne Hall, pushing themselves out of the air and growing darker, thicker, and closer with every second. Lightning sparked within the murky depths, blue and shimmering, more like glowing orbs in the clouds than the sky-splitting white flashes that were normally part of violent storms. And, most odd of all, there was no wind and no rain.

He knew immediately that this storm was not natural.

Mathias lifted his head from the pillows and blinked sleepily. "What is it?"

"I don't know."

"Olyr, perhaps? They would test this morning."

"Perhaps." Olyr had returned late the night before to be confirmed a full wizard and Orlan's first thought, like Mathias's, had been that this must be a test of the mage's powers. But this was nonetheless mysterious, for Olyr was not best at the manipulation of light; he showed strength and passion in his finest spells imposed upon the material medium, but nothing of this magnificence.

Orlan pulled his hose and tunic on over his nightshirt and went down the stairwell behind the Great Hall. The thick, oaken doors were shut, but there was a barred ventilation panel set high on one door and if he sat halfway up the stairs and ducked a little, he could watch the proceedings as well as hear them.

Olyr was not casting spells; the mage appeared defiant and strangely near tears as he knelt in a pentacle painted red on the floor. Lord Redmantyl, standing before him, looked dark and angry. It was his storm then. But why? Then Orlan heard Olyr's anguished cry:

"It was only once!"

"That is more than enough. You know the consequences." Redmantyl's face was set as firmly as stone, but his eyes seemed to glow and the storm outside showed the fury that was suppressed here and unleashed beyond.

"Can't something be done?" Olyr pled. "My Lord, I have lived this last year in penance. I fasted a full sennight and did not sleep 'til I fell in a faint. I have crawled about, so afraid that everyone could see what I'd done. So ashamed, My Lord." The young mage's tears fell unchecked; he did not even try to maintain control over that. "I would have scourged myself if I thought it would do me good." He looked up at Redmantyl hopefully, but the wizard would not look at him. "Can I do more? I beg you tell me. Is there else I can do to recover myself?"

"No," the wizard answered. "All you may do is leave your magedom and renounce all hopes of wizardry. That must be your last sacrifice to reclaim honor, then you need not be troubled again."

"Need not be troubled!"

"For one not a mage, such a thing is no crime. There is no shame in it."

"I shall be cut with the shame of it all my life."

"I think not, Olyr. In time, you will see that this is best. You are not fit for wizardry."

"I am not fit for anything else!" Olyr sobbed. "I have trained for no other position since childhood. Please, My Lord, I will do whatever you ask to save myself this. Not my wizardry. Anything, I beg you!"

"There is nothing," Redmantyl answered softly. "Olyr, your sign."

Olyr surrendered it, looking up at his former master with a last desperate plea, but Redmantyl would not acknowledge his distress. He tore the talisman from the black browband, which burst into flames in his hands. The fire died quickly once Redmantyl threw the burning mass to the floor. Outside, thunder roared so loudly that the castle walls shook. Orlan watched this baffling scene, frightened and fascinated.

Redmantyl spoke: "Hear me, Olyr Nightehauk. Though you are to be pitied for your weakness, there is no redemption. From this day, you will no longer be called a mage, nor will you be called a wizard. You have failed at your greatest test and you are hereafter outcast from the ranks of all magicians. Seek another profession, for this one is closed to you. You are expelled."

He knelt over the prostrate youth, gently took him by the forearms and raised him. Olyr clung to him, seeking comfort from the man who had brought this disaster upon him. Perhaps he still hoped for forgiveness and restoration. The wizard's fingertips brushed the fallen mage's temple, then he pressed his lips to the same spot as if he had inflicted an injury there and meant to repair the damage. But Olyr shrieked at the kiss.

"My Lord–!"

Redmantyl released him and rose. "Go now, Olyr. It is finished. May you find happiness and strength elsewhere."

Orlan crouched close against the stairwell wall as his father walked away. Within the room, Olyr turned at the wizard's exit, open-mouthed and sobbing like one heartbroken. The boy went to the open doorway and asked the terrible question: "Olyr, what has happened?"

Olyr wiped at his tears. Instead of answering, he asked, "Which way has he gone, Orlan?"

Orlan waved in the direction of the corridor through the Hall below. Olyr fled in the other direction, down the stairwell.

"Olyr?" Orlan went down after him, but stopped when Olyr did not reply. He returned to the empty room. An overpowering tang of ozone hung in the air and the ashes on the floor still smoldered. From the light through the tall windows, the boy found the silver talisman that Olyr had worn on his brow. It had been a small disk engraved with the delicate image of a hawk in flight; Redmantyl had made it a smooth, melted mass, as if never forged into any shape or engraved with any device, as if Olyr's mage-years had not existed.

Outside, the thunder rumbled.

He could not answer Godefroi and Mathias when they met in the Feast Hall for breakfast, though both apprentices repeatedly asked what he had seen and heard in that mysterious interview. They puzzled over it, each offering a different interpretation and arguing over Olyr's fate. All fell silent when the wizard entered. No one dared to ask, and while they fretted, Andemyon in his innocence was the first to speak: "Why is there this horrible storm?" He was not aware that this question might be unwise, for he had never seen Redmantyl in a fury. Not one of them had before that day.

But Redmantyl smiled gently. "It is a sad thing, Little One," he explained. "Olyr will not be a wizard. He has broken his mage-vows and brought about his ruin. At his testing, he confessed that he dallied with a maid from Lyges when he was last here, and so has been banished."

Godefroi protested: "But that's not fair!"

"It is the rule for all magicians," Redmantyl answered. "We must take vows of abstinence in magedom. It is a matter of control, to prove that you may maintain yourself strictly and are sufficiently disciplined to be a wizard. You will take these vows soon yourself, Godefroi, and you must understand their importance. You must know that one infringement will be your ruin. Olyr knew this when he made his vows and when he broke them."

"But for one mistake—"

"For a wizard of power one mistake can mean death. A few years of careful diet, vigilant nights, and celibacy are simple compared to the constant control and guardance that a wizard must have to survive. If you fail in your mage-years, you cannot survive long after."

"Clergy take vows of celibacy and simple life," Godefroi persisted, "but no one insists that they adhere to them. Priests, even bishops, are not cast out if they break a vow once or even a dozen times, and they promise for all their lives."

"This is not the clergy," Redmantyl answered tersely. "Their rules are not ours and their God is more forgiving than Others are."

The apprentice stood red-faced and ready to speak, but he had no answer.

"Godefroi, sit." The wizard's voice was grim. "There is nothing more to be said." But Godefroi left the table.

St. Khrystopher's bells struck midnight as Orlan and his friends crossed the empty bazaar. The merchants had departed hours ago. Beggars shuffled amid the abandoned stalls and heaps of rubbish searching for scraps and fallen valuables. Some were blind; others were Plague survivors, backs bent and limbs twisted, stunted, useless. The sighted glared up at the passing maid and youths, but the children ignored them. Their night games had ended; they'd run through the ports and shipyards, up and down the piers in search of Tades' ship, which sat waiting for an outgoing cargo, and left the young mariner there.

Reynalde lagged behind his companions and teased the beggars by juggling a silver shilling from one hand to the other, feigning to toss it to them and then catching it again before it left his grasp. As they drew hopefully closer, he made a grand show of pouring the coins in his purse into the palm of his hand and sorting out the silver and large copper pieces. He flung the rest, farthings and ha'-pennies, into the darkness. "Yours if you can find them!" he shouted, and laughed at the scramble and the fights that ensued whenever a coin was discovered. A few, less agile and lured by the promise of silver, crept forward, pleading, ready to grab.

"Fox, come along!" Eduarde insisted. "Let them be." He yanked his friend's sleeve. Reynalde stumbled backwards.

Orlan reached him before the nearest beggars could pounce. A little wizard's fire, ill-directed but sufficiently fearsome, drove them away. He helped Reynalde to his feet.

"Did you see! The wretches knocked me down!"

"No, that was Eddie." Orlan released the youth, who walked a few steps and fell to his knees.

His sister looked disgusted. "Leave him if he's too sotted to walk."

"I wouldn't," Orlan answered. "We won't abandon you to the streets, as you all left me last night."

"Left you?" Jepatha laughed. "Orlan, you left us."

"One moment there at the tea-table, and the next–" Goduin waved his hand. "I thought it magical."

"I don't remember," Orlan admitted.

"'Tis wonder Jep can," Reynalde said. "I couldn't say if you'd left before us, or if *I'd* left before us." He giggled. "God alone could say how a one of us came home."

Julia sighed. As they turned into the Mayor's Parade, Eduarde took Reynalde from Orlan's shoulder. "Come along, Darling. I'll see you home. And you, Julia, my sweet." Together, they walked to their homes on the Square. Jepatha and Goduin remained before the Mayor's Hall.

"I had a friend once," Orlan said as he watched the retreating figures. "The strangest boy. He called everything nonsense."

"What? Wizard's things?"

"All things, save honor and beauty. I never knew what he meant by that—'twas not what we would name right nor pretty. Wizard's Keep as worthless as prayers for God's intercession. He left us..." the thought trailed away.

Godefroi had been wonderful to listen to. Poet, dreamer, ever-questioning nonconformist, he went on about the most odd ideas, not all of them heretical. Godefroi had pictures in his mind. His perceptions, like Orlan's, were acutely sensitive, but where one boy was pained by what he sensed, the other was delighted. Godefroi burst into exclamation over the mist beneath the trees in the garden and the gray-green endlessness of the sea; the plaits of Laurel's silvery hair were like snowfall with sun bright upon it. He spoke of the Faerye and their deception of mortals: their magic made gold coins of pebbles, lovely maids of ancient hags, palaces of ruined cottages. What a talent that would be! Astronomy, Godefroi said, was a waste of time, but there was something in the stars, he knew not what. He had read of music from the Ether and he wondered what manner of creatures sang. He tried to reproduce the images in his illusions and when that proved inadequate, he drew them. He painted canvas screens for the troupe and illustrated the margins of his lesson-books. The sketch he had given Olyr was not his only portrait; Godefroi had worked at others, of Laurel and also of Lord Redmantyl, Olyr, Andemyon, and labored so that they were most like his models. He gave tender, frantic attention to one in particular, of Orlan's cousin Igren as a virgin with a unicorn.

Orlan kept that drawing, for he thought it appropriate to both the imaginative apprentice and the gentle maid. He had laughed at Godefroi's poetic fantasies and earnest artistic efforts, but he missed these same eccentricities once Godefroi had gone.

Jepatha and Goduin stood patiently, waiting for Orlan to continue, but he only said, "They've all gone."

The two grinned at each other. "Good night, M'Lord," Goduin answered, and they went off into the night, leaving the fair young man on the Mayor's doorstep, thinking of other things.

He'd seen Godefroi for the last time that day, not an hour after Olyr's exile. He found the apprentice in his solitary chambers in the Shadu Hall; Godefroi had changed into the gray tunic of a wizard's child, like Orlan, and left his apprentice garb and red ribbons on the chest at the foot of the bed.

"I'm going," he said. "I couldn't stay, not after– I want to be a wizard, but not if I must become so heartless and unforgiving as he is. If My Lord expels Olyr, he expels me too."

"But what of your magedom?" Orlan protested. "You are nearly at your confirmation and if you could wait so long–"

"I can't! I will not abide by useless, binding rules. They've ruined Olyr! You see what comes of them! He has no reason for such strictness, save that it has always been so and cannot be changed."

"If it has not changed, then it be must right," he answered, as he usually answered Godefroi's unorthodoxies. "'Tis horrible, I agree, but we would not cling to wrongful rules. Father would not."

Godefroi shook his head. "You don't understand."

"And you won't stay?"

"I won't stay in this house another day. I'll try to catch Olyr before he goes far from Lyges." He embraced Orlan quickly. "Farewell, my friend." Bundle tucked beneath his travelling cloak, he ran out. He was far from the castle before his absence was discovered.

Orlan still didn't understand. Godefroi must be mad. He didn't behave as other people, ordinary folk or wizards. He couldn't accept life for what it was; he had to know why. Why must he perform this common courtesy? Why must he repeat this ritual? Why was there magic? He questioned everything. The principles he took upon himself meant something to him. When he thought traditions were useless, he simply disregarded them. He lived by *noblesse oblige* because he believed that the powerful and privileged had a duty to aid the poor and subjugated. Godefroi loved without hope of reciprocation, took vows only when he intended to keep them, stood by his friends regardless of the circumstances—not because these actions were part of the ancient and debased chivalric code, but because he thought them right. He would follow his own code of honor to the end, even when it required that he leave his apprenticeship and his magic. Orlan could not imagine so great a sacrifice for friendship's sake or for a vague principle, whichever Godefroi had meant. He wouldn't do such a thing even if he thought it ought to be done. No one in their right mind would.

Of course, Godefroi would have gone that same summer, two years past, but both he and Olyr should have departed Wizardes Cliff under a better light. Their hopes had been destroyed, prospects ruined, lives blighted and turned into new channels they had not planned nor foreseen. Orlan knew that it was unlikely he would ever see either young man again.

The storm went on for days. Orlan watched it, terrified, and clapped his hands over his ears at each clash. It became worse, not more tolerable, with the repetition. He wanted to crawl away like a frightened animal and hide in the bottom-most catacombs of the castle until all the bright light and loud noise was gone, but he was caught by a different sort of fear and fascination, and he could not look away.

He had heard tales, as Julia and most of Christendom had, of the Lightmaster's storms, but he had never seen his father's fury before. In those days, he began to understand the mortal fear of magic. Wizards were not entirely human; they couldn't be. What human was capable of *that* fierce display? He had first believed that this was the reason for his own fear, but the truth was more terrible: he was afraid of his father's vast power, but he was more afraid at the knowledge that he was developing that same power in himself. He possessed such magics. One day, he would be as fearsome as Lord Redmantyl.

Would he be able to command his magic as his father did? Redmantyl never lost control; Orlan marveled at that still. The storm was a display of wizardly anger, disappointment, even heartache that he must banish a promising boy he had trained. Olyr had been Redmantyl's first apprentice. He'd been part of the wizard's household for years, loved as dearly as a son. Redmantyl had taken such pride in him. It must have wounded the wizard deeply to do what he had done. The storm was an emotional outburst, but not fury run wild. The wizard only released what he could not contain within himself, as a lesser man might weep or curse. His self-discipline was not relaxed.

Could Orlan keep himself so well? Even a little laxity, as Olyr had shown, could catch him off guard and ruin him. He too would be cast out.

Many of the household retreated to Lyges to wait out their master's fury or quit his service altogether. Mathias and Andemyon hid in their rooms. Simon bickered with the remaining servants, insulted Alfryda to tears, shouted at the boys until they ran to avoid him, but when Redmantyl was near the chatelaine was silent. The most stunning news came at the end of it: Nel was mother to a child.

"Gods above and below, a mage-child," Redmantyl swore in amazement when the story came to his ears. There had been no great fuss at Nel's baby until the frightened villagers discovered who its father was. Then, they had cast her out; her family ejected her from the house and the parish priest would not let her sleep in the church pews. Redmantyl also blamed the girl for Olyr's fall, but when he heard of her plight he was not entirely unsympathetic. He recognized her persistent petitions to be allowed audience in the castle.

His colorless eyes were icy when she entered the Great Hall.

"They say the storming's because of me!" Nel began. "Olyr's fallen and they say I'm at fault!" Her voice rose to an indignant wail.

"Not entirely," said Redmantyl. "Olyr has his share of responsibility, but a vow of celibacy cannot be broken by one alone."

"I've done naught wrong!" she protested. "'Tisn't fair that I'm blamed! I never–!" The air around the wizard sparkled and she stopped suddenly.

"Do you deny? Did he force himself on you, Girl?"

"N-no, M'Lord. 'Twas a simple wooing, as I have with any lad I take a fancy to."

"Olyr is no ordinary lad," the wizard told her. "You do not woo a mage as you would a cowherd! You knew what he was."

"I'm not at fault!" she cried. "I've done naught any maid past sixteen hasn't a right to and Olyr might've said yes or no as he pleased. 'Twas his choice, and if he's ruined that's his own too. It's none of my doing! And I've got the worst of it! I must stay here and care for a child with no father to name!" She was sobbing. "How can I live here? They'll kill me to make the storming stop! What'll I do?"

Redmantyl watched as she clutched her skirt and wiped away her tears. "Do you wish to leave Lyges, Maid?" And when she nodded, he said: "I will give you sufficient funds. Take yourself and your brat and go. Leave this day. I do not want you in my sight again."

Nel glared at him sullenly. "M'Lord, I won't be," she sniffed.

"Never."

Simon had been silent throughout this interview, but once the girl had been paid and escorted out, he spoke. "She wouldn't come to 'arm if not for ye. Trouble over Olyr? Bloody 'ell! We'd 'ave no trouble if ye'd keep yer own bloody temper." The words were muttered, but Redmantyl heard.

"What does that mean?"

The chatelaine hesitated, then burst out bravely: "Ye talk of the poor lad's control and ye–"

"Simon, enough!"

"It's not just!"

The wizard was furious, sparkling, ready to strike. Simon stood up to him, tight-lipped and terrified, but daring his master to lose himself in anger. Redmantyl surrendered first.

"Perhaps not," he said at last. "I had no choice."

"Seeing as ye're the best of all wizards," the servant did not conceal his sarcasm. "Ye cannot change–"

"No! Simon, leave me!"

"Aye, M'Lord." And Simon had nearly gone too. Only years of loyalty kept him, but their friendship was sorely tested by this quarrel and things were never quite the same. Orlan did not know which, servant or master, refused to forgive, but a cool formality crept into all their conversations afterwards.

The storm ended, but the dark days never lifted from Wizardes Cliff. Tedora, Laurel, Olyr, and Godefroi—all were lost, and Redmantyl became increasingly gloomy. The most distracting emotions had been burned away and the ashes did not trouble him. Nothing troubled him now. Orlan could only guess at the depths of his father's sorrow. He sensed the stormy surface, but the wizard's heart remained an impenetrable mystery. He could offer no comfort. Silence stood unbreakable; that had not changed from that first stormy day to this.

Orlan went into the Mayor's Hall. The porter in his cubby woke and blinked at him incuriously, then turned back to his sleep. A door opened in the gallery above and Ilset's large, silk-robed figure appeared at the top of the stairs.

"Oh, 'tis you, Chyelde. Is my husband with you?"

"No, My Layn. I haven't seen him tonight."

"You were with your friends among the local youths?"

Orlan nodded. "Shall I go and look for him?"

This was an empty offer. Certainly, Houarde was at a late-hours tavern, but Orlan had no idea which one. There must be a hundred about the city; he had visited more than dozen himself. And he was positive that Houarde was unharmed. This had happened before. Houarde had not returned from the Whitsuntide festival until long after the last stragglers had left the Square. Orlan had gone out then at Ilset's request and made inquiries of the servants who rolled away the empty kegs and pulled down the maypole; none had seen the Portreeve go. He did not dare to search further for Houarde that night, for the city had been new to him and frightening for its size. He'd feared being lost in the dark streets alone and so returned to Ilset with apologies. He knew his way about now, but he also knew that a search was useless.

Ilset must know this too, for she smiled. "No, Chyelde. That won't be necessary. He'll be home when he will. I bid you good night." As she returned to her chambers, Orlan went up to his own bed.

He woke late the next morning at a gentle nudging in the small of his back. The small servant-boy stood at the bedside. "Chyelde, there's a maid to see you."

"Maid?" In his drowsy stupor, Orlan thought it must be the drab from the Bag o' Nails with fresh accusations, but he rose and dressed with the boy's assistance. His head was splitting and his eyes sore and tender, too large for their sockets, but his training made him ignore the pain.

Ren stood in the front hall, looking about nervously as if she expected to be thrown out of this grand residence at any moment. She smiled when she saw him on the stairs.

"Rennie!" He came down to her. "What is it, Pet?"

"Mother sent me. You've not finished your business with her."

"Yes, I know. We had no time yesterday."

"She ask you to come along as soon as you may." Soft, brown eyes turned up to him, Ren touched the pomander still tied at her skirt. "Orlan, please?"

"As you wish, my pet." He gave the girl his most engaging smile. "I'll be along to the Whitelm soon, I promise you. Before the week is out!"

elfen

After the Salamander closed at midnight, the boys remained. It was too hot for them to go into the streets and they were not ready to go home. They had brought together the coins left in their pockets to purchase a jug of red wine before the alekeeper went to her bed; it was nearly empty now and resting against Orlan's knee as he lay across a table-top, drowsy and drunk into languor. He did not feel so strange as he had in his first days at Storm Port, nor like that time they had gone to the Jade Dragon on a lark and taken tiny porcelain cups of green tea, which had no taste beyond that of stale water but left his head spinning so that he had not known right from left. Tonight, the effects of the wine were quite pleasant. He was content to stay here until he was made to leave. The other boys were about the room, seated, lying on the floor, in a similar stupor.

Jepatha spoke: "Orlan, will you do some magic?"

"What?"

"Something magical. You are a wizard, are you not?"

"Not yet. But I can do some pretty tricks." He clapped his hands; the air above him filled with bright sparks like those spewed up from a stirred fire. This trick always pleased his friends, and they were amused again. The sparks fell to his chest, leaving a smell of singed linen.

"Do more," said Goduin.

"What would you like to see?" He took up the jug and drank cautiously; this tunic was the last clean one he owned.

"I have heard that you may light fires without tinder."

He had never dared to show them that magic. "Yes, I can."

"Will you light a candle?" Jepatha took down one from the wall, snuffed the flame, and set it on a table. "Can you do that?"

"Without moving from this spot, my friend." Orlan gestured dramatically, but the candle remained unlit. He blinked, then laughed. "I've missed the bloody wick! It may be too far away. Wait." He stared at the candle intensely, then waved again and the flame burned brightly. "There you are."

"Imps of Satan," Tades whispered.

"No such thing." Orlan tried to sit up. "I am a magician of some talent, no more. It will be my profession, as shopkeeping will be to all of you, save Reynalde, My Lord Mayor. The weight of a grown man's world will settle on us all in some way and sooner than we think."

Eduarde laughed. "God's thumbs, you sound like Houarde Portreeve!"

"The Portreeve is right, I think," Reynalde said with some reflection. "One has a certain time in youth to be spent in pursuit of good fun. But he has this time extend from twenty to seventy, and it cannot go on past thirty–" The youth paused to consider. "Or five and thirty, if you are allowed and inclined."

"It will end sooner than that for me," Orlan answered. "I must put all games aside this Christmas and it'll be five years before I resume any pleasurable pursuit."

The others were astonished. "Why?" Reynalde asked.

"I must avoid all temptations of the flesh. I shall be a mage—sober, chaste, sleepless."

"Is that why you won't–?" Jepatha grinned.

"Yes, that's why."

Eduarde took the jug from the table and sat at Orlan's feet, resting his cheek on the youth's upraised knee, winding an arm about his calf. "I've seen mages. They all look like such stiff sticks. Why would you take that path to wizardry?"

"It is the only path. You train in magic as you would for any profession, and when you enter magedom you become like a journeyer at the end of 'prenticeship. You must travel to perfect the craft and learn more than may be learned from one master. My master has always been my father. He is wise, but I should not learn all I know from him alone."

"But you must do it celibate?" Reynalde asked.

"And sleepless?" Tades added. "You'll never sleep?"

"Not as much as I would like to now. And yes, without a taste of wine or salt or sugar or good roast beef and without the company of any pretty maid. All for five years."

"For Christ's love, why?"

"Mages must vow to do so. Magic is built on self-control and magedom is magic's greatest test. It is the only way to become a wizard." But these reasons did not sound so convincing as they had when he'd discussed this with Mathias and Godefroi. These boys had no magic and no interest in wizardry beyond that of a spectator's curiosity in the unusual. "'Tis a test of will," he tried to explain. "If I keep to my vows I'll prove that I have command of myself in all parts and am fit to be called a true wizard."

"I could never do it," Reynalde said.

"You think you have so much will?" Goduin asked.

"I don't know," Orlan answered after a long silence. "'Tis easy to fail. My father's first 'prentice did. He broke his vows and Father banished him."

"Why go to such trouble?" Jepatha asked.

"If you have magic, you can do nothing else. I've never wanted to be anything but a wizard." But he wondered as he spoke: Why must he give over every pleasure? He was no less magical now, drunk, wanton, drowsy, than he'd been in his novice purity. Was unbending discipline really so important in every aspect of life? Weakness was not evil. He didn't abuse his power in his pursuit of amusement. He would not become a renegade. He remained a magician; he would be so even if the rules and restraints of wizardry cast him out for having fun. It didn't seem fair that the promising and talented, but not so strong-willed, were punished all their lives for one lapse.

"Then you'd best enjoy life's pleasures now." Eduarde offered the refilled goblet. The backs of his fingers rubbed against the underside of Orlan's thigh, sending ripples of unformed sexual thrill through him. "Drink up while you may."

"I think we've both had far too much. Stop that—it tickles." If the others observed this exchange, they ignored it.

"Were you ever taught to be anything else?" asked Reynalde.

"No."

"Hell, even for all the rules of wizardry, I think it'd be better to grow up in one place and know from the beginning what you are meant to be," said Eduarde. "I've never had an idea. I am fond of my father, but I do not wish to be like him. Reynalde, recall when you and I were first friends at Maryesfont? I was seven years old and you just six."

"He's going to tell you how I cried for my mother for days after they left me," Reynalde announced.

Eduarde chuckled. "No, I wasn't. I did too, you know, when I was first there, but that was more than two years before. No, Fox, I was thinking of the day my father and his steward rode up. I did not know which my father was."

Reynalde laughed. "I remember."

"He looked like all other men to me. I hadn't seen him since I was very small, and so forgot his face." He took the goblet from Orlan and emptied it. "I used to ask if I could come back to Storm Port with him, but he said it wasn't best and he left me. Oh, he had me come home eventually, but it didn't matter so much then."

The others nodded solemnly. Tades, seated on the floor beneath a table, looked ready to cry.

"At least you were never lodged in a Bishop's house," said Jepatha. "The pious bastard used to box my ears if I didn't answer to my lessons correctly. Horrid old brute. By Marye, I hated him."

"You'll never be a Bishop, I'll wager," Eduarde answered.

"Not I," the boy laughed.

"And I never wish to be a great merchant or Sheriff of any city," Eduarde continued. He reached for the wine, but Goduin had taken it. "But Orlan'll be a wizard, as his father is. He's only had the life he knows and he's happy in it. If I had lived in my parents' house, I might like them more than I do." He kissed Orlan's kneecap and smiled engagingly. "D'ye know, M'Lord, I've thought since I heard of your father's castle that it sounded grand."

"Yes, it was," Orlan said.

The keeper of the Salamander, a huge women with her hair unkerchiefed and wild and her figure in enormous bulges beneath her nightshirt, came down the stairway behind the bar and peered at them suspiciously. "Are you still here? I thought you lot had gone an hour ago, 'twas so quiet. No matter, you must leave now. I can't have this room such a mess in the morning." She shuffled toward the door and pushed it open. "Go on with you. And leave that glassware."

A little wine was left in the jug, so they passed it from mouth to mouth, each gulping until the last drop was gone.

"We'll be on our way, Goode Keeper." Reynalde flashed a smile and made his best bow. "Gramercy for your hospitality, and a good night."

"What's left of it," she muttered.

"Where do we go now?" Goduin wondered as he went out.

"Home," said Jepatha. "Right now, I want nothing so much as sleep." He blew out the candle and followed his cousin.

Eduarde exited last. As Orlan stepped down from the doorstep, the boy took him by the elbow and abruptly pulled him into the shadows behind the open door. Gently, he pressed two fingertips against Orlan's lips to silence him, then pushed him back against the brick wall and bestowed one swift, hard kiss.

"I'm not going home yet," he whispered. "Come with me?"

Orlan was not especially surprised at the playful invitation; he had caught more than one hint that Eduarde's tastes were broad enough to encompass boys as well as maids, and it had been impossible to mistake the young man's intentions tonight. Although he did not have the Christian upbringing to be shocked, and he was even a little flattered, Orlan's careful self-discipline had not yet relaxed so much to take him so far. He might drink to excess at Eduarde's encouragement, he might explore brothels, but he was not ready for this initiation.

"No," he answered and pushed away the hand lingering in his silver hair. "Eduarde, even if I were inclined, you know I couldn't–"

Eduarde released him. "'Tis pity. You are already a mage, My Lord." Still smiling, he went down the street after their friends.

The bells of St. Khrystopher's began to chime at sunset of the shortest night of the year, summoning all to the Midsummer Eve sermon of Samandramas. This was the highest holiday of the summer as Maryemas fell during the plague months. The Midsummer celebration had begun three days before, with the ancient Feast of St. John. A carnival raged in the city streets and bonfires roared in the bazaar; tonight, the festival would continue until the townsfolk gathered to attend Mass, then they fasted to take communion on Sunday.

Orlan had not been in the cathedral before, but he consented that evening to accompany the Mayor and her husband. He had not been at Mass since his confirmation. There was a chapel at Wizardes Cliff, but Lord Redmantyl did not insist that any in his household remain pious; he could not be called a pious man himself. The wizard did not accept Christian dogma as the whole truth of the universe and he had taught Orlan to be skeptical as well. But Orlan's friends would be at the service tonight and he was intrigued by the news that thespians would perform the tale of St. Samandra.

Orlan wore his long cloak to cover his informal clothes, for he would be highly visible in the Mayor's pew to the immediate right of the altar. The important folk of Storm Port were seated in pews before the great supporting columns at the front of the cathedral: the grim Justice Hugobarde like a judge of the Old Testament, and all his children; Leobolde Goldesmith, openly impatient; the ancient Damia Shinsplitter, retired Mayor and former Shieldmaid with the Redlyon, still fearsome though one hundred and eighteen; Ozualte Spicemerchant, his wife, and their children—Drusilla with her rosary and Julia and Reynalde whispering private jokes—the fabulous Amaris Silksmerchant, her own wardrobe the finest example of her trade; Rosamonde Lilie, who imported crystalware from Italy, and her daughters; Eduarde with his parents, and an uncle who had returned from a successful merchant's venture in Danemark and had taken too much wine in the afternoon celebrations. The lesser folk stood behind, crowding the vast floor of the nave. At Orlan's side, Houarde was nodding, nearly asleep although Mass had not yet begun, and Ilset read from her prayer book.

The bells pealed, solemnly, joyously, from the towers high above the vaulted roof. Within, St. Khrystopher's was ablaze from countless candles on tall stands, in votive stations, in the hands of the choir in the loft above the vestry. The Bishop of Greenstephan emerged from the little door beneath the painted crucifix, splendid in his ceremonial robes of purest white samite, his golden vestments, his tall, jeweled mitre and lengths of rosary that swung nearly to the floor. Priests in attendance followed, then the chaplains who assisted them. The sweet voices of the choir rose in clear, faultless notes, soaring into the darkness of the rafters and the heights of the cavernous dome, swelling over the bass voice of the Bishop. They sang a song in praise of the sainted Queen.

All who attended the Mass were familiar with the story. In the kingdom of Portugal, three hundred years past, the infant daughter of an impoverished noble family was orphaned by Spanish raiders and left to the sanctuary of the Sisters of the Sacred Heart; as a young maid, she had never been beyond the convent walls, nor seen any man except her Father Confessor. On Midsummer Day, this maid received a vision of the Blessed Virgin Mother, who told her that she was chosen to save her homeland from the Spaniards. In those days, Portugal was beset on all borders and nearly absorbed into the Spanish Empire. The King in Coimbra paid tribute to the greedy Spanish monarch and was considered a vassal who governed only by the greater King's grace.

The maid, Samandra, escaped from the abbey and the Mother Abbess who thought her mad. She journeyed, alone and on foot, to Coimbra, where she sought out the Vassal-King Julios and bade him fight against the unholy enemies who stood at their borders and lay siege to their ports. Then, as always, Portugal depended on its sea trade, and times were desperate. Julios was astounded by this maid, little more than a child, but he saw the holiness of her and believed the truth of her visions, and he prepared to do battle against Spain. Samandra herself did not fight; she would remain unstained by bloodshed. She was not the patron saint of warrior-maids, but the patron of all—wives and children, parents, lovers—who prayed for soldiers in battle. The maid never set foot on a battlefield, only prayed for victory and advised Julios and his captains to stay true to their cause, for God was on their side.

The performance would, of course, feature Samandra's miracles, the signs of her blessed state. She showed her true goodness with her first miracle: when the Spaniards learned of the maiden's influence over Julios, they tried to thwart the rebellion with her abduction and use as a hostage, but Samandra was not afraid and spoke kindly to her captors. The Spanish guards were so overcome by the gentle girl that they released her unharmed, and some joined her in the liberation of Portugal. Samandra then showed the justice of her cause with her second miracle: when the city of Lisbon was besieged and it seemed that all was lost, a storm arose from nowhere and destroyed the Spanish fleet. But the true sign of Grace was shown by the maid's third miracle, the most thrilling of all: when Prince Henri was wounded fatally in battle, the prayers of the sainted Samandra brought him back from the edge of death. With victory certain and his only child alive, King Julios rewarded the maid with marriage to Henri, so that she would be queen of the land she had saved.

Orlan knew that this tale was not entirely true. Yes, a war had been led by King Julios, who freed Portugal from Spain, and Samandra had married the prince, later Henri III, but it was doubtful that the miracles had actually occurred. However, the story was no less popular for its lack of verity. It was especially important to Normans, for St. Samandra was grandmother to Gabriela, the Dark Lady of Portugal, who was given in marriage to the Norman Emperor Robert the Good; together, they were parents to Eduarde Redlyon, grandparents to Duke Dafythe, and great-grandparents to the present Emperor. Sainted blood and the blessing of glorious victory ran in the royal family; Samandra was revered throughout the Empire and the Portuguese were welcome for her sake.

The song of celebration faded gently to silence. The Bishop gave his blessing to the congregation, and a flutter of activity in the west transept drew all attention. The play was beginning. A dark-haired maid meant to be Samandra in the Abbey, for she was accompanied by a group of white-cowled Sisters, spoke of her visions of the Virgin and of the victories poor Portugal would see. The Sisters expressed their disbelief, but not unkindly, until the Mother Abbess questioned Samandra's sanity. She asked the maid: "Would Our Lady choose you for such a fate when so many are more deserving?"

Samandra replied: "I do not know, but one must be chosen in a time of need and Our Holy Lady would bless those who did not expect to be blessed." The audience chuckled.

The Bishop spoke here, praising Samandra's humility, for she knew herself to be a humble sinner and proved her worth by calling herself unworthy. Was that not a lesson for all of them, both mighty and meek?

"Aye, but ye may be right for all that," Houarde muttered under his breath. Ilset nudged him to be silent.

As the pageant continued, Orlan thought that these thespers were not as good as his father's patronized troupe. The performers stood stiffly in their tableaus like paintings come to life. They showed little genuine motion, little feeling in their words, little truth in their tale. Of course, he could not expect the bawdy jokes and rough-house of street thespers in a church play, but Tedora had always done better no matter how religious or secular her subject. She would have done much better here. She would have given the audience more to see and had them hear words to truly feel the wonder of the tale. She would have told them a story and made it seem true. For all the drama presented here, the Bishop might as well read from a book of saints' lives.

Here in this cathedral, Tedora had made angels fly. Wires were run up to– there: Orlan found the thick, oaken beams that crossed the ceiling to support the transept roof, high above the scene enacted below. If one were to throw wires over those beams, then fasten them about the smallest maids in the troupe, the easiest to draw upwards, it would be a simple trick to have angels hovering over the Nativity. But how glorious it would have been! Storm Port would have talked for weeks afterward of the "flying" maids at Mass. It would have been Tedora's finest conjuring trick, as well as her last. Orlan was sorry she was dead—sometimes, he even missed her—but it seemed fitting that she should die for a spectacle rather than from plague or childbirth or eighty years hence, aged and enfeebled. The performance was her life. She was well-remembered by her troupe and honored as much by them as any saint or queen she had ever played.

The troupe performing this Samandramas had set up their storm scene during the last prayer. A city, Lisbon, was painted on rush screens and a blue cloth stretched across the transept to represent the ocean. Thunder roared through the cathedral most effectively, but Orlan could see the thin sheets of metal rattling behind the screens. Samandra and King Julios stood and watched the Spanish fleet, unseen, sinking, and they rejoiced. Orlan wondered if the maiden saint had been a powerful but unrecognized magician; her miracles were very like his father's spells. She had mastered the minds of weaker mortals. She had called up storms. If the tale were true, she had recovered the life of the Prince.

The irony was that the saint's powers first revealed themselves on a Midsummer, for Midsummer Eve was also a night of Wizard's Keep. This same night, while Christian folk celebrated Samandra's victory and perhaps recalled the seasonal festivals that predated even St. John, Lord Redmantyl was in the woods beyond Wizardes Cliff, enacting the rites of the wizards' private ceremony. Orlan would not know the secrets of this ritual until he was tested and confirmed a wizard; he imagined it to be a sort of vigil set up by the powerful. But against what? His training indicated that he was being prepared for vigilance. He knew that he should have fasted and spent these days between St. John's Eve and tonight in sleepless meditation, but he hadn't. How could he sit quietly when all of Storm Port was ablaze with festival?

Redmantyl sometimes referred to powerful Others in the universe, but Orlan had thought this only a magical myth. It was difficult to believe in things unseen, to understand the importance of the wizard's constant vigilance without knowing what dangers he stood against. Now, in this unguarded moment, Orlan knew that he should have protected himself; he was aware of the presence of some great power nearby. He looked up and around, as if it were outside the cathedral, pressing to the stained glass, trying to force an entrance. It sought him.

But there was nothing. No one else in the vast nave seemed aware of this terrible presence; they did not have the magical perception to feel what was there. Orlan didn't know what he sensed, but he was the only one who truly needed to know, the only one in danger. It reached for him; he could barely keep himself from drawing back. He felt the power of it, surging like a storm of unearthly brightness, flame and furies, all that would terrify and transfix him.

The tin sheets behind the painted screens rattled their thunder again, almost in mockery.

Orlan bowed his head, hands to his face, and said a prayer—or was it a spell?—his father had taught him for his protection. But even as he spoke, he knew that a Christian church, in the middle of High Mass, was not the place for this. He did not belong here. He was not part of this faith. His father had told him that a wizard should not serve any gods. Their touch brought madness. They could destroy.

"Chyelde?" Houarde nudged him. "Lad?" Others nearby, his friends and their families, were trying not to stare at him.

"I'm fine," Orlan whispered. "It's fine now."

In the transept, at the height of Julios' victory celebration, Prince Henri's battered body was brought in. No blood was allowed in the church, for that would be blasphemy, but the thesper in the role of the

Prince, lain across the arms of his fellows, looked dead. His face was pale and still. His limbs hung slack, enshrouded in a limp, white blouse, and his bright hair-

Orlan left his seat and ran from the cathedral.

"Chyelde, wait!" Houarde shouted behind him. Orlan stood and waited, jostled by the dancing crowds outside St. Khrystopher's, his breath in quick gasps. The cathedral reached into the dark sky; there was nothing but churchyard around it.

"Are you well, Orlan?" Houarde asked as he reached the trembling youth.

"I don't know," Orlan answered honestly. "Gods, I must be going mad. My head-"

"Aye, you looked odd at the Mass, and 'twas more than a sickness at that Bishop's long wind. Are you fevered?" He put a large, moist hand on the boy's brow. "Plague's about, you know. 'Tis said that two have fallen ill at the dockside this sennight."

"No, I think not." Orlan stepped back. "But I should go from Storm Port soon. I've stayed longer than I planned." A sharp, popping sound erupted nearby; Orlan flinched. A bright flare shot up into the sky and exploded into a fiery red ball that sputtered into sparkling droplets. "W-what's that?"

"Oh, 'tis rockets, made by the Orient folk with some sort of magical powder. They are popular here at festivals. Never mind that." He took Orlan's arm. "I know what'll soothe you, Lad. Come with me."

They found their way to a tavern; Orlan was unsure which one. Houarde ordered a glass of red wine. "This'll do you much good. Drink, Chyelde. Recall, you took your first drinks with me at Adyna's house?"

"It was not a month ago," Orlan said between sips. But it seemed much longer. He felt as if he had been here for years and Wizardes Cliff was no more than a memory from a long-past age.

"You're not so often in my company these days. Off with the lads, eh?"

"Yes, Syre."

"Ah, they're a lively lot!" Houarde laughed. "They've shown you a good time in your visit?"

"Aye, Syre."

"As it should be, my lad. You ought to run with boys your own age and not be shut up with old wizards and their books and spells as if your life had already flown. How do you feel? Still shaking in your boots, I think. Here, Keeper!" Houarde called to the man behind the bar. "Have you got a pipe? I know the places near the Jade Dragon barter for their weeds."

The man grunted, but he brought out a box from a shelf beneath and stuffed a fingers-grip of brown leaves into the delicately carved, stained bowl of a long-stemmed ivory pipe. Houarde took it up and lit the concoction with a wooden spill, then offered it to Orlan. "Here's the thing for you, Lad. If this cannot calm your quaking heart, nothing can."

"Tobacco?" Orlan asked. He had seen pipes before—they were popular among merchant folk, and Olyr had smoked during his magedom to ease his appetite and relieve fatigue—but the smell had always made him queasy.

"No, the leaves of another plant," the Portreeve was smiling. "Of dried flowers of the East. Oh, 'tis much more soothing than our western plants. It's not to my fancy, you understand, but 'tis wondrous for the nerves and I've never seen one in so much need of calming. Many's the time I've known Ilset tend to her headaches with this."

The smell was more acrid than tobacco. Orlan gingerly took the mouthpiece between his lips, drew the smoke in, and coughed.

Houarde pushed the wine goblet to his lips. "You must take it into your lungs, not your nose! The smoke takes hold quickly and there's not so much of that choking. You'll feel right again in an instant." He tipped up the glass; wine spilled over Orlan's cheek. "Go on, Lad. Down with it all! We'll get you another. Keeper!" The barkeeper poured more wine indifferently. "Better?"

Orlan nodded.

Houarde gulped his own ale and watched Orlan carefully. The queer, frightened look had gone and some pink colored his face again. His hands did not tremble as they lifted the wineglass. "Aye, 'tis good. How do you like our Samandramas festival? You've not seen one like it before, I imagine, to fuddle your head so."

"No, never," Orlan answered. "We do nothing at Midsummer at home, even if the thespers are there. Adyna taught me the story of St. Samandra when I was small, but we never had such a play at Wizardes Cliff." He took the pipe that Houarde offered again, drew in the smoke, coughed, and reached for his wine. The combined effect was relaxing. It was strange to think now that he had been so upset. He took a deep breath. "It seems to me that our most revered saints are warriors who led armies against Spain, or were made martyrs at Spanish hands. Does it seem so to you?"

"I've not thought much on it, Lad. Is it so?"

"I cannot say surely, for I have no copy of *The Lives of Our Saints* at hand. My father has such books. He would know certainly."

"You may be right for that," Houarde replied. "My good wife spoke only the other night at dinner—you were not there—of the damnable troubles of Europe. There's been another of those revolts in France, with the common folk setting themselves up against the Emperor. They cry about breaking off enough, but my Ilset notes that we never hear of them doing more than throwing rocks at constables. You know why that is, Lad?"

"No, Syre."

"'Tis that they know full well if they break away, they'd stay independent only 'til Spain claimed them."

"Would they?" Orlan asked politely, although he knew nothing of imperial or international affairs.

"So I've heard Ilset say. Oh, they'd be right swallowed up!" the Portreeve shouted. "That's why the German kingdoms cling together long after the last Roman Emperor's gone to dust in her grave, you see, and the Lombardy and Neapolitan kings gather about the Pope—to keep themselves safe. Look, my lad, at the little lands living 'tween our Kharles, the Czar, and bastard Spain. They must make themselves pets to one to keep safe from the others. If that Frankish lot ever broke away, they'd have to ally themselves with the Germans or be swallowed by Spain in a month and there'd be blood over their precious countryside then!" He dampened his throat with a deep drink.

"Aye, Syre," Orlan said, but he was scarcely able to concentrate upon Houarde's words. He felt as if he were both sleepy and drunk at once, as if his brain were shrouded by strange mists.

"Look at the Incans!" Houarde cried with enthusiasm.

"What of them?" Orlan lay his head on his folded arms.

"Bastard Spain's been battling for that little Empire's gold since we settled this half o' the world. If our good Kings Robert, the Redlyon, and old Kharles had not allowed to protect them, they'd be overrun with Spaniards as a carcass with maggots."

An alemaiden shoved his shoulder. "Here, what's wrong with ye, Lad?"

"There's naught wrong with the lad," Houarde laughed. "A maid in your place and you've not seen a lad deep in his mugs?"

She lifted Orlan's chin to study his eyes. "He's a queer look to 'im."

Houarde shrugged. "He's meant to be so. Wizard, you see, my girl."

"Wizard?" She stepped back, alarmed, but Orlan looked harmless. "Ye be the magical lad I've heard of?"

"That's him exactly."

"`Sblud," she said. "I've not seen a wizard before this. Are they all so oddly colored? Ye've no color t'ye at all."

"No, 'tis only me," Orlan answered. "My family."

"Still, ye look a lovely lad for that. And a wizard. Now, I'm wondering..." She sat down beside him. "Wondering what?" And she laughed.

Orlan blushed. "I'm afraid I couldn't tell you."

"What? A fine, big lad as yerself? Never?"

He shook his head and sent his thoughts fluttering wildly like birds in a disturbed cage. The wards he had set against unwanted perceptions were dissolving, devoured by the encroaching mist. Freed, his senses expanded beyond his control; it was as if he were gaining his first magics over again. Too much information flooded him: the stench of the tavern—beer, wine on leather, smoke, sweat, urine-soaked rushes. The sluggish porridge-like presence of Houarde and the warm, complacent energy of the maid. The abrasive texture of his own shirt against his skin. The bright-hot points of dancing flame on the candles. The lazy curl of bluish haze that rose from the pipe in his hands. The footfalls and shouts on the street. He couldn't shut it out.

A hand, cool, palm rough and calloused, touched his. "Now that misfortune's easily set right, if 'tis yer pleasure to."

Orlan looked up and tried to focus his eyes on hers. Her pulsebeat thudded in her fingertips. Her hair glowed in candlelight as if it were more alive than herself. She was smiling.

It was not as if such offers had never been made before—nor so abruptly—but he refused them all; he had his reasons. He could not entirely abandon the belief that he cheapened himself, his place, his honor, his magic with the careless act of bedding someone he didn't know. He was afraid of fathering a child on a woman he would never see again. When looked on such women, he saw his mother. The cajoling voices and caresses were more pitiable than enticing. He thought of Olyr; he knew what could happen. And he recalled the mage's maxim on mastering sexual urges: it would be far easier to endure five celibate years if he remained a virgin before. Orlan believed that this was indeed true. He had observed that the appetites of his friends were more articulately formed than his own, for they knew what they desired and he could only imagine. He shouldn't know. But that did not always belay his curiosity.

He wondered what it would be like to touch her, and the thought sent a warm thrill through him. He was aware of stirrings in his own body, not yet manifest in the flesh, but the first signs of a deeper awakening. If it were not for the approaching bonds of magedom, he would be ready, even eager, to explore this adult mystery. And why not? He was not a mage yet. He had tested his will against other temptations and he felt certain he could put them away from him at the appropriate time. He had sufficient control of himself to uphold his vows when he took them.

But this was different. Sexual desire was not the same as hunger for salt or wine or blooded meats; although the infringement of any one mage-vow would result in a young magician's banishment, the vow of chastity was held in higher significance than the dietary strictures, though less than the keeping of vigilance. There was danger, he knew, in flirting with sensual experience when he didn't fully understand its power over him. Here was something new and strange, its force unpredictable. Did he have the self-control to repress his sexuality once he had roused it?

And he hesitated for more than the sake of his magedom. Something in his sprawled awareness—though he could not locate the exact source—told him that this was not the right time. She was not the right person. He shouldn't do this. It was wrong; he told himself so. Yet, weighed against the impulses that urged him on, his fears, his cares, his long-trained disciplines didn't seem to matter so much. He couldn't think of them.

"What's your name?" he asked.

"Doesn't matter, Pet. You won't know it again by morning."

Houarde chuckled into his mug. "More to see to your nerves, eh, Lad?"

"Will ye come up with me?" She took his hand and Orlan did not resist as she led him to a curtained recess on one side of the room. He felt clumsy, large and heavy. His feet were unsure beneath him, as if he might move no more than slowly. He stumbled at the foot of a steep flight of stairs.

"Ye be light in the head, Lad?"

"I think I am." Orlan rested his head on one drawn-up knee. The world whirled, too fast for him to perceive. The floor, the boards beneath him, seemed soft. Dust crowded his eyes and nostrils, and for a moment he thought he was going to be sick.

"`Tis hard to say with ye, yer peculiar eyes `n' all. Can ye stand?" As she helped him up, her arm slipped about his waist and squeezed. "There y'go. Never fear, ye won't need to stand for long." They made their way to the top. "This room here." At the doorway she tugged him again and Orlan fell across the foot of the cot. She giggled.

He blinked, dazed. "What–?"

She knelt beside him and pulled at his tunic lacings. "Nothing, my darling. Naught for ye to worry over." She brushed the tangled curls from his face with tenderness and something like wonder. "Oh, ye are a pretty thing." She kissed him. The sensation surprised Orlan even in his stupor. Tales of romance and glory often spoke of the sweetness of a maiden's kiss, but all he tasted was beer. He thought of the women he had drunk with and joked with and patted as if he had touched many women before; he thought of jerkins and shifts left open to expose breasts, of dimpled knees revealed beneath hefted skirts, of Eduarde's more rough, insistent mouth on his, and of the pale, tight, flexing hindquarters of the mariner in the alleyway, and he reached up. He caught her about the waist and she yielded; another kiss, not so gentle, and she was soft against him. She took his wrist and pressed it to the blankets with a smile.

"Have patience, my lovely. Patience." She kissed his face again, then his collar as she bared it. His tunic lay open to the waist, and she pulled at his shirt, following the space of the gap with a succession of swift kisses.

Orlan wanted to respond, but the same influences which had relaxed his inhibitions now restrained him. His pulse pounded. His innards quivered at each kiss. But nothing more. He wasn't prepared to do this. In that void between impulse and action, discipline intruded. Remembrance of what he was and what he must be overpowered his first desire. He could not lose himself so easily. This was wrong; this was wrong.

"No," he whispered as he tore his mouth from hers.

She laughed. "Is it *No,* ye don't want to or *No,* ye mustn't?"

"I can't–" She sat astride him, feather-light, iron-firm hand on his chest. His wrist was still captive. So small a woman, all skinny arms and legs—it was impossible that she held him down like this. He ought to be able to push her away easily, but his limbs were too heavy to move. She shifted; the weight moved from his chest. Fingers searched for the breech-lacing at his hip, tugged at the strings in spite of his twisting beneath her. Surely she didn't mean to force him. She couldn't. Could she? He had to stop this before it was too late.

"Don't."

The word was soft; he could barely draw in breath. The mists—dust? smoke?—filled his lungs. The heaviness in his limbs was spreading, penetrating his flesh, permeating every inch of his body with inertia. His senses dimmed. He couldn't feel the weight of the girl on him. She blurred; her living energy was no more than a faint glimmer as he sank into darkness. Blood roared in his ears. He ceased to struggle. He felt as if he were drowning, yet he was not afraid. It was almost a relief to lose that painful awareness. Peace was nothingness.

Oblivion closed around him.

He dreamt that the alemaiden led him down the stairs, out of the tavern, and through the narrow streets. Suddenly, they were outside the city, wandering a still, night forest. No crickets chirped. No rabbits rustled in the underbrush. No sleeping birds nestled in the branches. His senses were baffled, muted one moment, flung open with blaring intensity the next; he could not trust his perceptions. A full moon rose over the treetops and a gentle wind flowed past tainted with the faintest pinks and greens like spilt wine. Water gurgled somewhere nearby. The River Lyn, thought Orlan. This was the wilderness to the north of Storm Port where he and his friends had ridden so often on nights such as this.

Then he was alone. Or was he? Though he saw no one, he heard the conversation of two women as if they stood over him:

"My Layn, I did naught ye asked. He fell to sleep as soon as I had him upstairs. I didn't even see him before this night. He isn't with yer– ah– husband so much as ye said."

"Never mind. I would rather be certain he was no longer virgin, but there is no time to ensure that now. The time is almost upon us. I must hope he has been so altered in other ways that the spell will not fail."

"What is it ye mean to do with him? He's a sweet lad—I wouldn't like to see him come to harm."

"He won't, I promise you. If you see him again, you may find him less restrained. That is no harmful thing, is it? But you mustn't remain here." Coins rattled as they changed hands. "You have done your service. Go."

Orlan lay supine in a grassy thicket. Ivy-heavy branches entwined over him and moonlight through the rustling leaves dappled his leathers. A circle had been etched in the dirt around him; he saw the gleaming curve of it as an unyielding metallic barrier. A magician's work.

Ilset knelt at his feet, the necromantic book open before her. Her hair was unbound, longer than the custom of merchant-dames, wizard-like in red streams that spilled down over her shoulders. She was out of her mayoral robes, in a flowing white shift that looked like a nightdress. The image was quite distinct, yet she was not near him. He was far from the city, but she was still in it—in fact, on the floor of her study. He could see the desk and wall of bookshelves behind her and glow of dying coals in the grate. Was he in the woods after all? Now that Orlan thought about it, he didn't recall passing a city gate; they must all be closed at this late hour. Had the maid brought him to the Mayor's Hall garden? The trees that sheltered him might be the bower near the ponds, though it was not as well-tended as it should be.

Ilset began to write at the rim of the circle—or, more precisely, the chalk letters were on the polished wood floor while he lay trapped in a grass-tufted clearing elsewhere. He tried to sit up and see what she was writing, but his head spun as soon as he lifted it and he sank back again before he could decipher one inverted word. The drug still confounded his blood, else how could he have such strange visions as this?

He wondered at the invocation that followed. What rite did Ilset perform? Her words were stilted and formal as any ancient spell. Her tone was almost a plea.

"Hear me, Lords of the Ether Between the Worlds, though I am lost myself, miserable and helpless in Thy Realm. I call upon Thy Powers to aid me. Restore to me what has been lost through battle with Thy greatest mortal foe and my most hated enemy. In return, I offer you the service of my humble magics. I shall do your work in this material sphere. I offer you this child, blood of Thy foe. He is weak of flesh and pliant of will. Take him as it is Thy pleasure. I offer you the most sweet taste of revenge against those who oppose Thy Purposes. Hear me, Lords of the Chasm! I charge in Thy unspoken names! Aid me! What is his shall be mine to wield and Thine to command."

Three candles stood around the open book. The middle one, of pure white wax, had already been lit so that Ilset could read the page before her. Now, she took up this one and lit the other two, muddy red-colored sticks, from its flame. She recited an incantation. The language was not Norman, but a demotic Latin neither classical nor contemporary in its grammar and vocabulary. A clumsy translation by an illiterate scholar of centuries past, Orlan guessed. Some phrases were not translated at all and their meanings were mysterious to him. It seemed to be a tortuous and repetitious series of related images: the spoiled meat of the lamb was most delectable to the carrion crow; the fruit that rotted on the vine was most enticing to the worm; the purest samite stained was the chosen garb of the devil's minions; the most virtuous and modest maiden outraged was the favored prey of the wanton.

Orlan had studied the structures of arcane spellcraft; he understood the application of symbolism. Similar images were in sympathy to each other, for they represented one object or idea. In essence, they were the same. Repeated variants of a single underlying theme strengthened the focus of a spell, at once disguising and elucidating its purpose. The motif here, as he interpreted it, was that all creatures of darkness delighted most in devouring a fallen child of light.

A child of the Lightmaster. She had caught him here to be consumed by some spawn of night. An offering for their favor. There were tales of pagans and witches who sacrificed the blood of virgins to their dark gods or demons, but that was not what Ilset meant to do. The fact that he had not surrendered himself completely dismayed her. He was meant to be ravished before he came to this. It was part of the spell. What, by all the right gods, did she offer him to?

In torpid, thudding panic, he tested the boundaries of his prison, knowing that he could not cross. The barrier held about him, solid as a wall of stone. His vague, fumbling fingers found no flawed spot he might breach. There must be a way to free himself before whatever Ilset had called upon came for him, but his mist-shrouded mind could not locate one effective counter.

It seemed that Ilset observed his struggles and smiled to herself.

At the end of her macabre litany of the despoiled, the Layn extinguished the white candle. Then she waited, braced against some violent blow, but the expected event did not occur. After a moment, Ilset frowned. She shut the book and rose from her ungainly crouch on the floor. "Worthless gibberish!" As she smoothed her rumpled shift, her image faded. No office, no book, no candles—nothing remained except the forest. Orlan sank back in relief.

A third voice, one he didn't recognize, called to him from very near his left ear. "Come. You must come with me." He turned his head, but saw no one in the close undergrowth. "Now!" It was the imperious, piping voice of a little child.

A pudgy, baby's hand reached out from the bracken and swept through the circle that imprisoned him. He could rise now, though slowly; he followed the insistent summons of the childish voice as it led him through the tangle of trees. "This way! Come with me." The little creature the voice belonged to remained invisible; Orlan saw no more than a slip of white in the underbrush, bending the tall grass in its wake as they escaped the forest and entered a wide meadow.

It was a cloudless night. The moon was now high overhead and the grass shimmered as the breeze rippled through it. In the distance above the bright fields a castle rose tall and white, high on pale cliffs. Home. This wasn't Storm Port at all. Somehow, he had traveled one hundred and twenty miles to the far end of Greenwaters Island.

His tiny guide rose from the tall grass: an elfish child, barely out of infancy, so fair as one of his blood and strangely familiar. Orlan knew that chubby, pretty face, the long, fair curls, the pouting rosebud mouth, the delicate, expressive arch of gilt brows.

"Andemyon?" he asked aloud. No; Andemyon had drowned in the sea. Pale and still, brought to his father's arms as the sacrifice for Orlan's carelessness. White shirt sodden. Yellow curls hanging limp. So much red!

"It is your fault," the child said reproachfully. "You slipped. You pushed him. You didn't come in time."

"It was an accident!" he cried. "I never meant him harm."

"It is too late. It is beyond a magician's power to restore the dead."

"Wait! There is a way to save him."

The little one nodded. "But we mustn't use it."

These were all his own thoughts; the child only echoed what was in his mind.

"Who are you?" he asked. "Are you me?" If he were so small again, there was time to make it right. No one need die. But, no, this was no boy. A little girl. She looked around the field, up at the silken sky, back toward the black line of trees, then she smiled at him.

"You are safe here, for a time."

"What's happened?"

"There are things she did not show you from her book. She means to recover her lost magics. The spell requires the defiling of an innocent. A full wizard is too strong to be taken unawares, but a young magician may be deceived and ensnared so he surrenders his powers to one of greater will. This transference must take place on a night of highest power. It is no accident that Midsummer is sacred to so many. Of course, it is sweeter for her that the innocent who falls to her hands is *his* son."

"Father," said Orlan. "She wants revenge upon him."

"As he destroyed her magic, she means to steal yours. Your corruption will be her triumph."

Kathryn L. Ramage

"But she hasn't corrupted me."

"She could not seduce you herself," the child answered. "But her husband, his companions, such friends as you have can only be themselves and do you great harm without knowing her design. She brought you to them, you must see."

"That can't be true. My Layn Ilset has been all kindness to me. She's done me no harm."

The little girl pouted impatiently as he said this, but she replied: "You are all so blind, poor mortal fools. You cannot see the traps she sets for you. Her pawns do her work in ignorance. And is *she* wiser than you? She doesn't comprehend the great peril she courts in her petty revenge. She no longer possesses the sensitivities to see what she has done." She glanced skyward. "There are Beings not of this earthly realm whose names the wise dare not speak, and she calls to them to aid her!"

What words from that infant mouth! Orlan marveled. Could so small a child pronounce such phrases, or even begin to comprehend their meanings? Unlike their first conversation, where she had thrown his own confused thoughts back at him, mocking them, she now spoke of things he had never imagined and did not believe. The absurdity of this cherub, to call him an innocent! Yet there was intelligence in her sing-song baby voice, surety and decision in her actions. She could be no human child; rather, she was like an ageless fairy queen who had taken this incongruous form for her own purposes.

"You are not of this realm yourself, Little One."

"Not yet. Soon." The night breeze swept up in a sudden gust. The little maid had been watchful since they first entered the meadow; now, she looked up, eyes wide with alarm. "It's coming! Quickly!"

She disappeared in a blur of white, flying with astonishing, impossible speed toward the ever-distant castle. Orlan ran after her, his nerves thrilling with that same sensation of danger he had felt outside St. Khrystopher's. Fierce winds screamed about him, battered him from every side. The grass tossed like a turbulent sea. The dark line of trees bent and danced frantically. In the wake of his elfen guide, he paused to look over his shoulder at the source of this commotion. The sky remained moon-bright, clear and starry, except for one black cloud— no, not a cloud. The darkness did not cover the stars; it was behind and between them, a rent in the heavens.

"Lords of the Ether between–" he whispered.

"Do not speak of Them!" the child commanded. "You are in danger enough! Hide yourself!" A chubby little hand tugged urgently

180

at the top of his boot and brought him down. He lay flat in the grass.

"What is it? I thought the spell didn't work."

"It did fail," she answered. "They have purposes of their own. She opens the gate but a crack with her summons, and then leaves it in her disappointment. Yet the way remains open."

Hidden in the writhing grass, shielded against the blasting winds, Orlan tried to grasp what was happening. His senses extended tentatively outward to receive a jumbled sequence of impressions:

The black gap spread across the sky, swallowing the stars, ripping the very fabric of time and space. Something sentient waited beyond that extra-dimensional void, an inhuman power past his comprehension. Monstrous, deformed, twisted and loathsome, measureless aeons old— to touch the rim of its existence made him shudder in repulsion and the little girl hissed, "Don't! That knowledge is madness!"

What was this? The danger he had been trained to guard himself against? The *They* the child spoke of? His awareness shrilled warning, but Orlan perceived only enough to be frightened. He could not explain what he feared. Students of magic whispered amongst themselves of the horrors they were forbidden to know, but Orlan had not truly believed. Demons? Antique superstition. The Pits of Hell? Mere myth. He had scorned, yet the source of a thousand legends was *here*, bursting through that doorway torn between their world and his. Lords of the Chasm. The Dread Nalro Saitham—but that was nonsense created by Mathias and himself. This was no game. What he sensed was the substance of nightmare.

Something touched the broken circle, snuffled eagerly, hungrily at its fragments and found it empty. A howl of disappointment rose into the wind They sought him! Ilset had offered a child of light and They had come to claim their prize.

It crashed through the trees in search of him. The form was indistinct—a small thing, dark, a shadow that did not leap with the others but moved of its own will. It was vaguely mortal in shape, yet it was not flesh. It did not connect with the material world, but wavered like a reflection on the surface of a disturbed pond. Orlan found it more horrifying than the unseen powers above, for it was part of that abomination, an incarnation of that energy.

His father, beacon-bright, walked the forest. Though the wizard was cloaked, the radiance of his being shone through, casting back the hungry night as he raced sure and swift on the errand to which he was summoned. He too had sensed the danger and charged to meet it.

Again, Orlan sensed the presence he had felt in the cathedral, all-seeing and all-powerful, elemental and savage. It reached for him. It called his name. Yet he was concealed; somehow, he was warded by this tiny creature sheltered beneath his arm. He would not be found. They could not touch him. But this evil was so ancient, so powerful beyond human scope. He was in no condition withstand it alone. Could his father and this elf defend him against that merciless engulfing force?

Other people were here as well: a lovely, slight woman with dark hair in a curly cloud and large dark eyes—Orlan was reminded of Godefroi. Her magic was so brilliant as Redmantyl's and she was as grim as she roamed the woodland, searching. An aged man with a long, snowy beard. Another man, also aged, of Asiatic cast. An ancient woman with a younger companion. A third man with filmed and sightless eyes, yet he moved as if he knew where he was going. A young man, red-haired and more wary than his elders as he poked at the shrubbery and peered up into the wind-whipped treetops. And, ever-so briefly glimpsed, a young maid as she slipped into the cover of the swaying greenery. Orlan did not know them, nor could he give all their names, but he guessed who they were—the ranks of wizardry. He understood that grown wizards were enemies, or at least associated in uneasy alliance; it was a surprise to watch them work together. They were linked in unspoken communication, their efforts coordinated like rural peasants beating bushes to flush birds or fox for a hunt. Their mission was similar, to drive one quarry from its hiding place, though the thing they searched for was far more dangerous than any earthbound beast.

It was discovered. Orlan heard the surprised yelp of a magician assaulted by the revealed night-thing. The others swarmed to confront their adversary. *Cast it out.* The single thought was shared by all. *It must not enter here!* Swiftly, they surrounded it, cast their spells and wards, drove it toward the broken circle where it had first appeared. The shadow-shape yielded before this line of defense. It had not had time to establish its corporeal form; it had little power in this realm. Though its masters held vast powers in their own sphere, their influence here was tenuous. Earthly magics were stronger. The wizards were vigilant. Their will was unbreakable. They would not flinch even though they were appalled and sickened by the hell-spawn they faced. The thing was thwarted; he felt its hatred and anguish as the bright beings relentlessly forced it back.

Then it was gone. In an instant, it flickered and disappeared. Blasts of rage followed. As if in retaliation, the storm redoubled its fury. Orlan shrank into the depths of the grass, trembling, eyes shut tightly, hands covering his ears. Lightning split the darkness. Thunderous roars shook the ground.

His father *was* the lightning. At the forefront of the battle, the wizard dissolved in blinding brilliance, became an arc of flame that shot into that cavernous maw. Dark and bright magics clashed. He held them at bay! Orlan could not help his admiration. What bravery! What powers wielded by one mortal! The boy began to hope he would survive unharmed.

But if Redmantyl was aware of his son's role in the appearance of this abomination, he did not acknowledge it. He fought for the sake of his world, not for his child. That was the nature of the wizard supreme, wasn't it? He was a man of strictest principles and highest duties. He acted as his place among the ranks of magical and wise compelled him. If he saved Orlan as well, it was by fortunate accident.

Abruptly, everything was still. The little girl sat up.

"It is done."

Orlan lifted his head. The winds were dying down in the aftermath of chaos. Streaks of clouds raced across the undamaged sky. "They're gone?" he asked. "Father drove them away?"

"They are eternal—they await. But the way is closed and They are banished for this night. You are spared."

"I don't understand so much of what's happened."

"You are still confused by the influence of your wine and opium," she answered. "Half of what you've seen is poppy-dream. At daybreak, all will seem so. It is no good for a magician to lapse as you have done," the pixie scolded as sternly as his father might in similar circumstance. "You forgot your vigilance on this most perilous night. You are too besotted to defend yourself. You've left yourself vulnerable to great danger."

"But I am unharmed. The spell failed."

"You did not fulfill its conditions and surrender in all. Chastity saved you. She could not take you virgin and unwilling."

"Yet They sought me."

"Not for her. If one is so foolish to call their names, They will hear. If the hour is right, They will come. Once the way was open and she abandoned her craft, They might claim you without giving her exchange. Remember the spell—they celebrate an innocent's corruption. The woman is no such thing. She comes to Them through no device save the lure of wrong magics. Necromancy promises you all you desire and leads you to betray all you hold dear, and so it is with this lost one. She offers her services—she is already theirs. You, however, are an appealing morsel. They would delight to see you enslaved. It matters not to Them if you are virgin, but They would be bound by the terms of the spell to receive you as her offering if all had gone as she wished. She would have the powers she desires."

"What was that dark thing?"

"A minion in human guise. It was meant to go unobserved among mortals."

"That horror? It would never be taken for a mortal being."

She smiled. "Yet it was once human, until it was chosen for their service. A human child. They stole it out and reshaped it at their will."

Orlan shuddered again at the thought of what those monstrous, depraved forces would do with a human child in their grasp. "Was that what They would make of me if I had been taken?"

The child didn't answer. "You are safe now," she said. Her smile was as oddly mature as her words. "You will not remain chaste long after this. You have already chosen the path which will bring you to me. If it were not so, I could not be here." Cherubic lips pursed into a pucker and softly brushed his cheek. "We will meet again." Then she left him.

Orlan followed. This uncanny child had spoken of foolish mortals summoning uncontrollable forces, and it occurred to him that he had somehow enlisted *her* aid. What was she? As he had sheltered her in his arms during the battle, he felt the brilliance of her tiny being, the enormous energies she contained. This little creature held magics greater than his own—so powerful as Laurel, so powerful as Redmantyl. She had broken the circle when he could not and had led him to safety when he was lost. She had shielded him from discovery. They would possess him now if not for her. But why had she come to help him when even his father did not intervene for his sake alone? How had he called upon her?

He was bonded to her. This little sprite had cast an enchantment over him. The essence of her being was wound into his as if she were part of himself—or he part of her. Did she sense his presence so clearly as he felt hers? Though her own mind was deliberately veiled, she seemed to know his thoughts and emotions as if they had been born in her own head. He had never felt such psychic affinity with another person before, save his father.

The tousled curls were barely visible above the waving grass. Behind her, Wizardes Cliff loomed on its cliffs against the dawn-gray sky. Clouds gathered about it with strange swiftness, as if they willed themselves there; they shone with colors he had not believed possible—bloody reds and misty lavenders, glaring yellows, deepest blues and livid greens. A spear of lightning shot from their depths, striking the highest tower of the castle and setting it to flame. Thunder rumbled like a chuckling bass voice. The storm had not ended. Had she rescued him from one power to betray him to another?

"Who are you?" he shouted into the rising wind. "What have you done with me?"

She turned back to him. Silvery eyes caught the moon. Though he must scream to be heard, her piping voice was a clear song that pierced the maelstrom:

"It is your doing, Father, and none of mine."

The storm descended in all its fury. Orlan recoiled as swirling colors enveloped him. They had him now! But this strangely gentle force did not tear him to pieces, nor did it violate his will, overpower his muddled perceptions, seize his magics. Pattering caresses struck him like raindrops—his face, his chest, his knees—and left him breathless.

He woke chilled and feverish, curled on a bed that seemed as hard and cold as rock beneath him. When he twisted to find a more comfortable position, he fell onto grass and gravel. His hand was scraped and his shirt sleeve torn. As he struggled to rise, a nauseating, spinning sensation overtook him; he moaned aloud and sank back, eyes shut tightly, wishing only that he might stay where he was– But where was he?

Hands fumbled at his shoulder, pulled him up. "No, don't," he murmured, and was lifted. His head fell back, and his first astonished thought was that so frail a maid could carry him.

A chuckle boomed against his ear. "Lad, you're sadly mistaken."

Orlan tried to open his eyes. "Houarde? What's happened?"

"I would ask you the same question, Chyelde. You dropped on our doorstep just minutes ago."

"Oh."

"I thought that one would have a better care for a pretty young lad. She's a wondrous girl, that. I knew her well myself, `til Ilset heard tales and put a stop to it. A fine lass."

"I don't remember at all."

"Ah, it must've been a merry tumble, to knock all memory of the sport from your head. Ugh, what's this you've got on your shirt?"

"Don't know. What?" His fingers brushed at something tacky and horrid smelling. Cooling red wax?

"You've been rolling in the gutters again."

"When have I–" he could not finish the question.

"Now, I've heard of you lads running the streets, mucking about, steaming the Sheriff, Eduarde's own father." He dropped Orlan suddenly, but the boy hit the soft featherbed before he could cry out. "'Tis all in fun, I know, but you must have a care for yourself, Chyelde." The walls of the chamber rumbled, as if with the knocking of a thousand tiny fists seeking an escape. Houarde looked around, baffled. "What's that? Rats?"

"Me, probably," Orlan laughed. "I thought I'd quit that years ago."

Houarde yanked at his shirt lacings, pulled the stained garments away, dropped them on the floor. "No matter. Sleep now, Lad. You've had the hell-raiser's night."

But Orlan was already sleeping. The house was silent again.

Ilset came up to his chambers later that morning. Orlan was up, in loose shirt and hose, and gazing out the window into the neat and ordered garden below.

"Are you recovered, Chyelde? I understand from Houarde that you were taken ill in the night." She glanced at the breakfast tray that had been sent up to him earlier, the bread and fruit untouched and tea cold. "Indeed, I was alarmed when you left Mass so abruptly. You seemed quite indisposed."

"I was," Orlan answered. "Because of the Midsummer. 'Tis a night of Wizard's Keep, you know, and it affected me strangely. But I feel much better now."

"Shall I send the boy to attend you? We are near midday and you should have dressed hours ago."

"My Layn, I am dressed, so much I may be."

Ilset's eyebrows came together. "Surely you do not mean to lay abed all day?"

"No. I've no clean tunics. I ruined the last, my riding habit, last night."

"Those laundry-maids are worthless in their lack of all haste," said Ilset. "I'll have to remove them and find a more industrious lot. Well, nothing can be done 'til the holiday is passed. I shall see what garments can be found for you 'til your own are returned."

"Gramercies, My Layn."

Some fragments of his dream were still vivid: the moonlit forest, the sage elf-child, the storm and the nameless and undefined danger.

When Orlan awoke in his bed at the Mayor's Hall, he'd been relieved, as if he had escaped some real threat to his soul. But this feeling faded rapidly. Now, all that remained was embarrassment that he had been so disturbed by a nightmare. In the light of day, he could look back on the terrors of the night with contempt.

But why, he still wondered, had he imagined Ilset as his foe? In all the weeks he had known her, she had never offered him anything but tenderness and generosity. Perhaps because she had no child of her own, she fussed over his comforts, lavished attention upon him, pampered him as a mother might. The Mayor's Hall was almost his home. Orlan felt as if he had committed some enormous breach of courtesy against his host when she visited him this morning; her concern was so touching that the witch-woman of his dream became obscene by comparison. Imagine Ilset a cruel and devious seducer of youth? Orlan blushed at his effrontery. So kindly a woman could never mean him harm.

Before dinner, Ilset knocked at his door and gave him a servant's kirtle and jerkin. "It's the best I can offer, Chyelde," she apologized. "But it is clean and I think it will fit you."

"It will do," Orlan said as he took the bundle of coarse fabric. "I've worn brown before this."

He dressed after she had gone. The costume recalled that earlier part of his life, when he had been a very small child playing alone in a stone yard. He had not always been a nobleman. It was presumptuous for him to wear noble garments, to speak proper Norman, to wear his hair in a free froth of curls to his waist. It was all a lie. He was the son of a whore. There was so much pretense in carrying himself as a young Lordling when, in truth, he was only his father's bastard. How could he begrudge Andemyon a place at Wizardes Cliff when he had no better right to be there? He disdained these commoner's clothes, but he had been born to wear such shabby garb. If his father had not acknowledged his existence...

He would have been an urchin, a beggar's brat, the son of a dockyard drab with no father to name. His life could be so very different from what it was. He had had little choice; the path had been set clearly before him. He knew exactly where he would go, from apprenticeship to magedom to full wizardry. He would establish himself as a powerful Lord, like his father. He had never questioned that fate; he'd always felt that it was what he must be. At the first sign of talent, he'd been taken into apprenticeship and prepared for the strict disciplines of a magician's life. He'd been kept from all normal pursuits, brought up in austerity, confined as carefully as a novice Brother, so that he could become a successful mage and steadfast wizard. Was it natural that a youth of twenty-two had never tasted ale, kissed a maid, played as he had these past weeks? He had been guided into narrow channels since childhood. Had he ever had a choice? His place had been determined before he was old enough to decide for himself. He was expected to be a wizard because he was a wizard's son.

How different he might have been if he'd been raised in a city such as this!

What might he have been if he'd never been recognized as Lord Redmantyl's son? Might he be a boy like his new friends? No, Reynalde, Eduarde, and Jepatha were the sons of wealthy merchants; they were commoners, but commoners who carried themselves nearly as well as the nobility. He would not have been brought up as they were. In all probability, he would have been like Tades, thrown out to work at an early age. He might have been a mariner, or a soldier like Kyarde. If his mother had died and his father never arrived to take him from Lammouthe, he might have been sent to the Abbey as an orphaned ward. Or he might have become like so many children here in Storm Port, a beggar who turned to service at a tavern. He thought of what happened to such children; if he had been a bar-boy and men like Eduarde made him offers, he might have accepted—not from desire or curiosity, but in hopes that someone would take him out of that impoverished life. His mother had lived on such hope. Could he expect more than to follow her?

No, that would not have happened to him. Never. In spite of his birth, he was intelligent and self-respecting, ambitious enough to want more than a miserable existence. Once his magic had emerged, he would have sought apprenticeship, if not with his indifferent father then with another wizard or at the College of Magic at Maryesfont. He would have escaped.

What if he were not magical? Would Father have cast him out? No. Andemyon was without magic and Redmantyl loved him best. Orlan would still be a nobleman's son, free of this terrible burden. He might have entered the court at Pendaunzel and taken up a raise-hell's existence there while he sought the favor of his liege. He might have gone to Maryesfont as a scholar in some less exacting course of study. He might have become his father's seneschal, visiting Greenwaters Island's towns and hamlets on Redmantyl's business and preparing for that eventual day when he would claim the title of Lord of the Isle for himself.

If his life had taken one of these alternate paths, he might be worse for comfort and social position, but he would gain so much for experience. He would make no embarrassing, naive mistakes, as he always made before his friends. He would not be so ignorant of the ways of the world beyond the walls of his own home, nor so provincial and clumsy; he would be able to drink without illness and laugh at girls' jokes without blushing. He would have more practical knowledge than could be learned from all the books in his father's vast libraries. He could do as he pleased without this unending guilt that his conduct was unmagelike and wrong.

He had dreamt of a spell that required purity spoiled and virtue outraged. What rot! He was not pure. What virtue withstood temptation only so long as it never confronted it? Orlan saw that he maintained his innocence only so long as he was shut away from experience. Left on his own, unrestrained, his self-command faltered immediately. He succumbed to every forbidden pleasure as soon as he met it. He knew his weakness. Did his father see it so clearly?

He was certain his father knew how he had been living in Storm Port. Their bond, enhanced by his amulet, remained intact in spite of the distance between them. He knew that his father must sense his heart race as he ran to seek adventures in the city's dark streets, his head whirl with drunkenness, his body awaken to new yearnings. But did Redmantyl disapprove? A wizard so powerful surely possessed more than vague telepathy; if Redmantyl wished him to stop, he need merely command—*Orlan, behave yourself*—and Orlan would feel it as if it had been shouted in his ear. But Father was wise enough to recognize that if Orlan intended to indulge in the games of young manhood, this was the time to do it. Such liberty would never be tasted again. They both knew that he would soon return to Wizardes Cliff, be scolded for his folly, and resume the disciplines of the magical. All would be forgiven. Such distractions as he met here in Storm Port would be put away from him. He would make his mage-vows at Midwinter and his career would continue without interruption. The episodes of this summer would be no more than exciting, embarrassing memories in the mind of a most austere wizard.

Would Orlan obey such an order if it came? Probably not. He didn't want to. Whatever vows he made in six months, he refused to submit to them now. So, Father was tolerant of his behavior? Orlan had to knock aside that complacency. He was no meek, monkish boy to be led through his life at his father's direction. He must throw out one act of defiance before he slipped forever into the implacable abstinence of a proper magician. There was so little time left! Orlan ached to do something unmagelike if not positively wicked. If he had not shocked Redmantyl yet, he meant to.

He went down to the Samandra feast, but excused himself after the second dish. He abandoned his silver amulet and sash on the chest at the foot of his bed, then went out to find Reynalde and Jepatha. They were to bid farewell to the young mariner, Tades, tonight and spectacular sport had been planned.

There was a riot at the garrison halls below the Lyngate. Kyarde, returning from his mother's tavern with some other young guards, heard the uproar and cursed their lack of armor. They were unprepared and vulnerable without weaponry, and they looked about the empty street for some makeshift—a board that might serve as a shield, a broomstick—before they decided that bare fists would be better than absence. They had heard of rebellions in the Empire's lesser kingdoms but never thought that they would see one here.

But it was apparent once they reached the scene that this rebellion was not what they had imagined. This was no insurrection, no clash of weaponry, only a gang of ruffians throwing rocks and rotten fruit and butcher's refuse. The older guards, awakened by the clamor, had come out of the garrison halls to make their defense, but the troublemakers slipped from them like shadows, running into the protective darkness, laughing maddeningly, and spattering their filth.

As Kyarde ran out into the confusion in the broad gateyard, something slimy struck his chest. He looked up and found the only face visible in the light of the guard's torches, a face framed by a froth of glossy white hair.

"Orlan."

Shame and embarrassment crossed the noble youth's face. He opened his mouth to speak. Then someone chuckled behind him, in the dark, and Orlan laughed too, and ran away.

Kyarde wiped at his stained tunic. The street end was filthy. Muck squished beneath his boots. Other guards around him were snorting at the stench and kicking refuse into the gutters.

The sergeant approached. "Bloody little bastards! Did you see them?"

"No," Kyarde answered. "No one I could name."

The man looked amused. "Cursedly you didn't—and I didn't

either. Not a one here will swear to it they saw the Justice's own son and that lagabout cousin of his, nor a one of that lot. No one saw that white-headed boy. Nothing'd be done about it if we did."

"That sort," Kyarde said. "They do as they please, and they never care who they hurt. Young raise-hells, and no fit companion for an honest guardsman."

"Ye're not hurt, Lad?"

"No, not hurt."

"Then you'll do yer part in clearing this mess. Captain'll have a bloody fit when she sees..." He walked off grumbling.

The others did not notice the young guard as he stepped back into the shadows, leaned against the solid wooden planks of the gate, and wept.

tuelfe

Ren stood and listened to talk from two traveling soldiers, a married couple; they grinned at her questions about Layn Margueryt and her unabashed thrill at the news that the Prince of Gossunge might pass through the city on her way to the frontier. She ought to know, she told them earnestly, if the Storm Port garrison would be called out. Her brother would go to battle, and so might she.

They smiled again. Her?

"I might," Ren answered, blushing. "My mother's promised I may serve as Captain Alyx's squire once I am sixteen."

"What will you do in battle, little maid?" the man, brawny and scarred, asked. "Why, I've broadswords as tall as you and twice as heavy."

"I may serve," she repeated, with a dreamy-eyed looked that touched the two even as they were amused; admiration for warriors and enthusiasm for the glory of combat were things all Normans understood and respected. "I cannot wield a sword, true, but I may carry one. I could lead a mount and hold it steady for the knight who would ride. I can watch the battle. I—" she paused. "I have a friend who will help me. A young Lord." Her blush darkened, for the soldiers' amusement redoubled. "I will go."

She looked up as her brother came into the Whitelm. "Kyarde." But he did not reply; the look on his face declared that something was terribly wrong. "Kyarde, what is it?"

"I must speak to Mother. Is she in?"

"At the back."

She would have asked more, but Kyarde stepped around the bar and pushed through the door beyond. "Mother, have you seen Orlan?" Ren heard her brother speak, then his voice was cut off as the door shut.

Orlan walked back to the Mayor's Hall in the hours before dawn, light-headed from the wines and ales he had swallowed that night—the number of mugs and goblets seemed countless—but he felt wonderful. He was able to stand and not ready to vomit. Only weeks ago, he could not have kept his head so well. It was strange that he should grow accustomed to this way of life so quickly, and stranger still that he should leave it so soon. He couldn't imagine going back to that quiet, studious world his father ruled; it would be so dull. He meant to go home, but the more he felt he ought to return the more reluctant he was to go. For what was at home? His father, Mathias, a handful of servants in the great, empty halls. What would he do there? Prepare for a life of restraint and intense self-control. He would much rather stay here a little while longer in the company of lively, pleasant people, his friends, and Julia, who had decided that she preferred fair-haired lads after all.

She hadn't cared much for his company before this, but Orlan took that to mean that she had grown truly fond of him. She was no ambitious maid seeking a fine match; she didn't care that he was a nobleman. Tonight, she had smiled at him, walked with him, taken his hand.

They walked hand in hand now, a little ahead of the others and for the most part ignoring their pranks. The boys had met a barmaid at an inn outside the city walls, where they had ended their night's riding, and she had agreed to walk home with them once the innkeeper chased them out. They sought to amuse her by leaping upon each other's shoulders, shouting, jostling in a playful assault, and laughing when she begged them to stop. Eduarde and Goduin outdid themselves in the competition.

Then a voice shouted from a window above, "Here, you! Quiet!" and they darted into the shadows like so many giggling imps.

"He'll set the guards on us!" the maid moaned in distress. "Hush ye! We'll be dragged off to the gaol, and I've done naught wrong! Oh, hush!"

"Hush yourself!" Jepatha hissed back. "A pox on your whimpering! There'll be no guards if you keep still."

"If they come, you'll be the cause of it, Pet," Eduarde whispered behind them. "You and your doe-eyes lead an honest youth to trouble."

"I never!" She turned to Goduin, but he was laughing.

"It's safe now." Julia's hand still in his, Orlan was the first to venture out. "Where are we?" They had hidden in the unkempt lawn of an empty house in the street before the Square. The shutters were barred and the chimney stones covered with untamed ivy. Orlan had only seen it in daylight before, the Portreeve's family home. Houarde and Ilset had lived there in the early days of their marriage and would again when she was no longer Mayor, whenever that day might be.

"What a fright," said Julia. "It was better kept once. I remember."

"An old woman lives there," said Eduarde. "The Portreeve's nurse, and deaf as a post these days. There's a garden behind, beneath the city wall, a fine and quiet spot. Shall we–?" He pulled the alemaid close to whisper in her ear, and she jumped away with a yelp.

"Oh, ye wicked thing!"

"What did he say?" Goduin demanded, but with no more than a pretense of jealousy. "Here, you came along at my invitation and if that lout's given you rude insult–" He shoved Eduarde, and Eduarde shoved back. The other boys leapt in and they were all soon pushing and kicking and yanking braids.

"Stop it," Julia said. "You are wicked boys, all of you. I've heard what you've done."

"We thought it the best way to see Tades off," Reynalde answered easily. "After all, the lad is French and that Frankish lot's famous for their assaults on the city guards. If he were Galsh, we'd have set a torch to the Council Hall."

"If he were Skottish," Eduarde added, "we'd ride down the Mayor's Parade, shouting as best our lungs might and carry off goods such as you, my pretty." He grabbed at her, and she slapped back. He chuckled. "And were he Irish– if he were Irish, we'd have to marry the Emperor's plain daughter as Prince Kat's father set up his rebellion." Shouts of laughter rose again and the alemaid looked up and down the street, expecting guards at any second.

"Jep may marry her, for he's no prize himself," Goduin grinned.

"No, Cos. `Tis Eddie's plan and he must carry it out."

"Horrid, the lot of you," said Julia. "Common as dirt and cruel as the deuce's own."

"No one was hurt," Orlan answered. "`Twas only in jest."

"The guards were given more excitement than they would see in a year. They are fat old toads for the most part and `twas time, my sister, someone put a match to their arses and made them jump," said Reynalde. "When Orlan goes home, what shall we do then? Fire-rockets, do you think?"

"`Twould make a spectacular show and our wizard might join it with his own fire and wake the whole city," Jepatha agreed.

"When are you going, Orlan?" Goduin asked.

"Soon enough. I meant to stay only a fortnight and I've been here more than a month. I expect Father will summon me home any day."

"We'll be going soon ourselves," said Julia. "There's Plague in the city and Mother's made plans that we should go to Maryesfont until the danger is past. I shall miss you."

"Yes," her brother agreed. "`Twas fun to have you with us."

"Great fun," Orlan said.

"You'll return?"

"If I do–" he began to explain his coming magedom to Julia, then he met her eyes suddenly. She had tried to speak to him alone all evening, but the others were always nearby. They had kept themselves to pretty flirtation and their real conversation remained unsaid. It could not be spoken now. Orlan blushed. "I might." The others smirked and nudged each other.

They made their way across the Square, tossing friendly jests, tumbling, teasing, always laughing. It was no time for a sober thought, but it was very late. When they passed the Justice's house beside the Council Hall, Goduin and Jepatha went in. Eduarde whispered to the maid, and they turned back to the abandoned garden.

"Poor wench," Julia said, but without pity. "He'll cast her aside once he's had his fun. Lads will do that to alemaids."

"I would not," Orlan said.

"And most will say that to any pretty maid," Reynalde, a few paces behind, laughed.

Julia scowled at him. "In truth, Eddie will pounce on anything passably attractive or willing. My brother can tell you—isn't it so, Fox?"

"Orlan already knows."

The maid glanced speculatively from one to the other, and placed a protecting hand on Orlan's arm. "Reynalde, have you nowhere to go?"

"Not I. At last chimes, the churchbells rang the hour before prime and there's nothing open `til dawn. You are going–?"

"To see Orlan to the Mayor's Hall. Good night, Reynalde."

"No, I'll come with you. Blessed Lord knows what might happen to our friend in the next twenty paces along this empty street if he goes alone."

Julia looked exasperated. "My brother!"

"Mine is as vexing," Orlan smiled. "Reynalde, go home."

"If you insist," the boy replied with a grin. "You'll be along soon, Julia?"

"Yes, in time." When her brother had finally gone, she said: "The brat! He imagines us like him and his lot in their filthy pursuits, with no better feeling. I have been in love now and again, I confess it, but I do not give myself wantonly at every whim, as he does." They were now at the front door of the Mayor's Hall. "You do like me, don't you,

Orlan?"

"Yes, very much."

She smiled. "And you'd not think me wicked if I said I liked you as much?"

"No, I would not," Orlan answered, and he was not surprised when she reached up to kiss him. Her hair was perfumed, her lips sweet, the fluting warmth of her breath against his throat more dizzying than wine. This was the way romantic tales and ballads promised it ought to be.

Only two nights ago he had predicted he would leave Storm Port as chaste as he had arrived, but now he began to think he had been hasty. In Julia's embrace, he felt none of his usual fears and hesitations. It wasn't wrong this time; he did not doubt himself or believe that his actions were improper. Once he gave his heart, everything was easy. This was no indifferent dalliance. He did like Julia. He wouldn't marry her—wouldn't marry at all—but he had spent this wonderful night in her company and it pained him to think he must leave her so soon. His spectacular summer was nearly over. They could not be parted! Not yet.

Arms around each other, they sat on the doorstep.

Julia took his hand. "For once, my mother would not protest my choice, but I did not choose you for rank or wealth. You must know that, Orlan. You are a gentle youth, kind, courtly, unlike the other boys, and I love you for that." She brushed her face against his upturned palm, then kissed the pulse at his wrist. "You mustn't let them lead you astray, for they will spoil you with their rough ways. Look at what you have fallen to already, this horrid garb you wear, as if you were a stable-boy."

"I have not been spoilt," Orlan promised. "I've only begun to learn what I truly am, what I want."

"And what do you—" She looked into his eyes, and suddenly became demure. "Perhaps we could go riding tomorrow, you and I, alone?"

"If you wish," he answered. "We must go back to retrieve our horses from the inn. Shall we meet there, if the weather remains fair?"

"Fair? It'll be another miserably hot day. See?" The sun was nearly up and the sky to the east a fierce pink. Julia kissed him again, then rose, smiling slightly. "I must go before our household awakens. Tomorrow?"

"Yes, I'll be there. Good night, Julia." He watched her walk down to her home before he went in.

Ilset broke the spelled seal, opened the folded note, and smoothed it on her lap. She read, and her brow creased deeply. She bit her lip.

"What's that, my Love?" Houarde asked over the breakfast table.

"A message from Lord Redmantyl."

"Orlan's father?"

"Yes. Where is our young guest?"

"Sleeping. He was out late last night, long after I retired. What does the Red-Lord want of us? That's not– ah– sent to the lad, is it?"

"No, the direction is to me. He rides for Storm Port—he wishes to speak to me. I suspect that My Lord has heard tales of his son's behavior that do not please him and he means to account for their truth."

"Why does he want to speak to you?"

"The Chyelde is in our house. His father may hold me responsible."

"Responsible?" Houarde pushed aside his empty plate and reached for another roll. "Responsible how? You said yourself that young Orlan ought to see the sights of Storm Port, and that's all he's done."

"Perhaps. But My Lord Redmantyl will not see it so. The nobility is not as we are, Houarde. They have codes of proper conduct that they must at least seem to obey. The conduct of wizards is especially strict." She frowned, for Houarde did not appear to understand. "As a magician, Chyelde Orlan has misbehaved. He has been indiscreet. Lord Redmantyl will much mind if his son drains every keg in our taverns and beds every maid, but he will be far more angry if his son becomes the object of gossip. I'm afraid that young Orlan has become a source of ill rumor."

"He's done nothing wrong."

"You are not with him all the time, are you?"

"Well, no."

"So you cannot account for all his actions. I have heard tales, Houarde. He has been encouraged by our local lads—you know of whom I speak—in creating all manner of unpleasant disturbance. He is a wild boy by his magical nature, and they a rowdy bunch and more than their share of trouble to us these past years. When he joins them–" Ilset shook her head sadly. "The Sheriff and Captain Alyx both have asked questions of our guest that I hesitated to answer. It may be no good for us, dearest." She folded the note. "We must disclaim responsibility. After all, we have treated the boy as an honored guest and it is no fault of ours if My Lord Redmantyl's son has behaved so badly."

"The lad's only had a bit of fun," Houarde said pettishly. "His father can't tell him how to conduct himself."

"He may try to," said Ilset. "Well, the boy has seen to his own ruin and we are not at fault. When My Lord Redmantyl arrives, I shall tell him that we have tried to uphold our duties as hosts, but his son is simply beyond our control. Yes, that's best. The damage is done. We must remove ourselves from this distressing situation. It is not our business to interfere. You will say nothing, Houarde. Do you understand?"

"Well, bloody hell, if a grown lad can't command his own lively amusements..." The Portreeve was still grumpy. "Will you prevent him going out?"

"I don't insist that he stay in, but I expect he'll wish to remain at our house if his father is here before Evensong."

"So soon?"

"My Lord's horse will not travel more slowly than the courier's. I shall bid Orlan stay. You, however, are free to go about as you choose. It may prove wiser if you are not here when Lord Redmantyl arrives."

"You know the way of wizards better than I," Houarde agreed. "But I think, my Love, that this Red-Lord ought to know–" Ilset looked up at him sharply, and he fell silent.

Houarde Portreeve was a man of few ideas, but the ones that he did possess were not easily dislodged. Throughout that morning, he sat and thought of Orlan and his odd, wizard-father and what service he might offer them both; the more Houarde thought his one thought, the more reasonable it seemed. At last, he went to his wife's study and, fingers clenched tightly about the unfamiliar quill and face screwed up in the effort to find the best words, he made his reply to Lord Redmantyl.

"After all, the boy's fully grown. No infant. He's a right to his pleasures. If the father's sensible, he must see that. Even great wizards have their fun. Yes, you may hold him no longer, M'Lord—I must say that." He smiled his satisfaction at the finished work. "There! Now, he'll take the Greenwaters Island Road past Narby... Boy!" he shouted. "Boy!" The small servant-lad scrambled into the room. "Boy, you know how to ride?"

"Aye, Syre."

"Then take a horse and go out of the Dukesgate and south to Greenwaters Island. I know not where on the path, but you will meet a man, a great Lord all in red and so fair as young Orlan." He gave him the message. "When you see him, you must give him this."

"Aye, Syre."

"Then go, and quickly. We know not when the Red-Lord will arrive."

His work done, Houarde went to the kitchens to find himself a cold beer.

Lord Redmantyl rode from Wizardes Cliff on Midsummer morning. He had met Kyarde's message at Midkrosse and immediately turned the courier back with his own warning to the Mayor's Hall. His worry for his son had increased at the news of Orlan's involvement with Ilset; she was no longer a magician of power, but she was not harmless.

He slowed as he approached the fork to Narby, fifteen miles from Storm Port. He had ridden the length of Greenwaters Island in two days and would reach the city by afternoon. The small servant stood in the middle of the main road, waving his arms hopefully. Redmantyl pulled his horse to a stop.

"Ye be the one? The Red-Lord?"

"I am he."

"The Portreeve sends this t'ye, M'Lord." The boy held up Houarde's note.

Redmantyl reached to take it. "The Portreeve?"

"M'Layn Ilset's husband."

"My son is in his company often, I understand," the wizard said darkly as he unfolded the single sheet.

"Not so much now, M'Lord, as when he first came to our house."

Kyarde had not mentioned this, and Redmantyl hadn't known. "He is in their house?"

"Chyelde Orlan's been our guest this month." The boy stood, watching Redmantyl's face as he read and wondering at his increasingly grim expression. "M'Lord," he ventured, "if ye wish t'stop awhile, I'll ride ahead and reply?"

"No," the wizard answered. "I'll reply when I reach the city."

Orlan shuddered as he woke. He had dreamt of the little girl again. It was time– No, the dream was gone. It didn't matter; he was awake and hungry and ready to attend the midday meal—if he had not missed it— before going out to meet Julia. He pulled on the rumpled, common garb he had been wearing and his riding cloak and went downstairs. Ilset stood in the hallway below and, as he descended, she threw a bundle of laundry at him, his own clothes. The words that followed doubled his astonishment.

"You must leave immediately. Return to that tavern and do not disgrace us with your presence again."

Orlan blinked at her, unbelieving. He had only known Ilset as a gracious host; he did not know this woman.

Houarde, beside her, was as baffled. "Why, what's the lad done?"

"What's he done? Houarde, you are a fool! This deceitful brat has abused our generosity since he first entered our house. While we have made him welcome, he has indulged in the most disgraceful behavior to be seen in any youth. We bid him enjoy himself and he insults the very people I am given to protect, and from my own home! All the city talks of it!" She glared at the boy, who stood staring, clutching the thrown parcel.

"I– You told me–" he tried to answer. "If I have done anything you did not approve of, My Layn–"

"Hark at his pretty lies!" Ilset laughed bitterly. "As if I had told him to assault our guards, corrupt our local youths, and lie drunken on our doorstep! Oh, we know more of your vicious ways than you think, my lad. We know you for what you are. What evil hides behind that youthful face! I regret I did not see it sooner, before harm was done. We are stained by this association, Houarde."

"The boy's done nothing so wrong–"

"He must go!"

"But–" Houarde made a last bewildered protest. "You can't send him out now, my love. It looks as if it will rain."

A sparkling, willow-wisp light in the woods beyond the city walls puzzled the guards at the Dukesgate; even after they heard the clomp of horse hooves and jingle of a bridle, they could not imagine what manner of rider would glitter so.

When Lord Redmantyl emerged from the shade of the trees, the guards could only stare; the air about the wizard shimmered with a myriad of tiny, bright sparks, as if he were surrounded by a retinue of fairies or fireflies. His whole being was radiant with light and fury. He drew his horse to a stop at the river and looked up at the towers flanking the drawbridge. His voice rang out:

"I wish to enter this city!"

The guards were too astonished to move immediately, and Redmantyl was impatient. He did not make another request. There was a roar of thunder and a blinding light; horses screamed and guards ducked and shielded their eyes. With a tremendous rip, the drawbridge chains tore from their locked wheels and the bridge crashed down. Redmantyl's horse reared and danced away, but the wizard brought it under his control and rode into the city as the guards rushed down from their posts to surround this remarkable intruder. One, Kyarde, ran from the ranks to reach the wizard and boldly entered the aura of light. His skin tingled and all the hair on his body stood on end, but he didn't step away. "My Lord?"

Redmantyl stopped. "Kyarde." His eyes were glowing like a cat's caught in candlelight. Power surged around Kyarde, making his heart pound, his breath draw in short gasps, his sight blur into a lavender haze of glamour. He was terrified, but he had grown up in this wizard's house and he trusted that this fury was not directed at him and he would not be hurt.

"If there is something we might do?"

"No, Lad. I do not require assistance." His horse shied again, then stood stiffly, abruptly still, but its eyes remained wild. Redmantyl swung down and gave the reins to the youth. "Hold her 'til my return. I have business within."

"Yes, My Lord."

He walked on, cloaked in his furious aura, leaving Kyarde and his fellows trembling in their armor. Over the city, clouds gathered. Thick, gray billows appeared from nowhere, quickly covering the sun. Storm Port was in darkness at midday. But none moved to detain the master of this display.

The Sergeant-at-Arms looked up. "I think we're in for a bad storm."

Orlan stood on the stairway, only now realizing that he was being blamed for all that Houarde and the boys had encouraged him to do, and wondering if they had planned this from the beginning, when a rage of thunder exploded above and Ilset fell silent; her face paled beneath the white powders.

"What is it?" Houarde asked.

"He is here." Her voice was hushed. The front door opened slowly, and they turned to meet Orlan's father.

Lord Redmantyl was afire. Living energies crackled from the ends of his hair, his fingertips, the snapping hem of his cloak. His pale eyes blazed white-hot. He towered on the doorstep, huge, red, dark and blinding at once, an incandescent sorcerer ready to call upon his minions to tear the whole of the universe to rubble and lay the ruins at his feet. He stepped into the Hall.

"Orlan, go out of this house and await me," the wizard spoke. Orlan didn't move; he was bound by no enchantment, but he stayed where he was. "Are you the cause of this madness?" Redmantyl continued. "Are you so proud that you flaunt it before me?"

Orlan thought that these words were also meant for him, but Redmantyl had turned to pin Houarde and Ilset under his gaze.

"Do you claim responsibility for the outrage committed against my son?"

"M'Lord–" Houarde tried to turn aside, but he was unable. "Well, damn my soul," he puffed, "a lad's got a right–"

"The youth is mine and you will answer to me for his seduction and debasement. If you have ensnared him for your designs–"

"No design," Houarde insisted. "No, M'Lord, no design! We drank a jot, and the boy kissed a pretty maid or two, but there's no harm in that. Your– young Orlan sported as any lad might. `Twas all in fun."

"Ilset?" asked Redmantyl. "Was it so?"

Ilset did not answer.

"Here," said Houarde, struggling in the magician's grip. "My Lady's–" The Portreeve's breath fell in little gasps. His heart was thumping; Orlan could hear the frantic, irregular beat.

"She knows what she must answer for," the wizard replied. Brilliant blue flashes spun about him as his fury increased. Some small, fragile ornament shattered; ivory fragments scattered over the floor. Orlan heard a sharp crackle, then a hush fell over the house. The bewildered boy looked up and around. He sensed the spellcraft. But what was happening? The air was stirring swiftly upward; a sudden, strange current of warmth coursed past him. Smoke followed. The Mayor's Hall was on fire! In the next moment, pandemonium erupted. Draperies burst into flame. The walls glowed red. Yelping, panicked servants raced down unseen stairs behind to escape.

"Yes! Yes, then!" Ilset screamed, defiant before this lightborn display. "I curse that I failed and he is put to no greater harm! Retrieve your precious child, but know he has been touched! No art of yours can remove that stain from him!"

Redmantyl's eyes seared through her. "I should not have pitied your life, Woman. You were past mercy's sake long ago and less deserving to continue now. Do you know the dangers you have invoked in your spiteful revenge upon my child? To damage him, you would endanger all. Such corruption cannot be suffered. Though you are fallen from wizardry, the rules of right magic apply."

Houarde stood agape. Though he did not understand the conversation which passed between Ilset and Redmantyl, he saw plainly enough that his wife was threatened. He could not hope to defend her, but the wizard's attention had turned entirely to Ilset and he was forgotten.

"No!" He stepped between them; Redmantyl glanced at him, for the briefest instant, but the Portreeve's damaged heart had already bourn more than enough. His eyes rolled back, blank.

"What have you done?" Ilset cried out, lifting the hems of her skirts and tripping back as her husband fell at her feet. "He was harmless!"

"He was your pawn."

She glared at the wizard with unmasked savagery, but Redmantyl met her eyes steadily, deliberate and unwavering in his intent. The Layn faltered first, as she understood that this blow against Houarde had been accidental; the killing strike was meant for her. Supreme wizard-lord, Redmantyl had his duty.

"It is the price," said the wizard, divining her thoughts. "Our highest laws demand that renegades be cast out."

Ilset fled; Redmantyl pursued—not quickly. He did not need to overtake her. Orlan knelt beside the motionless body that had been Houarde, disaster still too fresh to leave him more than stunned. He saw that life had already quit this flesh: the eyes were glassy, face frozen in an expression of surprise, the blue-tinted lips open in mute protest. He had heard often that the man's heart was weak, and it seemed that a single casual blow was enough to stop its beating. Poor Houarde. Poor hapless fool. He hadn't deserved this. He'd never had any idea what was happening, had been less suspicious than even Orlan. Orlan touched the rough cheek. Warm! Of course, Houarde had died only seconds ago. Was there time? Could he–?

Orlan did not witness Ilset's end, but he felt it. As he tugged at Houarde's tunic-lacings to reach that quiet heart and tried to recall the words to a simple spell which might recover the newly-dead, a pulse of stronger magics exploded, obliterating his small focus. In the next room, wizards battled. Orlan had heard of such conflicts: great powers tested themselves against each other. Devastating spells were cast. One will sought to weaken and conquer another. But Ilset was no wizard! She had already lost once and her magics were ruined. She hadn't stood against Redmantyl's relentless forces when she'd been stronger—how could she survive him now? What more could be lost? Then he heard the psychic shriek of a mind vanquished.

Orlan ducked his head and covered his ears to block out that anguished wail that was not sound. Gods, gods, what was he doing to her? Orlan felt it: magically, she was a faint spark; this was extinguished. The last of her power was siphoned from her. The defenses of her disciplined and well-guarded mind were torn away. Her will, her calculations and deceptions and prevarications, her anger, her malice—every thought and emotion was revealed, and eradicated. Her sanity dissolved; the fabric of her being unknitted and fluttered away like threads of loose-woven cloth. With merciless, inexorable, almost gentle precision, all that Ilset was was flayed from her strand by strand. And still she screamed, beyond pain, beyond terror, beyond human consciousness. He would go mad himself if it did not end. Then Ilset was gone.

Was she dead? Orlan didn't know. He couldn't sense her presence any longer, but it was impossible to receive any subtle impressions with his father's magic blasting through his head and the shimmering dance of fire all around. Flames shot down the staircase carpeting and ran up the tapestries. Smoke hung heavy on the ceiling. The walls curved slowly inward, drawn by the vacuum of that unnatural vortex which had sucked Ilset out of existence. The house would collapse. But Orlan didn't move. Why should he be so lucky to escape? Let them all be buried in the ruins! Houarde, Ilset, his father, himself—it was fitting that none survived the catastrophe.

Something crashed to the floor above, and boots thumped on the polished wood of the dining hall. Redmantyl returned alone, shining through the thickening smoke as he approached.

Orlan, trembling, sick, racked with coughs, did not resist as his father pulled him up from Houarde's body and led him out of the burning building. The sky was a murky, rolling mass, split by spears of light. Thunder rumbled continuously. A crowd had gathered on the Mayor's Parade. On one side stood the households of the best folk in the street: the Council, their servants, Orlan's friends—he caught Julia's eye and she ducked to hide behind a pale Eduarde. On the other side stood wide-eyed merchants and shopkeepers from the bazaar. Between them were the Mayor's heralds and housemaids in a wailing group and the guards who had followed Redmantyl.

The small servant-boy had returned to the city behind Redmantyl and stood now before the burning Hall with tears rolling down his face. As the wizard passed him, he shouted: "Witch!" Orlan stayed at his father's side, in tears himself, as Redmantyl took his horse from Kyarde.

"M'Lord," the young guard ventured. "The fire. It might spread." The upper floors of the Mayor's Hall were swathed in flame and the yard was brown and wilted. The garden behind had been made into a tiny wasteland: trees as bare as winter, unripe fruit shriveled to stone on the branches, fallen leaves in ashen-gray piles. The once-bright flowers were dead.

"Of course." The wizard did not look back, but the fire was quelled like a snuffed candle. The blackened rafters of the attic fell in. "Orlan, fetch your horse. We're going home. I will deal with your part in this later."

"No, Father!" Orlan struggled to pull himself free, awakened from his benumbed state by this final humiliation. He had been lied to on every side and had been too stupid to see. He had believed he'd engaged in a few harmless pranks—the best of the thrill was that he had behaved in an unmagelike manner—and he'd been betrayed. More was going on here than he had guessed. What dangerous game had Ilset played against his father? Had she brought him into it? Was Redmantyl's wrath for his safety alone? All the magical transgressions Orlan could think of had occurred in his strange Midsummer dream— but that had only been a dream. Hadn't it? What was happening? For incomprehensible reasons, his father had descended upon Storm Port like an avenging archangel. Houarde was dead and Ilset destroyed; people he had called his friends were horrified and the city folk crossed themselves as if they beheld an apocalyptic visitation. Then Redmantyl meant to drag him home as if he were a naughty child– "I can't let you do this! You walk away after–" Orlan wanted to scream, but laughed instead. "Will you scold me for some petty mischief when you've demolished the city? If I have done much wrong, I have not misused my magic. You tore her to shreds! What did she do to deserve that?"

Redmantyl heard this outburst in amazement, his raging brilliance only diminished a little. "Orlan, you can't know what she's done." His curtness made it plain that he did not wish to discuss this here.

But Orlan was too distraught to surrender meekly. He had gone too far to turn back. "It was my own doing!" he cried. "I chose my amusements. Whatever Ilset designed for my corruption, she never forced me to do a thing I did not want to. She was not there! It was my choice, Father! Will you not believe that? Can you not admit that your bastard child might be a stain on your honor?" He laughed and sobbed again. "Will you kill to deny it? Must my faults be blamed on anyone save myself? You murder poor Houarde for no reason but your pride! You could not care what I did, except as it reflects badly on you!"

"If I did not care, would I have come here to protect you?"

"You don't care! All you've done is keep your own reputation unspotted. You made me yours even to the profession to excuse my birth. Your mistake!" He no longer knew what he was saying, only that it was the lyric of the restless song that had been crying through his head these past weeks. "You've tried to make me like you, but I can't endure your unceasing rules. I am no wizard! I can't be so hard and cruel. I can't let you destroy them and walk away as if it were nothing. I won't go with you! You cannot lead me at your will any longer, for I am not yours to control!"

Fury burst from within him. He drew upon unused reservoirs of power; all his magic was gathered into his anger and focused at Redmantyl. He looked into his father's eyes, and stopped.

He had stepped boldly out and found himself at the edge of a cliff that dropped a thousand feet. There were depths he could not have imagined. Orlan thought he had witnessed a wizard's full power unleashed, but he had not yet seen all that Redmantyl could do. Unexpended magics burned in those colorless, gleaming eyes. All this light and dazzle was a spectacle to frighten fools and simpletons. The storm was a toy, a burst of temper. The burning Hall was no more effort than the sparkling fairylight. He could blight all of Storm Port, all of Greenwaters Island, as easily as he had blighted the garden. Ilset's destruction was no test of his abilities; he had fought true wizards with magics as great as his own, and always won. Magician-killer. Devourer of living energies. The furious storm of unearthly brilliance which held Darkness at bay. This was the power which Orlan had felt, and feared, all along, and it was at his father's command.

Orlan had lashed out in anger, but his anger was invalidated by this overwhelming force. He was far beyond his level. Redmantyl was not an old man past his zenith, but a premiere wizard at his peak; and he was not a strong, young magician, but an impudent puppy too arrogant in his little ability.

He was never afterwards able to determine if his father's words were spoken aloud or only an echo in his mind: "Child, do you challenge me?"

He retreated quickly. "I must get away from you. I won't live with this."

"You cannot leave."

"Will you stop me?"

Redmantyl blinked at these bitter words. "No, I could not. Orlan–"

"Then you won't." He turned and ran past the ruined house, past the maids sobbing on the withered yard. The crowd gave way before him, shunning contact with the Lightmaster's child. Orlan heard his father call his name, once, as he pushed onward to escape but he did not look back.

treten

Rain began to fall that afternoon and continued daily until the bazaar closed, the gutters flooded, the rivers swelled high against their banks and the dry farmlands and empty ponds were replenished. Storm Port was cleansed. Plague did not ravage the city that year and the pending drought, the poor harvest and the winter famine were averted.

Storms followed Lord Redmantyl home. He was no longer angry, but wound within deeper, more painful emotions that rages could not dispel. No lightning flashed nor thunder roared, but cloud upon darker cloud spread outward, covering Wizardes Cliff, covering all the sky. The castle stood empty, like a ghostly ruin that had not seen life in eons. Only Simon and Alfryda remained in service. Mathias became a quiet youth who watched his master with aching, worried eyes. The wizard never told them what had happened to his son at Storm Port. But the rain fell ceaselessly.

Orlan was not beneath the shadow of gloom that covered the coast of the Northlands from New York to the borders of Scandinavian Uinland. He was far from Redmantyl, and riding farther each day. He was miles from Storm Port, at the inn where he retrieved his horse, before he realized he still clutched his bundle of laundry. He was surprised too when he counted what remained of his money and discovered how much he had spent in the city; his purse had been nearly empty when he'd fled. He traveled with little thought of where he was going, knowing only that he must go. He went north because the road led in that direction.

He had ridden on for more miles before he recognized that this was the road to Oerykton, where his cousin Igren lived, and he made his way there. The Earl Geyraulte, Igren's husband, and his provincial court welcomed Orlan at first, for they had heard the Lady Igren's tales of her uncle's home and were fascinated by this representative of that fabulous castle. They were disappointed that the young magician would perform no tricks for their entertainment, but all agreed that wizards were apt to have strange and secretive ways. Orlan always wore his best clothes, faintly stained if anyone cared to look closely, and he played the role of a noble young dandy and knew all the while what a magnificent farce it was. He had no right to claim any position better than that of a dead drab's brat, but none of these fine folk saw that; they thought him one of their own. He amused himself by telling fanciful tales of Storm Port and Pendaunzel and flirting with the small court's most handsome Ladies, as any young Lordling might.

He'd been drunk often on his travels, but never so much as he was at Oerykton, for the wine spilled generously at the Earl's table so that all might have more than their fill. Orlan sat up with Geyraulte and his favorite courtiers into the late hours; he was sick every night and he ached each morning, until Igren began to look at him with pity, and he did not want her pity. He hadn't touched wine since he'd left Igren's home. He would not be a sot and there was no fun in drunkenness if he could not defy his father with it. It was no longer forbidden, and no longer sporting.

Even when news from Storm Port reached the provincial court, no one dared to ask the questions he dreaded, except Igren, who looked at him searchingly, spoke to him gently and tried to find him alone. This had finally roused Geyraulte's jealousy; although Orlan and Igren were cousins in the second degree and any more between them than the most innocent courtly graces would be incestuous, the country-bred, brash young Earl could not bear to see his bride extend her tender sympathies to any handsome youth. Orlan was sent from Oerykton.

He crossed the Yr River and presented himself at the Abbey of St. Yzra. Kaiberte, a student of the same arts which had saved him from infirmity, was delighted at his visit and the elder Brothers invited the traveler to stay. Orlan began by sobbing bitterly in Kai's cubicle and telling his childhood friend all that he would not speak of in Oerykton. That night, he cut his hair, cropping as short as he could before Kai intervened; he still bore small, healing wounds on his scalp from the brass scissors. The Brothers had treated the shorn locks as a precious thing, gathering them from the floor to roll into a long, silver coil and store in a carved, cedar box, for what purpose Orlan could not imagine. After this, he felt purged; it was as if he had confessed and stood in penance. He could be calm.

Throughout September, he stayed as their guest. He kept himself busy at the early harvests and the translation of medical books brought from Arabia; even the most pious Brothers grudgingly acknowledged that the infidel possessed wonderful skills in the healing arts. Orlan thought of staying within the peace of the Abbey; Kai and his fellows would have welcomed him, magician that he was, if he had wished to remain, but he could not share the spiritual faith that bound them together. Wizardry had been abandoned, but this faith was not his. He could not believe. He would always be an outsider here too. At last, he went on.

He wandered forests and mountain valleys of Yrfordeshire with no sense of direction, following roads and losing them, sleeping at inns or farm-cottages or, more often, at the roadside. He sold his horse along the way for much less than the animal was worth; lodging, food and drink cost so much. He was no longer an angry young man, but a weary child, miserable, dazed, and exhausted. The world was harder than Wizardes Cliff. The life which had seemed so boring only weeks ago was now comforting for that same familiarity and constant routine. He missed it so. He missed the castle inmates, all of them: Mathias, Simon and Alfryda, the maids, even Andemyon. If he saw Andemyon, he would embrace him. If he saw his father....

No, he did not want to see his father. He missed him, but every pleasant memory was overshadowed by that day of death and destruction and unforgivable betrayal. For years, he'd lived in that man's house, learned from him, admired him, hoped to be like him; how could he not see what Redmantyl was? The last memory was most vivid, and most dreadful, for he had glimpsed the terrifying, inhuman magics contained by a true wizard. Lord Redmantyl was incredible power embodied, more power than any mortal ought to command. He could rage like a demon. He could burn whole cities and lay waste to miles of countryside. He could kill at a glance, and with no more effort than he would use to swat an annoying fly. Houarde had only been an annoyance. He could– Orlan shuddered at the remembered sensation of Ilset's disintegration. How could he desire magic for himself?

Redmantyl had not misused his magic: Orlan knew now that that horror was a proper execution in accordance with the codes of wizardry. It was no more than a wizard's duty to eliminate the weak and malign, and Redmantyl had done it. Orlan had seen the merciless nature of a true wizard. So cold. So meticulous, even in rage. If he had been so foolish to challenge his father, he knew he would have met the same fate. Could he expect so stern and fierce a wizard-lord to be swayed by emotional concerns? No; Redmantyl would not relent even for him.

Orlan did not want any part of such powers. He wanted to forget that he had even seen them employed.

He wanted to go home, but he did not dare. He was afraid. If he returned, would he be welcome? He had defied Lord Redmantyl's will and had been banished as surely as Olyr; he had been forsaken by his own choice, as Laurel and Godefroi had been. He had no more hope of recovering his place at Wizardes Cliff than they. It was obvious to him that his father had disowned him. Redmantyl had not followed him out of Storm Port; he could have found him if he'd wanted to; he must be relieved to be rid of him. Orlan's defection had saved the wizard the unpleasant task of expelling his own child. Although Redmantyl blamed Ilset for Orlan's ruin, surely he must see how the flaws in his son had brought about the circumstances of his fall. Here was irrefutable evidence that Orlan was unfit. He was weak of will, temperamental, too soft and sensitive to endure the harsh codes which comprised a wizard's duty. A stronger magician would not have been so easily misled. A more resolute magician would not have fled when faced with the dread responsibilities of magic. He'd been an embarrassment all his life, but he was no longer Redmantyl's concern. The enchantment was broken. He was free of all restraints, and he was alone for the first time. He recalled his father's parting words to Olyr: *Seek another place, for this one is closed to you.* These were his now as well. He couldn't go back. His only choice was to go on.

The coins in his purse grew lighter each day; he spent the last on ship's passage the length of the Palefyt Sea, in hopes that he might fare better in Guylliamesburghe. His ship reached port before daylight, and Orlan began to walk. It was several days' journey to the inland city.

He woke that morning huddled in his cloak beneath a bower of saplings strangled by ivy. Shivering, he searched for the stream he had crossed at dusk the night before and, finding it, knelt on the damp rocks, splashed icy water over his face, and drank deeply from his cupped hands.

The sound of some huge thing approaching startled him, and he shrank back into the underbrush. A creature, an enormous stag with antlers like a broken basin and moss clinging to its shoulders, pushed through the trees. Orlan kept still for fear it would sense him, but the beast only lowered its grotesque head to snuffle at the water, then splashed through and lumbered on, never aware of his presence. Orlan remained silent after it had gone, for he had never seen such a monster before. Could it have been a buffalo? Until this moment, he'd thought it an imaginary beast.

After his cold-water breakfast, Orlan went along a narrow, beaten footpath. He was weary by midday, but he walked on as well as he could until he grew faint. He had left the main road for what looked like a less-traveled path along the seashore; after he had passed the sea's end, he was unsure if he remained on the path, but the sound of a nearby river reassured him; as long as he could hear that wild water— he couldn't see through the thick trees, but the abnormally loud roar made him think it wide and furious—he could find his way.

He stepped into a clearing at the edge of a cliff, and gaped at the waterfall before him; the river was as wide as he had imagined but the roar was from its great cascade. Orlan knew from his geography that this was Palefyt, the Great Falls, but no words could have created a satisfactory image of this marvel: a thousand, thousand barrels emptied at once, a great river spilling down, a huge froth-wall, a terrific roar that dulled his ears and a spew of mist and foam bright in the sunset as it churned the waters far below.

Orlan stood amazed for many minutes before he noticed a second thing as marvelous: a tiny island split the waterfall, and a castle stood upon it, partially hidden by trees and mist, a long, low place of wood and brick like a manor house with squat towers at the corners. Who, he wondered, lived in such a place? Was anyone there? How could they possibly reach it, set so between two fast-flowing flanks of water?

An hour later, after he had pushed through the vines and brambles and gone far upstream, he discovered a harbor cut into the grassy bank and a sleepy-eyed boatman who demanded payment before he agreed to ferry the young man to the island. Orlan gave him his empty, spelled purse.

They arrived at the back of the island, where the currents were not so violent; the ferryman was red-faced from his fight to keep control of his small boat and not at all willing to try the return voyage that night. He directed Orlan to the castle, through the wild-grown wood and gardens; a slight sense of order and the grassy flagstone paths indicated that they had not always been untamed. The boy struggled through the outsized hedges and rose bushes, and at last reached a sort of open yard between the extended kitchens wing at the back of the castle and the outlying buildings, fowl coops and sheds. Except for the agitated geese and chickens and the neat little patch of cabbages and carrots, the yard appeared to be abandoned. Orlan looked up to see a thin curl of smoke rising from a chimney; someone was in. He knocked at the kitchen door.

A maid answered, a girl with hair braided neatly around her head beneath a scullery kerchief, her apron and shirt cuffs wet. She looked at him curiously, this tall, fair stranger with his weather-worn cloak and bramble-scratched face. "What is it ye want?"

"If you please, who is master of this house?"

"Lord Alonz of Palefyt," she answered.

The name was familiar; Orlan had heard it before, but he could not think where. From his father? "A wizard?"

"Yes, Lad."

So that was his answer: a wizard would live here. Orlan considered turning back, but he could not. It was late. A chill wind was rising and the boatman would refuse to take him back before morning. He was too weary to go on and had to beg a night's lodging. "I would speak to your master, if I might."

"Ye have business?" She was doubtful of this.

"Please?" He tried to look charming and in need of help at once. "I'd be most grateful if you would ask him to admit me, Goode Maiden."

The maid considered him from clipped locks to boots. "I'll ask M'Lord," she said at last. "Come in."

The scullery was a single, low-beamed room full of copper pots and washing tubs. A man was cleaning the dinnerware, throwing refuse onto the hearth for the dogs and saving the better bits for himself. He scowled at the intruder. "Who's this?"

"No one to concern ye."

"The lad from Grandilse ye're always running off t'see?"

"I never! There's no such a one!" she cried, face coloring. "I'll have none of your rude lies, and you'll best keep your nose in your pots and kettles." She turned to Orlan with an awkward smile. "Stay here, Lad, as I go to M'Lord Alonz, and never mind this one."

"What about the washing?" the cook demanded.

"Never mind that as well!" She pushed open a door and flew down the corridor beyond.

The man turned to him, still scowling. "Sit ye there, Boy, at the chop-table, and keep yer hands where they'll be seen."

Orlan was disturbed at the way servants spoke to him, so different from the deferential tones they took with known nobility; no cook, no matter how uncivil, nor scullion, no matter how pert, had ever spoken to him so insolently before. But to carry himself as a wandering nobleman would create more questions than he was willing to answer. He sat and endured the insult until the maid returned.

"My Lord allows to speak with you," she announced. "Come along." Orlan followed her to the feast hall, where Lord Alonz remained after his table had been cleared. He was an aged man with a white beard over his chest and the black mantle of a lesser wizard, painstakingly embroidered with protective spells in red and white.

"Alen tells me you have some business with me," he said as they entered.

"Yes, My Lord. If I may request–"

"Have we–" He squinted fiercely at Orlan, then shook his head. "We do not know each other. Who are you, Boy?"

"If it please you, My Lord, I am called Orlan, a humble traveler in search of employment. I would be willing to work in your service, My Lord, or if you have nothing to offer, I ask a place to rest the night and some scraps from your generosity." This was Orlan's now-practiced speech of beggary. "The least lodging—the kitchen hearth or stable loft—would be welcome to me."

"You're not a child of common folk. Your speech is too well-formed." Alonz lifted an eyebrow. "Son of a Lordling, perhaps?"

"My mother was an alehouse drab," Orlan said.

"And your father?"

"I know no man by that name."

"Were you a scholar?"

"No, My Lord," he replied. "I served as a page at a great Lord's castle, and I learnt my speech and manners there."

"Who was this man?"

Orlan paused, then said, "He was a wizard of power like yourself. The Lord Wizard Redmantyl."

"That young upstart?" Simply the mention of the name distracted the wizard. "You served in the house of that whelp? He was little more than a beardless boy when he claimed the title from the Old Lord. 'Twas an outrage. A proper Redmantyl should be a gray-head of at least eighty." Alonz had just reached his eightieth birthday. "Not a youth less than forty."

He peered at Orlan suddenly. "So, if this boy-wizard was willing to take you, why did he not accept you as an apprentice to his craft?"

Orlan started. "My Lord?"

"It must be obvious to you, Boy. You glitter like a meadow of fireflies on a summer night. Would a wizard of honor refuse one of such potential?"

The boy scowled. "He would, if I had interest in his craft. I do not wish to be a wizard, My Lord Alonz. I did not come to enter apprenticeship. I only want to find honest work."

Alonz frowned thoughtfully before he made his reply. "Well, Lad, I must tell you that I would be obligated to accept you as an apprentice if you would ask it, but I have no reason to insist on training a youth who refuses his talents. Only a fool would seek to create another rival.

Do you read, Lad?"

"Yes, My Lord."

"Latin?"

"A little."

"You've quite an education for a pageboy," Alonz murmured. "That may be of use to me, Lad. You may stay in my service."

"Gramercy, My Lord."

"Alen!" the wizard barked, and the scullion who had admitted Orlan to the castle appeared at the door and curtsied. "Girl, show this goode youth to the servants' hall—any room fit for occupation will do."

"Aye, M'Lord." She bobbed again.

"Have Odo feed him and bring him to me before nightsfall. You will be my manservant, young Orlan, and learn the duties of your place then."

"Yes, M'Lord."

"Leave me now, both of you."

Alen took Orlan's arm. "I knew there must be a place for ye," she said. "We are only six here—myself, Odo, the laundry-man, and the groundskeeper and his boy." She paused to tie up a loose boot-lacing. "And there's Ruth, who tends M'Lord's table and rooms with me."

Orlan was surprised. Many of his father's servants had left after Olyr's fall, but more than twenty remained. He'd thought that Wizardes Cliff was terribly empty and understaffed; what must a house containing only seven people be like? The answer surrounded him as they left the main halls. The floors were swept, but the tapestries—too large for Alen and Ruth together—were ragged and dusty and the windows grimy. Cobwebs hung like curtains in the rafters.

Alen followed his gaze upwards and could not disagree. "It'll be a grace to have ye tending M'Lord, so me and Ruth can give some thought to the rest of the house. Oh, we try to keep tidy, but our work's never done. I'm glad of ye," she admitted, "for all you lied to M'Lord Alonz."

"How–?"

"I could see ye weren't telling him all." She struggled with the rusted iron catch on a tall door and pushed it open. Orlan followed her, feeling blind and foolish. He was accustomed to the bright energies of great magicians, but the lesser sort possessed their own more gentle glamour. Yes, this girl would know if he lied.

She led him into a courtyard with a dry fountain and bare trees rising from knee-deep grasses and piles of scarlet and golden-brown leaves. It was beginning to rain; they crossed beneath the cloister, then went through another door and up a steep stairwell.

"How did you come to be here?" he asked.

"'Twas my seeing. Mama thought I might train for magic. I get these fits, and I can tell what may happen, or where something's been lost. Sometimes I may see into folks' minds. Ye believe such?"

"Yes, I believe you."

"So I came here, but M'Lord said it takes a good deal more'n guessing games to be a wizard. But he'd have me stay in service. Mama said I might. I've nine brothers and sisters and she must find places for us all. She has her patch to live on, but if she tried to divvy it up between us, the little she's got would be even less. I can earn my keep and save to 'prentice. I've a fancy for silversmithing—'twould be pleasing to make such pretty wares. M'Lord Alonz helps me with my seeing fits–

"Oh!" She whirled on the stairs. "I know where I've seen ye before! 'Twas in a fit of mine, weeks past, I saw ye, or one like ye." She frowned, trying to remember. "'Twas at Midsummer. I saw a fair-haired lad like yourself, a bit older but not old. He was in robes as M'Lord Alonz wears, but all white."

"All in white?" Orlan wondered. "Like a priest?"

Alen shook her head. "No, like a wizard, but white. What can that mean? A true wizard? A ghost?"

"You don't know?"

"I never know 'til I see it come true. There's the flaw in my magic. My Lord said you have the talent too?"

"Perhaps," Orlan answered. "But I don't care for it. Wizards are too cold-blooded, too cruel. They use their power for destruction— They like to show how frightening they can be. And when their magic might truly do good..." Alen was watching him, wondering, and he explained: "I think my father let my mother die. He's killed others."

"You told My Lord Alonz you had no father."

"I don't, not now."

"Was he magical?"

But Orlan had said more than enough. They stopped before a door in the seemingly endless passage. "This one, I think," said Alen. "We've plenty of rooms, so ye needn't share unless ye choose to. Ruth and I are together, but we maids in the house must keep to ourselves." The room was the size of a monk's cell and furnished no differently: a single, narrow cot against one wall, a small chest pushed against its foot, a washing-stand in the corner. Rain patted on the window; Alen pushed the casement open a crack. "I'm sorry of the dust. I'll shake out the sheets and sweep tomorrow if you like."

"Gramercy, Maid."

"Now, ye must call me Alen. If ye'll need to find me, our room is across the way." She shut the door behind her. Orlan tossed his bedraggled bundle to the bed and selected a linen tunic; it would do for a servant's garb once he removed the girte and sash and sleeves. He stripped off his rumpled jerkin, hose, and boots—he had not been out of them in a week—and dressed again, then wrapped his silver amulet in his best silk shirt and placed it at the bottom of the chest. Other clothes, riding habit, red sashes, velvets and frilled shirts were piled on top, then the casket was shut.

He crossed the unkempt courtyard again, found the kitchen, and accepted the bread and cabbage broth the cook offered grudgingly. Odo insisted on standing over him as he ate, watching every move with a hostile glare, until relief arrived: the groundskeeper wanted to slaughter a hog and needed Odo's fierce grip to hold the animal; his own boy wasn't a match for the wicked beast. Orlan heard the struggle beneath the kitchen window, the profanity of the two men as they battered the pig insensible, the animal's cries until its throat was cut. He could not eat after that and left the unfinished meal to seek Lord Alonz's rooms. He tried to recall all the things Simon and Jem and the boy at the Mayor's house had done in service for him.

Without Alen as a guide, he was quickly lost, but he saw much of the castle and its sad state. The long hallways had not been inhabited for many years and he wandered under cobweb-laden rafters and dust-coated windows until he found the wizard's apartments above the great hall. Here, the corridor was swept, the woodwork polished, the carpets beaten clean. One door was ajar and a light flickered beyond; Orlan tapped discreetly.

"Enter," Alonz spoke.

The rooms within were also dusted, but not neat. Books were stacked on the floor, on the tables and chairs, and left in disorderly rows on the shelves. Papers and reused parchments scattered over everything. Quills were left to drain where they lay, spilling their red and black inks, and spells in chalk and charcoal were scrawled on the walls and floor. The place smelled musty and smoky and slightly like rotted eggs. Orlan was made queasy, but he bowed his head.

"I am here, My Lord Alonz, and ready to begin."

"So I see." The wizard sat on a stool before the fire, smoking a pipe. He smiled strangely at the youth. "Are you, then? Your duties,

Boy, will be to attend me as I require you and replace my books as they pile up, but do not hinder my way, and never—*never*—touch my writings."

"Yes, My Lord."

"I do not like ignorant clounes meddling in my work. Those illiterate girls would toss my most important notations into the fire as rubbish if I allowed them in here and let them sweep as they would. I am glad to find someone with a little learning." He paused to knock ashes onto the hearth stones—a small, sooty pile had already formed there—then fumbled at the vast pockets of his robe, brought out a copper piece a little larger than a coin, and tossed it to Orlan. "Are you able to read that?"

"*Cum hoc*," Orlan read easily, "*dicam in veritas.* `With this I shall speak in truth.' Is it your motto, My Lord?"

"No, only a helpful talisman." He touched Orlan's brow. The boy's legs yielded beneath him; he fell to the floor. Alonz stood over him.

"Tell me, Boy, what is your name?"

"Orlan," he answered. "What–"

"Where did you come from?"

Orlan was compelled to reply. "Greenwaters Island, My Lord."

Alonz's face wrinkled with suspicion. "Who is your father?"

"I– I have none–!" The last word ended with a yelp. Pain gripped him. Fire burst in his head; wrenching cold and heat tore his vitals.

"The truth!"

Orlan tried to resist the forces of Alonz's spell. He made a furtive gesture with his left hand, a ward against such assaults, but his agony redoubled until he gasped for every breath and curled like one unborn at the aged wizard's feet.

"Do not fight me, Boy," Alonz commanded. "I will have the truth from you." The chill and fire left him abruptly. "Who is your father?"

Orlan lay on the floor, weak and breathless, but trembling with rage. "My father is Yryd Lightmaster, Lord Redmantyl," he answered.

"Your mother?"

"I– I spoke the truth before. She was a tavern drab."

Alonz seemed satisfied. "So, you are the bastard son of that whelp?"

"Yes." Orlan tried to sit up; his head whirled and he was forced to shut his eyes and settle his head on his knees.

"An ill effect of the spell," Alonz explained simply. "It will pass. Tell me now, were you sent here by your father?"

"No–"

"Boy," the wizard began impatiently.

"It's the truth! I swear! I left Wizardes Cliff and my apprenticeship months ago, My Lord, and I do not plan to return. I am my father's child, but there is no love lost between us and he does not know nor care where I am."

He felt a lighter shock of violation, a sort of pressure behind his eyes as if a headache were about to settle in. Orlan wanted to fight this intrusion, but Alonz's powers were greater than his and he could only damage himself if he rebelled. He thought of what had happened to Ilset, how easily her wards, her very thoughts, had been stripped away. Alonz was no Redmantyl, but he had the skills and power to do the same. Orlan clenched his teeth and allowed the rifling of his mind. At last, the aged wizard nodded. "Yes, it is true."

Orlan sighed.

"I had to know the truth, for I saw at once that you were lying. You see, I challenged your father once, years ago, and I could never forget the look of that young wizard. You are too much like him." He held out a hand to assist the boy to his feet. "I have had spies here before. Oh, my home is small and not so grand, but the prospect is spectacular and remote and it is coveted by many, wizards and others. I cannot trust anyone. I apologize for your distress, but what is a touch of discomfort when it is compared with the safety of my home and life? No wizard would act differently. But I see that you are safe." He gripped the talisman between his own hands. *"Cum hoc dicam in veritas.* Young Orlan, if you wish to stay, you are welcome. I vow that you will come to no further harm."

This promise made Orlan look up with curiosity. He had experienced the potency of that talisman for himself and he knew that when the aged wizard spoke the incantation, its influence was invoked again. Alonz wanted him to stay. But why? Did he mean to hold him hostage? This was Orlan's first thought, but it seemed most unlikely. Redmantyl had no idea that he was here and, if he did, his presence would not protect this careful magician; rather, it would only serve to draw the more powerful wizard's attention and inexorable wrath. Surely Alonz knew the fate of those who tried to use him against his father and was too cautious to invite deliberate disaster. Or did Alonz want a companion? It would not be so odd for a miserable and isolated man with no company except a few illiterate servants to welcome an educated boy. Or did he intend Orlan to be something else? A subject of experiments? A source of unused magics which might be usurped?

A sexual plaything? The trophy of a young magician defeated and made to serve? Again, each of these seemed unwise. Alonz was not so foolhardy to toy with Redmantyl's son. He had some reason for wanting Orlan in his house, but Orlan didn't know what it might be. The wizard's mind was unreadable.

Orlan knew that the prudent thing to do was send him away as swiftly as possible. The suggestion of Redmantyl's retaliation ought to send Alonz into panic, yet Orlan did not use this threat to ensure his safe release. In truth, the boy was not absolutely certain that his father would intervene. He had left the great wizard's protection; did his father care now what use he came to at a rival's hands? The professional antagonism between magicians demanded that such insults as Orlan had already suffered not be tolerated. Pride would urge Redmantyl to act in his defense in spite of the breach in their relationship. But he could not be sure of this. Did he even want his father to defend him? Hadn't his folly caused more than enough damage? He had been caught once as a pawn in the games of two mysterious forces. Why hope to see that bloody tragedy repeated?

He had escaped one wizard's influence to become the prisoner of another. Was there truly any difference? Alonz was less powerful, but no less brutal, no less cold, no less ready to use him for personal ambitions. But, whatever this magician intended for him, Orlan was not afraid of it. The worst had already occurred. He had come here willingly. He had accepted this position of service. He was too weary to go on. Where else did he have to go?

"Shall I come to assist you in the morning, My Lord?" he asked.

Alonz nodded.

When he returned to his room, Orlan thought of writing protective wards on the door, but magical locks were easily broken and he'd do just as well to pile up his furniture as a barricade. Either might anger the wizard and incur punishment but neither would stop him for long. Alonz had vowed that he would not be harmed and he must rely on that alone. After he had undressed, Orlan reconsidered and made a circle around his bed, a simple spell to wake him if any danger approached. It might not help, but he felt more safe with it there.

That night, rain poured down and lightning flashed across the sky. Orlan kept his head under the blankets and his hands over his ears. He recalled his father bright with anger, the burning Hall and the wilted garden, Houarde's rolled-back eyes and Ilset's mindless shrieks. He wept at the memories that would not die. Each crash brought them back with painful clarity.

At the loudest rumble, he cried out: "Stop it! Please, stop!"

The door opened. "Orlan?" This was Alen. "Lad, are ye well? I heard ye calling."

"I'm—" Orlan sat up. "I was in a nightmare." He couldn't see her, then there was a flash of lightning—she was in a white shift, hair mussed, stepping toward him—and it was dark again. "I'm sorry if I woke you." He flinched at the burst of thunder.

"No, I was awake. Are you—" She crossed his wards without effort. Fingers touched his face. "You're crying," she said, immediately before him.

"N-no." But his voice betrayed him.

"Yes, you are." Another flash; she was beside the bed. The thunder was loud about them. "Orlan?"

"I can't bear this! Doesn't it ever stop!"

"Hush, my dearest," Alen whispered, as she might to a frightened child. She had comforted children before. "Don't cry. There's naught to affright you so. A grown lad as you are, weeping at the thunder? `Tis only a little noise." She brushed away his tears. "Please, don't cry." She brought him into her arms. "Hush."

The Magician
1960

quarten

When the Lord Mayor of Storm Port heard that Redmantyl had returned, he welcomed him warmly, as if nothing unpleasant had ever occurred between the wizard and the city. Indeed, Redmantyl and the young wizard with him were invited to a banquet at the new Mayor's Hall, a tall, white-brick building on the Town Square. The wreck of the old Hall stood at the end of the street, damned and abandoned. Nothing grew there even after seven years.

Storm Port 's citizens did not regard Redmantyl as an enemy. Of course, he was fearsome, but it was generally acknowledged that the doings of magicians were mysterious and often violent. Only the foolish and the dead make enemies of wizards, and this one was particularly dangerous to fall afoul of. Sensible folk did best to stay out of his business. If their former Mayor fell, well, that was the way of wizard-battle and even a lapsed magician must face such perils when she meddled with one of the great. No charges were brought against Redmantyl for Ilset's destruction, nor for Houarde's death. Law as well as long-standing tradition granted that a parent could take such extreme measures when a child's honor or safety was in question. The people of Storm Port didn't know exactly what Ilset and her reprobate husband had done to the boy—rumor varied from the breaking of some obscure magician's vow to lewd molestation to demonic sacrifice—but they agreed that it must have been unspeakable for the punishment Redmantyl had returned upon them. Undoubtedly, the woman had been evil. If Storm Port spoke of Ilset these days, it was not as their once-popular Mayor, but as the witch who had worked dark and blasphemous magics in their midst and paid dearly for it. They pointed with whispers to the Portreeve's empty house, where Ilset had been taken after they found her alive in the smoldering ruins. In the care of a nurse, she remained there, mute and glassy-eyed, until she died.

Redmantyl's most outrageous crime in the city's opinion was the destruction of the Mayor's Hall. Everyone said that something ought to be done about it, but none would have had the courage to challenge the wizard if the Duke himself had not interceded. Storm Port was surprised; Dafythe was near his century and known for a peaceable and civilized disposition. Who would have expected the old man to have the courage to confront that wild wizard? But all of the Northlands was under Dafythe's protection. Like his subjects, he recognized the depths in which family vendettas and the savage custom of wizard-battle were embedded in the history of Norman society. Though he disapproved their practice, they must be allowed. But he would not permit such personal conflicts to endanger bystanders. He found it especially deplorable that one of his noblemen had wantonly demolished civic property for the sake of private revenge. Here, Dafythe took a firm stand; the angry wizard could not ignore a rebuke from his liege lord. Reparations were made, and the matter was considered settled.

Few folk were so brave to sit with the famous Red-Lord for fear of rousing his anger, but the young Mayor's friends who dared to attend the dinner that night were disappointed. Redmantyl was not the thunderbolt in human form they remembered, but a taciturn, middle-aged man who appeared wizardly only by his crimson, rune-woven robes. He did nothing magical. He rarely joined the conversation, instead leaving the tales of magicians' quests and travels to his young companion, Mathias.

Other guests entertained as well. Alyx, now a pensioned Lieutenant, lean and battle-scarred, recounted her campaigns in the Spanish Marches with the present Duke Margueryt; the young officers at the table envied her adventures, for they had not been in the war. The eldest daughter of Rosamonde Lilie, betrothed to the Mayor, detailed her elaborate plans for the approaching wedding and her sisters flirted playfully with the unclaimed men at the table.

Julia the younger Spicemerchant, heir to the great Spicemerchant since her sister had returned to the Abbey at Maryesfont, made polite, correct remarks from time to time while her brother Reynalde amused with bright, cynical jests and drank through the meal. Both glanced often at the wizard as if they wished to speak with him, but did not know what to say. Julia's husband Eduarde was more bold. Discovering that Mathias had apprenticed with Orlan, he took up this most precarious topic.

"He played with us that summer," Eduarde said cheerfully as they advanced to the parlor for honey-cakes and brandy. "A charming boy, wasn't he, Julia? A bit reserved, but of course he was about to become a mage. He had a care for his conduct. We didn't. We were a wild lot once—can you believe it now? You had much to do with *that*, My Lord," for the first time, he addressed Redmantyl. "We were stupid, selfish children with no thought for anything but our own amusements, and you frightened the wits out of us!"

"And frightened some sense in, I might say," the Mayor added. Eduarde laughed but his wife and her brother did not look so amused at the joke.

"`Tis a marvel to me that we weren't all blown to bits as well."

"We wonder of Orlan, My Lord," Julia ventured in the pause that followed. "We were all very fond of him."

"We meant no harm," Reynalde, refilling his wine glass for the third time, muttered. His sister looked up at him anxiously.

"We were fond of him," she repeated. "He was a friend to us. Will you tell us what's become of him, My Lord?"

"I do not know," Redmantyl confessed. "I haven't seen him."

"What?" one of the other guests cried. "Not since that same day?"

"Not since." The dinner guests looked as if they would ask more, but Redmantyl's forbidding expression stopped their questions. Julia fell silent; Eduarde took her hand. The Mayor's betrothed resumed her pretty chatter and offered refreshments and looked plainly relieved when the wizard excused himself. Doors were left open to the garden; Redmantyl disappeared into the darkness of the tall bushes and trees. The younger folk sighed.

"I didn't mean to be unkind," Eduarde apologized to Mathias. "But 'tis odd to speak with ease to a great wizard and not offend. We all wondered what happened to Orlan after that disaster. He never came back, did he?"

"No. We had news that he'd gone to Oerykton and the Yzra Abbey, but My Lord wouldn't call him back. After that, Orlan disappeared. No one's heard from him since he left the Brothers. I searched myself when I first became a mage, but he doesn't wish to be found."

"Poor lad," said Julia softly. "And My Lord Redmantyl is always so melancholy?"

"Yes," Mathias answered. "He has been for years."

But when the wizard returned, his eyes glowed with expansive awareness and the electrical surging of revived strengths crackled in the air like a sudden storm arising. There was a quickness in his voice which had not been heard earlier.

"I must leave," he announced. "I pray you excuse my abruptness,

My Lord Mayor, but an important matter requires my attention. I must go."

The Mayor didn't know what had happened to Redmantyl during those minutes alone, nor did he care to. It was obviously wizard's business. "If you must, My Lord. I'll have your horse brought out."

Redmantyl made his farewells to the baffled guests, but Mathias followed him out to the door. "Shall I come with you?" he offered. "Is it Orlan?" He smiled at the wizard's nod. "I thought we'd never see him again."

The wizard did not reply to this. "I bid you await me at the inn. I cannot tell you more now." Redmantyl's horse was brought to the door and he rode out of the Narnegate within minutes.

Father, please come. Help me.

Orlan sat before his cottage hearth, amulet in his hands. Though he was still quite young, the softness of boyhood had worn from his face to expose the distinctive bones of cheek and brow and chin. The tender mouth had drawn into a tight line. Transparent stubble grew untrimmed—he had not shaved in days—and bruised-looking blue shadows underscored his eyes. A handsome young man, remarkably like his grim father, but taut and strained, with an unwizardly fragility born of weariness that permeated to the bone, to the very soul. Alen slept upstairs, quiet for a little while, and Orlan resumed his earnest summons to Lord Redmantyl.

The amulet did not require a magician to invoke its spell, only one who desired to use it. *Whosoever bears this is bonded to Yryd Lightmaster and may call upon him.* Poor Nann Dafodylle had worked its special power, but help had come too late for her. Father must not be late this time.

Please come, Father. Hurry. I need you.

Could the bond between them be reestablished? Until this time, Orlan hadn't cared. In fact, he had done everything he could to sever his connections with Lord Redmantyl and wizardly ways. He did not cast spells. He closed his mind against the unwanted perceptions he still received and cast up barriers to conceal the active energies of his heart and brain; this was primarily a defense against Alonz's suspicious prying, but it also cloaked him from the psychic gaze of his father—on the assumption, of course, that Redmantyl sought him. He suppressed every manifestation of his magic—he'd wanted nothing more to do with it—but now, in this desperate time, he must reawaken that hypersensitive awareness which had plagued his adolescence. The power had not been lost; as he focused on the silver disk pressed between his hands, he felt it stir again. He sensed the electric thrill of energy through his nerves and veins, saw the glimmer of magic flash upon his skin. His revived awareness pushed *out*, broadcasting his urgent message. Father must hear him; he must come and help.

He had not forgotten the destruction brought by a wizard's power, but he had to call upon that destructive force and hope it could be employed for an act of healing. There were spells to ease pain, to stop the flow of blood, to rejuvenate injured flesh. Orlan had not studied these medical arts, but Redmantyl must know something of them.

Alen herself had insisted that magic had a beneficial purpose. "It can't all be wickedness," she once answered his angry words. "Wizards'd be outlaws if they did naught but put curses on folk and blow things up, not such great Lordlings as they are. It wouldn't be allowed. I've heard tales of magicians who built castles and cured the sick and did other good works."

Orlan conceded to this sensible response. "No, magic isn't evil, but it grants too much power for mere mortals. Its potential is too dangerous. In order to control the magic, a wizard must cast aside all that makes him human."

They had talked often of magic in his first days at Palefyt. While he worked in Alonz's library, a tiny collection compared with the vast libraries of Wizardes Cliff, Alen accompanied him, examining the books on the shelves with unrelieved curiosity. She could barely read common Norman; these texts were more magical to her for the mysteries of written language than for any spells they contained.

On that day, she had taken down a small, white leather-bound book, not identical to the *Necromantia Perdyte* Ilset had kept, but containing similar tales of lost and forbidden crafts. The pages were filled with stylized Arabic script. "Is that proper lettering?" Alen asked. "It looks like a lot of curving swords and flying serpents. Can ye read such things?"

"Yes, I can."

"Well, what does it say?"

Orlan glanced at the bold red-ink strokes. "'Tis a spell by which a sorcerer may learn the secrets of a dead rival."

"How?" she pressed.

"The left hand is cut from the corpse and suspended over an open book of blank pages. If the spell is done properly, the hand will write down a true answer to every question put to it," Orlan explained reluctantly. "The sorcerer must kill his foe himself."

"Grisly thing!" Alen shuddered. "D'ye think M'Lord Alonz casts such spells?"

"I know he doesn't dare." He took the book; it distressed him to see that innocent-looking compilation of monstrosities in her hands. "Wizards call such crafts evil. The hypocrisy! They won't employ it. They shun its mention. Why then do they collect it?" He slapped the book shut, not pausing for Alen's answer. "They must possess the knowledge even if they never use it. They enjoy knowing they can do such horrible things if they choose. Wizards must make people afraid of them. My Lord Alonz enjoys the torment of weaker beings. He cannot not be satisfied 'til he displays his power over them."

Gently, unexpectedly, Alen touched his cheek. "What did he do to you?"

Only a few weeks had passed since Orlan's arrival at Palefyt; the humiliation of Alonz's assault was still painfully fresh. Whenever he met his master's eyes, he relived the agonizing, fire-and-ice sensation that had seared through him during that interrogation, the plunder of the most private parts of his mind.

He could not explain these outrages to Alen, any more than he could describe to her how his father had unknitted the living essence of Ilset. This young woman hadn't experienced the horrors which a powerful magician was capable of inflicting on a vanquished foe. She couldn't know. While his own talents were conspicuous and attractive to the greater powers who would use him as a pawn in their incomprehensible games, Alen's were unobtrusive. Possessing no physical manifestations of magic, she passed untouched beneath their notice.

He was in love with her then. He'd been half-mad when he'd come to Palefyt, and she had calmed him. When Orlan woke in terror from his nightmares, she held him and whispered sweet, meaningless words to soothe his fears. On stormy nights, she came to him as if she knew what memories he suffered at the thunder and lightning. She was there often enough that Orlan began to anticipate her. He lay awake, hoping she would return, dreading she would not.

She baffled him, this maid who met him during the day with demurely downcast eyes and timid smiles, but came to him boldly in the dark. He was shy himself; she had seen him trembling and tearful as a little child over a storm. But his night terrors didn't seem to lower her opinion of him. Quite the opposite, Alen seemed pleased that he needed her.

It surprised Orlan that he felt such desperate longing for the presence of a person he barely knew. In Alen's arms, he found a sense of safety that he had not felt since his childhood. And, in return, he wanted to protect her.

"Ye can't look upon My Lord Alonz as the sample for all magicians," Alen told him. "Ye think wrong of magic because he's hurt you with it, but it isn't always so. Magic is given by God for a better purpose—there must be some goodness to it in the proper hands. It makes a difference what sort of person you are to begin with. 'Tis good or bad. Ye can use your power as you choose."

But Orlan could not believe this. Magic, he insisted, changed the magician.

"All young magicians come to their apprenticeship thinking that they can never commit such horrors as they hear full wizards do in battle, but they all come to it eventually. Their training makes them so hard, or they are cast out. The talented ones that are too gentle are called weaklings and unfit. They are ruined. I've seen it myself. Only the most cold-blooded survive. No, magic itself is not cruel, but wizards make it so. They make themselves inhuman. They act without mercy. It becomes easier, I think, as they grow to greater powers. They know what they can do."

"Ye were 'prenticed, weren't you," asked Alen, "before you came here?" She smiled at his astonishment. "'Tis no trick to guess that, Orlan. Ye talk as if ye know many wizards and I can see ye know what you're about with M'Lord Alonz's books. Your last master, did he cast ye out because he thought you too weak?"

"No. I cast myself out," he'd confessed. This had been the first confidence he'd dared to share with her, but why should he not? Alen seemed to understand his troubles before she learned what troubled him, and he had revealed enough by his bitter words for her to guess nearly all his secrets. "If I'd stayed, I would have learned to be so cold and brutal as the best wizards."

"Not you," Alen assured him.

But Orlan knew himself better. "I have that same cruelty in me. I can do harm to creatures weaker than myself—I have done it before. Wizardry would only encourage that."

He remained in Alonz's service for two years to be with Alen, but eventually he became restless at Palefyt. He asked her to go with him.

"Go where?" she asked.

"Anywhere. Not here."

"I thought ye were happy at Palefyt."

"I am—with you, Alen. You've made it bearable to live in this musty old house, but I am not free of magic here. It's a magician's house! Oh, he never has me use my magic for his own devices, but I am all but his apprentice. I shall go mad as he is if I can't escape this blasted wizardry."

"You're going away," Alen said softly, sadly.

"Come with me. Please? I can't leave without you."

"You haven't thought this through," but she saw how impatient he was to quit his service and she finally consented to accompany him.

Then, with apprehension, Orlan gave his notice.

Alonz had not been so malevolent as Orlan had first anticipated. The youth had been terrified when he entered the wizard's service; daily, he expected spiteful acts of revenge, beatings, further violations of his damaged psyche, but Alonz never again threatened him with physical or psychical pain and, slowly, Orlan relaxed his careful guard. He was not treated as a hostage or a conquered plaything. Alonz never questioned him about Lord Redmantyl nor sought to overtake his unused powers. Indeed, the aged wizard seemed completely uninterested in his manservant's magic.

No, Alonz was not a bad master. But the wizard was past eighty, often irritable, peculiarly insistent upon certain nonsensical rituals. He sat and stared at the fire in his sitting room for hours, smoking, lost in impenetrable thoughts. Orlan suspected that the old man must be in his dotage or perhaps insane with loneliness. Magicians must remove themselves from every emotional bond to avoid distraction and to escape betrayal, and years of isolation had taken their toll on Alonz. Alonz remained unceasingly wary, awaiting his death at the superior magics of a younger and stronger wizard, but if he imagined Orlan to be this opponent he gave no indication of it.

The wizard never explained why he had asked Orlan to stay; he simply seemed satisfied so long as the young man continued in his service. When Orlan once asked, Alonz replied, "I know who you are," but Orlan thought that a pointless and absurd remark. His identity had been established long ago.

Alonz grew to depend on the young man he had taken into his household. Orlan began as a personal servant, but he soon became scribe and librarian as well. After he swept up the ashes on the hearth and relit the sitting-room fire, he put away the books Alonz had scattered the previous evening and wrote out the scribbled notes in a clear hand. Alonz trusted him to put everything back in its proper place and to make accurate copies of his most important writings. When the aged magician was too fretful to sleep, he summoned Orlan to his chambers and they sat up into the morning hours playing chess. Later, Orlan received greater responsibilities; he became steward of Palefyt and assumed the management of the little castle. He often went out to the mainland on errands.

From the beginning, Alonz required Orlan's assistance with his experiments. Orlan was not interested in these specialized studies of antique spells, which his master conducted endlessly, but they were the wizard's sole interest and occupation. Alonz sought to discover the true nature of spellcraft. He explained to his slightly bored assistant: by refining long-familiar spells, he exposed their essential components. Which elements of the rite were most necessary and which were mere theatrical trappings? What happened when some subtle alteration was made? The wizard chanted the same incantation for hours, changing a single word each repetition; Orlan took notes on each variation. For more than a fortnight, Alonz drew a series of standard warding spells on the sitting-room floor—the primary circle, circles containing triangles, five and six-pointed stars, and more complex geometric figures—to test which provided the most effective barricade. Again, Orlan took notes and kept his master supplied with chalk. Alonz sent the youth out to gather roots and leaves for potions, so that he could determine if the freshly picked herbs were more potent than dried specimens. The wizard was enthusiastic about the results of these experiments; though he didn't dare to publish his findings, he was equally anxious that the information he had gathered not be lost. He confided in Orlan as one who would understand the significance of his work. Together, they filled several volumes of carefully gathered data annotated with the wizard's own tortuous explanations of his methods, and Orlan stored them on the library shelves.

Orlan did understand Alonz's desire for secrecy: among wizards, personally gathered knowledge was considered too volatile to be disclosed to other magicians; their own spellcraft might be used against them if it fell into the hands of potential foes. Perhaps one of the universities that had colleges of magic—Padua, Wittenburghe, Maryesfont—might receive a copy of a wizard's private studies, but the danger that a rival might discover it endured.

Lord Redmantyl had written scholarly works that he dared not publish. All the great wizard's writings were left in his libraries for his students and succeeding Redmantyls to examine. The future could do him no harm. Even so innocuous a thing as his treatise on the bonding spells of this same amulet could not be released for outsiders; Redmantyl had feared to expose Orlan to the machinations of his rivals by revealing that he had a son.

It was an indication of the wizard's trust that he shared the results of his work with Orlan; he believed that his assistant would not use this most personal information against harm. Alonz was fond of Orlan, and indeed the youth might have felt some affection for the peculiar old man if his memory of that first outrage had not remained so vivid. For all Alonz's later benevolence, Orlan could not forget how this wizard had used his powers to overpower a weaker magician.

Orlan was not captive at Palefyt, but would that change once he offered an open act of defiance? Could Alonz prevent his and Alen's departure?

He was apprehensive as he approached their master, but Alonz only said, "I shall miss you, Lad. You've been of good service to me these months. The girl too. Well, go if you must, but do not ever return." Orlan agreed immediately to this odd condition—what need had he to see Palefyt again?—and he and Alen left. They were married at Guylliamesburghe.

Not for the first time, Orlan examined the devices engraved on the worn, silver face. He could no longer read some of them. Redmantyl had crafted this amulet thirty years ago; its enchantment had not been invoked in nearly twenty. Had the spell remained intact through all these years? Did it still hold any power?

He would not have kept the amulet at all, would have cast it away long ago or left it in his trunk at Palefyt, if Alen had not seen it while he packed his belongings. She didn't know its magical significance; to her, it was simply a medallion of nicely crafted silver. Of course, she wondered how a poor and nameless wanderer had come to possess such a marvelous thing.

It was then that he told her the truth about himself, who he had been, what his father was. He told her about his days at Storm Port and the deaths of Houarde and Ilset. Alen said she had guessed something of the sort, and she offered an opinion of Redmantyl's actions:

"Perhaps ye don't know the reasons for what he did. Ye were only a 'prentice yerself when you left and there's so much they don't tell you 'til after you've proved yourself through all their tests." Then she added thoughtfully, "If I had a child put to danger by a wicked magician and the power to blast her to the Everlife, I'd do it. Anyone would."

She made him keep the amulet. Magic or no, it was too valuable a piece of silverwork to throw away. It had been his mother's and his father had given it to him so that Orlan could call upon him whenever he had the need. Orlan might want to break that bond now, but what if he changed his mind years from now and the amulet were lost? She would not have him do a hateful, foolish thing he would later regret.

It was as if she had had one of her precognitive "seeings," had known that this day would come and had equipped them for it.

In Guylliamesburghe, they lived in rooms above a carpenter's shop; Orlan took work there as an unskilled laborer and Alen entered apprenticeship under a silversmith in the same little street. During the first year of their marriage, they held each other close, body and soul. They attained an intimacy which Orlan had not believed possible. He had always thought that the psychic rapport between magicians was the closest bond he could ever share: at Wizardes Cliff, he often touched the minds of his fellow apprentices, his cousin Laurel, his father, knew their thoughts and emotions as if they were his own. Now, he realized how they had shielded themselves against that intense affinity— Redmantyl especially. They put up barriers to protect themselves, for none of them could bear the inadvertent intrusion. The very nature of their profession made them shun such closeness.

With Alen, he did not need to guard his thoughts. Alen knew him; she knew his mind in a way which might have disturbed him if he'd thought she would use that knowledge against him. But she kept his secrets. She protected them for him. That was her magic, more gentle than any other he had known, except perhaps that of his cousin Igren. He was healed by her. His nightmares ended.

His father had warned him against marriage—for wizards. But he was no wizard. It was incomprehensible to him that Redmantyl and Tedora had maintained their affair when they were so often apart. How could they desire it so? When he and Alen were separated during the day, he missed her achingly. The hour when she returned to the shop was the happiest of his day. He couldn't sleep unless she was there beside him, head resting on his shoulder, heartbeat against his. For Orlan, *this* was love: he could not imagine himself alone. Alen was necessary to his happiness, his peace-of-mind, his daily existence. From the first, he gave himself to her without reservation. No disgrace in surrender—he belonged to her and she to him. It was the most natural thing in the world that their separate but incomplete essences should merge into a united whole. If this love were distraction, he was willing to lose himself in it.

He had not known that life could be like this with someone who cared for him. Orlan didn't mind that their rooms froze that first winter and ice formed on the inside of the windows and in the wash-basin. He didn't mind the sawdust that dried his throat nor the splinters that scraped and roughened his hands. He didn't mind that they had to keep count of every farthing and sometimes ate thin broth and stale bread meal after meal. He didn't mind that they went to bed at sunset to conserve their small supply of candles, even though they were often both too tired to do anything but lie close against each other until they slept. Alen softened the blows of the harsh, common-folk's world he had chosen to live in. He could not have endured without her.

They stayed on through that first winter and the next. At Easter, a thespian troupe visited Guylliamesburghe and Alen was eager to spend her Good-Friday holiday at the promised performance in the city square. Orlan, who had seen more thesper-craft, was not so enthusiastic, but he went with her. He sat through the usual Eastertide fare, bored and indifferent at the wooden scenes of the passion play. Even when the rest of the audience went furious with whispers at the transparent and mist-draped images of Heavenly Hosts hovering above the dead Christ in the Blessed Mother's lap, Orlan dismissed it as a clever trick with cheesecloth and hidden mirrors—ghostly, but less than impressive under the midday sun. Then he sensed the delicate spellcraft. He began to take an interest in the play, particularly the thespers. He studied the face of each performer, and at last recognized one of the apostles. Though the actor was swathed in robes and hidden by a flowing, sage's beard, those over-large, dark eyes were as distinctive as the familiar signature of misty, conjured illusion.

Godefroi.

After the performance, he led Alen back to the thespers' caravan where his old friend, stripped of costume and false beard, waited for him. Godefroi had seen him in the audience long before and hoped he would come. They embraced as brothers and a burst of questions and exclamations followed. Olyr was there too, but not as a thesper. He was one of the rough, apathetic vagrants who attach themselves to any band of Free Folk and serve as porters and backstage hands.

The fallen mage had never recovered. Whether his powers had been broken or, like Orlan, he had abandoned their use when he became outcast, there was no sign of magic about him. When he spoke of magic, his caustic tones declared how deeply he despised all things wizardly. But hadn't he reason enough for his hatred? Sullen, downcast, haunted by irredeemable failure, aged beyond his thirty-odd years, he was nothing like the promising young magician Orlan recalled. It seemed impossible that this wretched man had once been a handsome, dynamic, overconfident mage. Olyr had no will to do anything for himself. If Godefroi's unalterable loyalty and sense of responsibility had not made him take charge of his friend, shelter him, urge him to go on living, Olyr would have fallen to beggary, or worse.

Olyr had been expelled from the ranks of magic and been ruined. Godefroi had left voluntarily, and thrived. He had not changed; he was the same earnest, inquisitive, dreamy-eyed boy—or, rather, the man that boy had promised to be. Among the thespers, he had the liberty to explore his talents as wizardry would never have granted him, to become the weaver of enchantments he truly desired to be. His magic had not been abandoned with his apprenticeship, for he employed his illusory spells as readily as he painted screens and designed costumes for the troupe. He did not regret his choice. In fact, with his dislike of rules and meaningless rituals, with his artistic instincts, he was in his proper place here. The troupe imagined Godefroi to be the only magician among them.

Alen had said that magic was a power bestowed upon mortals for good purposes, even if it was occasionally abused. Godefroi believed that magic was a natural force without purpose, save that which the wielder provided.

"You never know the uses magic can be put to 'til you exercise it in a new capacity," he answered Orlan's assertion that his illusory displays for the thespers were unorthodox and somewhat degrading to his talents. "Soon after we left Wizardes Cliff, Olyr and I traveled with a carnival and I earned our way as a conjuror. My slight-of-hand tricks were pathetic, 'til I began to craft spells in the shape of doves rather than try to hide lives birds in my sleeves. After that, I experimented with more spectacular stunts, disappearances, levitations. Of things that didn't exist! You know my limitations—I can't lift a pebble nor create a decent spark to light a candle, but I can make imaginary horses fly and cast walls of flame that blaze so vividly as true flame. Wizardry would have killed me eventually. I could never be one of the great. Too tender-hearted. Too weak. Nothing pains me more than wanton destruction. So, I use my powers to astound and entertain and I do no harm. Is that a debasement of magic? Is painting canvas screens a misuse of the limner's art?

"The talent isn't a power holy nor satanic, but a human energy. We cause it ourselves. Remember the litany? The heart, the mind, the hand—and that is all. It is ours alone to direct as we choose. Magic has many uses wizards do not employ. They cast the spells they are taught—"

"While other spells are forbidden without reason," Orlan

interjected.

"Exactly so. They use their powers just as magicians have done for centuries without a thought of variation. No other possible function occurs. If it did, it would be heresy. The useless traditions of the magical are like all things Norman. Nothing has changed in a thousand years. Our glorious Empire is built upon tradition—the things we must and mustn't do and no one thinks to ask *Why*?

"Now I do not suggest that apprentices be given leave to experiment with dark necromancy, but why can't a master-wizard teach his students the distinction between what is and isn't right magic in a clear and sensible fashion? To tell curious young novices that certain things are forbidden without any reason only makes them more eager to learn the truth for themselves and may lead them to stumble into real danger in their ignorance. If the strictures of wizardry can be explained, fewer young magicians might fail or go wrong. Why can't the questions be answered: what is the meaning of Wizard's Keep? Why must we abstain from every simple pleasure that ordinary mortals enjoy? Why are mage-vows so harsh?" Godefroi's voice had been rising as he expounded on this favorite topic, but his last words were spoken softly; Olyr was not far away. "What," he whispered, "do chastity, sobriety and sleeplessness have to do with magic? He might have been an outstanding wizard if their damned inflexible rules had not destroyed him. And we still don't understand why.

"In truth, I believe there is no reason behind the things that wizards do—or if there is, it was forgotten ages ago and magicians repeat the old ceremonies without knowing what they once meant. Remember, Orlan, when I used to plague My Lord Redmantyl with my questions, he always answered *Because it is this way*. It is probably the only answer he received from his own master, and he doesn't know the truth any more than we do."

Godefroi had heard of the Storm Port disaster.

"It is difficult, I know, to forgive him his crimes. We all worshiped him."

"Not I."

"You especially, Orlan. He was *your* father. He was all that Normans admire—tall, strong, brave, a victor of many battles. A living hero. I loved him so dearly as a father myself. Olyr too, though he would die before confessing it. When we were boys, it seemed he could do no wrong, and when he did, it was a betrayal. For years, I hated him for what he did to Olyr, but now I think he couldn't help it. He is entangled by the rules of his blasted profession and he won't bend them even for those he loves most. He loved Olyr, but he expelled him without mercy. He loved Laurel, yet he let her go. The ranks of wizardry do not admit leniency to the imperfect. And, Orlan, I believe he destroyed the Storm Port Mayor for the same reason. He wanted to save you from her."

"I didn't need to be saved!" Orlan protested. "Ilset did nothing to harm me. And what of her husband? He was an innocent fool. Father had no right to kill them."

"But he thought he did. She was an old foe and imagined she meant you harm—it doesn't matter whether or not she truly did. He saw her so, and he retaliated in the time-honored manner of wizardry. He challenged her to battle.

"Your father isn't evil. Cruel, yes. Ruthless in his treatment of lesser magicians if they prove weak or malign. If it is true that the Storm Port Mayor and her husband meant you no harm, he has committed a terrible injustice. But he saw them as a threat to his beloved son– yes, Orlan! He would do such a thing to protect you. He dealt with an enemy as wizards have always done. For him, there was no other course. He *is* great wizard, the premiere wizard. He cannot break with the traditions which brought him to the place he holds, even if he desired to be peaceable. I can't hate him. `Tis pitiable."

Orlan spluttered. "Pity him! He killed them!"

"He's killed others. It never disturbed you to know that."

"Yes, but they were full wizards, able to defend themselves in honest battle. They challenged him—as you say, that is the way it had always been done. They would have killed him if he had not been the stronger. Houarde and Ilset were helpless. And he did it in front of me! I *felt* them–" He stopped suddenly. The memory of Houarde's white, rolled-back eyes and Ilset's dying screams returned to him as vividly as he had witnessed them on that horrible day. He had never spoken of this before; he had told Alen the essential details, but not all.

"He descended on the city like an angel on the Day of Judgement," he continued, "bright in his wrath. The sky was as stormy as the days after Olyr fell. He was afire with all the energies a great wizard is capable of, powers so vast and terrible no human could contain them— yet he does. He can scatter the essence of a living being to the tiniest fragments. That was what he did to Ilset. When he left her, she was nothing. Houarde, he struck down almost incidentally. Even if they had contrived at my corruption, they did not deserve that death. It is unforgivable!

"I *saw* him truly that day, Godefroi. He is an inhuman force of destruction, and there is so much more he refuses to do..." His voice was choked with a confusing muddle of emotions and tears blurred his vision.

Godefroi's hand fell on his arm. "It hurts all the more to love him in spite of what he is."

"Love *him*? After what he's done? You must be mad."

His friend had simply smiled at this denial.

Orlan went to the cottage door. The mists of early morning had not yet dissipated, but the road between the green hills was visible through the trees on the slope below him. There was no rider on the road, nor foot-traveler. Redmantyl was not in sight. But it was foolish to expect him to arrive so soon. Only three days had passed since Orlan decided to call upon his father for help; even if Redmantyl had left Wizardes Cliff immediately after that first summons was invoked and had ridden at his swiftest speeds, the journey would still take a week.

Was Redmantyl traveling at all? Orlan shut his eyes, from weariness as much as from his efforts to concentrate. He could not endure this vigil much longer. For three days, three nights, he had waited, his spellcaster's senses flung wide, calling, searching, broadcasting his urgent message. He had spent energies long disused and if Redmantyl did not come, he would collapse in exhaustion.

Father, do you hear me? he repeated his plea. *Please come. I need you.*

He wished he could perceive Redmantyl, wherever he was. Once, it had been so easy to sense that radiant life-force; the psychic blaze of the great wizard had seemed omnipresent, a comfort in his childhood, later, a disturbance and even an intrusion to his own more subdued magical identity, but always there. He had lived within it. He had felt truly alone for the first time when he cut himself away from the overwhelming presence of his father. Now, he struggled to reestablish that severed connection.

Had his awareness atrophied so much with years of disuse? No. He was receiving impressions he knew he would not be able to if his senses were closed: the stir and creak of the house around him; Alen's muted heartbeat, so near; the non-living brightness of the hearth fire; the tiny flickers of birds and other small creatures waking in the underbrush; the fresh, rain-like coolness of the dissolving mists; the glint of active spellcraft on the amulet still in his hands; the teeming life of Oerykton not five miles away. If he exerted himself, he might locate a specific person in the town, touch a single mind and impart his feelings of exhaustion and frantic worry to one sensitive enough to receive them, but this was not the time for such experiments. There was only one person he must reach now, but for all Orlan's reawakened awareness he didn't know if Redmantyl had heard his plea. There was no acknowledgment. He could not sense that brilliant presence anywhere. He couldn't reach him. Redmantyl might be ten miles away, or one thousand. Would he come, even if he received the summons?

He had scorned Godefroi's words, but now he had to admit their truth. He loved his father; he hated him because he did love him so much. Redmantyl's enormous powers had terrified him, not because they revealed the wizard to be alien to everything ordinarily human, but because such powers were wielded by the one person whom Orlan had imagined himself most like. Until that time, he had wanted to be everything his father was, without knowing what Redmantyl truly was. When he discovered the truth, it had been too much to bear. It had seemed impossible that he admired the master of that raging force unleashed for terrible purposes. It was as if Redmantyl had deliberately concealed this inhuman power, and then revealed it in the most brutal manner. He had never told Orlan that this was what magicians were—that this was what he too would be. That had been the most frightening thing. That was the ultimate betrayal of his love.

But that all seemed to matter so little now. He wasn't angry anymore. Orlan would forgive Redmantyl the deaths of Houarde and Ilset. He would forgive Olyr's ruin. He would even forgive him his mother, if the great magics he had witnessed could accomplish this one saving act.

He needed him—so much was obvious. Even if he despised the wizard, Orlan had no one else to turn to in this time of crisis. His own half-trained and nearly forgotten abilities were not enough; he required strong magics, the strongest available.

Magic had purposes wizards did not reveal to the uninitiated. Magic had purposes which had been forgotten. Magic was without purpose at all. Magic was a gift. Magic was a curse. Magic was a dread responsibility to those who bore it. Magic was a power for death and devastation. Magic was a power for creation and healing. Whatever it was, whatever it was meant for, Redmantyl possessed it. Redmantyl *was* magic embodied.

Yet there was more at stake here. He would never have called upon the great wizard if it were not for this emergency, but now that it had been done, Orlan found himself trembling at the prospect of seeing his father again. He was nearly in tears at the thought of reunion. What would they say to each other? What could be said, after all that had passed?

For so long, his father had been the center of his life, his law, his teacher, his master in all things. Everything he had done was for Redmantyl's sake, whether to please him or to lash out against him. He could not be indifferent. It was still so today. If Redmantyl did not retain some importance for him, why was he so apprehensive to face him again after these long years, and more afraid that he would not come?

Would his father never come?

Father, please come.

He had fought with Alen for the first time when the troupe prepared to leave Guylliamesburghe. He wanted to join them. After finding his friends, he did not want to lose them again, and Godefroi and Olyr were as earnest to keep in his company. When they were together, they relived a happier time when they had been boys and had planned entirely different lives for themselves. Olyr brightened as they laughed over long-ago pranks and childhood games, swims at Dubbs Beach, rides through the forest and tag in the Great Tower. He grew misty-eyed as they remembered Laurel. Orlan spent so much time at the caravan that he neglected his work and the carpenter threatened to throw him out. He didn't care. He was weary of his menial employment and eager to leave.

Alen was ready to refuse him—he knew she had more than enough reason to insist on staying where they were—but in the middle of the argument she looked into his eyes, and sighed.

"If it will bring you happiness, my Love."

When the troupe left, they went with it. Orlan became a thesper. It was not an occupation he would have chosen for himself, but acting proved to be a magnificent game. He was delighted to discard the monotonous browns of a peasant and at last put on fanciful garb again, for he had not entirely lost the dandified tastes of his youth. It was an amusement to wrap himself in colorful cloaks and paste false beards to his chin.

And more: in costume, he became another person. *You are who your colors declare you*—the old saying was always true in Norman society. Orlan knew he had been accepted as a noble-born Chyelde when he wore the scarlet and grey of a wizard-lord's legitimate offspring, and he had lost that identity by returning to the simple clothes of a commoner. He was what he presented himself to be, but as a thesper, the change occurred daily.

His first disguises were not exceptional. Because of his height, handsome face and nobleman's manners, he was given minor roles as attendant knights and lordlings in courtly dramas. As he developed his ability to learn lines—no more difficult to memorize than lengthy incantations—and relaxed his stilted and self-conscious speech, he played the heroes of romances: Tristam, Launcelot, Prince Denys. He became these bold and adventurous lovers; he saw it in the shining eyes and giggles of the maids in the audience, and in Alen's smile when the performance was done. After this, his role-playing grew more elaborate. With a variety of wigs over his short-clipped curls, he took up the guises of monks, merchants, thieves and, occasionally, women, for the troupe was predominantly male and all of them were required to play milkmaids or Ladies when the play demanded. Once, he and Godefroi performed as comic minstrels and if lute-playing was not among Godefroi's many talents and if neither of them could carry a tune, well, that was all part of the fun. The frequent change of costume and character gave him a certain freedom. For a time, he could be whomever he chose. He found forgetfulness of his true self.

This was the lure of the Free Folk: all of them sought escape from something in their former lives, a personal sorrow, an impediment to their liberty, a dissatisfaction with life that ordinary people did not feel. These were restless folk who did not fit in; they had no place in the rigid caste system of Norman society and so lived at its borders. They sought freedoms which could not be found elsewhere. Here, they were able to shed all but the moment and live in capricious gaiety; onstage and off, they created new personalities at a whim and discarded these disguises once they grew bored. It didn't matter what they had been before. They were wanderers, banded together. Among them, Orlan did not have to think of where he had been or where he would go next. He did not have to remember who he was. He lived the security of one who was nameless, reckless, forever in motion, yet always at home and in the company of friends.

Orlan marveled that Alen had stayed with him, wandering, for as long as she had. While he found the life of a thesper intoxicating, she was miserable. Alen was no traveler and no performer; she was unable to assume any personality but that which she had been born with. Though her literacy had improved with Orlan's help, she was never so confident of her abilities to read aloud in front of others. She was too timid to recite lines and did not like to draw attention from an audience. She only agreed to appear onstage when the troupe was short of players and needed all available participants to fill out a crowd.

She was lonely among the elfish thespians. The few other women in the troupe were too flamboyant to have much in common with the shy little silversmith. Godefroi befriended her, and Olyr too, but when they were all together, she was often excluded from the conversation. They didn't mean to close her out, but all three were educated men, former magicians, boyhood friends with memories of a common experience which Alen did not share. Godefroi and Olyr were part of that past which Orlan so rarely spoke of; they knew him in ways she did not in spite of the depth of their intimacy. Orlan was able to speak with them of things he could not explain to her. When the talk turned to Wizardes Cliff, she could only sit and listen.

Orlan saw that she was unhappy, and it stung that his discontent had caused her pain. He was forced to choose between his own life and hers. When the troupe passed Oerykton, they bid farewell to his friends and tried to settle again. Igren welcomed them and found them a gamekeeper's cottage outside the town. Alen resumed her apprenticeship in the town. They'd been happy here.

He was nearly asleep before the fire when there was a knock at the door.

His father had arrived.

"Orlan," Redmantyl said. "You wanted me?"

Relief brightened the young man's eyes, but he only answered, "I had no one else to turn to. My Lord– Father, help her, please."

"Help who?"

Orlan tugged him into the cottage and led him up to the bedroom, a loft beneath a low, sloping ceiling and barely large enough to contain the narrow bed within. Alen lay beneath sheets stained pink by water and blood.

"This is Alen, my wife," Orlan said bluntly. "She miscarried badly. The midwife–" But Redmantyl needed no more explanation. "Father, help her. Don't let her die."

The wizard knelt beside the bed. "Have you called upon anyone to examine her? The midwife? A healer?"

"The midwife's been in and out since the beginning, but this is beyond her skill. Igren's sent for Brothers from the Abbey. They've not yet come."

"Little may be done before I know her illness. `Til then," he placed his hand on Alen's perspiration-spotted brow. Her breath fell a little more easily. "She will sleep without pain."

"You'll save her?" Orlan asked.

"I shall try. I can promise you no more. She may have gone too far to be recovered."

"No."

"You'll have to face that possibility, Orlan. If she's been so ill for days, I may be too late."

Orlan laughed bitterly. "Yes, you are always too late."

"I came as soon as I knew I was needed and I will do all I can, but this healing may not be in my power."

"Then your power is worthless to me! I turn to you and your great magic for help, and you do nothing. It is so much more easy to kill, isn't it, Father?"

"Yes, it is!"

Orlan stepped back, abashed. He hadn't planned that his first words to his father would be harsh and force his father to speak harshly too. This was not at all what he wanted. "Father, I–"

The wizard waved his hand against the apology. "She mustn't be disturbed," he said. They returned to the lower room, but before either could say a word, there was another knock at the door.

The Brotherhood of the Abbey of St. Yzra was famed for its medical knowledge and Brothers were often called out to heal any illness or injury which the less practiced local healers could not. No man there was best known for his skill with the problems particular to women, but Brother Anselm had been married to a midwife before he'd entered the monastery and he'd learned his medicine from her. He was an aged, silent monk who crossed himself as he entered Orlan's home, then bowed to Lord Redmantyl; the young Brother who followed him, Kaiberte, did the same. The midwife Uinen accompanied them. Alen had been her patient up to this point, but she was an herbal healer and deliverer of babies, and she had little experience with this type of severe complication.

"I asked to come when I heard," Kaiberte explained. "Orlan–" But the youth's sympathies ended at a sharp look from Brother Anselm.

"Where is the patient, My Lord?" Anselm asked.

"Upstairs. Orlan, take them to her." He spoke to his son as he might to a servant, but Orlan obeyed without taking offense.

"Brother Anselm says we must wait," the young man announced when he returned.

"It will not be long before we have an answer then. Orlan, sit down."

"I cannot." He looked up at the closed loft door impatiently.

"You must. What more can be done? Here, tell me of Alen. How long have you been married?"

"More than five years," Orlan answered.

"Have you always been here near Oerykton?"

"No, I only returned last summer. Igren's husband agreed that we might stay. He wouldn't have us in the castle and I would not be at his court again. Igren gave us this gamekeeper's cottage."

"You tend the deer?"

Orlan shook his head. "They flee me. No. I know a little of woodcraft." He gestured toward a pile of unfinished, jointed dolls, hinged boxes and kitchen tools piled in the corner. "'Tis money enough to live upon." He did not want to answer any more questions; each reply brought back a memory he could not bear.

"You are here quickly, Father," he said instead. "I called upon you three night's past and you can't have traveled so swiftly from Wizardes Cliff."

"I wasn't at Wizardes Cliff," the wizard answered. "I went to Storm Port to meet Mathias on his return from Europe. He is a wizard now."

"Mathias? He was the most hopeless of all the `prentices."

"He's not remarkable," Redmantyl agreed, "but competent. He'll make his place. Of the four greater talents in my care, none did so well. We were guests to the city's Mayor." He saw the flicker of dread that crossed Orlan's face, and added: "Not Ilset. She died two years ago."

"She was dead long before that."

Redmantyl did not answer this. Instead, he said, "Things are quite different in Storm Port now. I'd not been there since–"

Orlan twisted to hear the whispered conference upstairs. "Do you think they can do anything for her?"

"They are the finest scholars of medicine in the Northlands."

"Even Brother Anselm is not so clever in his treatment of women's ills. He's summoned to feed Igren herbs and tonics in her pregnancies, and she miscarries and delivers stillbirths. Her living child is no credit to him. Kai is only an apprentice. They do not see women for months at a time. What can they know?"

"They know a good deal more than you or I," Redmantyl answered. "At the least, they will recognize the depth of her illness and tell me where I must direct my powers. If she can be saved, I will do it."

"You must save her," Orlan said. He was no longer angry, only desperate. "Please, Father. Alen– She is all to me. There's been no one else."

"I know." He patted his son's arm. "You have not slept in days?"

"No, not since before– the– er–"

"You do no one good with such torments, not yourself and not her. You must rest."

"But if she needs me—"

"If she needs you, you'll be called for," Redmantyl answered he led him to a chair. "I'll stay with her until you wake."

"You promise?" Orlan was too exhausted to struggle and sank back.

"Yes, I promise you. Sleep, Orlan." He touched Orlan's temple; the young man's eyes shut and he relaxed instantly. Redmantyl removed his cloak and spread it over his sleeping son, then went upstairs. The midwife was settling Alen's blood-stained shift over her knees while she and Brother Anselm whispered in consultation. The Brother shook his head sadly.

"You can do nothing for her?" asked Redmantyl, also in a whisper.

"The womb is badly torn and inflammation has claimed all the lower organs," Anselm answered. "In such cases, when the fetus has not fully descended before its growth, the mother usually dies within a day. 'Tis miraculous that she's lived so long as she has. Healer Uinen's been giving her a potion of bitterroot to lessen the blood-flow and we've agreed to continue that, but in truth she's lost too much to recover. See how pale she is, how cool the skin in spite of the symptoms of fever." This was spoken to Kai, who nodded as an attentive pupil but looked more distressed than the elder Brother; he had held Alen's hand through the examination and felt how cold she was. "We may do little to eliminate an infection so entwined within the body. If an arm or leg is putrefied, a poultice may be applied or the poisoned limb removed to save the patient, but the innards..." Brother Anselm despaired at the thought. "The attempt would end her life more swiftly and painfully than it goes now. We do not have the skill. If you can do more, My Lord?"

The wizard nodded. "Yes. Gramercy, Brother, Kai."

"We'll be at Oerykton if you have need of us, My Lord," Anselm said. "Brother Kaiberte!"

After they had gone, Redmantyl turned to the bed and found that Alen was awake and watching him.

"No need t'whisper, M'Lord." Her voice was faint. "I knew when the baby was lost. Doesn't take a healer's skill to feel y'self fading."

"I'm sorry." Redmantyl sat at the bedside. "Are you in pain now?"

She shook her head. "I wanted t'meet you, Lord Redmantyl. Orlan's spoke so much of you, his wizard father. He is bitter but I could see there was more'n that. He felt more than he said." She tried to smile. "I'm glad you came to his call, e'en if it would do me no good."

"Alen, I will use all the skill I possess. You must know that."

"Yes, I know, M'Lord. You'll try. I'll be glad if I'm healed, but I won't believe it truly `til I'm out of this bed. Orlan's tried too, y'see."

"Did he?" Redmantyl was surprised.

"When the midwife was first here. She said she could do no more. He said he could, `n' he tried most bravely for me." She sighed. "`Twas not enough. He called for you then, an' you might try too." One deadly-white hand moved on the stained sheets, shifting toward him, and Redmantyl took it gently. Alen squeezed his fingers.

"M'Lord," she said, "I must ask this of you, if I die soon."

"Yes, Daughter."

"When you leave, take them with you."

"Them?" Redmantyl wondered. "Orlan and–?"

"He didn't tell you of our daughter?" Alen smiled slightly. "No, Orlan wouldn't. She's up at the castle with Lady Igren, since I– M'Lord, my child should be a Lady. I was born to a home such as this, and `tis a harder life than Orlan knows. He's only played at common's life, like a pretty minstrel's song of woolly lambs and green fields. Fools no one with his tales of bastardry—always a nobleman in poor disguise. He's not fit for this `n' she won't be either.

"Orlan shouldn't refuse his own blood," she continued after a thoughtful silence. "I've seen him so angry and frightened like a spoiled little child, and for no reason. He won't have his nobility to spite. Won't have his magic nor his learning, and won't have them for the little one. She's so magical as he is."

"Little children don't have magic."

Alen nearly smiled again. "She does. But he says it'll bring her no good. I can't believe him in that, M'Lord. I love him dearly, ye must know, for the man he is for all his unsettled heart. I'll follow him through his troubles, but not at the price of her. He mustn't keep our girl from a better life for his pride. I don't want her to end here if she has the right to more. You'll see she has her rights? You'll take her from here? Take `m both where they properly belong."

"I shall." He set her cool hand on the mattress. "She'll be received as my grandchild."

Alen shut her eyes, satisfied. "She'll be a credit to you," she whispered. "Her father's child, stubborn `n' ye must be gentle with both for that, but she's as fine as any Lady. She's `customed to castles."

She slept again. The wizard gently placed a hand upon her inflamed abdomen and began to weave the first of many spells.

cinqueten

Orlan woke to the sound of his father chanting softly in the loft, and he went up. Redmantyl, one wrist bandaged, sat at the foot of the bed writing a final cipher across the sheets; other runes were painted on the walls, on Alen's nightdress and her face. Candles burned at the eight points of a double-square star drawn within a circle on the floor and a faint sickly-scorched scent hung in the air. Alen lay at the center of this craft; Orlan watched the gentle rise and fall of her breath with relief. "She's sleeping?"

"For now," the wizard answered.

"What have you done?" Orlan could feel the intricately woven magics of the spellcraft about Alen; he didn't dare to come closer for fear of crossing the wards and disturbing them. He tried to read the smeared device on the palm of Alen's outflung hand, but he had forgotten much of his education and his father had never taught him this spell. "Will she recover?"

"I have stopped the blood and removed the mortification from her flesh. So much can be done. But, Orlan," he lowered his voice as he led his son gently from the room, "she has been bleeding for many days and that lost blood cannot be replenished. The infection has taken much from her. I am no healer, but I can see as well as any midwife or trained Brother that she has no strength to restore herself."

"You can't give her the strength?"

"That must be her own. But I can hold her as she is. So long as Alen is within the circle, she is safe."

"And this will give her time to heal?"

"No. The spell is one of *statari*—the unchanging state. Alen rests within in it, but she remains as she is, out of pain, undying, unliving. You must understand, Orlan, that she is like a flower cut from its stem," Redmantyl explained as they descended. "If you put it into water, it may be suspended in its fresh state awhile longer, but it will not continue to grow and you will never see it bloom again. She was near the point of death when I cast the *statari* sphere about her. I'm sorry, Orlan. That is the most I can do."

"She is alive," said Orlan. "How long will the spell hold?"

"It requires great effort to raise such a temporal anomaly, but it may be sustained for many years if the outer wards remain unbreached."

"Can she pass the boundaries?"

Redmantyl shook his head.

Orlan thought of Alen lying there at the point between life and death. She would continue so for as long as Redmantyl's spell held her. She could not move. She would never change. With a tremor of horror, he imagined himself sitting at her bedside through those suspended years. Would she hear if he told her news of the world that passed around her? Would she notice that he grew older while she did not? Would she suffer her unhealed injuries? Or would she simply sleep, frozen forever like the entranced princess of a fairytale without the release of a kiss?

It was not a true life. It was not what he wanted for her.

"No," Orlan could not accept this fate. "There must be something more we can do to save her–" Then he remembered. "Father, there is a way! There is a spell to restore the dead! We can–"

Redmantyl cut this hope abruptly. "We can't."

"You won't?" Surely, he was still asleep and this was all a nightmare. He had wished against reason that his father would come before it was too late, and Redmantyl had come. He had seen Alen. He knew how ill she was. He had even cast spells for her. Now he stood here and calmly announced that he would not restore her life even though he had the means. This could not be true!

Yet, it was so. Redmantyl refused.

"You'll let her die? You could save her!"

"Orlan, I can't! Do you think I would do less than I could for her life?"

"You might have saved my mother and refused!" Orlan shot back. "It is always so—you use your magic to show how powerful you are, how easily you can destroy, but when you might act for good, you stand aside! You know the spell! You kept it from me so I wouldn't understand how she died! You'll let Alen die too. For all gods, why?"

"It won't work," Redmantyl answered simply. "Such spells are too dangerous to meddle with."

"Necromancy?" the young man replied. "You speak of evil-doing when you might give Alen back her life? How can it be evil?"

"Orlan, you don't know what you're saying. You must trust me in this. It will come to no good."

Trust him? Orlan could not. "If you cannot perform this one

simple spell for her, I will!" He turned to fly up the stairs; his father grabbed his arm and wrenched him back.

Orlan fought, but Redmantyl held him at the foot of the stairs. His shoulders were pressed to the wall with a force like iron. "Damn you! Let me go!"

"Promise me you will not inflict that spell upon her. It is an abomination to all right magic."

"I won't have her die for your scorn of improper magic. I will go! You can't hold me here forever!"

"I will stop you," Redmantyl replied evenly, "so long as I must. You cannot employ such dark sorcery."

Orlan flung blows and kicks and shouted incoherent curses, hating his father furiously, but Lord Redmantyl remained unyielding and pinned him as helpless as a child. His struggles were useless; he could not break free and his father would not release him. There was no help for it save surrender.

"Promise me," said Redmantyl.

Spent, he gave into that stronger will and answered through clenched teeth and outraged tears: "Promise."

His father watched over him for some hours but, at last, even a great wizard must rest. Redmantyl had exerted a great deal of power to weave his elaborate spellcraft and needed to rejuvenate himself; he meditated.

Orlan waited, submitted, suppressed his anger. He could not speak to his father without loathing and he rejected all overtures for explanation or condolence. What could be said? What of the wizard's promises that Orlan would understand when the worst was past? If there were reasons for this atrocity, he did not want to understand them. What reasons could there be? Nothing excused this betrayal. No apology was sufficient. Redmantyl's actions were unforgivable.

After awhile, the wizard wisely ceased to try to talk and left his son alone, but he was always nearby. Orlan felt himself under guard. He still stung with humiliation at how easily he had been overpowered and he knew certainly that Redmantyl would not hesitate to stop him again. If he tried to fly to Alen now, he would be caught. The watch over him would be redoubled. His father might even imprison him, shut him away or bind him entranced, until she was past all help. For Alen's sake, he must pretend obedience. He did not go near the stairs; he did not attempt to escape from beneath his father's vigilant gaze. He bit back his rage. If it were not for the spells that held her safe, undying, he would have despaired but, so long as she lived, he could be patient. There was time.

When the wizard set himself to his rest, Orlan also lay down as if to sleep. He watched as Redmantyl's eyes shut, listened as Redmantyl's breath grew deep and relaxed. He waited until the wizard's meditative state indicated that his mind was elsewhere. No longer observed, Orlan slipped from the room and went up to the loft. He had taken a small, sharp carving knife from his carpentry tools. He held it now as he sat at the foot of Alen's bed.

A promise made under such circumstances was not binding. He would not be held by it. Alen's life was at stake! Did his father believe he wouldn't do everything possible to save her? He was not afraid of necromancy. He was no sorcerer intent on seizing unnatural powers for himself. He did not act for evil; he simply wanted Alen alive and he would do whatever he must to heal her. Damn the consequences to himself! If he endangered his soul, he was willing. Whatever higher forces which condemned such sacrifice might bring on their retribution as they pleased. He didn't care. Alen must not die if he was able to prevent it.

Redmantyl would not remain in his trance much longer. Soon, Orlan's absence would awaken him; even in the deepest meditative state, the exercise of strong magic so near would disrupt the flow of energies about the wizard and draw his attention. This one opportunity must not be lost.

He had passed the wards about Alen without difficulty. They were powerful, but to protect her, not to prevent his entrance. No harm could come to Alen here. The spell could only be broken from within. Once inside, he felt the influence of his father's work: he perceived the temporal anomaly Redmantyl had created as a sort of bubble defined by the octogram on the floor, enclosing the dying woman. Within, there was no growth and no decay. Suspended precariously in a static point of time, Alen simply existed. He felt as if he too were frozen in time. He was immersed in some thick, transparent substance like liquid glass; he breathed, he thought clearly, but he could move no more than slowly. Every action required great deliberation. An inconsequential gesture made in real time here seemed momentous.

With the concentrated intensity of a spellcaster, he placed his left hand gently between her breasts, against the beating heart, and called upon the magic he possessed. Quelled for so long, it reawakened at his command: he felt it rise with each pulse of his own heart, rise to match the beating of Alen's. He held the essence of her life.

The last time he had touched her so, he had felt the life seep slowly from her, her energy diminishing with each drop of blood. He had felt the rupture of deep tissues where their unborn child had tried to grow and instead torn its mother apart. Where the child had been lost, the infection had taken hold. He had sensed that too, as a separate entity inside Alen's body, a virulent force with its own will to survive. Ravenous, it had consumed her. It had sapped her life and strength and left only dead tissue. It would drain her life away if it were not stopped. When he had first used his magic for Alen's sake, Orlan had known all of this, but he hadn't known what to do to counter it. He knew less than the midwife and monks; his skills were inexpert and his powers uncertain. The vague spells had failed.

But Redmantyl had known exactly what to do. The necrosis had been cut away with a skill no chirugeon possessed. That was the power of the Lightmaster: light could create a bright shield, a spark to light a candlewick, a pretty, dancing toy, an inferno to blast through stone as easily as wood, or lightning to rend the skies. Light could be wielded as a sword against an enemy, or directed as a delicate knife to slice away dead and damaged flesh with pin-point precision. The blood that trickled away Alen's life had been stopped. Orlan was not certain how; it seemed as if a multitude of tiny seals had been placed upon the wound. He marvelled at the work. An exquisite piece of surgery, and accomplished without cutting the skin. It was almost enough to ensure that Alen would live.

But this saving had come too late. Alen had fought with all her strength to overcome the illness which consumed, and she had lost. The threat to her life had been removed, but only after her own forces were depleted. The damaged flesh should regenerate. The lost blood should replace itself. These processes of healing were arrested so long as Alen remained within the spellcraft, but Orlan knew that she had no energy left for them even if she were free. Her life-force was tenuous. The infection had ravaged her. She had already bled to death before Redmantyl had intervened. The *statari* spell held her, nothing more. Father had been correct; she would die outside the influence of this powerful enchantment.

Only one hope remained.

Many years had passed since Orlan had read that book of forbidden rites, but the incantation was simple enough. The words were not forgotten.

He spoke: "Blood to my blood, life to my life, soul to my soul, I give myself to thee." The words were heartfelt; he would sacrifice all these things, and more. All he had to give. For Alen. He lifted the knife to cut his own wrist.

Alen opened her eyes.

With a cry like that of a wounded bird, she flung up an arm and knocked the blade away. Orlan reached for it and Alen twisted beneath his hands. They moved slowly; Orlan did not immediately realize that Alen was reaching for the rim of the circle, not the knife. He struggled to pull her back. Alen resisted with a determination that surprised him. She slipped from his grasp and fell half-off the bed, arms on the floor, and brushed at the lines drawn about her. The circle was broken. One candle fell over with a tinny clatter and went out.

Redmantyl came into the room.

"Father, help me!"

"What's happened?"

"She broke the spell!" With one fierce tug, Orlan brought Alen back to the bed. The sensation of frozen motion had vanished. They had returned to the swift movements of normal time.

"She broke the spell? Herself?"

"I would not have believed–" Orlan stopped there, for his father had seen the knife on the sheets. Redmantyl did not speak, only picked it up and looked at him, wondering.

"Yes, of course I did!" Orlan replied. "I'm not afraid, as you are. I'm willing to sacrifice myself in the black arts if it buys her life."

The words were spit with defiance. He was unprepared when Redmantyl, in answer, took him by the shoulders and shook him.

"Wretched little fool! Do you know what you have nearly done? In ignorance, you would scorn my intentions. You betray all trust! Enough! I have been too gentle with your grief. I have tried to make you listen to reason. If you will not hear me now, I will put you out of this house to see her safe from your madness.

"Listen to me! Do you think that this spell will restore your Alen to you as she was, in all her health to a long life hereafter? It will not! You may revive Alen's body once she has died, but it will not be her. Do you understand? Her body, warm and not decayed, but without light in its eyes, nor intelligence in its voice, nor emotion. Alen would be gone. *That* is the spell you would cast—to make a lifeless body walk, and no more. If you use it against one who is not yet dead, you will surely kill her!"

He released his son and Orlan sank back, stunned.

"Necromancy is a double-edged sword. It makes fair promises but does not fulfill them as you imagine. You are willing to give your soul, yes, but what have you won? Alen dead. Her corpse animate, but not as a living woman. You also risk your own life for your efforts—an unpracticed magician casting such a spell! Do you know the cost to expend so much energy, Orlan? You are drained. The shock of it might burst your own heart as well as hers. Will you forfeit both your lives for nothing?"

Orlan was too deeply horrified to answer. Was this true? Might he have killed Alen when he acted to save her? It was as if a cloud of madness had passed from him; with growing shame, he was able to look upon his father's behavior and understand.

His voice was tight and tremulous. "Why– Why didn't you tell me?"

"I tried. You would not hear."

It was all true. Redmantyl had spoken only the truth. He had done all in his power for Alen. Nothing could save her.

"Father, the chalk!" He leapt up. "We must reset the circle before it's too late." He scrambled for the charcoal stick on the chair in the corner and knelt to retrace the smudged lines.

"No," a hoarse whisper from the bed made him look up. Alen had spent the last of her strength to free herself from the spell. Without it, she faded rapidly. "If you write that again, Orlan, I'll break it, God help me."

"But you'll die!" he protested, unwilling to believe her.

"I`m not afraid. Wondered what you did t'me. Horrid. `Twas like a dream I couldn't wake from."

"It was meant to save you," said Redmantyl.

"Save me? `M not saved. Ye trap me like a poor ghost in a bottle rather'n let me go as was meant by powers higher'n yers. Ye can't make me well again, can you?"

"There is always a chance."

"Truly?"

"It is very slight," the wizard conceded. "I cannot promise your life beyond the influence of that spell."

"What life is there in it?" Alen drew a shallow breath. "Without healing? If ye can't make me well again, please don't hold me past my time this way."

"Alen, no," Orlan moaned softly.

She turned her head on the pillow. "I thought you had love for me."

"I do!"

"Then you'll not suffer me these magical traps. If I live, I live. If

253

not... But no more of this, I pray ye." She shut her eyes. "Please, don't."

"As you wish, Daughter." Redmantyl took the charcoal from Orlan.

"No–!"

"Orlan–"

"You'll let her die!"

"She is dying. I cannot force her to continue against her will."

"You can't–!"

"It isn't our decision."

Orlan looked desperately to Alen.

"Please," she whispered. "Let me go."

The young man crossed the room and looked out of the window to the grassy hills behind the cottage and the mountains and bright sky beyond. He had thought as much himself: Alen could not live trapped in half-life. He'd experienced the inanimate existence within the *statari* spell and he knew that it would be impossible to endure that paralytic state for very long without going mad. Alen would abhor it. It was only right that she wanted to escape. But he had wanted her free of it to be restored to health; Alen expected to die. Rather remain within the spell than that! Yet she would break the enchantment and face her death, and he was helpless to prevent it.

Everything had been done for her. Everything had happened just as it should, but none of it was enough. How could it end so?

His eyes clouded with tears; he blinked, and water sprayed over his unshorn cheeks. "Father, w-what will happen now?"

"She will go in minutes or hours, as she would have before the spell was set."

"Are all the spells broken? Will she be in pain?"

"No. I can keep that intact."

"Then that is all I hope for." He did not look back at the bed. "Do it."

"It is done," said Redmantyl.

"The most powerful of all wizards," Orlan said in the bitter, anguished tone he had used that morning. "I've seen you tear open the sky with furies and fill a room with the colors of your magic for amusement. You could hold this world as a toy and do as you please with its people, bless or damn them at will. And for all your powers you are as helpless before death as any other man."

"My powers are great, yes," Redmantyl answered, "but not so vast as you seem to believe. I am only a wizard. Storms are simple things.

Fire is no more than a conjuring trick. I could tear down these mountains beyond us and raise them again overnight, if there were any good to it. But these are only pieces of unliving mass. Living beings are more difficult to command, and people more than all else because each has a will of his or her own. It is not so easy to kill—even a wizard will find a dagger more effective than magic against a strong soul. And no human skill can restore life once it is lost."

There was a choked sob from Orlan as he gave up his efforts to keep control. "I can't live without you."

"You'll have to," Alen replied. "It wouldn't ever be better if you kept me here, never as it was before, my dearest boy. Mustn't be afraid." She lifted her hand. "Orlan?"

He ran to hold her, head against her breast, as if he would never let go. "Alen—"

"Hush, darling."

Redmantyl took the knife from the foot of the bed and left them alone together.

A little later, an attendant in the Earl's blue livery came to the cottage leading a small child by the hand; he gaped at the red-robed Lord who answered the door.

"You are My Lady's uncle? The great wizard?"

"I am." Redmantyl studied the child, who stared back with curiosity. She was a tiny thing, perhaps four, her rosy mouth in a pout and her dimpled chin set stubbornly. Elaborate, delicate embroidery, Igren's work, edged the hem of her pinafore and the dusky, cornflower skirts beneath, a lace collar trimmed her blouse, and blue ribbons tied her silvery ringlets. She looked more like a little shepherd-maid in a courtly play than a woodlander's child.

"My Lady has had the care of this little one," the attendant explained. "We would keep her 'til she might be called for, but this morning she woke all the household with her cries to go home. She wouldn't be quiet for anything and howled so that My Lord Geyraulte bid she be sent away."

"She wanted to come home?"

"Aye, M'Lord."

"I want Mama," the little girl said.

"You will see her, Little One," Redmantyl promised, then spoke to the youth. "I'll take her, Lad."

The attendant bowed. "Shall I tell My Lady you are here?"

"If you would."

"I want my mama!" the child insisted.

"Patience," the wizard said. He looked into her eyes—water-colored irises rimmed by bright blue—and he smiled gently. "What is your name?"

"Anne."

"Then come with me, Anne." He offered his hand and the little girl took two fingers in her small grip. "Did you hear from your Aunt Igren that your mother was ill?" he asked.

Anne shook her head.

"Where then, Child?"

She didn't answer, and Redmantyl asked no more questions. "Orlan, Anne is here!" he called up the stairs as they ascended.

The young man sat up, surprised. "Igren sent her?"

"She sent herself."

Alen's mouth moved into the faintest smile. "Annie."

"She sent herself?" Orlan asked.

The child climbed onto the bed and nestled against the curve of her mother's arm; Alen touched her frosty curls and whispered words and Anne began to hum softly, as a comforted kitten might purr.

"Alen told me there was a child," Redmantyl said in a whisper.

"She does not live here," Orlan answered, also in soft voice. "Igren keeps her at the castle and spoils her almost as if she were her own daughter. There is so little room here and little money—we thought it best to have Anne in the care of such a benefactor. She receives a place in my cousin's home that a common-born child would normally not. Geyraulte does not like her much. He remembers when I was the youth fussed over at his court. I would wager he's the one to send her home, but I cannot be angry with him for that now. She might not have seen her mother again if she had been made more welcome."

"Orlan, the child asked to come."

Orlan ignored this.

After awhile, Alen slept and the little girl sighed, "Thirsty."

Orlan took up the pitcher beside the bed, but it was empty. "Father, would you–?" he requested as he lifted the squirming child to the floor. "The well is behind the house, and you might keep her outdoors awhile."

"Don't wanna go," Anne protested. "Mama."

"She is sleeping now, Pet," Orlan answered. "Hush. Don't fuss. Mama must have quiet. When she wakes, you may sit with her again."

"When Mama wakes?"

"Yes, I promise you."

Redmantyl took her hand. "Come along, Granddaughter. We'll give you water. Don't be affrighted."

"Not `frighted." The little girl twisted to look back at her mother, then consented to be led out.

Near sunset, Orlan left Alen's side. As the hours passed, he began to hope for her again. He found Redmantyl on a hill behind the cottage, beneath a cluster of trees. The wizard appeared to be asleep.

Orlan had not thought of anyone except his wife for days, and he was surprised to see his father so weary. But Redmantyl had reason enough to be exhausted. He must have ridden for days without pause to reach Oerykton so swiftly, and he had had little rest since his arrival. He had expended a great deal of energy in his efforts to save Alen. Orlan knew how difficult it must be to remove that killing infection so intertwined with Alen's flesh, and how much more taxing to weave the time-bubble to sustain her. Redmantyl had given his own strength for Alen's sake. He'd given his own life's blood. The crafting of such spells would strain even the greatest wizard's powers, yet Redmantyl had spent hours in their formation, then allowed them to be dissolved at Alen's word. He need not have done so. He need not have come at all to aid a son who had left him and a woman he had never met—but he was here. He had not healed Alen, but he had tried to his limits and Orlan could not fault him. The wizard had fought fiercely for Alen's life. Even if he must be hated for it.

Orlan was sorry he had been so ungrateful. If Alen chose to be released from the enchantment which sustained her, they had to abide by that. His father had done all he could. *He* had done all he could.

He saw too that Redmantyl had aged. The wizard was a young man no longer. How old? He must be past sixty, perhaps near seventy. Orlan had never learned exactly. He'd always thought of his father as an ageless being, continuing unchanged for as long as he kept his powers, but Orlan could see that deep lines had cut into Redmantyl's brow and fainter ones touched the corners of his eyes and mouth. If his hair had not always been silvery white, it would be streaked with gray.

The wizard's eyes opened. "Orlan. Is she–?"

"Sleeping, Father." Orlan sat down. "Where's Anne?"

Redmantyl gestured to the lower slope and the little figure in the tall grass, pulling up handfuls of flowers. She stared back at them, then resumed her pursuit. "She's a pretty child."

"I knew I would have a daughter. Alen too—she said it felt like a girl—but I dreamt of Anne exactly once, years before she was born. I would have called her Nann, after my mother, but Alen thought it common."

"Anne is a fine name. Emperors and Queens, Dukes, brave knights have been called Anne. Wizards as well—Anne Suifte, Anne of Orkeney." Their eyes met briefly, and the young man knew surely what his father was thinking. More must be said here, but Orlan was unwilling to speak.

"It is in our family," he said. "Magic. You've told me often enough."

"My Aunt Loren might've been a wizard of no little power, if she would use it," Redmantyl answered. "Others in the family carry the talent too: Kaiese, Laurel," he sighed, "Igren. But they cast it away. My grandmother, I have been told, was a wizard. When she is remembered at Tremontegne, they call her fairy, changeling, witch, demon."

"Why? What did she do?"

"That, I have never been able to discover."

"It must have been horrible, for such names."

"She was very powerful."

"As powerful, Father, as you?"

"I think not. Her name is not recalled among the ranks of the magical as the best wizards always are. But there are times that I wonder–" He considered the little girl thoughtfully, watching as she waved to the shepherds driving the Earl's flocks in from the nearby hills. "Power, true power in its most pure form, would not be thunderbolts and fire and the casting of elaborate spells. The most powerful being may be the one who never shows what it can do. It would have no need to awe lesser beings with arrogant display, for it would know its own abilities and that would be sufficient." Then he laughed. "Ah, Orlan, such a thought would not have come to me when I was younger. When I defeated the Old Lord, I thought *now I am most powerful*, and I never wondered how I might use my power best.

"As a young wizard, I made great plans. I believed that my years as Redmantyl would be glorious and later wizards would look back on my day as a time of magical excellence. I thought to see all my apprentices become magicians of great repute. Instead, I find that I've done nothing I meant to. My scholarship has come to scratchings in books that no one will read. I am no great teacher—all of you, save Mathias, are past my reach. I've failed at each duty my wizardry demanded, and so I must wonder if I am truly powerful or wise after all."

Orlan was astonished. Lord Redmantyl, so cool and strong and self-assured, spoke of such deep self-doubt? Impossible! This was not the unwavering master wizard Orlan remembered. What had changed him?

Tentatively, the young man reached out to reestablish the bond which had once linked them. There was contact; although Orlan only touched the still surface of the wizard's mind, he received more information than he thought he ever would.

He felt the sadness, the bitterness. Redmantyl's exalted power and position had become a gall. His magic, his knowledge, his strict discipline had not been enough to prevent the series of disasters which had befallen him. He had lost everything he cared for, and he did not understand how. What had gone wrong? Had these matters been under his control? If so, how could he have altered them? Redmantyl felt himself responsible, but he did not know precisely how he had failed. This mystery still stunned, bewildered, and pained him. He wanted to repair his mistakes, somehow, if he could. Most were past recovery but here, with Orlan, he continued to hope. He was ready to make reconciliations, to forgive and be forgiven and have peace again, but he didn't know what words must be said.

So little was revealed by the wizard's thoughts, yet so much of significance to Orlan. For the first time, he understood his father. Sorrow, pain, regret—these were the frailties of any human. By possessing them, Redmantyl ceased to be a being of vast incomprehensibility to his son. He was a great magician, but a man like any other.

"Why do you persist then?" asked Orlan.

"I cannot abandon what I am. I must be a wizard. I'd rather keep that which I possess than have nothing at all."

"Has it made you happy?"

"Happiness is not the goal of wizardry," Redmantyl answered. "Command is. Magic must be employed to the best abilities. I have given my best. I am above all other magicians, and must be satisfied with that. I could not explain this to the magicless, but you must understand."

Orlan didn't answer. He wished too that he had the right words to say, but they had not yet come. The most important conversation remained unspoken.

Anne returned with a bundle of weeds and wild flowers nearly her own size and threw them down. "Mama's waking," she announced. "We'll go in now, Da?"

"Yes, Annie."

Alen lay awake for a short while, never speaking, then resumed her sleep. Redmantyl reset the remaining spell which kept her from pain and kissed her cool cheek. "Fare ye well, my child. May you have peace." At the sound of footsteps at the doorway behind him, he turned to look up into his son's troubled eyes. "I do not think she will wake again."

The words confirmed Orlan's worst fears. Alen was healing herself, but too slowly. He knew that this moment was coming, yet so long as she continued to breathe he did not surrender to the inevitable grief. "Will you stay with us 'til the end, Father?" he asked.

"I would not leave now."

A fire was lit and the food left in the pantry brought out for the evening meal. Orlan ate little, then returned to Alen. Anne accepted spoonfuls of porridge from her grandfather, then beamed up at him and climbed into his lap. When Orlan came out onto the landing, she was resting in Redmantyl's arms, asking questions.

"Why do you wear red, Gran'ther?"

"Black and red are the colors of wizards. The greater the wizard, the more red. Do you know what a wizard is, Anne?"

She nodded solemnly. "You."

He smiled. "Yes, that's right. I am the most powerful of all living wizards, and so I am called Lord Redmantyl, for I wear this."

"'Tis truly magic, Gran'ther?"

"Yes, truly. Would you like to see?"

"Da doesn' like magic," she told him, then looked hopefully up at her father; Orlan did not protest. The little girl twisted around, smiling. "Show me!"

Redmantyl turned his hand slowly, fingers spread as if to hold a small orb, and a circlet of sparkling silvery-blue light appeared. It grew larger and fanned out from axis points at the top and bottom until it became a ball of shimmering fairylight. Anne cooed in delight and reached for it with her pudgy, baby fingers. Orlan watched them, his father and his daughter, and recalled when he had been the small one so easily pleased by the simple playthings of magic. Hadn't he once been as delighted by a glittering globe?

"You may touch it, Little One," Redmantyl said. "Go on. See how it glows brighter? Can you change the color? Yes, I think you can. There!" He smiled at her triumphant laughter as the sparkles flared into fluorescent pink.

"Can I play with it?"

"Of course, darling. It is yours now." The wizard rolled the fragile spell from his fingertips to the child's cupped palms.

Orlan was not familiar with this part of the game, but he watched it with a growing feeling of nostalgia. He remembered a room filled with colorful lights and the warmth of his father's arms about him as he cried. Even now, although he was nearly thirty, he would have welcomed that same comfort. He recalled how safe and strong his father had seemed in his childhood. He remembered, with a pang of jealousy, how he had seen Andemyon held as tenderly. He thought of the first time he had seen his father, how tall and splendidly red, how awed he had been at that magnificent being who could perform such wonderful tricks. He remembered the last time he'd seen Redmantyl, also bright, but a raging force of destruction. He remembered his sickened fear as he'd watched Houarde Portreeve fall and felt Ilset's mind dissolve. He remembered a storm over Wizardes Cliff, and Olyr's lost, hopeless look as Redmantyl walked away from him without remorse. He remembered a night when his father had wept, and another when he had flirted with some handsome Pendaunzel Lady, and so many years when they could not speak to each other. All his memories were here, now, in this room, in this quiet man with another child cradled in his arms—a little girl who held a spell of light in her hands as if it were a solid and ordinary toy. Could this all be his father? Which was the true wizard?

"Orlan," Redmantyl spoke softly as Anne settled herself to sleep, "what will you do now?"

He was surprised by the question. What would he do? "I don't know."

"Have you thought of returning to Wizardes Cliff?"

"No," but that was a lie; he knew that once he had decided to call upon his father, Redmantyl would try to take him back to that magical world he had left so long ago. Once, he would have been grateful to return, but he'd been a frightened, exiled child then. He was not that child now. "Do you want me to?"

"Yes, I would be glad to see you come home."

"So I must obey you, as I if were unable to know the best for itself. No, Father. I am no longer an unworldly apprentice to be led along your chosen paths."

"You are an unfinished magician," Redmantyl replied.

"I shall remain so. I would have become a wizard only because you wished me to, Father. I wanted to make you proud of me. But I would have been miserable. I cannot be so harsh and brutal as wizardry demands. I can't be so strict with myself. Do you think I would throw aside all my 'prenticing if I cared for it? I'm sorry if I disappoint you, but I will not be a wizard. I'm not fit. I do not wish to use my magic."

"Nevertheless, it is there and it must be dealt with," Redmantyl answered. "Orlan, you used magic to try and save Alen. Do you see? You say that you do not want your magic, yet you'll use your powers when you believe they will do some good."

"But they didn't," Orlan cried, eyes glittering with fresh tears. "Not mine, and not yours. Our magic was not enough."

"Then nothing was. Alen had half a day more—time for Anne to come home. You cannot deny the good of that. Orlan, whether you choose to exercise your power or no, you do possess it. You bear the responsibility of it."

"Responsibility?" said Orlan. "I have been ignorant of the most important matters of that craft. Why didn't you warn me? For years, I thought you let my mother die rather than use that spell. You might have told me what it was."

"You would not have listened any better than you did today. It is the nature of evil that it touches our greatest weakness and leads us to betray all that we care for in goodness. If you had gone on to wizardry, you would have learned the dangers of necromancy once you proved yourself able to resist the temptation. There would have been a proper time to reveal the truth. Outcast magicians do not usually possess the powers you have. They cannot cast such spells, so they are not so dangerous as you have been."

"Magic is dangerous in the grasp of any magician," he answered. "Even you. You have power and will far beyond mine, yet I have seen how responsible *you* may be. Do you believe you have never allowed weakness to lead you to error? It isn't so. If I should fail to command myself in anger as you had, I could not bear the consequences."

"I was very angry that day," his father agreed, "but I was never out of control. I had reasons for my fury."

"But, Father," Orlan protested, "I did not disgrace us at Storm Port so much as you may believe. You heard gossip from Adyna? She didn't know all of my conduct—only what Kyarde told her."

"I was told that you were a frequent companion to youths with a reputation for wild and rough play. With them, you met the lowest whores and most unsavory scoundrels and ran the city at night in all manner of outrageous disturbances. Kyarde found you lying in the streets too besotted to walk without help. You joined an assault on the city garrison. Was this not true?"

"No, it was."

"Then Adyna did not lie. However, I knew all this before I received her message."

"You knew—?"

"But I was resolved to let you do as you would. If you were truly unfit for wizardry, it was the time to discover it. I did not like it, but I could only see it through and have you find your own strength—or lack of it. I did not intervene until I felt that you were in great danger."

"Midsummer," said Orlan. Something *had* happened that night.

Redmantyl nodded in answer. "I saw then that you had been deliberately introduced to this vicious overindulgence. That woman led you to abandon the honor and discipline of a magician for her own malign purposes."

Orlan would have responded that he'd sought his own ruin without any help, but he knew it wasn't true. In seven years, he had had time to examine Ilset's motives. He had to believe that all he had witnessed in that strange dream was true. She had prepared him as an offering to whatever powers she had summoned that night. The despoiled innocent was their favored prey. With this knowledge, he now saw machinations in everything; Ilset's words were filled with malice and her smile was like a knife drawn against him. He had not chosen. He'd been so long afraid of his father's disapproval that once he came to Storm Port he'd fought against it, spitefully, childishly, and Ilset had encouraged his defiance because she knew how it would injure Redmantyl. She'd observed his vulnerabilities and used them to her own advantage. The choice, the deception, had been hers. He'd sought his ruin, but she had helped; he'd been her willing dupe.

"The woman called upon dark forces to aid her," said the wizard. "Such evil cannot pass unpunished."

"Then you did not do it for my sake?"

"It had to be done," Redmantyl replied. "Renegades must not be suffered. All rules of wizardry insist that we act without mercy. I know this seems harsh to you. You are so sensitive. I was once too, but that was killed in me long ago. Wizards must surrender some part of their humanity for the sake of higher duties. I cannot tell you more of what these entail. You know too much for the uninitiated as it is. Believe me—all we are required to do in the expulsion of the weak and malign is necessary.

"I was obliged by my duty as a wizard to deal with that viperous creature, but it ought to have been done dispassionately. Then I discovered that you were involved. She brought you into it. She touched you with her taint, then flung your corruption at me in triumph.

You cannot imagine my rage."

"Father, I felt your rage. All Storm Port did."

The wizard smiled at the undisguised irony in Orlan's tone. "I loosed more upon the city than I should have in my wrath. Ilset's obliteration was required, but the storm, the blighting of the Mayor's Hall—these were mere self-indulgent acts. A wizard perfect in his discipline would not have needed to make such a display of anger. Had I not been so outraged at the peril she placed you in, I would have—" He paused and looked at Orlan. "I would have conducted myself with greater discretion."

"Do you regret the Portreeve's death?"

"I did not intend to kill him," the wizard said. "His heart was weak and the blow too strong for him. Whether he was Ilset's tool or her partner, he was an inveigling knave. I cannot pretend to lament the death of such a man, but I am sorry I was the cause of it. I do not destroy anything wantonly, Orlan. Power bears that responsibility. I can only explain myself by agreeing with you. I allowed emotion to sway my actions. It is my weakness to love you as I do.

"Orlan, what would you do if your child were in such danger? What would you feel if she were so corrupted and misled?"

"I would be distressed," Orlan began carefully, knowing what his father implied.

"You would be more than distressed."

"Father, I know you think me wanton and lax in my disciplines, but I was not truly corrupted. I did nothing so wrong! I— I drank too much and was sick, and I hurt Kyarde. That was the worst of it."

"Would you have Anne behave so, with such pursuits and such companions?"

"But she's a girl. It's not the same."

"There was a maid in your company in those days."

"Yes." Julia. Orlan had not thought of her in years. When he did, he forgot her snapping, dark eyes and the thrill of his first true kiss; he remembered how frightened she had been once she'd seen how very different he was.

"Imagine Anne to be such a maid. She is defiant, profligate. She believes she is playing at harmless pleasures, but it is not so. Through her games, she is misled into great peril. No, Orlan, you did nothing so wrong, even for a magician, but that woman set you on the first steps to a depravity I think you are still too innocent to imagine. You cannot know what she meant for you. What if another such as Ilset meant to seduce and ensnare your child for the same unholy purposes? What would you feel?"

"Fury," Orlan admitted. "I would hate them."

"You would act to protect Anne?"

"Yes. But to kill them-!"

"I have tried to explain that to you."

"What of what you did to me? I would not cast out a child of mine, no matter how unwizardly she had been."

Redmantyl blinked at him in surprise. "Orlan, I never made you outcast. You fled."

"You were glad to be rid of me. You didn't come after me. Do you care where I have been these years?"

"You didn't want me to know."

This was true; Orlan could not answer. He had not wanted his father to find him. He had deliberately concealed himself. Then why was he so angry that Redmantyl had not searched?

"You have always held the power to summon me," said Redmantyl. "If I had pursued you, would you have consented to return to Wizardes Cliff with me? You will not return now, and you are not so angry as you once were. I cannot drag you back unwilling."

The wizard rose, gently cradling the sleeping child, and carried her to the little cot near the hearth. "I never quit my love for you, Orlan. You must know that. I have never been ashamed of you, unwizardly or no. I was proud to call you mine and I sorrowed to lose you.

"I cannot fault you entirely for abandoning your magic, nor Ilset. I have my share of blame. Your training was flawed. I did not teach you all a proper wizard must know. Perhaps if I had spoken more of the perils of necromancy, you might not have been so easily deceived. We are not permitted to tell apprentices many of our secrets, but I neglected much that might have been said. I did not teach you to be wary. I told you to be firm of will, but I didn't instruct you to anticipate the forces you must stand against. You never met temptations. You were so young, a boy, and ignorant of the world, and I sent you out to face its snares unprepared. I never warned you of the wiles of such foes as Ilset. I didn't think to tell you of her. She was a magician stripped of powers. I did not expect that she would keep such necromantic devices. Even so, she was once my enemy and a powerless magician may still do great evil in her quest for revenge. You were not suspicious. If you had known that the well-respected Mayor of Storm Port meant you harm, would you have taken so readily to every pleasure her husband and the local youths introduced you to? Her plans failed, yet she took you from me all the same. Once you faced mortal diversions, you doubted wizard's ways. You challenged me."

"It was foolish," Orlan answered.

"Certainly, but it was an opportunity to look into your mind. I would not before, and saw that I did not truly know you. I did not foresee the flaws that brought about your rebellion and correct them earlier—but I ought to have. I would not, and did not understand until it was too late."

"Is it too late?" asked Orlan as he came to stand beside his father.

Redmantyl smoothed a blanket over the child, who embraced her new toy, now of softly glittering gold. "You will not return to Wizardes Cliff. You refuse to complete your training. I am dismayed to see such talents as yours lost—or worse, misused—when they might be employed. It is a most critical time. Magicians are greatly needed now."

"Wh–" Orlan began to ask, when an image from his father's thoughts flashed in his own mind—an image he had seen before. A dark horror in the semblance of a mortal being, small, yet surrounded by an aura of nullity which made it seem monstrous. It *was* monstrous. The spawn of nightmare. All the power of that unearthly and malign force which dwelt in the place between the stars lay behind it. He had last seen it crashing through the trees of his forest dreamscape, in pursuit of him. In his dream, the wizards had hunted out this devil's minion, fought it, banished it from this world. But the conflict had not ended there. The masters of this unspeakable creature were eternal. They waited for further opportunities, and other battles had been fought since that night.

"It got through," he whispered.

"We have need of strong magics," Redmantyl reiterated. "Laurel is gone and Olyr is irretrievable. But you were never formally outcast. Your magics remain as they were. I had hoped I might be able to convince you to resume your apprenticeship and prove yourself fit to join the ranks of right magic. I believe you have a place among us if you will take it."

"I cannot," Orlan answered. Though he was gratified to hear that his father thought him fit for wizardry, he could not believe it of himself. "I don't have the power to fight that kind of abomination."

He expected his father to argue with this, but Redmantyl only sighed.

"I must abide with your decision. As you say, you are not a child to be governed. You may refuse your own talents, if that is your wish. But what of hers?"

"Her?" Orlan glanced up at the bedroom door.

"No." He stroked the curls of the sleeping child. "You retain the ability to see another's power, Orlan. Look at your daughter and see what she is."

Orlan looked at Anne and saw what he knew his father must see. All about the child, shining from the heart of her tiny being, was a radiance of infant glamour. He'd known about it for months now, although he tried to pretend it wasn't there. He could not ignore it any longer.

After the birth of his daughter, Orlan often recalled that dream which had not been a dream at all. The dream-daughter who led him to safety had been no unspecified girl-child, but Anne as she was. He had watched her grow into the cherub's face, the imperious, piping voice, the first manifestations of that willful personality which were already familiar. He had met her; he had seen the child, heard the woman she would become, long before her birth.

You have chosen the path which will bring you to me. Had it been destined from that Midsummer night that he would not return to Wizardes Cliff, that he would meet Alen, that he would father this extraordinary little girl? But how was it possible? He would not have survived the ordeal of that night without her help, yet she would not have been able to come to him had he not survived. He would not have lived to father the child who had delivered him from mortal danger if she had not been there to deliver him. Yet she had been there. Could she have been if his survival were not predestined? He could not have escaped alone.

It made him dizzy if he thought too much about it.

He had heard numerous tales of magicians who extended their powers beyond death. What sort of magic extended its influence to a time before birth, even before conception? What must await a child who had such magic? Anne was already conscious of so much: she understood things she was not old enough to articulate. *How* she understood, Orlan could only guess. She had the perceptions of a mature magician, as well as precognitive abilities more subtle than simple mental magic. And she was yet a baby. Very soon, she would be beyond his control and too young to control herself.

Redmantyl had followed his thoughts. "She is growing rapidly into her powers, Orlan. She shows them already. She will be a wizard of great ability one day."

"No," he answered. "She will grow, but not into wizardry." He thought again of the battle his father had alluded to. Strong magicians were needed. That infant power– "You will not use Anne!"

"She will be a magician, to one use or another," Redmantyl replied. "You know well how innocents are made tools in this. If she is kept ignorant, she is only so much more vulnerable."

"You cannot mean to bring a toddling little child into this. You were ready to kill Houarde and Ilset when they tainted me with it."

"Orlan, I do not speak of employing her talents now. Twenty or thirty years hence, when she is a grown woman and has come to her full powers, she will be ready. Before that time, she must be properly protected and taught to guard herself."

"Not if I can prevent it," Orlan persisted stubbornly. "I do not want her to live a magician's life."

His father frowned. "What then, Orlan? Will you raise her as Igren was, so that she fears her powers and lets them fall into disuse? Will you see her grow into a stunted woman married to a cloune miles beneath her because you wish to keep her from knowing what she is?" Anne murmured and he lowered his voice so he would not awaken her. "Orlan, magic is a wondrous gift and a dread responsibility. It cannot be banished simply by wishing it were not so. Is your dislike for it so great that you would refuse the talents of your daughter? Would you mar her face to prevent her from growing into beauty? Stop her mouth if she were gifted at singing or storytelling? Crush her hands if her fingers were too nimble for your liking?"

"Father!" Orlan was aghast at the accusation. "Do you think I can be so cruel?"

"You maim her as surely by refusing her legacy. When she is of an age to learn what her power is for, she will wish to use it rightly and she will hate you if she feels she has been crippled. You have crippled yourself so. Do you remember any of your training?" He took up an empty mug from the table. "Catch it, Son." He threw it and Orlan caught it in his hands. "You know that is not what I meant."

Redmantyl picked up another object, the silver amulet left lying there hours ago. "Try again." He tossed it at Orlan, who scowled, but the amulet hovered in the air between them until he snatched it down. "Yes, it is still there. I knew it must be."

Orlan paced the end of the room like a trapped beast. He threw the charm aside. "Even so, I will not join your magician's battle! Will you understand? I will not allow my daughter to enter it. Our magic is not like these other talents you speak of. If she were like Godefroi or Igren and used her magics for pretty, pleasing and harmless arts, I would not object. But this thing you suggest is dangerous!" Anne turned restlessly in her sleep, and he lowered his voice. "I know evil for what it is, and I avoid it."

"Orlan," Redmantyl said softly, "it cannot be avoided. You are in this. It will seek you out—you, and your daughter."

"I have been safe so far. No harm has come to me as an inactive magician, and Anne will be safe with me until she is of an age to decide for herself."

"You may be safe so long as you refuse to use your magics and conceal yourself," Redmantyl answered, "but Anne doesn't have that self-command. She shines bright and undisguised. It will draw them. It may have already. There has been much magic here."

Orlan realized he had not thought of Alen for nearly an hour. Was she–? No; he felt her heartbeat. She was still alive, but it was only a matter of time. He started for the stairs.

Redmantyl seemed to understand. "We will talk of this later."

"There is nothing more to be said."

Orlan sat up through the night, watching his wife as her breath fell more and more faintly and her hand in his grew cool. In the early hours of the morning, Alen died, and he was alone.

Something was wrong.

Orlan woke abruptly. It was the hour before dawn; he had fallen asleep at the foot of the bed. His reawakened senses thrilled with an overwhelming sense of danger. Alen? He touched her cold ankle. No. She was past that now. But he *felt* the disturbance in the air, the unrestrained energies expelled. Downstairs, there was a riot of crashes, bangs, and thumps. But what–?

"Mama!" Anne's voice.

Orlan leapt up.

Redmantyl was barely visible in the glow of the dying fire in the room below; Orlan heard rather than saw the sobbing child shadowed in his arms. Commotion erupted around them. Pots and crockery leapt from the kitchen shelves and rolled on the floor. Tables, chairs and benches danced, hopping from one leg to another. The front door burst open and shut. Shutters slapped the windows, cracking the panes.

"What's happening?" he shouted down. "Father, are you–?"

"No. Not me. Has she ever done this before?"

"No, Father." As Orlan descended, the little girl reached out for him.

"Dark girl!" Anne cried out. "She was here, Da! For me!"

A chill ran through Orlan at these words. He looked over the small curly head to meet his father's eyes.

"She is only four, Orlan!"

"It was a bad dream," Orlan insisted, though he knew this was not true. "That thing can't touch her. `Tisn't a Keep-night. Midsummer is weeks away."

"It doesn't need the gateway any longer," Redmantyl answered. "Their agent moves freely in this realm. I feared as much—it senses what has passed here. So much spellcraft draws its attention. The invocation of Dark powers."

"But Anne's only a baby!"

"Evil will not hesitate at the corruption of one so young. The one they have taken was a little maid not yet sixteen. They will not be less cruel–"

The wizard stopped abruptly. "Christ's Mercy," he whispered.

Orlan would have been shocked to hear such an oath from this austere magician if he had not felt Redmantyl's dread at the sound which prompted it. Soft but distinct from the loft above, bare feet padded on the floor.

The wizard clutched the child protectively and made a sweeping, warding gesture with his free hand to encompass all three of them.

"It is here! Orlan, guard yourself! It will use its worst trickery to torment and deceive you. Do not succumb!"

Above, the bedroom door opened. Orlan looked up.

Alen stepped out onto the landing in her blood-stained white nightshift. Orlan knew that she was dead. He'd felt the last of her life's warmth drain from her. Her heartbeat had stopped hours ago. It was not beating now. The thing before him was devoid of living energies, as lifeless as a wooden puppet. It moved like a puppet, an inanimate figure jerked into activity by unseen rods and strings. Not Alen. Not a living woman. Before him stood all the horror his father had foretold in the enactment of that simple spell: a corpse reactivated, mindless, insensate, but in motion.

It came down the stairs, slowly making its way as if the path and the movement were unfamiliar. Its steps were jolting, ungainly hops; the knees were stiff. Orlan made a soft, sickened sound, and his father lay a cautionary hand on his arm. The wizard whispered an incantation to increase the wards he had cast and he could not pause to repeat his earlier warning.

The body which had been Alen persisted undaunted into the thickening barriers until it was forced to stop at the foot of the stairs, unable to advance further. Redmantyl's spells held it at bay. The arms, which had hung limp, lifted in their direction. The lips fell slightly open as if a catch had been released. There was a voice, not Alen's.

"Come to me, precious Little One," it spoke without inflection. Eyes turned toward the child, but did not focus upon her. Alen's familiar hazel-grey irises were filmed over. "You shall have your mother again. We will be together. We will be happy. My baby." The corners of the mouth were tugged up into what was meant to be a smile, but the expression held no more affection than the words.

Anne stared back uncertainly. Orlan sensed her confusion: she could not doubt that this was her mother's physical form, but its movements, its words, the repulsive sensation of its presence felt as wrong to her as it did to him. "You're not my mama."

"I am, my darling. Will you not have me back?" it said. "Come to me."

Orlan could not bear this another minute. He wasn't terrified—he was infuriated that this inhuman *thing* had invaded his wife's defenseless body for a ghastly trick that fooled no one and only furthered the sorrow of himself and his little girl. He was certain it had chosen this tactic only because he had desired Alen revived. Father had said it was drawn by the invocation of dark magics: it knew what spell he had tried to cast and enacted it for him. It taunted him with the fulfillment of that obscenity he had nearly committed himself. It mocked his pain.

Hadn't he endured enough? Wasn't it sufficient that his daughter lose her mother without this creature flaunting the cadaver before her? Its entreaties were no enticement; even if Anne were willing to cross the barriers at its beguilements, they would never let her go. Redmantyl would not release his hold on the child. Orlan would block her path. It couldn't touch her so long as she remained under their protection; surely the thing must know it would not ensnare her by these means. It was grotesque, pathetic, outrageous. He would not have it in her sight.

"Leave her alone!" he shouted. "Begone from my house and back to Hell with you!"

The sightless eyes rolled to him. "Will you not have your wife again?"

Fury overwhelmed him. No more of this travesty! Orlan heard his father shout as he leapt through the wards and struck the body with the full force of his anger. His hands met cold flesh and his magic blasted into it, as if he could burn the invader from Alen as his father had excised the infected tissues. Instead of retreating before his unleashed powers, it grabbed his wrists with Alen's hands and held him away. A tingle like an electric shock raced up his arms. Because it inhabited Alen's frail body, he had assumed it to be physically weaker than himself, but the icy fingers encircled his wrists like manacles. He struggled to break the grip, but he was trapped.

It occurred to him then that he had committed an act of disastrous folly. His father had warned him not to be deceived by its subterfuges, yet he had done exactly that. He had been provoked into abandoning the safety of Redmantyl's wards, giving it this opportunity to capture him. It had sought Anne and her powers, but it wanted him too. Its masters had been cheated of him years ago. They had not forgotten Ilset's offering of an innocent and they meant to claim what was theirs. *This* was the trick it had intended all along: his desire to see Alen alive had not betrayed him; his unwary rage had. Now he paid for it.

For an instant, the filmed eyes met his and he thought that they held a hint of amusement at his stupidity and his belated knowledge of it. Blood-chilling energy which contained some fraction of vast, malevolent and unearthly magics ran along his skin, seeking to work its way into his vitals and insinuate its influence upon his soul. Orlan resisted this onslaught. Did he have the power to keep it from engulfing him? He didn't know. He didn't believe so. But he could not submit! It wouldn't take him without a fight!

Unused magics welled within him, rushed through forgotten channels and burst so violently into dazzling manifestation that he gasped aloud at the surge. A haze of lightborn glamour surrounded them; he blinded himself with his own incandescence. He had no idea he possessed this much power. It was a heady, invigorating sensation. This was what his father must feel when he cast himself into a lightning bolt or wall of flame. He was the power.

Yet the thing in Alen's body continued to hold him. Regardless of this newly discovered power, it was stronger than he was. It meant to persevere until his magics were spent and he must give in. Again, he heard his father shout, but the words were lost in the thundering of his own pulsebeat in his ears.

Fair promises echoed in his mind: *Cease your resistance. You are Ours. Great rewards await you. Surrender, and you will have all you desire and more than you dream. You will have powers beyond his and liberty to do as you please. You will have no restraints. Pleasures unlimited shall be yours. Mortal laws will not contain you. Surrender, and you shall be free.*

But these promises were lies. It could give him nothing he desired.

It could not return Alen. It could not give him freedom, only eternal bondage such as this wretched creature suffered.

If it came to that, he would not allow it to conquer him. He could make this untapped power flare into an explosive heat to consume himself and the body of the woman he loved. If he could not destroy this evil thing, at least he could banish it by blasting the flesh it had captured to worthless ash. He could place himself and Alen beyond its contaminating influence. Better that sacrifice than slavery. He must not let it take him. He had the power to accomplish that if he were not afraid.

Anne would be safe. Father would care for her.

Then it yielded abruptly. Orlan had been fighting to resist the persistent assault on his mind and body, when the hands loosened their grip and the corpse fell away without a sound. Off his balance, Orlan fell with it.

"Orlan, are you uninjured?" Behind him, Redmantyl put the little girl down and crossed the wards.

His clothes were scorched. His skin had a pinkish, sunburnt tone. His vision was somewhat obscured by the aftereffects of the lightsome dazzle. His head throbbed, his wrists ached, slightly swollen, and his limbs were too weary to lift with ease, but there was no severe damage. "I'm not hurt," he answered after a moment. "If you hadn't stopped it—"

"I didn't stop it." The wizard gestured to the first shafts of light which shone through the cracked windows. The sun was rising. With the growing light, the rattle and clatter slowed, then stopped. The feeling of danger subsided. "Creatures of Darkness cannot endure daylight. We needed only wait until its powers were diminished at dawnsbreak. I could not have destroyed it, Orlan, and I did not wish to destroy Alen's body to drive it away—nor you until I knew certainly that you were lost. That was insanity! Do you know what could have happened to you so unprotected? What possessed you?"

"Alen," he answered.

Gently, Redmantyl touched his son's shoulder. "Orlan, it was not her. She has been dead for hours."

Orlan knew this, but of course that did not ease his pain. The limp body lay still beneath him. Whatever had inhabited it had departed. But so had Alen. Tenderly, he smoothed the rumpled shift, stroked the tangled hair from her peaceful face.

He screamed his grief.

His father knelt beside him and took his head between his hands. Orlan recoiled, certain that the wizard meant to erase this horror from his mind. The grief he had felt at his mother's death was slight in comparison with the mind-searing pain that cut through him now. He braced himself: oblivion would come again and it was not entirely unwelcome.

But Redmantyl did not cast this enchantment. Instead, there was unexpected rapport. The wizard's thoughts were revealed to him; a series of images moved swiftly through his mind, memories the significance of which he didn't understand. He saw Andemyon, the grown lad of twenty he was now, his fair curls tinted red. He saw a tall, steel-spun young woman with a sword. Laurel? No, this was another, a kinswoman long dead. He saw another woman, small and pretty, her yellow hair tucked beneath a serving-maid's kerchief. She was smiling up at him. Suddenly, the memory dissolved into one Orlan knew well: that same pretty maid lying pale and still beneath bloody sheets.

I know, Orlan. A wordless message accompanied the image. *I know.*

His father's arm went around his shoulders and Orlan wept, heart-rent and lost.

"It's over now," Redmantyl whispered.

syseten

The funeral ceremonies took place in the yard of Isolde Chapel. Women of common birth were not often buried where Oerykton Ladies had prayed and been laid to rest in the vault beneath for centuries, but Igren had insisted. Others lay in the churchyard: a Mother Abbess who had accompanied Geyraulte's grandmother at the event of her marriage, the unacknowledged daughter of the long-dead Earl Kharlyet, a favorite court bard, Igren's own stillborn infants who, unbaptized, could not be received into the vault. Alen would be in beloved company.

Neither Orlan nor Lord Redmantyl spoke of the night after Alen's death. The mourners who attended her funeral knew only that she had died in her sleep. Brother Anselm had returned at mid-morning with the castle chaplain to find the body returned to the bed, and they performed the last rites. At most, the aged Brother thought it strange that Orlan requested this ceremony when he had not seemed to consider a priest's services necessary before.

With a final prayer for the soul's lasting peace, the chaplain closed his prayerbook, crossed himself, and returned to his rectory. The Earl's tenants and city folk who had known Alen and the courtiers who attended Igren made their quiet farewells, and the gravediggers finished their work and went home to dinner. The wizard, his son, the little girl, the young Brother, and Lady Igren remained, all in long mourning cloaks of white gossamer with hoods pulled forward and hems dragging on the grass so that they looked as if they were ghosts themselves. Rain fell, quiet, soft, and dismal; it was not a display of sorrow created by anyone present, but it surely reflected the mood of all.

Redmantyl had not joined the funeral rites, but stood beneath the nearby willow trees; as at Tedora's death, he donned a mourning cloak as a compromise between two millennia of Church tradition and his own beliefs. When the rains grew heavy, Kai quickly retreated to the shelter after him. Igren stood at Orlan's side a little longer before the fresh mound of upturned earth, as if she would speak, but she was a timid young woman—unlike her cousin Laurel—and not one for eloquence. With one gentle touch at his shoulder, she too left him.

"I must go," she whispered to the wizard apologetically. "My husband will be impatient if I am gone long. You understand?"

"Yes, Niece."

"Will you stop with us at the castle tonight?"

"No, I think not. I'll stay with Orlan until my departure tomorrow."

"Yes," she said. "He shouldn't be alone. Then I bid you farewell, Uncle. When Orlan will listen, tell him I am sorry. Alen was–" The Earling was at a loss for the word. "She will be much missed. I did love her dearly."

"I too, My Lord," Kaiberte added. "I offer my apologies that Brother Anselm was not here today. He says he finds folly in mourning for an honest woman who has certainly gone to a better place, but I think he sorrows that he could not help her. He does not like to fail."

"He did all his medical art would allow," answered Redmantyl.

"Shall I tell him that? It will comfort him to know that no human art could revive Alen and he is not to blame." He glanced at Orlan. "Pray that it will comfort him also."

"We must go," Igren said softly. "Kai?"

"Fare ye well, My Lord." The young Brother and the Lady walked together to the gate at the end of the churchyard and into the lowest gardens of the castle. Orlan had not yet moved from his silent vigil in the rain.

"Orlan," Redmantyl called to him. "We ought to go too."

Orlan came reluctantly; the wizard lifted the hem of his own cloak and dried his son's face.

"You are as soaked to the bones as a brine-potted eel. Mourning-garb or no, we must find you dry clothes as soon as you are home, and Anne too." Throughout the funeral, the little girl had wandered among the rose bushes and headstones, not knowing their significance but marveling at the strangeness of the place. Her white cloak, too long, trailed on the ground behind her.

Orlan turned to watch her. "Do you think she understands what's happened?"

"She knows her mother is dead, but she is too young to comprehend what that means. She does not sorrow as you do."

"She doesn't seem to remember," said Orlan. "It might all have been a bad dream."

"It is best that she believes it so," Redmantyl answered. "Let her forget until she is of an age to understand. She shouldn't remember her mother as she last saw her."

"You put spells upon me to make me forget my mother."

His father sighed and said: "You grieved so and I could not bear to feel with you, the little boy that you were. I knew no better way to ease your pain. I did what I could."

"A child has the right to cry for its mother."

"Do you wish her to suffer if you may provide some comfort?"

"No, Father."

Redmantyl summoned the child, "Annie!" She ran to him and smiled up as he offered a hand. The little girl adored the wizard; Orlan knew his daughter's awe exactly. Redmantyl must seem so tall, so splendidly bright and colorful, so marvelous in his magic and mysterious in his ways to her in her small experience of the world. He had held her and offered her comfort when she was frightened. Orlan had built his understanding of his father on these first impressions himself.

They walked down through the town mindless of the rain. Beyond Oerykton, they were careful to stay on the grass beside the road rather than in the muddy ruts. Redmantyl went slowly, Anne trotting to keep apace with him, and Orlan walked ahead, huddled and miserable, mourning cloak muddied to the knees, clothes sodden, hair in dripping ringlets against his brow and throat. Tears rolled down his cheeks and mingled with the raindrops.

At last, he turned back and cried: "I don't understand! Why did we let her go?"

"We couldn't have kept her imprisoned against her will," Redmantyl answered gently.

"If she'd remained in the circle, she would still be alive. That *thing* would never have been able to touch her."

"If it comforts you, Orlan, Alen departed the flesh long before that violation occurred. Her abandoned vessel was occupied. Her spirit was not tainted."

"Her spirit?" Orlan wondered. "Do you believe she continues then?"

"I know that she believed it. She sought freedom, not oblivion."

"But is she free? Is she safe? What happens with death? Tell me, please, if you know."

"I think that we survive after we quit our bodies, but I cannot prove it so. I know much of this universe and its secrets, Orlan, but I know not what waits beyond."

This was not as comforting as Orlan would have liked. "Death is horrible to me, Father. I must weep or I shall scream, and when I weep I feel as if I cannot stop." As he spoke, fresh tears fell. "Will it always be so unbearable?"

"It will ease in time," Redmantyl assured him. "You are very young, Orlan. You may live ninety years more and be happy again, but you will not think of Alen hereafter without pain. You may come to love another woman so well, but because you seek to recall Alen in her. When you look at the child, you will remember the mother."

Orlan knew that his father was not thinking of Alen and Anne, but of another woman and her child and a time when his own happiness had ended abruptly. Until he had seen Andemyon through his father's eyes, he had not realized how much the boy resembled Tedora.

"You loved her," he said after awhile. "And Andemyon for her."

Redmantyl looked up. "You understand that now? You do not begrudge it?"

"I– No, I cannot. I have no reason." Had he ever, truly? "You must know what I feel, then, for Alen."

"I know."

I know. This was the message Redmantyl had conveyed to him the night after Alen had died, but now Orlan understood that it was meant as more than simple condolence. His father did know. He had felt this same pain. *I know what it is to lose the woman you love.*

"Will there always be this ache, unhealed?" he asked.

"Always. I wish I could promise that you will not suffer this loss throughout your life," Redmantyl said, "but it is not so."

"If you had promised, I would not have believed," Orlan confessed. There was a bitter tone to his words that he regretted immediately, but his father did not seem stung. Instead, Redmantyl's eyes held a look of sympathy which Orlan had not expected, but the young man was grateful for it. He was encouraged to go on.

"Father, I have a request. You are right—Anne must learn to defend herself. She needs protection and guidance as she comes into her powers. I won't have her helpless before such abominations, and I cannot– Will you take with you when you leave?"

"Alen also asked this of me," Redmantyl told him.

Orlan's mouth trembled. "You see, she knew the education our daughter would require. She knew I would not be fit. I am too distraught to care for Anne myself. Annie, you must go with your gran'ther. He lives in a most beautiful castle on cliffs over the sea, and you will be happy there."

"Will you come too, Da?" the little girl asked with a thoughtful frown.

"No, I'm going away, but I promise you will always know where I am. You both will." He opened his soggy mourning robe to reveal the silver amulet tied at his throat; it had been scratched and tarnished, its spells worn to nothingness, but it was now engraved anew at his own hands. "Father, I won't abandon my bond with you again."

"What will you do?" Redmantyl asked. "They will seek you out as well."

"I'll hide myself," the young man answered. "I plan to return to St. Yzra with Kai and Brother Anselm. I'll take work as a lay-brother, tend the Abbey's goods and gardens, the sheep. It is a house of God. I'll be safe there."

Redmantyl looked doubtful. "Christianity is not always a haven, Orlan. It may afford some security to its priests and adherents, but for you it is mere superstition. I know why you insisted upon the last rites and allowed Alen to be buried in the churchyard. Neither holy oil nor consecrated earth will bar diabolic forces unless firm belief in the sacrosanctity of the object bestows such power. It is not something I understand—it is not a magic we possess. Abbey walls will not shield you, Orlan. You attempt to conceal yourself among the Brothers, but you will reveal yourself eventually and the artifacts of a religion you do not profess will not protect you. For you, they are meaningless material. You lack the faith to give them power.

"The masters of that perverse creature will not rest, Orlan. They are relentless. They will return again and again to try to claim you so long as you might serve them, so long as you retain your powers unguarded. But you do not need to be a heedless victim of their wiles. You do better to keep vigilant rather than hide yourself as frightened prey and hope to escape notice. There is no hope of that for any of us in these perilous times. Much of your education will prove useful if you choose to recall it. Or, if you are determined to discard magical practices, you must do so completely and never use your powers again. Without magic, you are in no danger. There are ways I can assist you if you wish."

Orlan thought this sounded ominous. "As you assisted Olyr?"

"It isn't a pleasant procedure," Redmantyl agreed, "but at times it is necessary. It may leave you with headaches or dizzy spells. You will feel as if part of your fundamental self has been torn away. I don't enjoy the contemplation of it. I should hate to see you so mutilated when there are other alternatives available.

"Orlan," he concluded, "Alen asked that I take you with me as well."

The young man looked up in surprise.

"I promised I would. My son, I wish it too. You require protection as well, more so than Anne. You are vulnerable in your grief and you should not be left alone. Nor should she lose both her mother and father at once."

"It's for the best. I can't care for her–"

"Perhaps you won't be able to give Anne all that she requires. I will take charge of her education and protection, but I will not act as her father. She needs you for that. She needs you to be with her. And, Orlan, you must admit that you do not want to leave her either."

This was true; Orlan could not deny it. He dropped to one knee to hold his daughter close.

"I do not command you," Redmantyl continued. "You are a man able to choose for yourself. I offer counsel. Orlan, come home. It is where you belong. You are not suited for common life. You think to be a shepherd? A carpenter? I suppose you've been among the Free Folk as well. But have you been happy in these professions? They are not for you. You are meant for more."

"Not for wizardry, Father."

"Even if you will not be a wizard, you are a young nobleman. You have a rightful place. You may disguise yourself as a peasant, but your manner and speech declare you plainly noble-born for all to see."

"Noble?" The bitter note returned to Orlan's voice. "No, you are a nobleman of rank and wealth, but I have no right to claim such position. For all presumptions of education and manners, I am only your bastard."

"Orlan, you are not a bastard. Not before the law." The wizard's reply was measured in its clarity. "Norman law maintains that any child born to a man and woman before they are wed is legitimate once the two are married, so long as neither is otherwise encumbered between the child's birth and the wedding day. `Tis true, I did not marry your mother, but she was never married and My Lord Dafythe— rest him well—had me swear before his lawyers and clerks that I would have wed her had she not died. A piece of legal chicanery, perhaps, but My Lord Dafythe had sympathy for your situation, as his own son Ambris cannot be rightfully claimed. You were proclaimed legitimate by royal decree."

Orlan was astonished. "When was this?"

"The month after I brought you to Wizardes Cliff."

"You never told me."

"I think I did. Orlan, you've been properly named for as long as you were known to me. Even a bastard has a right to be recognized. A rightborn child deserves more than that."

Orlan sat back on the grass, holding his daughter tightly. He had not expected this, of all things. In spite of Redmantyl's professed love and pride for him, he'd always believed that he'd been kept at Wizardes Cliff chiefly because his father was obligated by honor to take responsibility for his mistake. He had always been insecure of his place in Redmantyl's household, and in the wizard's affection. Yet he had been acknowledged long ago and never considered an object of charity or repaired shame. He was a rightful son. The stain of bastardry he had felt all his life did not exist for any except himself.

Abruptly, Orlan recalled the image of the pretty, smiling alemaid received from his father's memory. Though the face was familiar from his own memories, he saw now that resemblance between his mother and himself was more marked in Redmantyl's mind. The arch of his brows, the shape of his nose and mouth, his curls—and more, his high-strung and sensitive nature—were all hers. *When you look at the child, you will remember the mother.* Redmantyl had spoken these words only minutes ago and, fool that he was, Orlan had thought of Andemyon's red hair, so like Tedora's. He hadn't understood what his father's thoughts had revealed: he was as much a reminder as Andemyon. When Redmantyl looked at his elder son, he saw the silver-fair complexion and aura of magical energies which reflected his own, yes, but also the more delicate features and temperament which recalled a woman he had known long ago and sorrowed for.

"Father, was she anything to you?"

"Your mother?" Redmantyl considered for a moment before he made his answer. "I will not lie and say I loved her greatly, Orlan. I was fond of her. She was a sweet and gentle maid. I expected to see her again."

"But you never came back."

"When she did not summon me, I assumed she had taken another lover or perhaps married. Under such circumstances, I would be unwelcome. I did not wish to intrude if she were happy with another, and so I did not return to Lammouthe. I had almost forgotten her. I never expected to find her as she was, and with a child."

"It might've been different if you'd come to us sooner."

"It might've been different if she had called upon me sooner, instead of waiting until she was at the point of death. Do you blame me that she died, Orlan?"

"No," Orlan answered honestly.

"That she fell to whoredom, then? It was not my fault. I am not responsible for the follies of her life. Orlan, what do you imagine I would have done if your mother had lived?"

Orlan opened his mouth to answer, then shut it again. What indeed? It would be foolish to expect Lord Redmantyl to marry a barmaid he had dallied with years before. It was more foolish still to confess that he had once imagined exactly that. He had built his own fantasy from his mother's promise: one day, the wizard would return for them and everything would be wonderful. But that would not have happened. Redmantyl would have provided for them in accordance with the obligations of a nobleman's honor, would have seen them better housed, perhaps taken charge of his son as Orlan's magic emerged, but Nann Dafodylle would not ever be the wizard's lady.

"You must see that your mother's death gave you a place she could not give you in life."

"Would you have left me in Lammouthe if she hadn't died?" he asked.

"I don't know," said Redmantyl. "I had never taken up the responsibility of a child before and I think that at that time, if the option had remained, I would have left you in your mother's care. As it was, I had no other choice."

"You might have sent me away."

"I thought so myself. If I had been so impartial as a wizard must be, I would have. But I couldn't. You were not so much older than Anne is now. It would have been remarkable callousness to leave one so small and so very helpless alone among strangers. And so I took up the obligations of a father. I might've been a greater wizard without such distractions as you have provided, but I do not regret it. Please," Redmantyl repeated, "Come home with me."

"Into apprenticeship? That is what you wish for me, isn't it, Father?" Redmantyl had not spoken of Orlan resuming his magical career, but it was plainly in his mind.

"Yes, but that shouldn't be the reason you choose it. If you decide upon this course, it must be because it is what you desire above all else, not because you consent to conform with my expectations. Know that I love you, and shall even if you refuse me.

"Nothing will please me more than seeing you attain full wizardry, but I must allow you to choose for yourself in this matter without bias. Perhaps it was inevitable that you quit your apprenticeship. Endure five years of magedom? You did not survive two months before you cast aside all magical disciplines. With so fragile a resolve, you surely would have failed if you'd taken your vows. Yet you have changed much from that foolish and ignorant boy. You've learned much I could not teach you—there are secrets a wizard may not reveal to a novice. You hold great promise if your talents are developed to fulfill their potential. You alone know if you have the will to do so. Will you try?"

Orlan knew that he was being persuaded to return to the training of his youth, but he didn't resent Redmantyl's persistence, for he was beginning to believe that his father was right. The wizard's conviction clarified the confusion in his own head.

He remembered Wizardes Cliff. White towers and sunlit plazas, the apprenticing room at the top of the Daune Tower, Redmantyl's secret-cluttered sitting room. The place he had once belonged. Home. It surprised him how ardently he wanted to see it. He looked up at his father, standing over him, waiting for his reply. Could he return?

He had left too soon and he was incomplete. Even though he felt a thousand years old today, he was as frightened and unsure as a small child. He could not pretend to full manhood after he had wept in his father's arms exactly as he had twenty years before. It was a fool's transparent bravado to say he could stand alone. If he were proud and angry and he walked away from his father again, he would wander without direction, as he had before he'd met Alen. He had never stayed in one place for long and invariably left dissatisfied. Alone, he would be pursued by malign forces which he was unprepared to guard himself against. Always vulnerable. Always in flight. Always afraid. He did not want to live that way.

He didn't hate Redmantyl any longer. The circumstances which had driven him from Wizardes Cliff seemed insignificant; he couldn't think of them. They didn't matter. All that seemed important now was that Redmantyl had been there when he'd needed him. While Orlan had been incapacitated by grief, his father had tended him with gentleness, yet firmly urged him to care for Anne himself, to direct the funerary arrangements, to straighten the disheveled cottage in preparation for their departure. Together, they'd kept vigil through the night, watching over the child in her crib and the corpse in its coffin lest the invading alien agency steal in again. Without Redmantyl, Orlan knew he would not have survived the past days. He would not have maintained his sanity. He would not have recovered so swiftly if he'd been alone. Even now, his father made him believe that he had something to live for.

In order to defeat that monstrous thing which had invaded his wife's body, he must have the means to engage it. It was useless to rail against it; blind anger would ensure his doom. He needed self-control, direction, full knowledge of the nature of his foe. A wizard's education would give him that.

If he returned to Wizardes Cliff for a year, his apprenticeship would be complete and he might swear the oaths of a mage.

The rigid codes of magedom did not seem so confining as they had seven years ago. Then, he had been young and reckless and eager to experience all that the world offered; now, he knew the world and was weary of its pleasures. Physical gratification was meaningless. And what were the diversions of drink and sport? He wouldn't miss them. His days of wild release were over. The forbidden fruit had been tasted and found sour. There was no temptation to break his vows.

The one prize the Dark Lords of the space between the stars could offer was power—a portion of their own vast and unearthly magics. But he had never desired power. He'd always been afraid of it, afraid of unleashing forces he could not control.

"I'd like to prove myself," Orlan confessed. "But what if I enter wizardry and make another such mistake as I did when I crossed the wards? Neither you nor Anne were so stupid to be goaded into exposing yourselves to its influence, and I could have cost us all dearly. I would not be a proper guardian—only a hindrance to wiser and stronger magicians."

"You are far stronger than you realize. A lesser man might have gone mad with what you have endured. I do not approve your means of confronting that creature, yet you withstood its assault. You were not conquered. That is no simple feat!"

"Yes." It terrified Orlan to think of the intensity of the power which had risen so swiftly at his command. He had not possessed that ability when he'd been a boy; the blasting force had developed during the quiescent years. It had grown within him, waited for the time when he would need to use it. Even now, he felt it; it might overwhelm him and burst forth in an unguarded moment. It would do so if he did not check its undirected limits. His early discipline had shaped his magic, directed into channels that were entwined with his heart and mind, given it inextinguishable existence. In spite of years of suppression, it survived.

"The codes which govern our actions are harsh and unforgiving of mortal flaw," his father continued, "but you now have some idea of the reasons for them. You see how easily unrestrained emotion and physical sensation mislead us into error and you know why we take such pains to eschew these distractions. An honest and very natural impulse compelled you to cross my wards. I do not fault your motives, Orlan, save that they led you to an imprudent action. No, a wizard in his strictest discipline would not have made that mistake. If you had kept your head in spite of your outrage, you would have abided until dawn and had the satisfaction of outlasting that creature's power without effort and seeing it banished. You learned this once, and forgot. Do you think it likely you will be so impulsive if such circumstances are repeated?

"It is no small battle I ask you to join. The nameless forces we combat are a danger to life and sanity and even to the soul, but the task of driving such evil from this mortal realm must be done by those who have the power to accomplish it. You have the power, Orlan. I do not doubt that, nor your bravery in the face of such monstrous evil. If you also have the will to command your magic, you are one of us. You know the peril as few uninitiated do. You have fought, and for reasons that the finest wizards offer themselves unflinching to this battle. We guard, for we would not see our world spoiled.

"That is the true purpose of wizardry: our highest duty compels us to defend what is truly important in human life—this world itself, the freedom to live unfettered, that which we love best."

"I have lost what I love," Orlan answered.

"Not all."

No, not all. He lay his cheek against his daughter's silvery curls.

One day, Anne would be a greater magician than he was, perhaps greater even than Redmantyl, but for the present she was only a baby. And the fact that she was threatened by this same danger made him view his position differently. He was reluctant to wield his powers; he felt little obligation to defend this world simply because he had the ability to do so. But Anne conferred more heartfelt responsibilities. For her, he was willing to fight as he would not for an abstract concept of good and evil. He would undertake whatever duties his magic required to ensure that no malevolent nor corrupting influence touched her.

She had done as much for him. It was a debt he had to repay.

Anne struggled in his lap. "Le' me down, Da! I wanna go home now."

"We'll be home soon, Pet. I promise you." He threw a fold of his drenched cloak about her for shelter. "Soon."

It was just as Redmantyl said. A proper wizard protected what was important. Alen was. Anne was. Though he feared of the power he possessed, Orlan acknowledged that the exercise of that power in defense of those he loved made him feel like a grown man—a state that leaving home, marriage and fatherhood had not imparted. He felt as if he had discovered what he truly was in that explosive moment, as if his timidity and uncertainty and dependence on stronger wills to guide him were only facades and another Orlan lay dormant beneath, a mature and resolute man. As if he had disclosed the man he might become if he had the courage to recognize it, a wizard in his own right, more than Lord Redmantyl's son.

As long and as far as he traveled and looked elsewhere, he could not avoid that in him which was like his father. To be like Redmantyl had been all he desired in childhood, and he still found some of his father's qualities admirable, especially now that he understood the motives which prompted them and the steadfast resolve required to maintain them. He faced the same questions he knew his father must have confronted in his own struggle for magical discipline.

Could the tender elements of his nature survive if he did attain the fierce and unwavering conviction of a wizard? Would he ever be certain that he acted for good when his actions seemed extravagantly harsh? He wanted that stronger magic once revealed in battle, but not at the price of compassion. Could he channel his passions into his magic without losing himself in uncontrollable rage or wanton brutality? Orlan knew what cruelty he was capable of without that restraint and he dreaded the possibility of unleashing such destructive forces, for that was exactly the sort of power his foes delighted in and looked to eagerly to employ for their own purposes. It was theirs. If he were so cold and ruthless he would be no better than the evil he meant to expel and might give himself over to malign influences even while he opposed them. Nor did he want those gentle qualities to undermine his self-command. Anger might easily strangle reason, but the weakness of doubt and hesitation and misplaced forbearance which permitted such evil to flourish was likewise fatal. He must tread carefully and find that perfect balance.

Could he do it? The prospect of failure was terrible, but Orlan saw only one course which might save him from disaster. It was no matter of what he desired, but simply what must be done. Whether he had been trained for nothing else or he had been born with the ability, he was magician. He could not ignore it nor abandon it; the thought of allowing his magic to be torn from him as Olyr had suffered disturbed him profoundly, as if Redmantyl had suggested he pluck out his eyes. One was no less a mutilation than the other. Magic was beyond choice. The power was so much a part of himself that it was plainly his nature to fulfill its promise. It was inescapable. He *was* the magician Orlan.

"Very well, Father," he said at last, "I'll come home."

The End